"I thoroughly enjoyed this original ar future . . . great story, good ideas from ar forward to a sequel."

Eliot Coleman, farmer and author

"A lifetime of passionate dedication to genetic preservation and the principles of nature has supplied Will Bonsall with a vision for a low-tech sustainable future . . . takes one on a captivating adventure into a post-apocalyptic world rich in earth-awareness, filled with social metaphors critical for our time. I can hardly wait for Book II!"

David Cavagnaro,
widely published photographer, author, and futurist

"Will Bonsall's new novel joins a line of novels of the post-petroleum future, from Ecotopia to A World Made by Hand. Unlike those, Bonsall gives the details of the choices made along the way by one group of people trying to create a sustainable world for themselves. He tells you how the windmills work, how the barter economy has developed, and takes you on trade routes along the rivers . . . well thought out, well told, gives you a practical roadmap to a workable future; full of interesting characters and thoughtful solutions to the problems we are all facing . . . appeals to the intelligence and creativity of the reader."

Gary Lawless, Gulf of Maine Books

"In Through the Eyes of a Stranger, Will Bonsall creates a world that builds on his own experience as a homesteader. Nut trees, orchards, trading within the community, sharing seeds, group housing, they're all part of a new world that could develop from pieces that are already happening. You'll enjoy seeing what might come next."

Russell Libby, Executive Director of
Maine Organic Farming & Gardening Association and poet

"In structure, Through the Eyes of a Stranger is most like early modern works of utopian allegory such as Austin Tappan Wright's Islandia, or David Lindsey's A Voyage to Arcturus. As it's title indicates, Bonsall's book is told through the narrative perspective of a stranger who is a stand-in for the reader, and who shares the reader's background in something like our world. Yet at heart this book shares more with William Morris nineteenth-century allegorical fantasies, such as The Roots of the Mountains, and their admixture of a barter economy and a socially responsible ethos."

Kenny Brechner, Devaney, Doak, & Garrett Booksellers

THROUGH THE EYES
OF A STRANGER

THROUGH THE EYES
OF A STRANGER

YARO TALES: BOOK ONE

written and illustrated by

WILL BONSALL

To order additional copies of this book, contact:
Xlibris Corporation
1-888-795-4274
www.Xlibris.com
Orders@Xlibris.com
57389

Acknowledgements

Whenever innocent trees are felled to provide pulp for the publishing of yet another book, the author is never the only guilty party. Others must share the blame for enabling him to impose his thoughts upon the reading public, and this case is no different. Unwilling to take the rap by myself, I'm prepared to finger some others who were in on it.

Over the years, countless friends, workers, and apprentices have been subjected to oral versions of the Yaro Tales, and many have even encouraged it by adding their own ideas, from broad critiques to useful minutia. Those culprits include Harriet Brickman, Francis Bliss, Mike Burd, Bonnie Campbell, Dan Chard, Steve Conaway, Denis Culley, Noah Gottlieb, Kehben Grifter, Mike Hermann, Joe Hodgkins, Selma MacHenry, Heather Patrick, Kim Roberts, Tom Vigue, Raivo Vihman, Bennett Steward, Katheryn Sytsma, and others who are spared only by my flawed memory. Chuck Boyer and Katheryn Dunham and Charlie and Helen Buzzell were pivotal in getting the story into submissible (i.e. digital) form, and without the aid and abetting of my friend and editor Kathy Beaubien, Through the Eyes of a Stranger might still be a harmless heap of spiral notebooks. If I had been more diligent in following her good advice, a fair number of spruces might still be standing. To give some idea of just how long this thing has been festering, Canaan Bernier, who played the part of Juniper (originally Willow) in our first Squirrelfolk Day celebration, along with brother Amos Burd, are both now grown to parenthood themselves. Countless other children have passed through the bough-huts on their way to adulthood, adding their mite to a not-yet ancient tradition. They too must be held accountable.

Some liability also lies with Ross Donihue and the folks at the Center for Community GIS, who contributed a lot to the preparation of the main map. How many sticks of pulpwood were ground up for that alone?

Would that my own family were blameless in this business, but brother Charles, in the midst of a dismal economy, offered to invest in this shakiest of all ventures (his idea, not mine!). Youngest son Kindle, growing up amid the Esperian vision, had many useful comments on both the text and the artwork, as did my wife Molly

Thorkildsen. Perhaps the greatest burden of guilt lies on elder son Fairfield, whose inadvertent pushing of a computer key kick-started the process of self-publishing and forced an end to my procrastination.

The folks at Xlibris are of course totally culpable for this story coming to light. No excuse there, they should have known better. Indeed their extremely helpful staff guided me through the process with towering patience.

So you see the fault isn't all mine, and if anyone feels this book is not worth the paper on which it is printed, they should stop me before I write again. But be warned—there is a sequel in the works.

Oh, by the way at www.yarotales.com you can access a full size, full colour, version of the map of Esperia, plus other features to be added over time.

You shall be blind to what you know too well; only through the eyes of a stranger shall you truly see

—First-century prophet Rainwalker

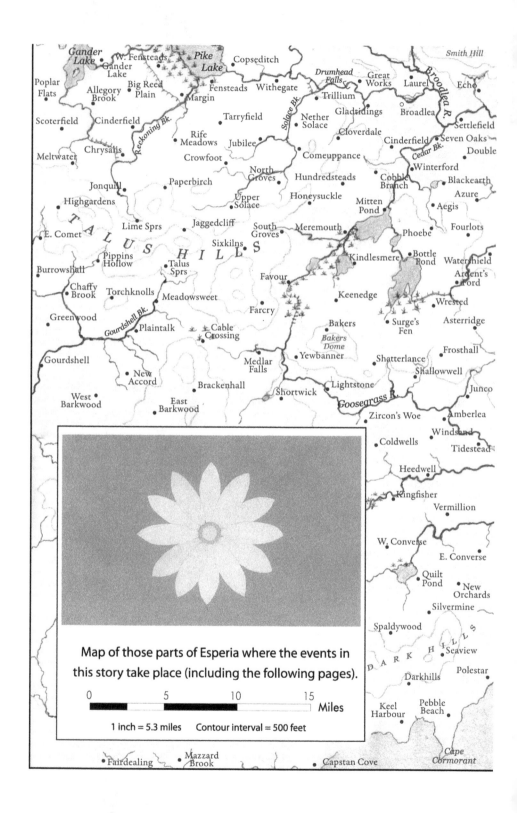

Map of those parts of Esperia where the events in this story take place (including the following pages).

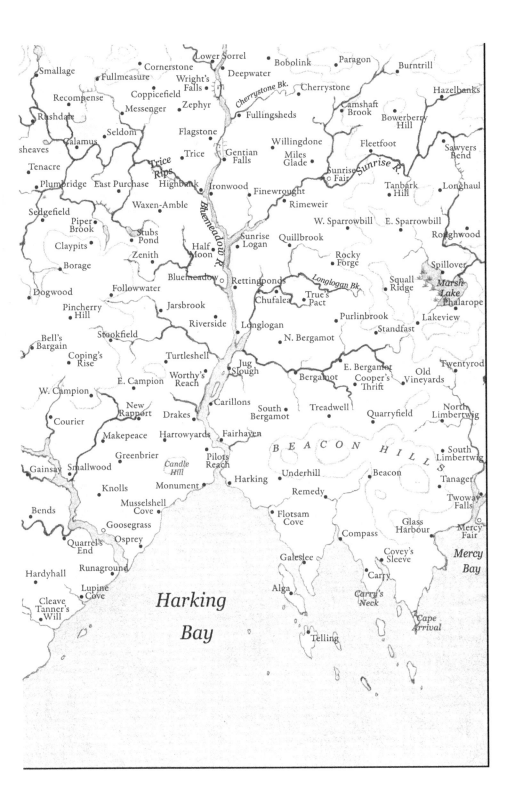

Chapter 1

14th of 12th month, 547 AC*

At first it was invisible, lying somewhere beneath the distant waves. Nothing indicated its presence except a rumour started in the crow's nest by the predawn watch.

Three of us stood on the foredeck, heavy collars raised against the keening breeze which drove us northward. I had hastened up from below only moments earlier, awakened by the announcement that the Esperian coast was hoving into sight. Joining the other two at the bow, I yawned and strained my eyes to glimpse what was already visible from the rigging.

Beside me, Arnica, the *Minkey*'s swarthy captain, leaned against the rail to steady the glass as he scanned the gray-green horizon. Beyond him stood Wren, the dusky-faced youth who only days earlier had rescued me from CADS (that is, the Anagaian secret police). None too soon either—somehow they had learned that I was hiding out in the back alleys of New Chalice, and with a price on my head for two murders, they had orders to shoot me on sight. If Wren had not believed my story and convinced Arnica and the rest of the crew of my innocence, I would surely have been dead by now.

Glad as I was to be away from that dismal country, there was much that wasn't easily left behind. I now had plenty of time to reflect on how I got into this situation; here's how it happened.

I was in love—that was it, you see—my first real love, I suppose. Of course I never would have fallen in love with my half-sister if only I had known. But I didn't know, neither did Fawn—how could we? Nobody in town knew except Jasper Gates, and he wasn't telling.

You might wonder how he even suspected I was his birth son. After all, Archer Seekings had gone all the way to Cleftridge, some eighty miles away, to adopt me

---

* please see Appendix for Calendar Conversion

from the orphanage run by Steward missionaries. Jasper himself probably never even knew that he got Serene Miller pregnant. You see, he hadn't always been the second richest landowner in Dryford; no indeed. He started out modestly enough as an itinerant mechanic, repairing equipment for the many cotton-growing estates throughout the "autonomous region" of Umberlands. He got around, Jasper did, and who knows how many others he begot in his travels? However, to give the man his due, it was probably not wholly his fault, certainly not his intention. I later learned things about Jasper Gates, things which he himself would not reveal while he was alive, including this: Serene Miller, a poor country girl of sixteen, had accused a live-in uncle of making sexual advances. He had denied it, the parents believed him, and she continued to live at risk. When the young rake Jasper Gates had come through town, she had practically thrown herself into his arms. It probably had never occurred to Jasper that she would deliberately get pregnant in a desperate attempt to thwart the incestuous relative. In any event, Jasper soon moved on, and Serene was left with the consequences.

A year or so later, Jasper had another dalliance, this time with Rose Hunter, the lovely daughter of an "old money" planter family in the West Umberlands village of Dryford. Mind you, Jasper Gates was a handsome and energetic fellow, and Rose was not the class-conscious snob she was brought up to be. Nevertheless, her parents were scandalized and tried to get rid of the upstart suitor; but when Rose became pregnant, the elder Hunters resolved themselves to make the best of it with a quiet wedding. Actually, it solved another tricky problem for them: under Anagaian law, women cannot directly inherit property. Rose was an only child, and should the Hunters die before she married, the estate would go to Rose's uncle, and they were not on good terms.

Truth to tell, Jasper never gave them cause to regret it. He proved to be an attentive family man as well as a hard worker with a shrewd head for business. By the time the senior Hunters passed away, Jasper controlled one of the richest estates in the district, second only to the Shacklefords'. Perhaps he had inherited wealth, but no one could deny he had improved upon it.

Well, anyway, their daughter Fawn and I would surely never have met were it not for Archer Seekings. He was a landed peasant who just happened to live in the same village as Jasper Gates. Seekings had only one child, a daughter, and because of the difficulty of the birth, Mrs. Seekings had been warned not to have more children. In Umberlands society, a son was everything and a daughter less than nothing. So they decided to adopt a son; not an infant, you understand (there would be all of the expense of rearing it), but a near-grown boy who could help out around the place.

The orphanage staff weren't enthusiastic about it, but government policy was specific: any white family was preferable to the care of those "foreign radicals." Within twenty-four hours, I was tearfully packed off to Dryford.

I was eleven when I came to my new home, but it was several weeks before I had occasion to meet Jasper Gates. I was carrying firewood into our kitchen one evening in late fall when he reined up in the yard, and I overheard him arguing with Archer.

"Well, I can't see paying that price for them next year. My workers complain that they're too scraggly, all rind and fibre."

"But, Mr. Gates, sir, you know sweet potatoes can't size up proper with no more rain than we've had this year."

"So irrigate more. I can't control the weather for you."

"Truth is, my old pump's broken, and I haven't the money to replace it just now. I've been watering what I can haul, but if the river dries up anymore, we can't even do that."

"Didn't I hear you went and took in a new boy? I suppose you got him helping out too?"

"He isn't cut out for it yet. Too young. He tried it and got heatstroke. Believe me, I won't coddle him, but I can't whip him for what he can't do."

"Well, that's all none of my business. But I won't be paying so much for those cull yams next time."

"But I'll take a licking both ways, if I lose tonnage and rate."

"You can't expect me to . . ."

I had crossed to midyard when I realized he was staring at me, long and hard. I felt self-conscious. Never laid eyes on the man, but here he was, looking as if he knew me from somewhere. It was not like Archer to think of introducing me, nor did I expect this wealthy landowner to pay attention to some kid from away. But pay attention he did. Stepped right down and walked over to me.

"Well, hello there, boy. What did you say your name is?" He extended his hand with an unwonted courtesy. I dropped the armload of wood on my feet and offered my own hand awkwardly.

"Yaro, sir. Yaro Seekings."

"And what's your mama's name, your real-born mama, I mean?"

"I don't know, sir. I never knew her."

"Ah, what a pity. I'll bet you look just like her. And where do you come from, may I ask?"

"Cleftridge, sir. The Mid-Umberlands Children's Home."

"Oh, yes, the Flint Hills. I used to know that area, in a general sort of way. So tell me, when were you born anyway?"

"In 528, sir. I'll be twelve at solstice."

"Well, well, you're a fine young lad, anyone can see. Let me welcome you to our little village, and I hope you'll be very happy here."

Actually, he didn't seem all that happy himself. Behind his breezy, glad-handing manner, I sensed an unaccountable nervousness. Of course I had heard about this self-made millionaire (in fact I'd already met his daughter), but why he should tender such a personal greeting was beyond me. It just wasn't done. I was even more embarrassed when he stooped to help me gather up the fallen stovewood. Then he turned and walked away with his hand on Archer's shoulder, and as I went inside, I heard him continue.

"No, Seekings, those runty yams just won't do. We've got to get them up to size. Tell you what, I've got a spare pump I could probably loan you next season. Why don't you send the boy around to pick it up? A man can't stay in business without the right . . ."

I guess Jasper just put the facts together—he was no man's fool, after all. Apparently, he had little respect for Archer, but after I joined the family, he often did little things to help out. For example, he loaned us a mule when he heard ours died, and he sometimes hired me for odd jobs at good pay, even though he already had several servants. I know we should have been more curious, but when you're down and out, you don't question your benefactor.

Anyway, it was years later (I was eighteen) when Fawn and I got together. Melody—that's my adopted sister—she and Jasper's daughter were best friends, and Fawn often came calling. I didn't presume on her friendship, and anyway, I was usually busy at work, so we were only casual acquaintances. At least that's what I thought. Besides, Ash Shackleford, the richest, toughest kid in town, was known to be sweet on her. Anyone who knew what was good for them kept his distance.

Melody loved to manipulate things, and she knew that Fawn was interested in me, though I never had a clue. She jacked me up to invite Fawn to a New Year's party, and things went from there.

Now Jasper Gates, he'd been out of town a lot lately on business. What with the drought and cotton prices dropping due to the Esperian boycott, he was in a pretty tight fix, I imagine. Trouble is, he never let on he was over his head, so the family went on spending as usual. He returned from one trip in a particularly foul mood, according to Fawn. Rose tried to take his mind off business by mentioning that their daughter had had a lovely time at the New Year's dance. I guess Jasper assumed she'd gone with Ash Shackleford, but when he learned that I was her date, they say he about went through the roof. What really confused everyone was the reason he gave: I was below her class, he said—what did she know of my origins? From Jasper, that was strange talk, as they hastened to remind him; for despite his wealth, he had always disdained what he called those "inbred aristocrats" as much as they loathed him. But the more his wife pressed him, the more he insisted that we not see each other again. That was the end of it as far as he was concerned, and he continued to treat me in as kindly a manner as before, assuming as he did that the matter had been put to rest. But we continued to meet, Fawn and I, arranging our trysts at a secret place on the oxbows of the Possum River beyond the village. Our love was like a bud which blooms in the dark and therefore is not subjected to the more critical scrutiny of day. Quite aside from our blood-ties, if our love could have blossomed in the open, perhaps we might have had a more balanced view of the whole thing, possibly even reconsidered. But the need to conceal our affections only strengthened the attachment, blinding us to anything which might pull us apart. Oh, the fool, Jasper Gates! What shameful things might have resulted from his closed lips, if our passions had been as unbridled as his own! As it was, our lovemaking never went beyond hugs and kisses, but I blush to think what might have happened had our courtship not been curtailed by unforeseeable events.

As I said, Jasper Gates was away frequently on business, or perhaps it wasn't always business. Maybe the pressure of his financial woes was grinding down his character; who knows? What was known, albeit much later, was that one of his tenants had fallen way behind in rent payments; not unusual, given the failure of one cotton crop after another. The unusual part was that Jasper didn't force them off—mind you, Jasper was not softhearted in business matters. The tenant had a wife who was exceptionally beautiful, and apparently there was unsavoury gossip about her and Jasper—I heard nothing of it at the time.

Our family (the Seekings) was having financial worries of its own. Mrs. Seekings had died a couple years earlier, and Archer was increasingly hobbled by his arthritis and a weakening heart. Melody and I were doing most of the work now with some help from Melody's boyfriend, Crag. There was a real danger we could lose the farm, and that would mean moving away from Dryford, away from Fawn. There was no money in cotton or sweet potatoes, and I had a desperate plan. I discussed it with Fawn, and she warily assented, but now I had to lay things before Jasper.

As I turned into the Gates driveway that sultry evening, I saw a fellow stump off angrily in the opposite direction. I gave him little notice at the time, preoccupied with my own business. I noticed a lamp burning in a small outbuilding across the yard. It had originally been the overseer's office, but Jasper was his own overseer, and I knew he would be in there now. I suppose he was going over his account books, trying to marshal his resources against the relentless drought. However, I now know he was also working on another document there, and perhaps that was what I interrupted—I'll never know. The door was discreetly closed, and when I rapped lightly at the window, I thought I saw him shove something hastily into the desk drawer in front of him. As I entered, he seemed to make a conscious effort to brush away the shadow that was upon him, and made his usual affable greeting. I got right down to my business.

"It's about our family, sir. Archer is just not making it, you see, and I'm worried . . ."

"I know, boy, I know. It's tight for us all just now, isn't it? Frankly, I'm a bit strapped myself, so I'm not sure I can do much to help . . ."

"Oh no, sir, you don't understand. You've done so much for us already, I wouldn't ask . . . and anyway, we need more than a loan. What I mean to do is go up to Tramont for the winter, if I can get travel permits. I hear they're hiring workers for the coal mines there. It pays better than farming does nowadays, and maybe I can help the family out. At least, I'll still have a home to come back to."

"Bad idea, boy. Do you realize how many workers get maimed or killed in those pits every week? Why do you think they're always hiring?"

"I do realize that, but I mean to take the chance anyway. I've been talking it over with Fawn . . ."

Jasper stiffened. "What has Fawn to do with any of this?"

"Well, sir, I don't expect you to be enthusiastic about this, but Fawn and I are planning to be married some—"

"Never! It's impossible!" The man seemed to be choking, but less from anger than from horror. "She's not even supposed to be seeing you! Just what has been going on behind my back anyway?"

"Nothing dishonourable, I can assure you of that. But after all . . ."

"Dishonourable? What do you even know about dishonour? You just don't know what's involved here, I tell you. You don't know . . . you can't . . . look, Yaro," his tone was softer now, almost pleading. "Look, it's not your fault, boy, none of this is. Believe me, I really like you . . . hate to hurt you. Hey listen, you've had a tough time ever since you came to this town. Now here's an idea: I've got this old friend, a business partner actually, who raises prunes out in the Sixth District on the Great Muddy. His crop is boycott-exempt, so he's making good money from export. If I gave you a recommendation, you could take the whole family out there to work for him. It would be a fresh start in life. You could forget you ever saw this dust-hole."

Now I felt my own temperature arising. "You mean, forget I ever saw Fawn? Let me tell you, sir, if I'd go for a deal like that, I really would be unworthy of her love. In a few months she will be of age, and we won't need your permission. We would like your blessing, but with or without it, we intend to be married! I'll leave town, all right, but I'm coming back!"

I was fairly shouting by now, and with the door left wide open, I realized the entire household must have heard the quarrel. I didn't much care; in tearful frustration, I slammed the door and stormed off homeward.

I woke next morning feeling like the world's biggest jerk. I had gone to seek Jasper's blessing, not to pick a fight with him. Eventually, things would surely smooth themselves out, but I must at least offer apologies. Although Jasper probably wouldn't accept them now, at some future time, they might serve as the basis for reconciliation.

Without waiting for breakfast, I hurried over to the Gates place, but I saw that his spring wagon was gone. I was hurrying on past when Rose called out to me from her flower garden. Gesturing me over to her, she said, "Jasper has gone out already, Yaro. He went over to the west field early—didn't even take breakfast."

"Yes, I'll go right over there. I need to apologize for something."

"Very well," she added. "But I'm not sure it's you who owes the apologies. I just don't know what's gotten into my husband lately."

"All the same, it's no excuse for me. I was rude last night and lost control of myself."

"Well anyway, I want you to understand something: I don't know what my husband's problem is, but you should know that I think very highly of you and would be proud to have you in our family."

It was the first bright light in a day that promised more dark clouds, so I responded as warmly as I felt. "Thank you, Mrs. Gates, I can't tell you how much I appreciate that right now."

I continued on past the Gates place. I knew right where I would find Jasper: at a new field they were preparing about a mile to the west. It had lain fallow for a year (not nearly enough to support cotton), and the well to irrigate it had gone dry as the water table retreated. Jasper proposed to deepen the well and hopefully squeeze out enough of a crop to keep him afloat until rains came. Of course, rains might increase the yields, but not the prices. Those would remain low as long as the boycott held, and now Esperia's allies were beginning to reject our cotton too.

It was very hot and dry, as it had been for months. Behind the field was a slight ridge, and I knew the wellsite was situated partway up that slope, so the water could be gravity-fed to the cultivated land below it. The ridge was wooded, meaning the skimpy puckerbrush that passes for woods in that region. Part of that had been new-cut by the fuel sellers (another attempt by Jasper to raise quick money), and fine dry twigs lay all around. They snapped loudly under my feet, but then I wasn't trying to be quiet. I saw no one at the well. Probably the workmen hadn't arrived yet, but I figured Jasper must be around somewhere. So much the better if I could talk to him alone. I heard some noise in the brush nearby, but when I called out, there was no reply, so I took it for a stray goat or something. I settled down to wait, looking around at the piles of dirt and rocks, various lengths of pipe, and assorted tools. I examined two pumps lying there; apparently, Jasper had tried to cut corners at first (unlike him) using a locally made pump. But it was poorly machined and constantly lost prime, especially at the new depth. This time he had bought the very best: a Carillons Double-Valve Liftmaster, imported from Esperia. But even that couldn't pump water that wasn't there, so they were digging deeper yet.

I took a look down the deep hole, but at first I saw mostly darkness. I shielded my eyes to block out the glare, and as my pupils adjusted, I could make out more detail. Near the top, the dirt was dry as ashes, then it got darker with dampness, and farther down, my adjusting eyes could see trickles of water seeping down the wall. I could hardly make out the reflection from tiny puddles formed in the muddy heel prints when suddenly, my blood froze in horror. There was somebody down there, an inert figure slumped against the wall by the ladder! Beside it lay a cabbage-sized boulder. I could now see the head, or what had been a head. The skull was horribly crushed, and its contents spilled out onto the well floor. The figure was that of Jasper Gates.

You might suppose that I would have sprung into action: called for help or even run away, but you were not in my shoes. I was paralyzed, too rigid with revulsion to move a muscle; I could only stare transfixed at the gruesome scene.

At some point, voices began to penetrate the swirling mists of my brain. "Well, Yaro, you're up and around early . . . hey, what's up?" "He's talking to the boss. Is Jasper already down there?" I looked up. "Say, what's the matter with you? You look . . ." another arrival was peering down the hole. "He . . . oh, my God!" One of them turned around quickly and puked on the ground. Another turned toward me, his face pouring sweat, and gasped, "What's happened here, Yaro? Did you . . . ?"

"No!" I fairly screamed as their meaning became clear to me. "I just got here myself. He . . . he was . . ."

"Well, who did do it then?" demanded the first one quietly. "Because I don't see anyone else around here, and you sure turned up at a curious time."

23

"It was no accident," confirmed a third man. "I was real careful yesterday to keep all those rocks well back from the edge."

"But why would I want to kill him?" I protested. "He was my friend."

"You didn't sound too friendly last night," contested the first one. "I was in the tack room when this guy came by to chew him out. Something to do with Fawn."

"Yeah, I know he's been sneaking around with her. I never could figure out what the boss had against him. But I guess Jasper knew something we don't."

Despite my loud protests, I was soon bound and carried off to jail, accused of willfully murdering a pillar of the community.

Chapter 2

"There it is," announced one of the deckhands, as we followed his pointing arm to a sliver of darker green that peeped over the waves from our left. It still felt like we were on the high seas, but Arnica's chart showed that we were now in the Esperian Gulf, surrounded on three sides by land. These were the *Minkey*'s home waters.

The ship lurched slightly as we tacked shoreward. We could see land all along our port rail, and farther off to the right and abow.

So this was Esperia, the smallest and most populous of the Steward Alliance. I leaned heavily on the rail to take the weight off my injured leg. Arnica turned to me and commented, "It must all look very alien to you."

I nodded.

"How much do you know about our country?"

I was just asking myself that question.

"Not much, I'm afraid."

"Do you know anyone here?"

"Not a soul. The only Esperians I ever knew were the missionaries who raised me, and I assume they are all still down there."

"Quite probably."

"Do you think I'll be welcome here?"

"Oh, you'll be treated kindly. After all, it's the law, you being a refugee. Anyway, I doubt you'll stay long."

I jerked my head around in surprise. "Not stay long? Why? Where else would I go?"

"Wherever you wish. We're obliged to provide you free passage to the asylum of your choice. Borealia, for example, you'd probably be a lot more comfortable there."

"Because I'm white?"

"Perhaps, although that's nothing to us."

"What then?"

"Well, it's just that this is a very different country from what you're used to. I guess we Stewards have a way of seeing things that doesn't set well with others. No one here will send you away, but you may decide for yourself that it's not to your liking. Others have. Anyway, don't worry, we'll get you to wherever you want to go."

I thought hard. Here was a new slant on things: I might not *want* to stay here. How absurd! He seemed to be saying I would be a misfit here, which was likely enough, but he didn't realize how much of a misfit I'd been among "my own people." You see, while I had been taken from the orphanage unwillingly, I was fiercely determined to keep it a part of me. Therefore I had slavishly observed various customs and manners without hardly understanding why—if you think that wasn't awkward!

What then did I know about the people whose land I was about to enter? I knew there were some six million of them in a land one-twentieth the size of Anagaia. They were neither white like me nor as black as the Palmettoans. Some of my countrymen referred to them as half niggers, and those same people usually insisted that all Esperians were communists and atheists. Frankly, I didn't know whether that was so or not—they certainly had not tried to raise us up to be either. I did know that any Stewards I'd ever met were vegetarian, and that they were averse to saluting flags or other symbols. I had also heard that Esperians didn't live in cities, but in such a densely populated country, I knew that couldn't be. Beyond such random details, I was quite ignorant of those people, even more so their "way of seeing things," which I would supposedly find so distasteful. For now, however, I had more immediate concerns, and Arnica seemed to read my thoughts when he suggested, "You'll be needing a place to stay."

"Indeed, and it will have to be someplace very cheap. I have only one piece of silver left, and it may take a while to find a job. Of course, if the inns are too expensive, I'll have to live on the street, but I'm used to that."

Arnica merely blinked as though I'd just spewed out a string of complete nonsense. It made me nervous. Wren intervened, "You see, Yaro, there are no inns here, although any place would put you up for a few days. They won't take your silver, but they'll give you a job, or several, as soon as you're well enough."

Now it was my turn to do the blinking. Arnica added, "Communication will be a problem. Plenty of us speak your language, but by no means everyone. I think your greatest need is to be around someone who can help you understand what it is to be Esperian, and it would help if they understood what it is to be Anagaian."

"And so?"

"Well, I was thinking of my cousin Hewn who lives on the island of Alga. He used to be an ambassador to the Onyx Court and he speaks your language fluently, better than I. He has spent his whole career explaining one culture to the other, and I think he and his wife could be very useful to you."

"Of course, it would be wonderful, but why would he be willing to help me, this ambassador?"

"Retired ambassador. He's more of a consultant now. Why would he be willing? Well, that's not really the question, it's more a matter of whether they have room to accommodate you since their house is rather small. The only way to know is to ask, so since you seem interested, I'll send ahead to inquire."

"Send ahead? But we're at sea! Are you a wizard?"

"Matter of definition, I suppose. We'll send a dispatch to one of the signal towers on shore. They'll relay it to Alga, and hopefully a reply will catch up with us at Fairhaven, in time to put you on the late ferry."

Signal towers! We had those in Umberlands too. Ever since the Amanita Uprising, the Central Agency for Domestic Security, or CADS, had erected a network of communications beacons using a combination of mirrors by day and lamps by night. There was a tower on the ridge outside our village, but you didn't snoop around there if you knew what was good for you.

"But are ordinary citizens allowed to send messages? Where I come from, the system is strictly for police use."

"Ours is a public system," Arnica replied crisply. "There is a small fee for personal messages, but we can charge this one to the Refugee Fund. The only problem is we'll have to wait awhile now. There is a downtime between the lamps and the mirrors. Right now, it's too light for one and two dark for the other."

Fortunately, the sky was clear, and by the time the sun had climbed high enough above the horizon, the shore we were following loomed up high, only a couple miles away.

"There is the Dark Hills station now. Wren, would you be kind enough to fetch the transmitter, and we'll start."

In a moment, Wren returned with a contraption resembling a large lantern mounted on a floating disk on a small supporting table. After adjusting a windowlike sliding lens to the appropriate angle for the sun's position, he rotated the reflecting barrel toward the tallest of a cluster of hills on shore.

"This apparatus is only for local or short-distance transmitting," Arnica explained. "But it will be visible to that station once we get their attention. They in turn will use their much-stronger beam to relay the message up the coast and over to Alga. There it will be picked up by a local receiver, that is if anyone is on duty there. Wren, would you operate the shutter while I dictate? You are better at this."

I looked on in wonder as the device blurted out a series of flashes, which were answered a moment later by similar blips from the crest of the far-off hill. "Aha, that was quick!" Wren gloated. "They must have been watching us already, waiting to announce our arrival." He next began a staccato of flashes as the captain read out a message to him.

I watched spellbound as the tower on the hill blinked furiously for several seconds. A moment later, we saw another light on a much more distant hilltop, which duplicated our signal toward yet another receiver, somewhere beyond our view. In less time than it took to clear our own wake, the entire message was sent speeding on its way.

As the freighter continued to plough its way up the narrowing bay, Wren pointed out various landmarks. "There is Runaground on the Goosegrass estuary. Within a half hour, we'll be entering the Bluemeadow River where our homeport is."

From our sea level perspective, the land looked to be wholly forested; but where hillsides faced into the waxing morning, I could see an intricate patchwork of woodland mixed with farmland. On many of the hilltops—no, all of them—I could see towers comprised of segmented vertical cylinders, which turned as we watched. Windmills, Wren explained.

"Ah, look over there!" called Arnica, who had moved over to the starboard rail. "That long island, see? You can just begin to distinguish it from the shore. That's Alga, the largest of the Random Islands where my cousin Hewn lives. If things go well, you'll be there by tonight."

I turned my attention to the island, a wall of sheer rock rising abruptly out of the surf. Along its crest, we could barely make out more of the ubiquitous windmills; but otherwise, the place looked quite uninhabited.

"You mean people actually live there?" I shuddered. "It looks like an enormous slab of rock."

"Much of it is," agreed Arnica. "But plenty of folks live there nonetheless. I believe Alga banner counts over eight hundred residents."

"Mustn't they be wretchedly poor?"

The captain broke into hearty laughter. "Indeed, they're right prosperous there, every one. It's said you can't grind your meal nor salt it without trading with Alga. No, they lack nothing but good deep soil, and time and the wind will give them that too."

I was about to ask more questions when he excused himself. "We're coming off Harking banner now, and we'll soon be in shallows. I must attend to things." I knew I was in no shape to help, even if I had known the first thing about seamanship, so I tagged along with Wren to watch. He had already gone amidships where I watched him and two other deckhands undo a heavy line. As it eased through a large wooden pulley, a cross spar was lowered and an upper sail was reefed until it caught no wind. Gradually, we felt the ship lose speed as they moved on to another line. By the time the huge vessel nosed into the broad section of river mouth called Pilot's Reach, we were cruising slowly enough for the helmsman to keep us in the channel. I watched the low silvery blue mudflats glide by us as we navigated through a winding maze of reeds and salt grass. At this point, the channel was hundreds of feet wide; but after five days on the high seas, it felt terribly cramped. The mudflats were crowded with flocks of wild geese, mallards, and other migratory birds. They were gorging on the reed seed in a last-minute feeding frenzy before heading south. I wished them well and rejoiced that I was going in the opposite direction.

Only a couple miles up the Bluemeadow River, the *Minkey* made a final scraping bump against its waiting pier. That solid contact with the new land seemed momentous to me. You see, when the *Minkey* had slipped its moorings at the quay in New Chalice, I was not on it. The police were watching the harbourfront closely, and every outgoing vessel was carefully searched for stowaways. Not only on my account; it must be remembered that there were many dissidents eager to leave the country, and of course, the government suspected everyone of smuggling weapons to the Amanita or to guerrilla groups in the Coquinas. It was Wren who came up with the plan: for two days I stayed hidden under the quay while the *Minkey* was loading. Stevedores, merchants, and night watchmen all came and went without realizing that a wanted criminal crouched on a stone piling only inches below their feet. Each night, one of the *Minkey*'s crew sneaked me a bag of food and water. On the night of departure, I watched uneasily as my savior ship cast off on the outgoing tide. Obeying instructions, I waited exactly a half hour, by which time the police and customs inspectors had all left for a nearby tavern. I came out from my hideaway and ran for all I was worth; past the docks, past the warehouses, past the squalid slums of Hell's Hollow, down the shore road among the dunes, all the while my knee throbbing and my lungs bursting. Down a rutted side lane that vanished among the reeds, where a gaunt phantom arose in front of me and beckoned with silent gestures. Who knows what goods he smuggled on other nights? Tonight I was his contraband. He motioned me into a shallow skiff, which he rowed noiselessly along the lee of a sandy point. Watching, waiting, we scanned the moonless expanse of Great Oyster Bay, ears straining for the sound of patrol boats. Soon, the faint glimmer of a shielded lantern, once, no more. We darted out into the open water, into the path of the dark-looming vessel. A rope came over the side, someone tossed down the second half of the rower's fee, and I was hoisted onto the deck of the northbound freighter.

Chapter 3

A knot of waiting friends and family stood on the pier to catch lines and help secure the two gangplanks. They had heard of the *Minkey*'s imminent arrival from the same signal tower that had carried my message to Alga, and they now crowded around to welcome my shipmates. At that moment, more than at any time during the voyage, I was struck by just how alone I was. To the rest of the ship's company, these swarthy faces were well-known, their language intelligible, the surroundings familiar. To me it was all strange and unsettling.

A gentle tug at my elbow drew my attention to a boy of about twelve who had just boarded and now stood beside me. He held out a note, and I could barely understand his faltering words, though they were in my language.

"You refugee Anagaia? Very good, I have message. Your ship steward he can read." Having delivered the note, he turned and left at once. He didn't seem to expect any tip, which was lucky for both of us. I took the paper to Arnica, who was giving directions for securing lines and unbattening hatches. He paused long enough to scan it.

"Leaping limpets, this got here quick! As I expected, Hewn says you're welcome at Stonesthrow, at least for a while. You are to take the *River Harp* this afternoon. Someone will meet you at Alga landing."

Wren, who had been organizing some papers nearby, piped up. "I can see that you get on the ferry and tell the pilot where to let you off. I'll be busy unloading until then. If you want to poke around and see the place, fine, only be back here at noon if you want to eat with us."

To tell the truth, I had little interest in "poking around" at this point. Prolonged walking, or even standing, made my knee throb from a nasty cut I'd received while fleeing the border patrol in the Foxfire Mountains. I sat down on a bench near the wharf to watch the unloading. It would take days to finish, I knew very well; I had watched, or rather heard, every item of cargo be carried onboard. Yet what a contrast; the New Chalice waterfront was such a teeming place, backed by a market district with its hawkers and beggars and prostitutes. How different was this place—other than a row of warehouses and a dozen or so men and women dockworkers, there was no indication of any great population centre. And what about security? At New Chalice, armed guards watched out for pilfering while doing a bit of it themselves. Here, no one seemed to worry about theft. The only concern was for getting cargo sorted and under cover before the weather changed.

For hours, the *Minkey*'s hold continued to disgorge itself onto the long pier where it was Wren's job to record and organize it all as it went ashore. There were piles of crated figs and apricots, cases of glass and bars of copper, bolts of flannel and denim, and bales of raw cotton. Back in Anagaia, the carting had been done mostly by horse- and mule-drawn vehicles, but here I saw no draught animals. The cargo was loaded onto conveyor belts which extended right out onto the pier. These were driven by a tidal-mill via a series of cables and pulleys. Branch conveyors delivered each load to its designated warehouse where people used handcarts and dollies to move everything into its place.

Wren scurried from one pile to another, writing things down on one list and checking them off another. Every few seconds, he would call out instructions to the air in general, and someone would show up to either load it onto a conveyor or take it off. He was far too preoccupied for me to disturb him with the obvious question that was on my mind.

*   *   *   *   *   *   *

"So where is it?"

"Where is what?" Wren took another bite of his lunch as we leaned back comfortably on the bench.

"The port. I mean, the *Minkey*'s homeport is Fairhaven, so why are we unloading here instead?"

"Oh, this is it. You're in Fairhaven."

"But where is the city proper? Is there nothing but docks?"

"Well now, there's more than docks, of course. But there is no city. You see, we don't have any cities in this country."

"Oh, come on now. I've heard all that before, but how is it possible? There are millions of people here—they can't all live in villages?"

"Actually, we don't have any villages either."

"You expect me to believe the whole country is rural?"

"Not that either. At least not like you're used to. This area is fairly typical. Maybe if you walk around the neighbourhood, you'll get some idea of what I mean."

"Maybe later. So you're saying there is no town of Fairhaven?"

"There's a community of Fairhaven. Actually, we call them banners. But none of them has what you'd call an urban centre, unless you count the bannerhouse."

"Bannerhouse? What's that?"

"A large community building. It combines administration offices, library, school, meetinghouse, and other functions all under one roof. It is always identified by the community banner that flies in front of it—not that you'd mistake it for anything else. Fairhaven's is up that way less than a mile."

"What can you tell me about Alga?"

"Real nice place, friendly folks. Rather cosmopolitan too—you'll find lots of people who speak your language fairly well. It's a small community, but very prosperous—rich, you might as well say, what with their chemicals and bay wax and stuff. They're too crowded though. Much of the soil is thin and poor, so they can't feed themselves. They are chronically in violation of the Vine Laws."

"Vine Laws? What's that all about?"

"Oh, hoot, it's too complicated for me to explain now. Wait until you get to Alga, and you'll see for yourself. Anyway, Hewn is the one to ask about that stuff—it's right down his line."

"Hewn—that's Arnica's cousin, the retired diplomat?"

"I don't think he's really a cousin, more like a distant kinsman. And I'm not sure about the 'retired' part either. They keep him pretty busy here at home."

"Well, what's he like, he and his household? After all, I'm going to live there."

"I don't know any of the household, except Hewn and his wife, Ermine. They're both in their midseventies, I'd say. Last I knew she was stead steward—you'll learn about that—and she's also a healer. She is originally from Longlogan, which is how I happen to know them. Hewn is an expert on foreign affairs, especially trade issues. He is a liaison with the Vision Fulfillment Commision, so his opinions are very sought-after by the Anagaian envoy. Hewn and Ermine are both very intelligent and active in the community at many levels. After all, they dwell in a very Large House."

"Oh no. Arnica himself said that their place is very small. They hardly have room—"

"Don't be silly. I'm not talking about their house."

"You're not? But you just—"

"It's just an expression we use: 'dwell in the Larger House,' you know?"

"No, I don't know. What does that mean anyway?"

"It means . . . hey, look, I'm no good at explaining that stuff—it's part of the Vision. That's why you're going to Stonesthrow. Arnica figures it's the best place to learn, and I guess he's right. I've got to get back to work now. You've still got two hours until the ferry."

After lunch, my curiosity began to outweigh my discomfort, and I decided my knee was up to a short exploratory hike. I walked a ways along the road Wren had indicated and immediately felt I was in a different world. I now saw a face of the country that was not so easily seen from the river.

I would say my first impression was of compactness. Within a mile I passed two farmsteads, a small factory, and a brickyard. Each farm had a windmill, and I saw several others in the distance. I passed a field of about five acres, which was divided by stone walls into several smaller plots. Even at that late season, one could see that they were or had been planted to a variety of crops. There were no sweeping panoramas, at least not in that neighbourhood, but always a closer, more intimate landscape. The road was very narrow—about eight feet—yet well graded and ditched. It was considered a two-lane highway, yet an Umberlands farm wagon would hardly have fit in the whole road. (Of course, such a wagon would have been useless here since Esperians keep no horses or other draught animals.) Two people passed me with handcarts, and several bicycles whizzed by. I had seen only one of those before in my life: Ash Shackleford had once cajoled his parents into importing one for his birthday. He had bounced over the rutted and dusty roads of Dryford for a few weeks before tiring of it, after which it was relegated to a corner of an equipment shed. Here in Esperia, bicycles were obviously a serious means of transportation.

Everything I saw here seemed to be on a smaller scale, all except the houses. Those were unusually large and solid—I wondered where the poorer people lived. I didn't venture as far as the bannerhouse, though I could see it ahead of me. So this was the centre of town, yet here were farms, albeit small ones, right in the middle of it. I saw what Wren meant about there being little "rural" here, or rather a very dense "rural." I saw no vast fields of grain or anything else but lots of gardens, orchards, and woodlots all compressed into what seemed like a model—a miniature version of a real country.

The exertion soon wore on me, and I returned to the dock where the unloading continued unabated. There were several long piers jutting out into the tidewater. Some were empty, a couple held small coastal freighters. There was a newly built gunboat, which Wren said was commissioned by the Palmettoan government to patrol its coast, and a curiously designed vessel which was used for oceanographic research. Only one other ship was comparable to the *Minkey* in tonnage: a broad-beamed freighter carrying the flag of Borealia. The Borealia language is close-akin to Anagaian, so I got to chat with one of the sailors. It was called the *Spruce King*, and they were not there to trade, but for emergency repairs. Their cargo consisted mainly of furs, which Esperians did not want, and lumber, which they did not need. The sailor grumbled that it was unfair that Esperia was so self-sufficient; they only imported a little resin and zinc and potash from Borealia, whereas the latter was wholly dependent on Esperian manufactures. I had heard similar complaints back home about Esperia's lopsided balance of payments. Some of the local bystanders seemed to assume I was from the *Spruce King* because of my light complexion, yet I wasn't dressed like them. My worn-out leather shoes had been tossed into the *Minkey*'s galley stove days ago, replaced by stout linen canvas boots with braided rush soles, and my disintegrating cotton shirt was concealed under the loose quilted coat Wren had loaned me.

The day had grown cooler, and my leg wanted rest, so I hunkered down on the sunny side of a stack of cotton bales. They, like myself, were newly landed, and the warm lint felt familiar against my back. However, its touch carried me back to a time weeks earlier when I was altogether too warm.

Chapter 4

Standing on the courthouse steps in Shoatmart, I hesitated only a moment. It seemed I had been granted a new lease on life, but I wasn't sure what that lease was worth. Judge Strider was very clear about the sentence: the curse of banishment did not mean I was free, but rather that I was dead in the eyes of the law. The implications of that were clear to anyone who wished me harm: no one could be held to account for killing a person who was already dead.

I couldn't help noticing Ash Shackleford's black gelding hitched to a post across the street, yet I hadn't seen him at the trial. If anyone wished me harm, it was Ash.

Despite the torrid heat, I ran down the street and out of town. If I wanted to live, I must put miles between myself and that place. No going back the four miles to Dryford to get my stuff, no last words to Melody or anyone else unless I wished to put them in jeopardy too. The curse was quite explicit: anyone who helped or comforted me in any way also incurred the curse. Running madly down the provincial highway in that blistering heat was foolhardy, but to dally was suicide.

I soon moderated my pace, if only because heatstroke was staring me in the face. I had no food, no water, no money, no weapons, no extra clothes. I was totally vulnerable. I kept looking over my shoulder, expecting to hear the hoofbeats of pursuers, but none came.

The road was surprisingly empty, considering that there were usually peddlers or drovers bound for Shoatmart or other towns on the river plain. Only toward late afternoon did I spy a caravan of wool merchants coming toward me from the east. As they neared, I approached the lead carter beseechingly.

"Water! Please, I need water!"

He drove on past without seeming to notice me. More aggressively, I implored the second driver, "Please, I'll die without water!"

He appeared to waver slightly, but a mounted escort spurred his horse forward, knocking me backward off my feet. I lay sprawled in the dust until they were past. They knew—it was plain in their faces they knew, just as if I had a brand on my forehead saying "accurst." Those men didn't hate me; they probably weren't even afraid of me.

They were afraid of the curse. But how could they know, coming from the eastward only hours after the trial?

I'll never know how I survived that first day and night. I hadn't been overfed when the whole ordeal started, but right now, thirst was my biggest problem. I had passed a few farms, but they were always barred and shuttered; and once when I approached a pump in the yard of one place, a couple of vicious dogs came snarling after me. At another place, a rifle barrel was poked out through shuttered windows to wave me away. Nevertheless I kept trying—I had no choice. Once, I thought I was in luck when I passed a place that really was abandoned, but when I pulled on the pump handle, the squeaky gasp of a dry leather washer told me why the place was deserted.

Of course, all this time I was following the Possum River, which often overflowed its banks in the spring. But during those drought years, the flow was usually reduced by irrigation to a mere trickle by late summer. Within the old streambed lay pools of stagnant green water, roiled by livestock and choked with algae. Anyone knew you couldn't drink that stuff, yet in my extremity, I was tempted. In a very short time, I was doubled up on the roadside, puking my guts out onto the parched red earth. It was worse than thirst—I never tried that again. But I did have to get water soon or die. A pair of turkey vultures were circling overhead, and I feared they knew more than I did.

Eventually, an idea occurred to me, and I scuttled down the bank to the riverbed. Ignoring the foul pools this time, I looked around till I found a gravel bar formed when the river was in flood. With bare hands, I picked away at the gravel for several inches, and then I found sand. That was easier to scoop out, and I enlarged the hole but came to a layer of coarse marly clay, which my fingers could not attack. I found a jagged piece of rock and scraped away more, all the while feeling my energy seep away in the enervating heat. Finally, I was relieved to strike sand again, sand that was bone dry at first; but as I dug deeper, it became damp. I sat back to rest a minute and was ecstatic to see that drops of moisture had actually formed a tiny puddle. I dug deeper and waited longer—my hole was nearly two feet deep now. There was only about a half cup of water in there, but it was safe water, filtered through the marl and trapped in the sand. With no cup to dip with, I craned my head into the hole and sucked up what I could, taking in a good deal of grit along with it. If I hadn't thought of that trick, I do believe those vultures would have had their reward within hours.

It didn't seem to matter which way I turned, the whole world seem to anticipate my every move. Every farm shut up tight, no travelers on the road, no sign even of the ubiquitous shepherds on the marginal lands. Why was I headed this way anyway? Today, I am well aware that it was only three hundred miles westward to the Prairie Federation and less than that south to the Palmetto Republic. I didn't have a very good knowledge of geography, but I had a vague notion that somewhere over the mountains eastward was the sea, and there were great cities where a person might lose their identity, ports where ships sailed to other lands. Rational or not, my instincts guided me in that direction. If I could just get to some place where no one knew me, I might have a chance, but how?

For no good reason that I know, I kept to the provincial highway, ignoring smaller roads to one side or the other. However, late on the second day, I came to a fork in the highway which required a decision: continue along the Possum River toward the south end of the Flint Hills or turn northeast onto a small cut-off road that climbed over a gap in those hills. The first option offered continued access to drinking water, but a drawback was that it led toward the orphanage. To even appear to be going there could be bad news, for them and for me. The other road seemed to pass over the hills well to the north of Cleftridge. I knew that area was relatively wild and unsettled, which might be a help. At this point, any change seemed propitious, so I chose that road. It was another fluke decision which I believe saved my life.

* * * * *

My thoughts were rudely interrupted by the blast of a horn at the third pier over. It was the ferry *River Harp* on her downstream run. Wren dropped what he was doing long enough to see me onboard and say a few words to the man at the helm.

"All set, Yaro. I think you'll do just fine now," he smiled reassuringly.

"I can't thank you enough," I stammered, choking up at the thought of leaving him.

"Glad to help," he shrugged. "I'll keep in touch to see how you're getting along. Hang onto that coat for now—I'll get it back sometime. I must tell you, though, I think Arnica's wrong about you not staying. From what I've seen of you, I think you may grow to like it here."

It struck me that this short ferry ride down Pilot's Reach was momentous in one respect: I was backtracking. During all the weeks since leaving the Shoatmart courthouse, I had rarely retraced my steps. It was turn this way or that way, but always keep moving or risk death. Now I could travel a few miles upstream or a few miles downstream—it was all the same.

I had examined the scenery pretty carefully on the up-trip, so now my attention was directed to the curious vessel which carried me. I learned that the *River Harp* and its sister ferry, the *Bluemeadow Mist,* were operated by something called the Lower Valley Commission. They plied the river from Worthy's Landing to Harking and both shores of the bay. Passage was free to the public; only freight paid a fare. That is to say, getting onboard was free; actually going anywhere depended partly on the passengers' own effort. I shall try to describe the craft's curious means of propulsion.

It required at least eight people of average weight to propel the vessel, of which four were supplied by the crew; the rest depended on the enthusiasm of the passengers. I was intrigued by the mode of converting human power into forward motion. On the broad deck near the stern was a huge paddle wheel or treadmill. A chain sprocket drive linked the treadmill shaft to a parallel camshaft below deck. From each cam, a drive rod projected out the stern board and slanted down into the water where was fastened a "thruster" (also called a squid), a device resembling an umbrella which has been blown inside out. That is to say, a number of smaller rods were hinged to the drive rod end and connected by a pleated covering of rubberized canvas in the shape of a forward-pointing cone. When the rods were pushed outward by the cam action, the cones spread open wide, giving a maximum thrust against the water. As the rods were withdrawn on the return stroke, the cones collapsed onto themselves, giving minimal resistance. At any moment, a number of thrusters were pushing while others prepared to push, generating a steady forward motion. The entire assembly could be tilted up out of the water if rocks or shallow bars threatened to damage the squids.

What really puzzled me was that under a tarp right behind the treadmill was a small charcoal-fired steam engine. It probably could have driven the ferry all by itself, yet it was not even fired up, and the clutch was disengaged.

The last leg of the trip was from Galeslee across the Strait to Alga Island, which looked much less forbidding from this side. Unlike the seaward cliffs, the inner shore was low and approachable with cobbled beaches and ample signs of habitation.

It was late afternoon when the ferry bumped lightly against Alga landing. I stepped ashore and looked around for the person who was supposed to meet me. Across the pier, a small beamy craft was tied, and several people were forking its contents onto a sort of wagon mounted on rails. The stuff was seaweed; and when the wagon was full, someone pulled a lever and the wagon pulled away, seemingly of its own accord.

I had other concerns just now: someone was supposed to be here to guide me to the ambassador's house, a place called Stonesthrow—I didn't even know how to say that in Esperian nor how to ask for directions.

Presently, an elderly workman detached himself from the group and approached me. He wore a bast-cloth apron coloured by an ugly purple-brown stain that matched his hands. Despite his apparent age, he was erect and vigourous. His long wind-tossed grey hair and piercing eyes seemed part and parcel of the island's ruggedness, and I could well imagine that this old-timer might never have set foot off this rock-girt place. On the other hand, he must surely know the way to . . . what was it? Stonesthrow. If I could only think of some gestures to explain my need. However, he spoke first.

"Would you be the gentleman who is expected from the *Minkey*?"

Incredible. Flawless Anagaian, not like my singsongy Umberlands dialect, but proper, like the urban gentry.

"I . . . I was seeking the way to the home of Hewn . . . I don't know his family name, but you must know of him. He was the ambassador to . . . ."

"Ah, Hewn, yes, I know him well. But you see, he doesn't have any family name, nor does anyone else here. The closest thing we have is stead names, so Hewn of Stonesthrow is what you'll have to call me."

"You? Why, I mean, I . . . ."

"You expected something a bit grander, no doubt. Sorry, but we don't go in much for that here. Besides, I'm home from the embassy nowadays, except for consultation, so I work on the wrack boats whenever I'm able. They're about finished here, so let's you and me go up to the house."

I was still incredulous. I had expected a messenger, some household servant at best. Was this really the former ambassador, representative of Esperian interests at the court of the Olotal Blaze II, come to meet me in person? I might have suspected a hoax were it not for his impeccable use of my language. Seeing that I had no luggage, he turned on his heel and started briskly up the road, with me hobbling along trying to keep up.

Chapter 5

For two whole days, I ate and slept and loafed. Yes, and wept; now that my troubles finally seemed over, the floodgates opened, for only now did I have the luxury of venting those weeks of tension and despair. My own people, my community, those who knew me and should have trusted me had rejected me, thrown me out to perish. Only the most improbable series of flukes had preserved me alive, here on the shores of a strange and far country.

In fairness, not all of them had turned on me. Melody, after all, had kept me off the gallows. And what about Fawn? There was reason to believe that Rose, her mother, doubted my guilt; but I had no idea whether Fawn trusted in my innocence, or whether she was among those who despised me as her father's murderer. Ash Shackleford would certainly be there, doing all he could to poison their minds against me.

You see, I had no way to contact her—Anagaia has no public mail service, and private couriers are often in collusion with CADS agents who open and examine the mail for suspicious content. Merely receiving a letter from abroad could get Fawn into a lot of trouble. Even assuming Fawn wanted to join me in exile, it was quite impossible. One needed official papers just to travel outside the district; surely the authorities would not allow her to leave the country, knowing her intent. There was simply no way to let them know I was alive and safe.

I was putting on weight, and my knee was mending, albeit slowly. Still, I was depressed, and I knew I needed to do something about it. Sitting on my bed in the bachelors' dormitory, I looked out at the low clouds scudding over Galeslee Strait. A stinging rain pelted the windows, driving nearly everyone inside. Harvest was all gotten in now, and some of the household were downstairs, dealing with food-processing chores. Sounds of cheerful laughter and the mingled aromas of cooking wafted up to me as I turned to bury my face gloomily in my pillow. *Quit being foolish*, I told myself, *people here have made great sacrifices to get you this far, so get on with it*.

I climbed down the narrow back staircase to the large kitchen and stood blinking a moment. Half a dozen steadmates were seated at two long tables, working at various projects.

"I want to do something . . . to work. What can I do?"

"Are you sure you ought to, dear? We don't want that sore to reopen now."

Ermine should know; she had cared for it since my arrival, draining the ulceration and swathing it in poultices.

"But too much resting is wearing me out. Maybe if I'm sitting down . . . ?"

She smiled understandingly. "I suppose we can use more help. Let's see, they have enough hands drying leeks, so you can either shred cabbage for kraut or help me clean out these pumpkins."

I chose the latter. I enjoyed being with Ermine who, like her husband, spoke fluent Anagaian and knew a lot more about my homeland than I did. For all her seventy-two years, she was an exceptionally beautiful woman, with high cheekbones framing dark and expressive eyes. Her skin was smooth and swarthy, even for an Esperian. She had a quietly assertive manner that helped her get things done without antagonism. Whenever others were squabbling, she could say a calm word or two, and it was like oil poured on boiling water. Frankly, I found it easier to imagine her mixing with the fine ladies of Anagaian society than as she was now, up to her elbows in pumpkin shells.

"Here," she said, handing me the cleaver. "Your hands are stronger than mine. Why don't you split these open while I scoop out the seeds?"

The pumpkins Esperians grow are mostly used for their seeds, which are green and free of hulls. I had already developed a great liking for the rich oily kernels.

The spacious room was snugly warm from a massive brick stove in the centre, which contained ovens and a thick cast-iron plate for cooking. Everything to do with the kitchen was on a large scale; after all, it was expected to feed seventeen mouths, thrice a day, mostly with food grown on the premises.

A great iron cauldron of apple butter plopped invitingly on the hot range while racks of sliced vegetables and fruits dried overhead. High along one wall hung bunches of sage, savoury, and other herbs together with long braids of garlic and onions.

The dour skies outside seemed to make the group only merrier as all joined in the communal work. Where I come from, such gatherings are rare; and although the chatter was mostly incomprehensible to me, I felt a strong glow of pleasure in being part of such an intimate group.

Wren's description of Stonesthrow had given me some misconceptions, all of which were cleared up upon my arrival. It was not a small house at all, at least by any standard I was used to. It was a huge and solid structure, which could be considered small only in comparison to other homes on the island. If it indeed seemed a bit crowded, that's only because there were seventeen members of the household, not counting myself. You see, the place wasn't really Hewn's or Ermine's, rather it was a communal dwelling called a stead. The occupants, who were not all related to each other, shared the surname of Stonesthrow by virtue of residence, not lineage. I've said enough about that for now.

There was one of our workgroup who wasn't a household member, but she visited often enough that she almost seemed like one. Myrica was Hewn's and Ermine's granddaughter, and she lived with her parents on the nearby island of Telling. She too spoke pretty good Anagaian, though with a thick accent, and she was eager for opportunities to improve her skill, so we became good friends. Anyway, Myrica now sat at the table behind me, part of the sauerkraut bee.

"You sure must have liked those buckwheat cakes we had for breakfast," she teased. "We couldn't cook them fast enough."

I grinned back sheepishly. "They were good, even better than my sister makes. That's one of the few familiar foods I've had since coming here."

"Yes, I was thinking it must be a difficult change for you. I mean, since we don't eat meat or milk and such."

"Oh no, that's not . . . I myself have never tasted those things, though I've smelled them often. Actually, the food here is much more varied than I'm used to. I really love it."

"But I thought Anagaians ate lots of stuff from animals. I read that they have more livestock than people there."

"That's probably true, but most poor folks sell the meat they raise and eat cheaper foods like sweetpotatoes."

"So your family was vegan?"

"Certainly not. They ate whatever meat they could afford. We always kept a pig or two, but the Seekings mostly used the lard and cheaper cuts. I never ate any of it."

"But why not, if your family did?"

"You see, I was raised by your people until I was eleven. It was an orphanage, run by Steward missionaries. They never ate animal foods, but they never told us not to. When I was taken away from there, I was really unhappy—I always considered them my real family, especially Faring. I was hard-bent on doing everything they did in my new home, even if I didn't understand why. It used to drive Archer wild."

"So you never knew your birth parents?"

Ermine cleared her throat and made a look of reproval.

"No, it's okay," I assured her. "I'm happy to talk about it. I don't even know who my birth father is, but I did see my birth mother, only a few weeks ago."

"Really? How wonderful!"

"Well, not really—it was pretty sad. You see . . . she's one of the people I'm accused of murdering."

Myrica and Ermine gasped, and as my words were translated, a shocked silence fell over the room. I knew I needed to explain further, so I began by taking a thin waxed cloth wallet from my pocket and carefully withdrawing a small scrap of paper. On one side, it was a nineteen-year-old lading bill from a textile factory in Sycamore, Umberlands. Crumple marks suggested it had once been retrieved from a waste bin. On the reverse side, I pointed out this faded pencil message: "Pleez take gud care of my child. I cant no longer. When he grows up, tell him I luv him and am sory. I hev cald him Yaro." I explained to my listeners that the note was tucked into the swathing rags, which protected me from the freezing cold on the early morning when I was left on the back steps of the Mid-Umberlands Children's Home. I've always carried it, and that's why I always spell my name Yaro, even though I'm named after the herb. Next, I told them the story about the day I decided to live.

Chapter 6

As the days of my banishment went by, it really seemed that I was doomed—there was no way of escaping Judge Strider's curse. I didn't know what lay ahead for me, but I knew it was dreadful. In my more reflective moments, it occurred to me that this must all be a colossal nuisance for the police too. Apparently there was some system by which everyone knew just where I was heading, and it must be tying up a lot of resources. There was, after all, nothing to prevent anyone from killing me—at what point would some impatient CADS agent decide to be done with all this foolishness and save the taxpayers some money? At what point might I wish it for myself?

As I approached the Flint Hills, there were towering banks of cumulus clouds and occasional rumbling, but the heat went on unabated; and I expected that if it ever did rain, it would be on my vulture-picked carcass.

I passed another farm, probably the last before the uninhabited hills. It was shut up tight like the others, though I felt eyes watching me as I plodded past. I couldn't help noticing that the corn was not completely shriveled and that the yam field was unusually green for so late in the year. There was no sign of a well in the yard, so I put two and two together as I continued on by, appearing to ignore it all. Just beyond the farm fields, the land changed abruptly as a series of steep ledges arose from the flat silty river plain. Just like that, the road began climbing into the Flint Hills. I walked only a few hundred yards up that slope then turned off sharply to the right. Although the plain was close cropped and bare overall, the rocky hills were grown up here and there to brush and sparse woods. I dodged into a coppice of blackjack oak and doubled back to where I could look down over the ledges and observe the farm without myself being seen. Sure enough, just below me, a clump of young growing aspens and a streak of lush grass meandered away toward the yam field. There had to be a spring there, just out of sight; I could even make out part of a fence that was no doubt meant to keep livestock from roiling it. That alone explained why the place looked fairly prosperous when so many other farms in the neighbourhood were withered and abandoned. Right here below me were the two things I most craved: clear cool water and food, although I had never in my life eaten a sweetpotato raw. I resolved to lie in wait until I could venture out under cover of darkness.

I hunkered down to watch the place. A teenage boy came out and looked up the road. I assume he returned to tell the rest I was nowhere in sight because the farm immediately came back to life. The father resumed threshing a pile of millet from which I had probably distracted him, the teenager went back to digging sweetpotatoes, while two younger kids wheeled a barrow of culls over to a pigsty. The woman of the household carried a load of wash over to a trough in the side yard, and everything looked as normal as ever.

Twilight brought a profound change to the farmstead. The air became cooler and more humid than it had been for weeks. Clouds of insects flitted and hovered over the spring while a pair of bats swooped back and forth through them. Crickets chirped, and I even thought I heard frogs croaking. I was impatient to go down yet too timid to hurry. Gradually, the whole family withdrew into the farmhouse, including both dogs. I was careful to note that: with a criminal loose in the neighborhood, I wondered why they weren't tied outside. I waited still longer until the lamps were all out, then I crept down the slope. As I hoped, the spring formed a shallow rock-lined pool which I could approach without leaving tracks. As I lay on my stomach to lap from it, my shirtfront got soaked, but I had never before felt or tasted anything so satisfying. I didn't hurry, letting the drops seep into every cell of my being. After a while, I slinked over to the nearest row of sweetpotatoes. I collected a half dozen, but none from the same hill, lest anyone notice the loss. I smoothed the soil and tried to tread lightly so no prints would show. Back in my hideaway, I ate one of the sweetpotatoes before dropping off to sleep. I was in no hurry to leave the place. I told myself I would hole up there for a couple days at least and eat and drink my fill before moving on.

Next morning, I peered out of my brush-fringed nest to see the farm wife starting toward the spring with a couple of buckets. Her husband called her back and took the buckets himself. I saw him inspect the rows of sweetpotatoes then hurry back with the full pails. The man was no fool; in spite of my care, he had seen something which aroused his suspicions. Still, no one seemed compelled to act on those suspicions. A short while later, I saw a man arrive on horseback from my direction. Even at that distance, I could recognize his CADS uniform. He was berating the farmer who was clearly intimidated. Finally, the farmer pointed off in my general direction, and the officer uttered a few stern words before turning his mount and galloping back eastward. The farmer called to his teenage son, and they both went into the house. I knew what was up even before they reemerged with their guns, and I was quick to get out of there. I didn't run too hard though; my shirtfront was stuffed with sweetpotatoes, and I'd just as soon get shot as drop them. Anyway, I realized by now they didn't care where I went to as long as it was away from them. Like everyone else, it wasn't me they feared so much as the curse. As long as I didn't settle down and get comfortable, most folks wouldn't bother about me.

I knew now that this man, or some other officer, was always ahead of me, warning residents of my approach and no doubt threatening them as well. Perhaps there was a second rider somewhere behind me who somehow notified the front rider where I was and when I took a different road. Apparently, that last fork I took threw them off a bit, but not for long. How did they communicate? No one had passed me. All I knew for sure was that without some answers, I was in a trap, and nothing I did would get me out. Legally dead really meant as good as dead. Perhaps it seems obvious now; but in those days, peasants understood little about how the government operated, and it wasn't always prudent to inquire. Therefore we saw things every day without being fully aware of the role they played in our lives.

All day long, the thunderheads piled higher and higher. It was clear they meant business this time. I would want shelter, so I kept an eye out. It was also getting darker fast as I ascended the gap. Big scattered drops were falling, stirring up the dust. Around me rose jagged pinnacles of hard chert, bared like sabres where the softer chalk had eroded away around them. Some had toppled over with time into jumbled postpiles, impenetrable except where the road had been squeezed into a narrow defile. There were no wheel ruts; only pack animals could get through here. The wind was mean and the lightning nonstop, and now the rain really let go. I was so intent on scanning the rocks for some cave or overhang, I didn't see the crude knapsack until I nearly tripped over it. I glanced anxiously around, but seeing no one, I rolled it over with my toe. The ground underneath it was rain spattered, so it had lain there less than ten minutes. The storm was breaking in its full fury now, but I was no longer intent on finding shelter. Curious but wary, I knelt and untied it. Only a few items but all terribly useful to me. A cheap pottery jug, corked and filled with fresh water. A round loaf of coarse dark bread and a small cloth bag, apparently containing some coins. Emptying them into my hands, I saw that they were not copper bullheads but silver falcons, nineteen of them. In my astonishment, I had dropped the empty coin pouch by my feet. As I reached down to pick it up, a prolonged flash of lightning revealed a single word stitched onto the bag; the word was Yaro.

Chapter 7

I threw myself down on the road and hastily crawled behind a group of rocks. I felt sure a rifle barrel was pointed at me from somewhere, but nothing happened and I began to reconsider; thus far, no one had tried to kill me, so why now? And why would an enemy carefully stitch your name onto a bag of money? It wasn't bait. Here I was, alone and vulnerable; there was no need to lie in ambush. Less afraid now, I peeked out to see if anyone was around. At first not, but then I spotted a fleeing figure darting among some boulders high on the slope above me. It looked like a skinny little girl, out here in the wilderness, far from any village or farmstead. She clearly meant me no harm but was in some danger herself. The rocks here were very jagged and hard, and the rain turned the thin chalky soil into grease. There probably wasn't much I could do to help her, but I had to talk to her, to find out what this was all about.

The storm was in full crescendo, driving great gusts of rain into my face. When lightning flashed, it seemed to flash everywhere, making the whole world brighter than noon; but in between flashes, the land was plunged into deep gloom. Grabbing the knapsack, I scrambled up the slope after the fleeing girl when a sudden thought brought me to a halt. Snatching the waterproof wallet out of my pocket, I hastily unfolded the talisman note, which I hadn't even looked at for several years. Not only was my name similarly misspelled, but it ended with a slight flourish, exactly like the stitching on the pouch. That was not a young girl up there—that was my mother!

I ran after her, shouting wildly to reassure her. My voice was annihilated by the wind. She was not very fleet, and I hoped to conquer the distance between us before she got herself hurt. But I was hardly in peak condition myself, and it was hard to keep her in view as she darted among the great boulders. One moment it was pitch dark, the next it was blinding bright as the giant forked arrows of electricity slashed open the sky. By one of those bursts, I spotted a figure dashing recklessly along the crest of the ridge. I was closing the gap. Once she turned to glance back, and I saw the terror in her eyes. She seemed to be coughing convulsively, which caused her to slip and fall. I was nearly to her, but she sprang up with frenzied energy and was off again, babbling incoherently. I hesitated. If she were afraid of me, my pursuing her could only compound her danger.

Still, I couldn't just turn back and leave her in this forbidding place, especially in her condition. I had to catch up with her before she came to harm.

It was hard to see where she had gone, but the rough terrain limited the possibilities. I came to a narrow crevice formed by two overarching slabs, and I stumbled through into the confusing blackness. Just as I emerged from the other end, a renewed burst of light made me recoil onto my own footsteps. I had almost stepped off a sheer drop of nearly twenty feet. Peering over the edge, I could make out a contorted figure sprawled on the rocks at its base.

More quickly than was prudent, I picked my way down around the cliff until I was squatting beside her. I didn't need to examine her to know she was dead. It was also evident that the fall was not the sole cause of her death—I probably could've leaped off the cliff and sustained no more than a broken ankle. Although she appeared to be in her midthirties, she was unnaturally aged. Her hair was matted and lustreless, her eyes dark and sunken. From her shriveled body, I deduced she was badly malnourished. Clearly this woman had suffered much at the hands of life and was perhaps little worse off now.

There were unanswered questions: if she were in such wretched health, how had she come by herself to this remote place? And if she were so starved, why had she not eaten the bread herself? And if she were as addled as she appeared, how had she known where to find me and when?

Many questions, but only one answer presented itself: a mother's love. For me, or rather for the thought of me—after all, she had not seen me since infancy. At least, not that I knew of. But I dimly remembered a story Faring had told me shortly before I was taken away from the orphanage. I had been asking him questions about my birth mother; and he told me that soon after my coming there, Bracken, another of the keepers, had noticed a woman standing across the street from the head of our alley, watching us kids at play. No one knew who she was, but she only showed up on holidays, and they assumed she came from one of the textile sweatshops over in Sycamore. One day, Faring said I suddenly left the group and ran up the alley, crossing the street amid a throng of traffic. Of course, I don't remember this, but they say I walked right up to the woman and asked her if she wanted to see me. About then, Faring caught up with me and picked me up, apologizing to the woman. She was very flustered and hurried away. Of course there were lots of other kids at that orphanage, but Faring said I was the spitting image of her. Anyway, she was never seen there again.

The body lying beside me bore an unmistakable resemblance to me. I cried. On a freezing morning in 528 AC, this woman had left me on the back steps of the Mid-Umberlands Children's Home. Left me there, not out of neglect, but because she knew my life depended on my getting better care than she could provide. Faring had said I was underweight, and they assumed she had taken sick and dried up during the flu epidemic. But she had not abandoned me. I now know she found opportunities to watch me, to see how I was doing. For some reason she was afraid or ashamed to meet me face-to-face, now as then, and it had cost her life. Apparently, she had already been giving her life for me, long before this. She had been saving money for me out of her meagre pay—nineteen falcons for a textile worker was quite a hoard. She had paid with her health, including I suspect, her mental health. I don't know how she found out where I was or how she intended to get that money to me—she probably didn't know either. But then one day, apparently, she learned of my banishment—who knows how, but everyone else seemed to know about it. She made her way to where she hoped I would pass, and the rest was plain.

Did I mention that I cried? I cried a river. I screamed at the death-dealing rocks. I screamed at the heartless wind, which only hurled my screams back into my teeth.

I had often wondered about my mother; I had imagined the things I would ask her if I could. And now, just when I had come to be in the same place with her, to ask her what she was and what she had done, now here she lay lifeless before me.

Unaware of the passage of time, I kept a lone vigil over my mother's corpse. There was no funeral; only the hours came and went in subdued grieving, tendering their futile condolences to the sole human mourner.

A brief lull in the rain was accompanied by an ominous silence followed by a new downpour, this time of hail. As the clouds slung down a barrage of icy bullets the size of grapes, the hailstones rattled off the rocks like drumrolls and stung my sun-chapped skin like buckshot.

I wasn't willing to leave my mother's body exposed to the elements like that, so I dragged her into a shallow crevice near the base of the cliff. I huddled there myself to wait out the storm. The hail was again replaced by a miserable cold rain, which beat down like a flapping of heavy curtains. I wrung out my clothes and ate some wet bread and the only sweetpotato I hadn't dropped in the chase. In a while, I shivered myself into a fitful sleep. When I awoke, the storm was over, and I could look out over the broad Umberlands River Valley to the east. Here and there, stars peeped through the rifting clouds. I watched one particularly bright star low on the horizon until I realized it was not a star at all, but a distant lamp. Too bright to be a farmhouse, and too late at night to . . . but wait, it blinked off then on again, over and over. Of course, I thought: the signal towers! The storm had shut them down, and now they were . . . I felt a sudden jolt of realization. We peasants didn't know exactly what the towers did, except that they had something to do with police communications. Could it be that CADS was now using them to monitor my own movements? It never occurred to me that this whole system might take notice of me, a nobody. But then I wasn't a nobody, was I? I was a convicted murderer, fully deserving of official scrutiny. Yes, it was . . . how stupid of me! Now it all made sense. I now knew not only how they were tracking me, but I also realized I had the key to a new strategy. I could change course radically for a few days, traveling at night when possible. I would avoid traveled roads and shun strangers before they could shun me. If only I could break a few links in their chain of surveillance, I just might drop out of their sight altogether. As an unknown vagabond, I might use my coins, which otherwise were useless, to buy food or other needs. At least it would give me a chance. I was really excited now, almost hopeful.

At daybreak I gathered all the rocks I could move and improvised a sort of sepulchre over my mother's body. I dared not tarry there any longer since they would soon miss me and they would search the area. I carefully retraced my steps to the road, retrieving most of the sweetpotatoes I'd dropped. I didn't get back on the road but hurried across it and struck off cross-country in a northerly direction. It mattered little that I was immediately lost—it wasn't as if I knew where I was going before. And if I wandered for days without seeing anybody, well wasn't that the whole idea? The point was that I had a plan. There was a hope, however slim, that I might live a while longer.

As I finished the long narrative, it didn't occur to me that I hadn't addressed the obvious question in everyone's minds. Myrica brought me back to it. "But your mother's death was an accident. How could anyone accuse you of murdering her?"

"Oh yes, it was strange how I found that out. You know Wren, who rescued me?"

"That nice fellow from Longlogan. Yes, I've met him."

"Well, when I met Wren on the pier in New Chalice, he and Arnica wanted to take me onboard the *Minkey*, but you see, they had to prove to the rest of the crew that I really was innocent."

"That makes sense" confirmed Ermine. "Under our Refuge Laws, they were obliged to help you if innocent, yet forbidden to abet a murderer."

"Well, I told him my story, but how could I confirm it without leaving my hiding place? Without my knowing it, Wren went to the CADS office, supposedly to arrange for predeparture inspections. While there, he found a desk officer who was inclined to gossip, and he picked up this tidbit: a week earlier, a bounty hunter was in the Flint Hills, tracking coyotes, when he noticed ravens circling over a cliff. Upon investigating, he found the half-buried remains of a woman, which he reported to the police. It was about the same time and place they lost track of me, so they assumed I had struck again. By the way, that was the first time I learned my mother's name: Serene Miller. That was also the end of my banishment. Now instead of merely isolating me, they immediately offered a reward for my capture, dead or alive. So you see, I had changed my strategy just in time."

Chapter 8

On the evening of my fourth day at Stonesthrow, Hewn returned from a trip to Goosegrass, whither he'd been summoned on urgent business. The next morning at breakfast, he proposed we take a walk together. My knee felt considerably improved under Ermine's expert care, so I accepted, hoping he would moderate his pace for me. He tried to, but he still had to pause often for me to catch up. We went up past the stone yards where grindstones were cut, up past the orchards belonging to our neighbour stead, through a belt of young woods, around the granite quarries and across the tram rails where a great gallymander was being eased down toward the dock with a four-ton slab of stone. Above there, the island showed its bare bones in many places, with small shallow depressions of thin gritty soil corseted by protruding ledges. Although the soil was too meagre to support usual crops, sea roses and bayberry seemed to thrive in the damp salt wind. These gnarly bushes comprised the island's only agricultural exports: rosehip purée and bay wax.

After a steady climb to the southwest, the land dropped off abruptly to the water in a series of cliff. This seaward face was thronged with the nests of various seabirds. Along the island's crest stood a row of huge windmills, and we stopped so I could examine one of them. Its tower was full forty feet tall, and in the centre were three giant wooden turbines of diminishing size. To describe their shape, imagine a large barrel sliced in half vertically then rejoined so the edge of one half meets the centre of the other. Mounted together on a single vertical shaft, the three turbines caught the wind from whichever direction it might come at the moment. At the bottom of the shaft was mounted a tightly sealed drum, which floated in a tank of brine. The salt served as antifreeze while increasing the buoyancy. Just above the float drum, a huge wooden cogwheel transferred the force to a horizontal shaft which projected outside the tower frame. At its outer end, a large spool served as a power takeoff pulley, and a stout cable was warped around this several times before going off to wherever the power was needed and back again. Anywhere along its length, a takeoff pulley might be engaged in the cable and used to cut wood, grind grain, haul stone, or many other mechanical tasks.

These windmills, together with the waterwheels, did much of the work which in other countries is done by horses, mules, or oxen; and I needed no one to tell me the advantages of that. Our mule had required three and a half acres to maintain, land that otherwise could have fed humans.

Near one of the windmills stood a stone building which Hewn called a saltworks. Stepping inside, I saw how the seawater was pumped up from below by a wavemill. A huge solar reflector focused the sunlight on coils of pipe carrying the pressurized seawater which was boiled away to leave dense brine and eventually salt. The salt, I later learned, was not only for food use, but supplied a whole range of ancillary chemical industries, on the island and elsewhere. And this saltworks was only one of many along the coast.

We went back outside and sat on a sheltered bench. Hewn pointed out the various islands and translated their names for me: Brassbound, Mast, and Inner Chicory lay in the closer distance; Two Kettle and Kittiwake farther out. Over to our near left, the large low-lying mass of Telling Island was separated from Alga by only a narrow channel. Practically at our feet, the waves crashed violently over two barely exposed islets, which he identified as Bellows Shoals and Iceman's Ledge.

Finally, Hewn got around to things that I knew were on his mind, and mine too.

"So how do you like it here so far?"

"Very well, indeed," I answered quickly, hoping to forestall any unpleasant news he might have. "People have said I probably wouldn't like it here, but I confess I don't see what there is not to like, and I should hate very much to have to leave."

"I for one never suggested you wouldn't like it here, and no one is saying you should leave. I guess the concern is that you might find life here too different to be comfortable."

"How comfortable do you suppose I was before?"

"I understand that. But before this banishment business, things must have seemed familiar there at least."

"Not altogether. You see, I've always been sort of a misfit. As a child, I was raised by Stewards whom I loved and admired, but I never quite understood what they were all about. Then I was adopted by what you call 'my own people,' but I never really fit in there. I was too attached to the memories of my early childhood, and I tried to carry them with me, which was difficult. Sometimes I think I don't really know what it means to be Anagaian, even though I am Anagaian by birth—I never quite know how to play the part, and anyway, I no longer want to, even if I could. I want to live here."

Hewn leaned back into the bench and stretched his feet toward the sea. For several moments, he was silently thoughtful, and I knew better than to interrupt him. At last he began carefully. "Much of my life has been devoted to foreign affairs, not to philosophy. However, it would have been impossible for me to do my work without understanding some of the profound differences in our ways of thinking—and believe me, they are profound. Likewise I expect *you'll* have difficulty adjusting to life here unless you at least get comfortable with those differences."

"And just what are these differences?"

"We'll discuss that sometime, but not today. For now, we should deal with daily details rather than the big ideas which begot them. I brought you up here partly because we have some immediate matters to consider."

"Oh yes, I realize I must find another place to stay. I've already burdened—"

"Would you stop jumping ahead of me?" he snapped, reminding me that I was acting quite out of character. After all, I was the one who always hung back, watching the game until I understood the rules behind the rules. Now here I was, charging ahead without even knowing the shape of the playing field. But Hewn continued more patiently. "Actually, that's not quite what I meant to discuss, at least not yet, but since you bring it up, we may as well speak of it first. It's true we're a bit cramped at Stonesthrow, not so much now as in the summer. You see, we have two stead members you haven't met. They spend every winter living up north and working at an enterprise we co-own there. When they return in the spring, we'll need to make other arrangements, but for now, you're entirely welcome to stay with us. Everyone here seems to like you fine, it's just that we are in violation of the Vine Laws and must impose limits on ourselves."

"The Vine Laws?"

"Yaro, believe me, there are so so many things for you to learn about us, I just don't want you to be overwhelmed. It will all come with time. For now, we must give thought to your schooling."

"Schooling? But I'm almost twenty. I'm too old for that."

"Too old for schooling? What a novel idea. I'm seventy-five myself, and I'm beginning a course in invertebrate zoology—worms and such, in addition to my lifetime interest in oceanography. Listen, by your own reckoning, you've had only the most rudimentary education: you read and write fairly well in your own language and are capable of basic math. But that won't do here. You know little science, less geography, and no history. You know nothing about art or music, and you speak only a few words of Mok."

"You mean Esperian?"

"Well, yes. Esperian is merely a dialect. The language spoken by most Stewards is called Mok, although the Bisonian dialect is barely intelligible to us. Anyway, you'll need to learn it. Here on the island, there are a lot of bilingual folks, but you won't find that everywhere."

"Well, of course I'd like nothing better than to study all those things, but it would take so much time. Unless I can work to repay you, I'll just be a burden."

"Yaro, without education, you'll always be a burden, to us and the whole nation. Esperian workers are highly skilled and knowledgeable. We don't raise cotton or sweetpotatoes here. You must learn to do many things."

"I don't mean to argue, but it is you will bear the burden of educating me, and others who will benefit from it."

"Well after all, I should hope we dwell in a Larger House than . . . well, let me put it this way: as you may have noticed by now, we're a very communalist society. Our compatriots are already investing a great deal in us, surely we can invest in them.

Although there is a Refugee Fund we could draw on for your expenses, we can reap greater honour by covering the cost ourselves, which the household has already voted to do. You will indeed have occasion to work in our various enterprises. It will be part of your education, but it will also relieve part of your burden, as you call it."

"Well then, how do I go about this education? Shall I attend school with the ten-year-olds?"

"Now that's what we must figure out. In general, I think it's best for you to be tutored separately. For one thing, I expect your rate of progress may be much too fast, given your maturity and motivation. Once you become fluent in Mok, you could join the teens at the banner school for things like science and advanced math. Our school classes are not age-graded, so you can just slip in or out of whatever classes seem appropriate. Meanwhile, you could do what everyone else does: supplement your formal studies with your own personal reading and questioning. But after all, this is just my recommendation. How do *you* wish to go about it?"

How *could* I wish to go about it? It was all too wonderful for me to have any opinion about the details. Peasant boys from West Umberlands simply did not study science and advanced math. I stared out pensively across the cobalt expanse of Harking Bay, my mind's eye seeing far beyond the southern horizon to the rat-ridden alleys of New Chalice where even now, the police were searching for me. Half to myself I muttered, "Two weeks ago I was going to die. Now I'm going to school."

I felt Hewn's hand light on my shoulder, and and I knew he understood.

* * * * * * *

Immediately after lunch, my education began with an hour of language study with Hewn. The "retired" ambassador had many and diverse responsibilities, but since my time was wholly flexible, we managed to cobble together a schedule which dovetailed my lessons with his busy agenda. He was to be my primary tutor for language and history. I wondered that he could squeeze me in, but he insisted.

I learned some fascinating facts about Mok, or Moktok, as it was originally known. For one thing, it is a totally artificial language. Whereas Anagaian evolved from classical English and tries to retain elements of that ancient tongue, Mok has no such linguistic tradition; the very name is said to be a corrupted form of Mock-Talk, a sort of argot devised during the Calamities for secret communication between Stewards. Of course, after the Calamities it became unnecessary, but by then a new generation of Stewards were accustomed to its use and eager to distance themselves in every way from the mother culture which had sought to destroy them. The language developed its own syntax and vocabulary so that today it is a highly nuanced idiom, capable of expressing all the subtleties of thought found in any other language.

There is one word-forming device which is not widely used here as it is an Anagaia: the use of acronymy. For example, the ruler of my homeland is called the Olotal, which is acronymic for *Overlord Of The Anagaian League*. The dominant established religious sect is called MOTHS, from Masters Of The Holy Shrines. And of course, victims of the cruel contract-labour system are called bucs: *bound under contract*. This lexical device harkens back to the Ancient World, which may explain why Anagaians have carried it to such a degree, whereas Esperians avoid it.

I should probably mention here that education, even literacy, is a rather rare possession where I come from. There is no tax-supported public education whatever in the interest of "streamlined government." Instead, people are allowed to have "educational choice," which means the peasants have no schooling at all while the aristocracy have their private tutors. The main exceptions to this are the scattered mission-schools operated by Stewards from Esperia. Those few peasants who can read are often viewed askance by the authorities since they clearly have been under the influence of "pernicious foreigners."

Anyway, my own schooling was cut short at age eleven, although I made some small gains on my own at Seekings'. My adopted family had a library of over a dozen volumes—quite impressive for a peasant home. For my part, I devoured those books avidly, struggling through difficult passages and no doubt missing the full meaning of much I read. At Stonesthrow, I became like a learning machine run amok. I spent spare moments digesting whole pages of vocabulary, even learning many new words I never knew in my native tongue. I tried the words out in conversation, and chafed inwardly whenever anyone smiled at my malapropisms.

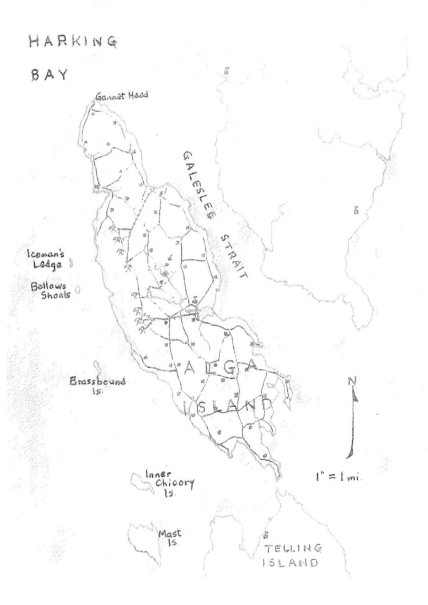

HARKING

BAY

Gannet Head

GALESLEG STRAIT

Iceman's
Ledge

Bellows
Shoals

Brassbound
Is.

ALGA

ISLAND

N

1" = 1 mi.

Inner
Chicory
Is

Mast
Is

TELLING
ISLAND

Chapter 9

I should probably describe the actual household of Stonesthrow, as these were to be my extended family, as it were, for the foreseeable future. Although Hewn was undoubtedly the most renowned member, he was not the "head of the house." If anything, that honour would go to Ermine, by virtue of her being "stead steward," an annually elected position. Neither of them was the oldest among us. Hewn's sister Alaria was seventy-six, and her husband Grebe was seventy-eight. Both of them were quite active; Grebe often worked in the stone yard while Alaria oversaw the "broom factory." Although age had stiffened her hands somewhat, she still tied the straw for others to trim. It was certainly not poverty that kept them both at work; it just never occurred to either of them to be idle.

Hewn and Alaria had a widower cousin, Discern, who also lived with us, although I understand he came from the mainland originally. He was ninety-six, and the year before my arrival, a paralyzing stroke had left him bedfast. His mind still seemed pretty clear though, and I really enjoyed spending time with him. It seems he had spent much of his younger years at sea, and he spoke both Anagaian and Coquinese passably well. What especially attracted me to him were his stories, of which there seemed no end. Although he was frequently vague about events of the previous week, he could recount personal experiences which happened well into the past century. Now history was a topic very dear to me, if only for my ignorance of it. In my homeland, historical studies were suppressed, creating a sort of cultural amnesia from which I yearned to be cured. Therefore I spent many spare moments by his wheelchair, prompting his recollection.

Hewn and Ermine had a daughter, Unison, and a granddaughter Myrica, but they lived at the son-in-law's stead over on Telling Island where they both worked in a publishing cooperative.

Alaria and Grebe had three children, which was itself cause for remark and not altogether favourable. Their middle child had joined his wife's stead on the mainland. Their youngest was a forty-six-year-old single son, Fulmar, who only lived part of the year at Stonesthrow and the rest of the year up north. It was his seasonal absence that made it possible for me to be there. The eldest of Alaria and Grebe's three was a daughter named Dawn. At fifty-two, Dawn was more powerful physically than many younger men. She was married to Freeheart, a quiet-spoken mechanic who spent much of his time maintaining and repairing the many windmills on the island. He was pleasant enough, but I found him hard to get to know. His mother, a widow, also lived with us, although I believe the family was originally from somewhere in Goosegrass fair. Despite her age and being "from away," she was a very active and influential member of the household. Personally I found her a bit overbearing. Having said all that, I'm embarrassed that I cannot now remember her name, and it's not in my notes.

Dawn and Freeheart had a twenty-two-year-old son named Marten (after the Concordian poet). He was tall, slender, and scholarly. He had a deep fascination with adventure but seemed to keep himself far from it. I would grow to like him a lot, but at first I just found him puzzling. Like most Esperians, he had several occupations, but one in particular intrigued me: he was a "Keeper of the Numbers," which is to say, a sort of statistician. He was always bicycling around the island with a knapsack full of notebooks, collecting data on crop yields, healthcare, industrial output, just about any information that was expressible in numbers. He explained that he periodically met with other number keepers to collate data and forward it to the appropriate interest groups.

All the individuals described so far were more or less related, but there were several other steadmates who belonged to a completely different lineage. Sixty-one-year-old Vervain and her husband Teal had a daughter Corolla, who was married to Elan. The younger couple both worked in the saltworks and the related caustic soda plant, and Elan also cut grindstones. They had a nine-year-old daughter Thistle.

Besides these, there were two other residents, a midthirties woman named Tilia and her twenty-five-year-old cousin Burnet, who were unrelated to anyone else in the stead. Their family had once constituted a large part of the household but had either died out or moved away. You see, a stead does not appertain to a particular family but to whomever lives there. A stead is never sold, although families or parts of them may come and go. Everyone living at our stead had the surname "Stonesthrow," regardless of kinship ties. If anyone brought a spouse to live there, the newcomer automatically became So-and-so of Stonesthrow, regardless of gender. Except myself; due to my sojourner status, I continued to be Yaro Seekings. Now Tilia was the other resident who, along with Fulmar, spent winters living inland. Tilia and Fulmar were both engaged, though not to each other. Tilia already planned to move to her fiancé's stead up at Chagrin Lake, but it was expected that when Fulmar married, the couple would reside at Stonesthrow, and the resulting housing shuffle would leave little room for me.

It was a good thing for Stonesthrow that Esperian longevity is usually accompanied by remarkable vigour since more than half of the household were over sixty.

It might seem strange that eighteen people, related or not, should all live together under one roof, even allowing that it was a very large roof. I must point out that Esperians are accustomed from birth to communal arrangements and have long ago worked out an etiquette which enables them to rub elbows daily with a minimum of friction.

The steadhouse of Stonesthrow was an imposing edifice of cut granite quarried on the island where stone was more plentiful than timber. It had stood for over three centuries, not at all uncommon here. The main wing had a second story, capped by a massive roof whose rafters soared upward to a heavy oak ridge pole, much like the ribs and keel of a ship turned upside down.

The lower floor of the main wing held a spacious dining hall which doubled as meeting room and, on occasion, workplace for temporary projects. Next to this was an equally large kitchen and off that a separate pantry where most of the dried or canned foodstuffs were stored. Through the pantry one passed into an outside chamber, which was a root cellar. It was hewn into the solid ledge, and its roof, or ceiling, was also of thick granite slabs covered with three feet of earth and sod. The solid stone walls and floor kept it cool in summer, yet frost-free in winter. Against the hard damp walls were stacked bins of carrots, beets, cabbages, turnips, and potatoes as well as apples and many other foods which were unfamiliar to me.

Off the central dining area was the laundry. This room connected in turn with the smaller wing. One of the products which Stonesthrow manufactured for trade was rainproof coats. These had to be treated with a mixture of linseed oil, pine tar, and beeswax; and part of the process was done in the laundry as well as in the wing.

You see, Stonesthrow was like most steads in that it was more than a dwelling or even a farm. It was also a sort of industrial centre. Beside meeting most of its own food and fuel needs, the stead produced rose hip purée, candles, rainwear, brooms, and brushes, while it cooperated in the production of salt, grindstones, bay wax, and chemicals. It was obvious at a glance that the entire household was busy and prosperous.

The second floor was divided into six bedrooms for the married couples. Above the smaller wing, two dormitory chambers housed the single men and women. I shared one with Burnet and Marten. The room was subdivided by woven rush screens, giving each of us a personal space of only six by eight feet. Esperians are accustomed to less privacy than other peoples and make their own adjustments. I must admit I never felt cramped, but then I was raised in an orphanage.

Still higher up in the house, a commodious attic nestled into the roof peak. The gable ends were not of stone, but timber-frame sheathed inside and out with matched planking. The space between was stuffed with bundles of cattail rushes as was the roof itself, making a warm dormer-lit garret. Most of the space comprised the so-called broom factory, including a small overhead crawl space, which was crammed with bundles of broomstraw and other supplies.

Over all this arched the great vault of the roof, clad in split cedar shakes. An enormous stone-and-brick chimney rose through the centre of the house. Most of the building's windows were oriented to the south side, and rooms were laid out accordingly. I was amazed at the widespread use of window glass. In my native Umberlands, the possession of one or two glazed windows was a sure mark of wealth, yet here I saw dozens of windows, all doubled-glazed for fuel efficiency.

The immediate grounds were occupied by late remains of fall flowers, and a small orchard of bare-limbed trees whose fruits were even now drying or simmering cozily in the great kitchen. Garden and orchard were all bracketed by shoulder-high walls of carefully laid stones, which brunted the sea winds and moderated the climate. Nestled into the angle of two such walls, a stack of beehives hunkered down out of the wind. Beyond lay larger gardens, recently harvested and, in some cases, sown to winter grains. None of these fields was over two acres, and they were all level. That is to say, the land was not at all level by nature, but every rod of ground had been shaped into terraces of various sizes. Even hayfields and orchards marched up the slopes like broad staircases, and everywhere stretched the buffering walls.

Behind the main house was a large stone barn whose ample interior housed a cider press, a threshing floor, a storeroom for tools and machinery, and a loft area for curing and scutching flax.

Then there was the forest land. None of the island's woodlots seemed to exceed ten acres, yet they were scattered everywhere, forming a mosaic of wall-girt groves separating the croplands. They provided most, though not all, of the island's domestic fuel. They also provided much more than that, as I would learn later.

I guess I could best sum it all up by saying that Stonesthrow was a citadel—a bastion against want and insecurity. Its seventeen residents did more than reside there—they worked there, gave birth and died there, and finally their ashes were buried there. Yet these people were not parochial—how could they be, with so much coming and going? At Stonesthrow and everywhere, there seemed to be an endless schedule of shared activities for every taste. Cultural and athletic events, hobby clubs, professional meetings all crowded the calendar—some felt too much. One could attend public lectures on everything from Anagaian pottery of the Tetrarchy Period to the hybridization of daylilies, and they were usually well-attended. Larger events were usually held at the bannerhouse, but smaller groups often met at individual steads. I remember a handbell choir that used to meet for practice at Stonesthrow every week, even though none of us belonged to it. Apparently, it was founded there by some long-deceased stead member, and they had never seen fit to move their meeting place, much to our delight. Of course, we served them refreshments, whereas a bagpipe-and-drum band was obliged to meet for practice at the wrackplant.

Alga is a long pod-shaped island, low-lying on the east shore facing Galeslee Strait, and rising slowly toward the west where it ends abruptly atop granite cliffs. It is six miles from Gannett Head on the north tip to the Narrows at the south, and two miles at its widest. Most of the usable farmland lies at the north and central sections of the island while the southern end is dominated by cranberry bogs. The island's soil is thin and poor by nature but greatly enhanced by human effort.

Although the island has no streams for waterpower, the wind is comparatively strong and steady, especially atop the cliffs. There is also extensive use of wave and tidal power, as well as solar, for some applications. The population at the time of my residence there was 794 (not counting myself), occupying 5,145 acres, of which 1309 acres consisted of bare rock.

I should also mention that Alga banner is part of a larger unit called the Bluemeadow fair. Now *fair* has two meanings here: it is roughly comparable to a county or province in other lands, and it also refers to a regional outdoor market which is held weekly in the milder seasons. More about those later.

I was quite comfortable at Stonesthrow, despite the constant need to adapt my individualistic outlook to a communal lifestyle. I could well imagine how that tension alone might make most foreigners wish to move elsewhere, but for me at least, it was well worth the adjustment. I realized from the beginning I could not remain at Stonesthrow indefinitely. Other parts of the country were less crowded, they said. I was already anxious to find a place where I could be more than comfortable, where I could sink roots as deep and strong as those great bur oaks up beyond the orchard. I knew there were obstacles, things I must learn, but I hungered to be more than a refugee, more than an immigrant. I wanted to weave myself into the very fabric of the nation, not to remain a pasted overlay. I frequently met people from other parts of the country, and they told me things that made me hanker to see it for myself. On the wall of the dining hall hung a large-scale map of the country. I spent hours wistfully scanning the outlines of rivers and mountains and the myriad names and dots that represented communities. If the features limned on that flat dry sheet held such fascination for me, how much more splendid must be the land itself!

Chapter 10

It seemed to Ermine that my knee was not mending fast enough. She was a good healer, and the infection was gone, but the ulceration was slow to close up. She suggested I go over to Heathstead at the south end of the island where lived another healer whose advice she valued. Marten offered to drive me over there in the banner's drawchair, a long low tricycle used for transporting the sick or injured, but I refused. I didn't want to tie up anyone else's time, and besides, I rather felt like exploring more of the island at my own pace. I knew Ermine would object to my making the five-mile walk by myself, so I didn't mention when I was going, figuring I could rest often on the way. As I ambled along with a slight limp, I recalled the night weeks earlier when I had sustained the injury.

Apparently, my strategy of traveling nights and sleeping days had served me well. For two days I had veered north, sticking to empty back lanes and drovers' trails. I had seen no one, and more importantly, no one had seen me. Occasionally I would hustle off into the shadows at the approach of some nightfarer. That itself was encouraging; no one seemed to be watching out for me. But as I trended eastward again, a major obstacle loomed before me: the Foxfire Mountains. They, of course, formed the boundary between Umberlands and Hither Anagaia, and one might assume that being an internal border, they would be unguarded. But uneven tax laws made them a smuggler's haven, not to mention a refuge for subversives, and so the boundary was heavily patrolled. There was no way I could take any road through the gaps, all of which were blocked by customs stations. Yet going cross-country through the mountains without a guide was foolhardy, especially at night. Even if I eluded the patrols, I could easily get lost in the jumbled terrain. I knew all this, but there was no choice, if I wished to reach the seacoast. Impatient to start, I broke my routine and began traveling long before sundown. I was anxious to at least get into the high country before dark so as to have the whole night to make the crossing in stealth.

I've read that in Ancient Times, the Foxfires were densely forested with towering sweet gum, tulip poplar, and dogwood; but what I saw then was almost as denuded as the land around Dryford. Centuries of grazing and stripping firewood had left the slopes gullied and bare in places, with coarse grasses interspersed with scant patches of brush. There were countless goat paths, if one knew which ones to follow, but little cover in which to hide.

Once in the high country, I came across a herdsman's stone hut set in a remote hollow. It was surrounded by stone corrals, and it appeared to be deserted. That wasn't surprising since most of the flocks had begun to move down to lower pastures, but I saw something beyond the hut that made my heart leap: within a high stone fence, an acre or so of amaranth stood nearly ripe and uncut. I had eaten no grain for many days, and the temptation was overpowering. I crept up to the enclosure and pulled down one of the drooping heads. Threshing and winnowing away the hulls in my hands, I nibbled on the tiny hard grains as I walked down the rows. I selected the ripest heads to stuff into my knapsack. To my surprise, the tall plants suddenly ended in the middle of the patch, replaced by much-shorter plants. These had pale green seedpods from whose gashes glistened tiny beads of amber gum, or what little had not already been collected. Suddenly I was terrified, realizing I had wandered into someone's opium plantation. Was it my imagination, or were there rustling sounds in the breezeless amaranth? Without looking, I ran; but in a moment, I was hurled down by someone much heavier than I. We rolled over amid the dust and poppy stalks, but I was soon pinned to the earth by powerful arms, and I felt the razor-sharp steel at my throat. I was certain it was the end for me and only wondered why the attacker hesitated. Evidently, he wondered too, for it was another voice that called out to wait. The speaker stood directly above us both, but in the dust and glare, all I could discern was his voice. There were other voices murmuring in the haze, but the first voice was clearly in command. The knife went no deeper, nor was it withdrawn

"Who are you, anyway?"

I was too terrified and winded to do anything but gasp for a moment. Before I could muster a reply, another voice grumbled. "Who cares who he is? He's a prying busybody, probably an agent. What else do we need to know?"

"He's not an agent. You saw him grazing in the amaranth. He didn't know what he was looking for. Besides, he's practically a kid, no weapon."

"Well then, what's he snooping around here for?"

"That's what I want to know too."

The leader, a grizzled mountaineer, came into my field of vision, his creased face showing all the predatory fierceness of an old mountain lion. "Speak, you! Who are you and where from? One lie and his knife will decide the rest."

What was I to say? That I was banished and anyone could take my life with impunity? Then it occurred to me that these men weren't on the safe side of the law themselves. They were testing my honesty, not my innocence. Candour seemed my only defense.

"I'm running . . . I was banished. They were tracking me by the signal towers until I learned to dodge them . . . by . . . I'm trying to get over the border . . . to the coast . . . to get away."

"From where? Where did you come from?"

"From Dryford, near Shoatmart."

"Go on with you! That must be two hundred miles west of here. If you were banished, you couldn't buy food or drink. How could you travel so far? How did you know the way?"

"I didn't . . . I still don't. I just headed east . . . toward the coast."

Another voice chimed in. "Well, we can believe that anyway. If he'd known where he was going, he surely wouldn't have come this way. Any other direction would have got him out of the territory in half the time."

"If that's so, I didn't know it. Anyway, I've been living off stolen food when I could. But mostly going hungry."

"He don't look too good, that's for sure. What did you do? They don't banish anymore."

"They say I killed someone, but I didn't. I found him dead. The judge didn't believe me, but maybe wasn't sure, because he banished me instead of hanging."

"Who are you supposed to have killed?"

So I told them; I told the whole story. I had not spoken to any living person in almost two weeks, and it was almost a relief to tell what really happened, whether they were sympathetic or not. At least, while they were listening to me, they weren't killing me.

They were indeed well inclined to be skeptical—it was a most unlikely tale. The burly fellow who had jumped me was least inclined to accept my story.

"It smells funny, Uncle," he argued. "And anyway, there's too much at stake. We've got to go over tonight."

"It sounds weird to me too," agreed the Old Cougar (as I mentally named him, never knowing his real name). "And I probably wouldn't believe him either, except for something else I know. When I was down at Goodman's place yesterday morning, I heard some talk. They say CADS has been tracking a fugitive, and they've lost the sniff of him. Everyone's having a great laugh over it. No one seems to think he may be heading up this way, but there's that much of his blubbering that fits. I'm of a mind that this is him, that it's just as he says. You all know I'm not squeamish, but I've never killed a man they didn't need it, and I don't mean to start now."

I was yanked roughly to my feet. These were clearly members of a mountain clan, and the Old Cougar was the patriarch, but perhaps not undisputed. He looked around at every face, taking the measure of his own authority.

"It's not for me alone to decide this. We'll vote on it. Who says he lives?"

He punctuated his question by thrusting out his upraised palm. A couple others slapped their hands on his, then after some hesitation, three more followed. The burly nephew looked around at his kinsman before reluctantly adding the unanimous vote. The old mountaineer was a cagey leader; by manipulating a traditional democratic gesture, he had created the illusion of consensus. He turned abruptly to me. "All right, kid, get out of here."

"No, I won't." I could hardly believe I was saying it, nor could anyone else. But in the few seconds since reprieve seemed possible, my mind had been racing ahead to my larger dilemma. There was no time to weigh risks.

"I won't go. I'm staying."

"What!" The Old Cougar was incredulous. "I give you a chance for life. Take it!"

"What chance? As you just said yourselves, it's an incredible fluke that I've made it this far. How am I to cross over mountains I don't even know, in the dark yet? If I don't get shot by the patrols, I'll surely get lost. After all, you've shown me more mercy than the authorities. I'm going with you."

"You will do no such thing, you fool!" snarled the leader impatiently.

"I'm a bigger fool if I try it alone. With you I might stand a chance."

"A chance to expose us and get us all killed," countered one of the men. "How he gets across is his problem, not ours. He'd just slow us down."

"In the past week, I've gotten pretty good at traveling fast and quietly in the dark, often cross-country. If I hold you back, you can just leave me . . . and I'll pay you."

This last suggestion was conceived on the spot—it slipped out without time to consider its wisdom.

"Pay us? With what?" The Old Cougar's eyes narrowed shrewdly.

"I haven't told you quite everything. Before my mother died, she left me a bag of silver coins, her life savings, I expect. I'll give you . . . whatever you demand, if you'll take me along."

"Where is this silver?"

"In my pack, just over there."

"Get it."

"Will you take me?"

"Get it!"

I walked over to where I had dropped the knapsack among the amaranth. My position was awkward in the extreme. Now they would not release me without having my money, yet there was no guarantee of help in return.

I handed the pouch over to the Old Cougar, who examined it thoughtfully before emptying the contents onto the ground before them all. Nineteen falcons glistened in the late afternoon sun, but the men seemed less impressed than I'd expected. A bony man sneered, "That's how he'll pay us for risking our necks. How fine—we can each build a palace and retire." The others chuckled scornfully. The Old Cougar tossed the empty bag onto the scattered hoard.

"No doubt it's a fair bit of coin for you, boy, but if our business tonight goes well, we'll have many times that. If not, what use would it be? You'll be needing it more yourself. Now pick it up and be gone."

"I told you I'm not leaving you," I insisted, amazed at my own audacity and fully expecting to get my ribs whittled.

"Don't be stubborn!" he hissed. "It won't work. I've done all I can, so get out of here fast!"

"We should take him with us."

All faces whirled in surprise at the burly nephew. "I still have doubts—that's why we should take him along. If he's not that fugitive, he might take it into his head to collect a reward. We can't afford to turn him lose, knowing what he does. We need to be able to watch him. One wrong move, and we slit him open for the coyotes. If he's level, then he can help carry the load, so we can move that much faster."

The others seem to approve of his reasoning—surely no one else could have swayed them. Since they were planning to move out immediately, we made a hasty reloading of the contraband, so my knapsack held its share. I was not pleased with that part of the plan. I had been raised by the Stewards to despise all such "consciousness thieves," and I had seen Mrs. Seekings waste away from her laudanum use. Yet I was resigned to the imperfect means of my own survival, and I shouldered the burden without comment.

The stakes were high in this cat-and-mouse game. These men spent most of their year herding goats and cutting wood, yet this night's work would dwarf their other earnings. All this raw opium gum was not from their own small patch. They had bought up all of the neighbourhood production as well, figuring a huge profit on their investment . . . if they got through.

A hasty conference was held, reviewing routes, signals, contingency plans, etc. Then we were off, climbing hastily into the gathering twilight.

I was disoriented from the very outset as we ascended one ridge after another, skirting open areas and avoiding gullies where we would be exposed to ambush. I never knew which of the crests was the actual border—we didn't stop to celebrate. We were descending one of the long slopes when the Old Cougar pulled up short, and we all listened intently. Somewhere on the height behind us, a faint yelp was followed by an eerie ululating howl, and that was taken up by others. A patrol had crossed our path, and the hounds had gotten our scent. We could hardly see each other's faces in the gloom, but we all knew the plan. We began running now, and soon came to a fork in the path where we split into two groups. Shortly after, we divided again, and now it was just the old Cougar and myself. Several times we paused to dust the trail with cayenne from our pouches. At one point, I tripped on a root and sprawled headlong with a gash in my knee. It was shallow and bled little, but it hurt badly. There was no stopping now, so I sprang up and limped after my companion, who was very fleet for his years. Apparently, the patrols had a strategy of their own because our splitting up caused them only a little delay as they did the same. The cayenne likewise bought us a little time as it threw off the lead hounds, but they were soon on us again. Once we heard a shot from far off to our left and wondered if one of the others had been hit. The dogs were only moments behind us when we came to a deep and narrow gully. We scrambled down one side and up the other where the old man paused and pulled out another pouch. From this he took out a palmful of little clusters made from wood slivers tied together so they could not lie flat. He strewed them on the ground at the edge of the wash. I didn't have to ask their *purpose: the hounds wouldn't go into the gully but would leap over it, inevitably landing on the sharp clusters which would injure their feet and hopefully disable them for the night's work. It was our only hope. Our pursuers were so close we could hear the men's voices urging the dogs onward. We would soon be overtaken unless our tactic worked. The frenzied yelping seemed almost at our heels when a piteous howl of pain cut it short. A human voice called to the other dogs to halt, but in the mad rush of pursuit, it was futile. More squeals from other dogs, loud curses, and random shots; but we knew we were safe as we hurried on at a more reasonable pace. The men would give chase for a bit farther, but without the hounds, we could easily lose them on the many bypaths. By the time the eastern sky had begun to brighten, we had buried ourselves in the mountain fastness of Hither Anagaia, too far from the border to attract attention.*

Chapter 11

I was greeted at Heathstead with great cordiality while a child was sent out to fetch the healer and someone to translate. When they arrived, she examined my knee, asking questions and doing all the things Ermine had done: checking pulse and temperature, poking and flexing the joint itself. She also did some other curious things: examined my eyes intently with a lens and poked various points on my feet. Finally she conferred briefly with the interpreter who said, "She feels that Ermine is doing everything right. The poultices and hydrotherapy are having good effect. Perhaps Ermine is dissatisfied because she underestimates your overall debilitation—we don't usually see patients in your condition here. But she thinks there is no cause for concern, only persistence. Perhaps you should eat more kale and parsley, which are plentiful now."

I nodded agreeably, not bothering to tell her about the mountains of dark greens Ermine had been force-feeding me like a layer hen.

"Before you leave," the translator continued, "she needs to fill out a report to be filed along with Ermine's. Now you say this happened in the AL—which province, please?"

"Either Umberlands or Hither Anagaia."

"But surely you know where you were when you got hurt?"

"Not exactly. It was somewhere near the border. We were fleeing from the police."

The healer's eyes widened at this item, and she asked through the translator, "So was the injury sustained in the course of committing a crime?"

"Well yes, but no. It wasn't me they were after so much as the people I was with. They were opium smugglers." Both of them caught their breath and a whispered consultation followed. Finally the translator said, "We suppose there is no point in asking whether you were wearing proper safety protection at the time, and presumably no heavy machinery was involved. This is all hard to fit into the categories of her form. So she is writing that this accident was not occupational, but the result of 'expedient haste.' Under preventative suggestions, she recommends that you henceforth avoid the company of opium smugglers."

I grinned widely. "I shall follow her prescription to the letter!"

After she replaced the dressing, I started back home. I picked a different route from which I had come. The road sidled along a low ridge which overlooked the Strait to the right. It was a moraine, I later learned, a place where the continental glacier had once dumped its burden of far-flung debris. There were boulders of all sizes strewn over it, many big enough to fill a wheelbarrow. The packed and sterile gravel was clad only in tough sedge-grasses and gnarly sea-roses, among scattered clumps of stunted pin cherry. It looked as barren as any place in Umberlands, yet at the far side of it, the land was suddenly free of large stones and there was a healthy young grove of nut-pines alternating with chestnuts. There was no gradual merging of one soil type into another—a sharp straight line demarcated the two areas. The productive zone was clearly not natural. I thought I heard a low rumbling which was certainly not thunder, and just over the brow I found the source. A crew of men and women was working in a large shallow depression scooped into the flank of the ridge. It looked like a gravel pit except nothing was being removed. Rather the excavated material was being transferred from one side of the pit to the other. In the process, it was screened and sorted into piles. Between the piles and the pit-face stood a battery of large machines, perhaps a dozen of them, all rotating noisily. I went closer to look and a worker greeted me, but he spoke only Mok, so I just stood and watched. After several minutes, I began to figure it out: the machines were huge mortars, or grinders, driven by cables which came from nearby windmills. I saw one worker pull a lever, and a machine stopped turning. He emptied the contents into several wheelbarrows, which were trundled over to the other side and dumped. The hopper was refilled with fist-sized stones, and several balls of hardened steel were tossed in with them. Now I understood: they were grinding up the sterile gravel to make soil, which all went back onto the ground again. I had to move away from the machine since I had no earplugs. I walked up to the rim to watch the overall process. Bizarre. Such a gargantuan expenditure of labour and for what? To make dirt? At the rate they were going, it would take decades to convert the whole worksite into whatever it was they wanted.

But then I looked at the area beyond the pit. The first rows of planted trees were about waist-high, the next ones about ten feet then fifteen feet and so forth. This was a "rolling" gravel pit; those trees were growing on what had once been nearly bare moraine, and the skimpy brushland on the other side was also destined to become productive forest, given a generation or two. Mind-boggling. I resolved to ask Hewn or Ermine about it at the first opportunity.

A couple miles farther, I found myself on a familiar road. It made a sharp bend around a high walled terrace, and when I saw the lone figure approaching me, he was only a few yards away. I didn't recognize him, but I felt a twinge of panic when I realized he was white. And no Borealian sailor, I could see; his apparel left little doubt he was an Anagaian nobleman. On the streets of New Chalice, a man of his rank would never have deigned to acknowledge my presence, yet this fellow addressed me almost like an old acquaintance.

"Well, hello there! What a pleasant surprise to see a fair complexion in this place."

With slight hesitation, I shook the hand he so warmly proffered. I was at a loss for words, but the stranger seemed quite willing to carry both ends of the conversation.

"I am Brownlea Lord Amberson—just Brownlea between us, no need of formality here, of course. And you . . . ?"

While on the lam in New Chalice, I had hidden behind the alias of Dusty Wells, which I took from a village signpost. I was tempted to resurrect him now; but no, this was Esperia, and I would never again be afraid of the truth.

"My name is Yaro Seekings. I used to live in West Umberlands."

"Indeed, such a lovely place—splendid sunsets and all. You must be as eager as I am to return home. I'm posted here with the trade delegation, you see. My first season and quite an adjustment, eh? Oh, it's a nice place in its own way, but well, surely you know what I mean."

"Not sure that I do, nor do I care much." I was astonished at my own bluntness. "I think Umberlands a most dismal place, and have no intention of ever going back."

"Well, well, each to his own," murmured the stranger, refusing to be ruffled. "You obviously haven't been here long enough to know its darker side. Believe me, these people don't think like you and me. In time, the weirdness of it all will get to you, and you'll long for the old homeland. I only hope it won't be too late then. I assume you know that anyone who lives in Steward lands for twenty-four consecutive months forfeits their rights as an Anagaian citizen."

"What rights? It's only your class who have any rights there. You may as well know, I'm wanted there for crimes I didn't commit. If I set foot back there, I'd be dead."

The stranger acted surprised at this revelation, though I had the feeling I wasn't telling him anything new.

"Ah, so that's who you are! I've heard something about that case. What a pity—so you don't know then."

"Know what?"

"Such a terrible mistake, really. Quite recently, some new evidence was brought forth, confirming your innocence. The real murderer has confessed, you see. All that's needed is for you to appear in court to sign some release papers. You're as good as free!"

"I am free here. What makes you think I'd be so foolish as to believe you?"

"Because you yourself know you're innocent, right? Why then do you find it so unlikely that new evidence would support your case?"

"I know my innocence, but I also know Anagaian law."

"Bah! What you know is bungling provincial bureaucracy. Do you know that the judge—Strider, I believe, yes, you see I do know something about it—he was fired from the bench for mishandling your case? I can prove that to you when the records arrive. Now if you were to come back with me, I could personally arrange a hearing of appeal, at the Onyx Court itself, which I guarantee would be in your favour."

I had heard enough nonsense. I brushed past him and hurried on toward Stonesthrow. He called after me.

"You're going to be extradited, you know that, don't you? I've just come from Stonesthrow. There's going to be a hearing, and they're going to send you back. You'll have a hard time of it on your own in a CADS court. Return with me on my yacht, and I'll see that you are well spoken for. Otherwise, my hands are tied . . ." His words trailed off in the wind as I sped toward the house.

Despite my bold retorts, I was unnerved. I hastened to find Hewn and demanded an explanation. He tried to calm me.

"There, there, relax now. Here, have some hot mint. Yes, I owe you an apology for not telling you he was coming today, but then you did run off without a word to anyone. It could have gone ill too, if he had managed to hoodwink you. I'm sure he meant to lure you onto his boat and conceal you there until he leaves next week. We couldn't have proved you didn't go back of your own free will. Of course, you weren't so naïve, but I'm sorry to cause you alarm."

"But what's it to him anyway? Why should he take such a personal interest in taking me back? He must not only be very zealous, but completely convinced of my guilt."

"Not necessarily. I doubt he cares much one way or another about your innocence. He's playing a bigger game. It would be quite a feather in his cap to return with a fugitive in custody. Couldn't hurt his standing at court."

"You can't mean that. With all the weighty affairs they have to consider, what can a single criminal—guilty or not—matter to them?"

"Ah, but you don't know the administration of Blaze II like I do. To them, there is no 'weightier matter' then the totality of their control. Every single malcontent who manages to wriggle through their net is a serious challenge to their authority. Conversely, every one that is brought back is a new chink in their wall of repression. It says to the people: 'There is no escape; even in other lands, we will find you!' So you see, you mean quite a lot to them."

"I see what you mean. But he said you might send me back. What's that about?"

"Like everything he told you, it's a lie wrapped around a grain of truth. You won't be sent back, rest assured. But there is to be an extradition hearing—a mere formality—so the Anagaian government can present its case."

"But I thought I gave them the slip back in New Chalice. How did they even know I was here?"

"We told them."

"What?"

"Yes, of course. Yaro, you must understand, we're not a permissive society. The very fact that you've been charged means that an investigation must be made. I have not yet explained to you that our society is power-heavy at the bottom like a pyramid. It is not Esperia that assumes responsibility for you, but Stonesthrow. We are to protect your rights, just as the banner protects ours, and so forth. It's not enough that we, your steadmates, believe you. We must also be prepared to certify your innocence to our higher levels of alliance if it should ever come to that. The same law which requires us to shelter refugees also forbids us to abet murderers. We may not err either way, you see, or we risk having blood on our own hands. We need facts, and so far everything you've told us has been supported by CADS' own evidence, so unless they come up with something new and convincing, Lord Amberson's yacht will sail without you. I suggest you quit worrying and concentrate on your algebra."

I let the matter drop, but it was hard to be at ease with this new information.

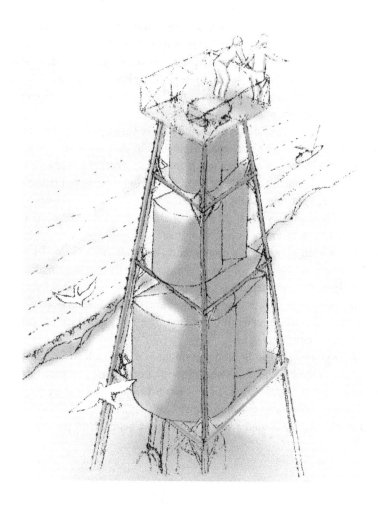

Chapter 12

That afternoon, I tired of my studies quickly, or rather my assigned studies. I went into the kitchen where Ermine and a few others were slicing apples to dry. No one objected when I grabbed a coring tool and joined in. Turning to Ermine, I asked, "Do you mind explaining something to me?"

She smiled expectantly at me, which I took as a go-ahead.

"Well, I keep hearing about these Vine Laws, and it always seems to have nothing to do with vines. What's it all about?"

"A good question, and a very big one. I'll try . . . let me start with this: you understand that our values system is rooted in much of the same Holy Scriptures which Anagaians use?"

"I've been told that, though it confuses me. The very use of words like *Holy Scriptures* strikes me as contradictory for atheists."

"Really? How so?"

"Well, after all, it has God saying this and God saying that. The whole thing is all about faith."

"To Anagaians, it is about faith. In fact, most of it is about how to live. In any expression of mythic vision, you'll find plenty of things which are not meant to be understood literally. They tell a bigger story, a concept that may be difficult to grasp abstractly, so it is expressed in models with types and symbols. Our people see the very notion of Godhead itself as an example of that. The problem with all symbols, though, is that they tend to take the place of the thing itself, which may be why the Holy Scriptures are so careful to warn us about them."

"You mean idols?"

"Well, just for example."

"Let's see if I get this straight: Stewards don't believe in God because God commands them not to since that would be idolatry?"

"When you put it that way, it sounds like quite a paradox, doesn't it? Of course, Anagaians are not very comfortable with paradox, or at least with other people's paradoxes. But yes, I think you described it well enough. And by the way, it's not quite accurate to equate Stewards with atheism. Concordians for example are believers, and yet they're quite decent people. There are even many Esperians who have their own concept of things, including God. I mean, it's not a mainstream idea—in fact, it's considered kind of kinky—but I don't know anyone who has a big problem with it, especially if they're well-behaved."

"I'll have to think about all that. But now, the Vine Laws?"

"Okay, as I said, the scriptures tell us how to live, sometimes in great detail, sometimes not. For countless centuries, people have seized on some passages and elaborated them while ignoring or downplaying other parts. We're no different, although maybe we can afford to be more candid about it. Now there's one little line in a prophecy—not even a commandment, mind you—that refers to a man living in security under his own grapevine and under his own fig tree. Through interpretation, this obscure reference has been expanded into a whole body of legislation, which basically mandates a high degree of self-reliance. Probably nothing to do with the prophet's intent, but it has served our purpose well. I can't think of any other set of laws which has impacted our culture quite as much as the Vine Laws, especially one part of it called the Staples Rule."

"Yes, please keep going. I'm very interested."

"Well, the Staples Rule requires that every household—every stead—be self-reliant as to basic foodstuffs and domestic fuel. We can bring in wood and charcoal for industrial uses, but we're supposed to grow our own firewood, which by the way, Alga is failing to do."

"Then how can you get away with breaking the law?"

"Who says we are getting away with it? The law is meant for our own benefit, and we are the main ones hurt by neglecting it. Any community not living within its resource base is unstable—witness Anagaia."

"But is such a law wise? I mean, this island has plenty of resources. What's wrong with just selling your salt, wax, and grindstones, and buying in grain and wood from those who have lots of it?"

"Yes, we could have such a system, couldn't we? But then what would become of our beautiful gardens and forests? Instead, we'd have huge cities with their overfed elites and starving masses. We have dirty industrial zones and backward peasants, stripping the wooded hills bare to buy the goods they are forced to need. In short, we'd be like Anagaia. What we have instead is a system where everyone has to account for the resources they consume. We like that."

"I have to admit, I do too. Still, when you have a crowding problem, what else can you do?"

"Well, there's plenty we can do, and are doing: we can improve our yields, we can heat more efficiently. And the bottom line, of course—we can control our population. In fact we are working on all those things and more—do you know we're actually creating new cropland?"

"Yes, yes, I saw that! Strangest thing—grinding up the very rocks to make dirt!"

"You're probably talking about the Lightning Knoll Project, which is an extreme example. But also, we're dredging silt from Galeslee Strait and the Narrows to build up soil depth in ledgy areas. Those projects are designed to serve other purposes as well, but ultimately, they'll make land for producing more food and fuel."

"I just don't see how it can make sense. I mean, the people working on that project will never live to see it completed."

"That's only one way of looking at it. You know that little stand of yukomnia I pointed out to you above the orchard?"

"Those elmy-looking trees that give you rubber? Yes, I remember."

"What you probably don't realize is that part of that area is built up from quarry rubble. It was once nearly bare bedrock, and now it's a valuable piece of ground. Our rainwear enterprise depends on the latex from those trees, and the oak-coppice in between gives a significant addition to our firewood.

"The point is, we didn't do all that work, our ancestors did it over a century ago. True, it was an enormous investment in labour, but the long-term benefits are even greater. I know in Anagaia, if an investment doesn't repay itself in a year or two, it is considered unprofitable. However, our time frame is much longer than that. We're not a slash-and-burn civilization, Yaro, we're here to stay. That project you saw is adding a quarter acre each year to the island's area. That's tons of food or fuel we must otherwise buy from the mainland. Unlike Anagaia, we do not grow by conquest, but rather we improve on what we already have."

Her reference to Anagaia set me to thinking: while back in the Umberlands, whose valleys were decimated by drought and dust storms, people here were thinking in terms of quarter-acres. We had always been told that our problems were due to the climate—something we have no control over—and that our nation's survival depended on endless wars of conquest to wrest the resources we needed from "inferior peoples." Yet I have also heard that our country was once a land of towering forests and lush prairies—that was before the Calamities, of course. Archer once commented that there wasn't enough rain to grow trees, but Dr. Borestone insisted there weren't enough trees to grow rain. What was behind it all? I wondered. What was so wrong about Anagaia, and what was so right about Esperia? Was Anagaia truly doomed to be a predator nation, or could it become a place where people confidently invested in future centuries? I had entertained these questions long before coming to Esperia, but it was different now; discussing such grand matters with Dr. Borestone in his garden had seemed like a mere exercise in fantasy. Here there seemed to be a possibility of making a concrete difference, however modest. It might occur to others that it wasn't my problem anymore, yet Hewn had made me see clearly that Anagaia's problems were ultimately Esperia's problems. He also hinted that because of my peculiar situation, I might have a unique perspective that could prove useful.

Chapter 13

The knowledge of my upcoming extradition hearing preyed on my mind constantly. I decided that as long as I had these plagued thoughts, I may as well organize them at least so I might testify more cogently if called upon. I rehearsed my memories of the dreadful ordeal as I went about my daily business.

The Dryford jail was unpretentious, even as jails go. The rough sandstone-slab building was uncomplicated by windows or furniture, unless you count the urine-soaked pile of straw in the corner. In truth, it was rarely occupied, except by Briney Hames, the town drunk. Ever since Constable Pierce had been replaced by a CADS agent, as happened everywhere after the Amanita Uprising, Briney had become the new jailer. We always joked that the only change was in which side of the door Briney leaned against to sleep off his binges.

From Melody I learned the disappointing news that Archer was not wholly convinced of my innocence. Others in town were berating him for his foolishness in bringing into the community a child who had been perverted by those foreigners. Instead of stoutly defending me, he had caved in and refused to have anything to do with me. Melody had wanted to sell one of the pigs to hire me a lawyer, but Archer balked. Only when she pointed out that they certainly would lose the farm without my labour did he relent.

Folks kept hogs to be fattened on the culls of the yam crop, which was just beginning to be harvested. It was still late summer, and people don't butcher until colder weather, so a hog sold then wasn't going to fetch the price of a first-rate lawyer. In fact, I didn't even get a third-rate lawyer—he never so much as came to see me during the whole time I awaited trial, only four miles from his office. Meanwhile, Briney didn't feed me any too generously; he explained that under the streamlined government's "self-supporting" system, he received a molecular salary and was expected to make up the rest out of his prisoners. I was even more alarmed at his revelation that the judge was also on the "self-supporting" system, picking up most of his pay wherever he could, which of course saved the taxpayers a bundle. They were not called bribes, but "judiciary fees." Briney hinted darkly that he'd heard there was some serious money put up against me, which at first I took to mean Mrs. Gates, but Briney reminded me that Gates weren't the only folks in town with money. I asked him if there were any way I could get my case before another judge, and he said, sure, I could always claim I had killed Jasper because he was a landowner, and I hated all landowners. That would make it a PMC, or politically motivated crime, which carried an automatic death sentence without further trial. I decided to stay with Judge Strider even though according to Briney, he had made out "real good" on the self-supporting system. It might take months, Briney added, but he wouldn't let me starve to death—that could cost him his job.

In fact, I only had to wait a couple weeks. When the trial date finally arrived, I was manacled and loaded onto a mule for the four-mile ride over to Shoatmart, the district seat, under armed escort. As I was led into the back door of the courthouse, we passed the scaffold which stood there. I noticed that there was no stinting of hardware; drop hinges, hooks, and slide bolts were all of the highest quality steel. It was perhaps the only piece of fine machinery in the territory that wasn't imported from Esperia.

The courtroom was packed with spectators, mostly townsfolk attracted by the case's notoriety. There were also many Dryford faces scattered through the crowd, several of whom I had counted among my friends, but now who could tell?

Judge Strider was a gentleman of mature years and impeccable grooming. I was led to an enclosed bench at his left and ordered to sit. The proceeding began with a reading of the indictment, after which I was asked if I intended to represent myself. Before I could answer, another voice in the room announced that he had been retained to represent me. Turning to the voice, I saw a slender and dapper man with a prominent Adam's apple and a pronounced deficiency of chin. So this was my lawyer who proposed to defend me without ever having taken the trouble to make my acquaintance.

"Attorney Meech, I presume you have already taken counsel with the defendant?"

"Your Honour, I have not yet found occasion to meet with my client. However, I have here a number of depositions and other information bearing on the case, which have been largely supplied by the defendant's sister. I consider them adequate to present his case, if he wishes."

The judge frowned at him then, turning to me, said, "You, sir, stand accused of a most serious offense. Do you wish to accept the services of this counselor, under the circumstances? The choice is yours."

I had only a moment to ponder: the man showed little commitment to my cause, yet he had already been paid, and doubtless, his understanding of judicial affairs would make his poorest efforts more effective than my best.

"Yes, I do."

"Very well, we may proceed. Mr. Prosecutor, would you please commence."

Thus began the criminal trial of Yaro Seekings, age nineteen, adopted son of Archer Seekings, smallholder, of Dryford, West Umberlands, accused of willful and malicious murder in the death of Master Jasper Gates, landowner, also of Dryford. In keeping with Anagaian court procedure, the prosecutor was to present evidence and arguments against the accused, after which I, personally or through my representative, was to present evidence and arguments in my defense. Following these, the judge might opt to put questions to either party before passing judgment and sentence. This was much speedier and cost-efficient than the old-fashioned jury trials which had been abolished since 539. Those of noble rank could appeal his decision to the Territorial High Magistrate, or conceivably to the Court of the Olotal. For commoners, decisions made here were final, to avoid frivolous delays.

"Your Honour," began the prosecutor. "We have first examined this case, as was our duty, in the light of possible political motivation. However our investigation has revealed no compelling evidence to suggest that this is connected to any class struggle or terrorist conspiracy. So far as we can determine, the accused has no links with the Amanita or the Land Reform Movement or other subversive organizations. Furthermore, it must be noted that his own family are landowners, in a modest way, and therefore entitled to full recognition of his rights under the law.

"I believe it is worthy of comment that the defendant, prior to the age of eleven, was raised in a Steward-run orphanage in the Twelfth District. As is well-known to the court, these people practice a godless egalitarianism, which is detrimental to an orderly structured society. They neither pay homage to the respected symbols of authority, nor do they show respect for the proper distinctions of class. Although the defendant was removed from their influence at a tender age, and has since been raised by decent and God-fearing parents, it must be remembered that more than half of his life has been spent under the dubious guidance of these foreigners. Of course nothing said so far comes as evidence, rather I offer it merely as an explanation for the set of mind which might be susceptible to such behavior.

Now if it pleases the court, let me try to reconstruct the events which have led to this tragic event: Some time ago, the defendant presumed to establish intimate relations with the deceased's daughter, despite the great disparity in their social ranks. Now one might assume a degree of genuine affection, but there were surely other motives. Of course, the wife and daughter may not inherit directly, but the deceased may provide for the estate to be held in trust or guardianship, to devolve on the daughter's husband if she be married within a prescribed time. It is a common enough practice, and when the deceased's will is found, I expect we will find that some such provisions have been made. However, we have strong reason to believe the deceased did not wish for the defendant to be his heir. We know that he expressly forbade the relationship, no doubt recognizing defects in the defendant's character, which have only recently become obvious to the rest of us. Indeed on the night before he was killed, he and the defendant had a violent quarrel on the very subject of that relationship. From that moment on, the young man stalked his erstwhile benefactor like a beast of prey, watching for his chance. It came the next day, when he found the man working on his own land, repairing a faulty pump in a new well. Lurking in the bushes until his victim was alone, he crept up to the hole, and grabbing a nearby stone, he crushed the unwary man's skull in a savage and premeditated assault. He no doubt expected to get away from there and deny his guilt, but he was surprised by the returning workmen before he could effect his escape. There was no indication that anyone else had been there—the defendant himself admits as much. All the facts—the testimony, the circumstances, the motives—all point to the defendant, Yaro Seekings. I submit to the court, therefore, that he is guilty of willful and malicious murder and should pay the supreme penalty."

I felt a chill go down my spine. It was no different than I expected. Who could refute it? I would have had to agree myself had I not been there.

As the judge had no questions for the prosecutor, it was now Attorney Meech's turn.

"Your Honour, although I must concur with the honourable prosecutor on many of his points, I intend to show the court that one may arrive at a very different conclusion. It is my hope that the court will recognize the appropriateness of a humane and charitable treatment more suitable to the defendant's condition."

What's he getting at? I wondered.

"It has been pointed out that the defendant was removed from his familiar surroundings when he was eleven. One can imagine what a traumatic experience that must have been for a developing young mind.

"It has been remarked by several that he is a quiet, shy type of person, an inward-dwelling sort, not given to sharing his problems but bottling them up inside. And yet it is universally said of him that he is cheerful, hardworking, considerate of others. How can we reconcile this picture with the horrible deed which is at the heart of this case? I would remind the court that the defendant was deeply in love with the deceased's daughter. Evidently they had made plans, and these plans were thwarted by the girl's father, for whatever reason."

I wondered where all this was heading. I saw that Melody was plucking at the lawyer's sleeve, but he was ignoring her.

"I have a deposition here from Mrs. Rose Gates, the deceased's window. She is in bereavement and unable to attend today, but she states here that Yaro Seekings was always a helpful, respectful young man, for whom her late husband felt a genuine attachment. In fact, she says that on the morning of the murder, the defendant spoke with her and gave every indication of repenting the previous night's argument. These are her exact words: 'If he is the one who killed my husband, then he is not the Yaro Seekings I have known.' And therein, Your Honour, lies the crux of the matter: the Yaro Seekings whom everyone in Dryford has known for the past eight years is not the Yaro Seekings who killed Jasper Gates. When he went to the wellsite that morning, he had no intention of harming anyone. But they had more heated words, and in the defendant's love-crazed mind, something snapped and—"

"No!" I was on my feet before the bailiff could hold me down. "No, that's not it at all! He's trying to say I was insane, but I wasn't. I didn't do it at all."

"Silence in the court!" bellowed the judge. "Attorney Meech is your appointed lawyer. Will you not let him represent you?"

"No, he cannot. He is wrong!"

Meanwhile, Attorney Meech was shrugging his shoulders and shaking his head in frustration, as Melody continued to tug at him.

"Young man, you say he is not working in your interest. For insanity, you could spend your life locked inside a madhouse, but murder is a capital offense."

"But how can I agree to either? They are both lies."

The judge looked at me very steadily before saying quietly, "I believe you're making a great mistake. Sit down."

After I was forced back into my seat, he continued. "It is not customary to allow a defendant to change his mode of defense in midtrial, but neither is it illegal. Against my better wisdom, I'm going to allow the accused to treat on his own behalf. Proceed, if you will, sir."

I realized at once that I was in the thing well over my head. I had no understanding of court protocol nor any skill in debating. Worst of all, I had no hard evidence to support my statement. Nevertheless, I proceeded to tell my story. I was careful to relate every detail, admitting that I didn't know what was relevant or not. For instance, I mentioned in passing the ill-tempered man on the road the night of the quarrel, but admitted I had never seen him before and couldn't say whether he had been to see Jasper.

Melody was on her feet now, trying to say something.

"Quiet!" The judge rebuked her testily. "You are not allowed to speak!" Turning to me, he added meaningfully, "Unless of course the defense wishes to call you as a witness."

Taking the hint, I promptly called my foster sister to the stand. I had no idea what she would say, but I trusted her a lot more than Attorney Meech.

"I have some information," she began. "I went up to the wellsite a couple days after with my boyfriend, who's a tracker. As everyone knows only too well, there hasn't been any rain for weeks, and the ground is dry and hard everywhere. We looked around the clearing for footprints, but there weren't any. Around the well, where it was muddied up some, there were lots of footprints, all of which matched the boots of the workmen—we checked them all. Out near the edge of the damp area, we did find one single print that had a nick out of the heel, and it doesn't match with anyone else's. Including Jasper Gates—Mrs. Gates helped us check that."

I glanced at Judge Strider, but his face was inscrutable. If he was impressed by this latest tidbit, he didn't show it.

Melody continued. "Then we looked around the area above the wellsite where the woods hadn't been fully cleared yet—maybe it has by now. My boyfriend found where someone had trod on a bunch of dried broken twigs before entering the woods. He says whoever made them was tall and they were running real fast—"

Judge Strider interrupted her incredulously. "Wait a minute, young lady, you did not see this purported intruder, yet you could describe his build and his movements?"

"No, sir, I couldn't tell anything. My boyfriend could though. Like I said, he's a trained tracker and he knows how to find stuff like that, which nobody else sees. I could see it too, once he showed it out to me."

"And this boyfriend, why isn't he here today to testify for himself?"

"He couldn't, sir. He was hurt."

"Hurt?"

"Injured, sir . . . beat up."

"By whom?"

Melody *flushed very red. "I couldn't say, sir."*

"Couldn't or wouldn't?"

"I . . . I just don't know, sir. He'll be all right now, and it will end there."

"And no one has tried to hurt you? Threatened you, perhaps?"

"Yaro is my brother, sir. He's innocent. Somebody's got to give him justice."

Dear Melody! *Did she know as well as I did whose name was on the cheque in* Strider's *back pocket? The magistrate now seemed to take her more seriously, and he used his prerogative to quiz her further. "So did this boyfriend find any more knicked footprints in the wooded area?"*

"No, sir. The ground was too hard everywhere, excepting around the well."

"And does he—this boyfriend—have any suspicions of his own who the murderer might be?"

"No, sir. He just knows what he saw."

"Thank you, you may sit down."

Then turning to me, he asked, "Young man, this fellow you mentioned seeing on the evening before the murder . . . walking angrily away from the Gates place, could you describe him better for us?"

"Not really. Like I said, I wasn't paying much attention to him, absorbed in my own errand."

"Well, would you say"—coached the judge with a significant look into my eyes—"that he was very tall and, perhaps . . . athletic?"

I took his meaning but could do nothing with it short of lying, and I didn't trust lies to get me anywhere.

"He was tall enough, I guess, but not so that I noticed, really. And sure, I suppose he would have been capable of running a few yards through the woods, but who wouldn't? I tell you, I only mentioned him because I'm trying to think of any useful details. I'm not out to pin the murder on someone I don't even know. All I know for absolutely certain is that I didn't kill Jasper Gates."

The judge peered at me very thoughtfully, almost pityingly. "A knicked bootprint, some broken twigs . . . that's your main defense?" I don't know if anybody else sensed it, but I heard a subtle alteration in his voice as though he were no longer talking to me or anyone else in the courtroom. I remember his exact words, though I didn't quite understand their relevance, then or now. "Justice is not served by intuition or speculation. It is served by information, by testimony, by forensic data. Justice may not err on the side of caution. Error in either direction is still error, it is not justice."

He had seemed to be looking not at me, but at something far beyond me, but having said these words, he seemed suddenly aware of me, sitting in his foreground, awaiting his judgement, the judgement that would end it all.

"Before giving my verdict, I shall retire to my chambers for a few moments to do some research."

There was a murmur in the room as others asked the same question I was thinking: research? Either he believed me or he didn't. What in his law books could help him decide that? I took it as encouraging that he needed to consider anything at all, in light of the "judicial services fee" the Shacklefords were supposed to have given him. Nevertheless, I dreaded his return, which was not for several minutes. He gave me a rather peculiar look as he entered. I can't explain it, but somehow he looked older and younger, all of the same time. It was almost as if he had found himself on trial for his own life, and somewhere in those books he had sought, and hopefully found, something that would acquit him.

"Order! Order! The court will resume. After considering all the evidence that has been presented here today, there seems to be little doubt as to the defendant's guilt. That therefore is my verdict: guilty of willful and malicious murder. Silence! Now ordinarily, the punishment for that crime is death by hanging. However, there are some disturbing inconsistencies in the case which bother me. They are too slight to merit acquittal, but worrisome nonetheless. There is another punishment for capital offenses, one which leaves execution up to the god of justice himself. I find it has not been used for many generations, but neither has it been abolished. That alternative sentence is banishment. Now stop your murmuring, everyone—bailiff, quiet them down!

"Now, everyone understand this: the defendant is not being acquitted, rather he is henceforth dead in the eyes of the law. Do you all understand? He is dead. From this time forth, he lives under a curse. Whosoever should aid or comfort him in any manner brings the same curse upon themselves. That includes giving him food or drink, shelter or transport, or any communication whatsoever."

Turning to me, he intoned solemnly, "Yaro Seekings, I hereby sentence you to lifelong banishment from your people. If you be guilty of this crime, may your life be short and filled with suffering, and may you die in misery far from the solace of your family and friends. If you be innocent, as you profess, may the good God you refuse to worship sustain you and carry you to a safe haven. This case is closed."

Chapter 14

During the night, the island was socked in by rain and sleet, driven by a strong southeaster. By morning it had tapered off, but the wind bore even harder and colder. The windmills had to be unpinned and shackled to keep them from spinning themselves to pieces.

Someone came up from the bannerhouse to say that a message had come across from the Beacon Hills station just before the storm broke. A signal had been received from the CADS office in New Chalice forwarding a copy of the proceedings of the West Umberlands Twelfth District Court in the case of the *State v. Yaro Seekings*. It also included police records of the murder of one Serene Miller, indigent, of Sycamore, East Umberlands, and of the murder of Jasper Gates, landowner of Dryford West Umberlands, and also the police search reports from New Chalice, Hither Anagaia. These documents were presented to Brownlea, Lord Amberson, who immediately requested a meeting of the household of Stonesthrow. Although it is not required, Hewn also requested that the banner steward and the Keeper of the Vision be present at the hearing.

I was actually much less nervous than I had expected to be. Indeed I was surprised at how quickly it all happened. Lord Amberson presented his evidence to Ermine, as stead steward, and demanded that the criminal described therein be turned over for safeguarding back to the Anagaian authorities. Ermine in turn read all the evidence aloud to the others and encouraged them to examine the documents for themselves. There was little comment at first beyond the observation that the papers offered nothing new or contradictory to my version, albeit a different perspective. Ermine did suggest however that a formal record of my own detailed statement (which Hewn had written down a week prior) be filed with the extradition request and that a copy be forwarded to the Anagaian government. Hewn also presented an affidavit from Arnica of Fairhaven, detailing his and Wren's conversations with me in New Chalice and the crew's reasons for deciding to help me escape. I was then asked to present as evidence my mother's note and the embroidered money bag.

Finally, Hewn declared there was something which needed clarification. "Whatever our personal opinions may be, we need to sift out something positive enough so that the rest of the nation won't hesitate to stand behind us at any future time. Something external to Yaro's own statement. We have some of that, but I find three more points which are beyond his knowledge, and to me they are the most conclusive. The authorities in Sycamore, who where unaware of any family connexion, reported upon investigation that the second victim, Serene Miller, had told a co-worker that she was going to '*see* someone whom she dreaded *meeting*.' Those are her exact words. Now if she dreaded the person themselves, then whyever would she go to such trouble to *see* him—you notice that it was the *meeting* that she said she dreaded. It's entirely reasonable she feared not the person himself, but the curse he was under. According to the decree, she would fall under the curse by helping him. Yet despite her fear—despite it, mind you—she went to see him and was discovered by him. Yaro's statement confirms that she never intended to meet him. It is a curious situation. Yaro's explanation, and only his, accounts for these facts in a way that he himself could not have known. Secondly, the police record quoted a coroner's opinion that she died from a severe blow to the head, but it ignores the fact that he also recorded several broken ribs and a fractured left femur. This combination of injuries would be more indicative of a fall than of foul play, a fall onto jagged rocks such as Yaro had described before. Thirdly, there is the matter of the trial judge, this fellow Strider. For some reason, which is not clear to me, this man was absolutely convinced of Yaro's innocence—"

"Objection!" interrupted Lord Amberson "That's preposterous! It says right here that he considered the evidence damning, else he would have acquitted. Apparently, he had some tender scruples, which were swept away by later events."

Inwardly, I had to agree with Amberson. How did Hewn arrive at that idea?

"My friend," continued Hewn, addressing the courtier but looking at the ceiling. "If that judge had any doubts whatsoever about Yaro's innocence, do you seriously believe he would be sitting here among us now with his neck still in place? Yaro has suggested that the case against him was strongly influenced by monetary considerations."

"Objection! Are you trying to imply that one of his Munificence's magistrates is corrupt?"

Now Hewn looked at Amberson with cold disdain. "If a representative of the Onyx Court will stoop to kidnapping, what are we to expect from a provincial judge?"

"As I was saying," Hewn continued, "if this Judge Strider was as bribable as my experiences with the Anagaian judiciary would suggest"—here he pointedly ignored the envoy's indignant spluttering—"he had much to gain and absolutely nothing to lose by having Yaro executed, nothing but his conscience, and I seriously doubt whether that troubled him much before. But this time, apparently he heeded it, though it seems to have cost him dearly. It says here that he has since been removed from office for 'judicial indiscretion.' He sacrificed a lot, and for what? Not even to acquit Yaro—he knew that was impossible under the circumstances—but only to give him a fighting chance. Why? All I can say is that this man knew something we don't, and it convinced him, as it convinces me, that Yaro is innocent."

I looked over at Amberson. The argument seemed all gone out of him, as if he had given it his best shot and realized that it was a futile effort. He didn't even seem interested in the outcome. Ermine looked around at every eye and quietly concluded, "Unless Lord Amberson can offer some convincing counterexplanation, I recommend that we deny the extradition order and accord Yaro Seekings refugee status under Article II of the Refuge Laws. He will be allowed to remain in Esperia, under protection of the Covenant for as long as he chooses, and if and whenever he desires to seek a different country of asylum, he will be carried there at the expense of the Refuge Commission. Any attempt upon his person or freedom by Anagaia or its agents will be considered as an act of armed aggression against Esperia itself. Is there agreement here?"

There were universal murmurs of assent, and Ermine declared consensus. I was surprised to see that the envoy who had prosecuted the case with such vigour now accepted their verdict with a casual shrug.

"I will deliver your decision personally when I arrive in New Chalice in a few days. I'm sure we can put this matter behind us now and press on with more important issues."

Now I saw what Hewn meant about Amberson. As soon as it was clear he could not carry off his little prize, he took care that it did not threaten his larger career objectives. He turned to Hewn as though they had never exchanged less-than-cordial words.

"Now, sir, I wonder if I might consult with you a while on a matter of mutual concern?"

"Oh, I thought you had concluded your business for the season."

Lord Amberson sighed. "I wish it were so. There are still some loose ends that are too important to give up on just yet. I've been trying to negotiate some agreement with the Fulfillment Commissioners, but we can't seem to reach an understanding. I'm hoping you may help with some suggestions that will break the impasse. It's the . . . uhh, the cotton embargo."

"Well, I don't expect I can be of much help there, but of course, I'll talk with you. When?"

"Immediately, if possible. I have another appointment with the commissioners tomorrow morning and need to get back to Goosegrass in case the weather turns even worse."

"I'm afraid I can't quite yet. I have a little chore I'm supposed to attend to at the wrackplant before lunch. The only other person who knows how to do it right is Freeheart, and he just left to repair a damaged windmill rotor. It usually takes me a couple hours to do it alone, but with Yaro's help, we could probably finish in half the time."

"That would be fine. Shall I meet you here then?"

"I can give you more time if you meet me there. I realize your schedule is tight, but so is mine today."

The effete aristocrat seemed less than enthralled at the prospect, but he gamely replied, "Very well then, I'll meet you there in an hour."

Hewn's chore at the wrackplant was a routine end-of-season clean-out. I was glad to help him out, though I wondered that he would give the job priority over a potentially far-reaching trade negotiation. Anyway, he directed me to various pipes which needed to be dismantled and scoured while he himself descended into a vatlike depression and began scraping and scooping out some vile-smelling sludge.

Anyone who has ever whiffed a pile of rotting seaweed can just multiply that stench by a hundredfold and get some sense of the "ambience" in there. When in operation, the process was contained and fairly odour-free, but the cleanup was overwhelming. We both worked quickly, and when Amberson arrived, we were just finishing up.

"We're almost done," Hewn assured the dapper diplomat.

"But what is it? What does it do?" Amberson clutched his silk handkerchief over his nose.

"Ah, dear me, I'm no chemist. Let's see now . . . first they ferment all the . . . well, of course, it gets acidified before they distill—no, no, wrong process—first it coagulates, then the precipitate is evaporated . . . or is it centrifuged first? As you can see, I'm pretty vague on it myself."

"Well then, what does it make?"

"Make? Why, it makes everything under the sun, or so it seems sometimes. Depending on the process, they get iodine, bromine, potash, saltpeter, gelatin—whatever they want. This whole complex makes soap, matches, and blasting powder, to name just a few things. If we could grow corn or wheat on those ledges, they wouldn't repay us as much as this slimey stuff."

"Yes, speaking of crops." The young aristocrat seized the opportunity to lead the discussion in a more propitious vein. "The Olotal is quite offended at the new boycott of Tramontese cotton."

"Is he though? Then please take back our sincere apologies to him. The boycott is not intended to give him offense, nor anyone else. It is intended to induce policy changes. If your cotton planters will raise a product which does not violate our Blood Laws, we'll be happy to buy it."

"Blood Laws? But this is cotton, not beef! It has no blood on it."

"My friend, I'm sure your government did not send you up here without some understanding of our legal system. The Blood Laws are not half as narrow in scope as you would like them to be. The same goes for the the Slave Laws, the Nest Laws, and the Pits and Parapets Laws, all of which are being invoked against your cotton. It's your contract system, of course. Back in '46, our Council of Keepers of the Vision urged a boycott on all goods produced by workers who are bound under the contract system, or 'bucs' as you call them. So your government modified some of the more egregious features of the system, but only until the boycott was lifted. Then those clauses were gradually reinstated, with different phrasing but the same intent. Imagine yourself living under those conditions, Amberson—they're horrendous! Perhaps your Olotal cares nothing for the suffering of his people, but he cannot expect us to subsidize it with our imports."

"Sir, you are speaking of the internal arrangements of a sovereign state."

"So are you. If the Contract System is Anagaia's business, then the boycott is Esperia's."

"Well, of course you have the right to buy or not buy as you wish. But look at the harm this does to the common people of both nations. Your people need cotton, and they cannot grow it here. And what of the poor Anagaian peasants? You claim to be concerned for them, yet the boycott is costing them their livelihoods."

"We are finding numerous alternatives to your cotton. Indeed, our people are surprised how well we can manage without it. It is from the Banners, not the Commission that the boycott initiative arose. As for the Anagaian peasants, I have one right here. I've talked at length with Yaro, and he agrees with other peasants we've interviewed that the suffering caused by the dependence on cotton outweighs any benefit."

"Oh, so this is your consultant on such matters," Amberson sniffed. "A renegade who has abandoned his own people. Since when is he an expert on global commodities?"

"He certainly has hoed an awful lot of cotton. What about yourself?"

"Of course I haven't . . . what do you think I . . . anyway, what does any of that have to do with Tramont? They're not a major cotton producer, nor have the new regulations been applied there."

"True enough, they're a very minor producer, yet they've suddenly become a major exporter in the last couple years, haven't they? We haven't been fooled, Amberson. There are two reasons you haven't applied the laws there: first, Tramont is a hotbed of dissidence, a powderkeg you don't want to touch off just now, and second, they're much more useful to you as a transshipper, selling Umberlands cotton under Tramont labels. Your government has made a bad situation worse—now we can't even import legitimate Tramont-grown cotton. Practically every bale now comes from Palmetto."

"But theirs is far more expensive than ours!"

"Is it really? If you factor in the degradation of land and people, theirs is a bargain. After all, it's not the price of your cotton that we object to, but those hidden costs."

Softening his tone somewhat, Hewn continued. "Look, Amberson, we can argue all day, and you'll get just as far as you did with the commissioners: nowhere. But you did ask me for advice, so I'll try to help you. There are a number of small cotton producers in Hither Anagaia, which have a special exemption from the boycott. That's because they operate in ways acceptable to us. They are either worker-owned coops or plantations with profit-sharing. They have worker-safety programmes, they put a certain percentage of acreage in tree crops (which we also agree to buy), they mulch the soil to reduce irrigation; and various other stipulations. For this, they get to ship their cotton here, and we pay them a 40-percent premium. We would welcome similar arrangements in other parts of your country, like Umberlands, but we don't have enough certifying agents there, and those that are there are restricted in their movements. The local coop leaders are frequently harassed and jailed by CADS. The Olotal treats them as a threat rather than an opportunity. This is an area where our governments could work together to our mutual benefit."

"That's quite out of the question. His Munificence could never accept such a perversion of the natural relations between employees and . . ."

As Lord Amberson was speaking, the door of the factory opened, and two men dodged in out of the ranting wind. They were Amberson's servants, and they waited awkwardly to speak with him. After conferring with them privately for a minute, Lord Amberson came back over, shaking his head in sheepish consternation.

"It's the *Ruby Princess*—my yacht. She has snapped her moorings in the wind and been driven aground."

"How terrible!" commiserated Hewn with sincerity. "Has she gone down?"

"No, they say the hull is broken through, and it's stuck upon the rocks. The tide is going out, so it will hold for now."

"Good, good! We can patch it enough to float and tow it up to Fairhaven for repairs. They should know better than anyone how to mend it since they built it."

"But what shall I do meanwhile? I cannot stay aboard it, and there are no inns here."

"Well, I'm sure you're welcome to lodge with us while your ship is in dry dock, though I'm afraid the accommodations aren't what you're used to."

"Oh, I would be most grateful for that! I realize it is highly irregular, but we will try not to disturb your pattern of living. This really is a predicament."

To our surprise, Lord Amberson proved true to his word. Ordinarily, his yacht was his office as well as his residence, to avoid the complications of living among Stewards. But in his extremity, he proved remarkably adaptable. Throughout his stay, the pampered courtier fit into the household, after a fashion, rubbing shoulders cordially with people he inwardly considered his inferiors. He was dismayed to find that his gold sceptres were not acceptable as payment, but that he was expected to participate in household chores. We knew he found dishwashing especially humiliating, yet he pitched in with a cheerful façade that fooled no one, but impressed everyone. I'm sure it helped that none of his servants were present—that would have been just too much. Due to overcrowding, they were billeted at neighbouring steads. There was no grumbling from any of his staff since their master had strictly commanded them to say or do nothing to displease their eccentric hosts. In fact, the fair-skinned crew left no doubt that they had never had it so good, even in His Excellency's service, and they would be loathe to leave.

As for me, I was more than a little nervous about the new situation. Amberson was given the use of Marten's dormitory room (which was next to mine), while Marten moved in with Discern. That meant that Amberson, the man who had plotted to carry me back to Anagaia, was sleeping six feet away from me with only a reed mat partition between us. I expressed my concern to Hewn.

"If you wish, you could stay over at Straitside for a week. However, I think your fears are totally groundless. Lord Amberson is a fellow who unwaveringly pursues his own self-interest above all else. Before today, he might have abducted you, and we could have never have proven our suspicions. But since the hearing, he has very little to gain and everything to lose by harming you. If he were implicated in any foul play, his entire diplomatic mission, and thus his career, would be undone. He understands that all too well and will go to any length to see that you are unharmed while he is here."

Apparently Hewn was right. In spite of myself, I was often in the sole company of Brownie (as he insisted I call him.) Even then he treated me cordially as though nothing had ever happened to prevent our friendship.

All the to-do about my hearing and Amberson's stay with us made me even more mindful than usual of the people I'd left behind in Umberlands. Fawn was the most painful memory of all. It even occurred to me once to try to get a letter to her. Whether she loved or hated me, it seemed I ought to at least let her know where I was. She could read, after all—I had taught her myself—and she could pass along word to Melody. But I realized at once how absurd the idea was. It was not at all certain that a letter would even reach Dryford, but it was quite certain that it would be opened and censored by CADS, and that would be nothing but bad for Fawn. I didn't know what kind of troubles she might be having, but being in communication with a banished criminal would surely add to them.

I now seemed to view every aspect of my former life with mixed feelings.

Chapter 15

On the third morning after the shipwreck, I arose very early to join Vervain, who was already in the kitchen. She was preheating the great oven for the day's project, for which I had volunteered. I carried in armloads of firewood, enough to fill the capacious woodbox, yet it would need refilling at least twice before day's end. I thoroughly mashed the basin filled with cooked potatoes and dumped them into a crock with malted meal and fresh yeast. I set this starter in a warm corner by the stove to foam and bubble while I went on, grinding caraway seed and measuring out sea salt according to Vervain's directions. Before long, Marten and two others came in, barely awake, and began mixing dough in two huge basswood troughs.

What we were making, I learned, was flatbread, hundreds upon hundreds of crisp, large discs of rye, each with a hole through the centre. The large thin loaves would go into the yawning oven, emerging as ring-shaped biscuits. Stacked by the dozens to cool, they would then be wrapped in brindle-coloured paper, looking much like edible grindstones. A number of the bundled loaves would be threaded onto poles and suspended from the ceiling until wanted. Today we were baking the whole winter's supply, and quite a bee we made of it. During the day, others came in to relieve the mixers and rollers so there would be no gaps in the production line. Everyone struggled to keep the supply of raw dough heading toward the insatiable maw of the oven. It was real work, but a sense of gaiety pervaded the air, borne aloft with the scents of yeast and caraway.

Even the marooned Lord Amberson dropped by and helped in his own fashion. His energy was not sustained, however, and he soon excused himself on other business.

"I just don't know what to make of that guy," I admitted to Ermine, who was helping in the group activity. "He once tried to get me killed, now he acts like we're old buddies. Last night before bed, he was confiding to me all sorts of court scandals and gossip. He apologized for causing me any 'unpleasantness'—that's what he called it! And he said he wished we could have met under different circumstances. You'll think me terribly gullible, I know, but he really seemed sincere."

"On the contrary, I'm sure he was sincere. I've noticed that about him: he would slit your throat and expect you to hold no grudge because he would hold no grudge if you were to slit his. One mustn't let business interfere with friendship and vice versa. Now that you have no usefulness to him, he can afford to be your confidante. But if circumstances should ever change—beware!"

"I know what you mean. He is kind of a snake."

"A snake?" interrupted Marten, who was working across from me. "Why, what favour did he ever do for you?"

I was puzzled, but Ermine explained to him. "It's one thing to translate words, Marten, and quite another to translate foreign ideas. In Anagaia, the expression 'snake' implies treachery. That's just how they look at snakes—it's something of an insult."

"But how do you use the word then?" I asked.

"You see, snakes are not considered pests here—nor are weasels, foxes, or skunks. Since we don't keep poultry, such predators have never been a problem. But we do have problems with mice, rabbits, and squirrels. We would be overrun by them if they weren't controlled by those animals you despise. Therefore, we call a person a 'snake' or a 'weasel' who does our unpleasant work for us. It's not at all derogatory. I remember that when we were in Anagaia, the people there avoided calling me by name, for fear of offending me."

"I see. Well, call Amberson what you will, I wouldn't like to be at his mercy."

"I can certainly understand that," agreed Ermine reflectively. "And yet I guess he fits the Anagaian ideal of what an ambassador should be."

"Yes," I said. "And I guess Hewn fits the Esperian ideal of what an ambassador should be."

Several people, including Ermine, giggled loudly. "Tut-tut, Yaro! Do you suppose we don't know exactly what you're thinking?"

I blushed. "I mean, he's always very gentle with me, but I've noticed with certain people, he's . . ."

"Not a very diplomatic diplomat? Oh, how I do know it! I've pointed it out to him many times, but he insists his bluntness is his stock-in-trade."

"But how? Don't the foreign diplomats hate to deal with him?"

"You'd never know it. Esperia maintains a fully staffed consulate in New Chalice, but they insist on talking with Hewn. Before, it was old Lord Shatterlance, now this chap Amberson keeps traipsing up here to consult with him. They won't give him any peace, and sometimes he loses patience. Hand me that caraway please."

"Then why don't they seek out someone who isn't retired, someone who's easier to deal with?"

"I guess they just realize that pleasantries are of no use to them. You see, Esperia has a lot of complex trade regulations which arise from our Vision. Anagaians don't share that Vision, so it complicates their efforts to trade with us. They don't understand how things work here, and Hewn seems to have a knack for getting it across to them. They may be put off by his crustiness, but they know he can help them gain the understanding they need if they want to do business here. And they simply have to do business."

"Yes, of course, but so do we. What if they were to retaliate by boycotting Esperian goods?"

"That's just it, you see. They need our products more than we need theirs. With a few glaring exceptions, we could forego all foreign trade. For our part, it would be a bothersome inconvenience, but it would be crippling for Anagaia. As you know, their economy is completely market based and export driven. Even with the cotton boycott, we're still a vital market for many Anagaian goods. That's why we have so much influence in the Olotal's court."

"Then why not boycott them altogether?"

"There are a few things that Anagaians are doing right, and we wish to encourage their good practices. For example, we'll never boycott their dried fruits and nuts or anything that causes them to plant trees. We could manage quite well with our own, but if their sales depended on those few Anagaians who can afford them—after all, they're considered a luxury there—you know those trees would be cut down and replaced by cotton. We may be a tiny country, but we are populous and prosperous, so we can influence their land-use policies by our purchasing decisions. Here's a new batch to be mixed, thank you."

I didn't say anything at the time, but I had serious misgivings. I knew perfectly well that Esperia exported a torrent of manufactured goods to the Empire. Was I to believe that they could shut off that flow without ruining themselves?

Chapter 16

Hewn loved to walk. He said it helped him work off his frustrations. If so, he must have been frustrated often, because he walked whenever he could find time. I liked to accompany him. He walked fast for his seventy-five years, and though my knee was fairly healed, I was hard-pressed to keep up. He often left it to me to select our route, and I invariably began by passing the bannerhouse. One day he asked me why.

"Because of that," I replied.

"Oh really?" He followed my finger up to the blue-and-green flag with the frond of seaweed in the centre. "What's so special about that banner?"

"Only that it's not yellow and square."

He looked puzzled a moment then chuckled in recognition. "Ah yes, that. I remember it too."

We were both referring to the "Snotty Banner," so-called. When the present Olotal Blaze II had succeeded his indolent father, the grasping young ruler had consolidated his control by decreeing that henceforth, his personal ensign should fly over every public building and square, with the flag of the League placed below it. All citizens were to show respect by bending the knee and baring the head, failure to do so being treason, a capital offense. According to hearsay, when one of his courtiers objected that he had no personal ensign, the Olotal is said to have pulled a soiled silk handkerchief from his pocket and said, "Let them bow down to that!" Be that as it may, the flag was nicknamed the Snotty Banner, in secret, of course.

"Yes, as I recall, that created difficulties for all Stewards working in the League, since only we embassy staff were exempt from the edict."

"It nearly shut us down. The orphanage workers couldn't go to the town hall to pay our taxes."

"Couldn't they send in a local friend who didn't share our scruples?"

"I think the government was trying to force a confrontation. The law specified that taxes must be paid by the owner in person."

"I never knew that part. However did they get around it?"

"I barely remember, I was so little then, but I think they arranged something with Mr. Canes, the original owner. Maybe they put the property back in his name—I never really knew."

"Well, I'm glad it wasn't a problem for you personally"

"Oh, but it was. All my life I've avoided public buildings. Even in Dryford, I always took backstreets rather than cross the square."

"But why? What did you even know about our Idol Laws?"

"Nothing at all. I only knew that Faring would not bow to a flag, so neither would I. I was a true fanatic: rich in zeal, but poor in understanding. That's why it gives me such pleasure to walk by here and flagrantly ignore that flag, although it is rather pretty in a way."

We both laughed as we strode briskly on past the wrackplant.

Ordinarily I was on the receiving end of our interactions; whether I was being fed or housed or taught, it seemed I rarely had much to give back. But on this occasion, Hewn seemed to feel that there were parts of my young history that interested him. As we walked down the Beach Road, he said, "I suppose you're old enough to have clear memories of the rebellion. At the embassy, we were pretty much shut off from most information."

He was referring, of course, to the Amanita Uprising in 539. I explained that it had happened very shortly after my arrival at Seekings', and being only eleven, I wasn't directly involved; but I sure remembered it. Reportedly it began with a police crackdown on opium growers in East Umberlands, whence it escalated to include food riots and tax protests in a number of border towns. Within a fortnight, the revolt had spread like the wildfires that periodically swept the drought-ridden land. Nearly every outlying province, including parts of Hither Anagaia itself, was in turmoil. The aristocracy was aghast at the extent and ferocity of the outbreak, and the government reacted with unparalleled brutality. Several crack army divisions were recalled from the occupation of Upper Tupelo to counter the insurgency. For months, the Provincial Highway out of Shoatmart resounded to the boots of seasoned combat troops, crisscrossing the land in pursuit of the ragtag rebel armies. Although the rebellion exposed the depths of popular discontent, it also proved premature. The leaders of the Amanita Movement misjudged their organizational strength and lacked coherent strategy. By winter, the uprising had virtually collapsed, except for sporadic resistance in Tramont. Curiously, the area around Dryford was spared the worst ravages of the conflict, although it was a hotbed of opposition sentiment. Just as a tornado roars across the land at whim, wreaking havoc in one place while skipping entirely over another, so the sleepy village shuddered in the wake of devastation as the abortive rebellion surged back and forth around it, leaving it unscathed.

As winter progressed, local peasants trickled back into the community, with no one asking where they had been. Others were conspicuous for not returning at all. Neighbours quietly speculated about whether they were dead or trapped in prison camps. There was an unspoken consensus that the matter wasn't over yet, but it was completely certain that the leadership core was shattered and would not rear its head for many years.

"And CADS," Hewn reminded me. "That's when they took over everything."

Yes, indeed that changed a lot in the life of small communities like ours. CADS had originally been the Olotal's personal bodyguards. After the uprising, it was greatly expanded into a centralized police organization with unbridled powers. They were secretive and accountable to no local authorities. I remembered Carter Pierce, who had been the town's constable before the "reorganization." He was well liked, if a bit too easygoing. After being replaced by Agent Longwood, Carter went to keeping a general store, just off the square. But people continued to call him Constable, which vexed the CADS agent no end.

"Were the Seekings good to you?" I didn't know why Hewn was so curious about my background, but I was willing enough.

"They intended to be, I'm sure. I don't really know what Mrs. Seekings wanted in a son, but I know Archer was disappointed, at least at first. Whether he realized it or not, he was more interested in a worker than a son. At that age, I was not much use to him. Oh, I tried all right and was always keen to please—but when I went hoeing in the fields, I just couldn't bear the heat. One time they nearly lost me to sunstroke. I sincerely wanted to help out though, and soon I stumbled onto a way. Back at the orphanage, all of us kids were taught various handcrafts in addition to our basic studies. One day, a bale of cotton fell off a wagon in the street and burst open. The teamster couldn't get it back onto the load and Bracken, one of the keepers, offered to buy it from him cheap. His wife made us a bunch of drop-spindles so we kids could spin coarse yarn. Bracken and Faring improvised a couple of crude looms so we could make blankets for ourselves.

"Well, soon after I came to Seekings', I noticed that Melody's old wool blanket was badly moth-eaten. We couldn't afford a new one, so I got some crooked poles out of the woodshed and cobbled together a small backstrap loom that was even funkier than what we had at the orphanage, yet serviceable nonetheless. Then I went through the neighbours' harvested cotton fields, gleaning the bolls that had been missed or were immature at picking time. The quality was poor, and it took hours to hand-clean the seeds from the lint. Eventually, I managed to work it all up into three broad bands which I sewed together to make a single, lightweight blanket. Melody was ecstatic, and Archer was impressed. He was quick to see an opportunity to supplement the family income. He found me some smoother, straighter poles for an improved loom. Melody mentioned the plan to Fawn Gates on one of her visits and, and next day Jasper's gin-man dropped off a whole bale of short staple cotton—quite a gift. With that, I could work much faster and spin stronger, smoother yarn. In a few weeks' spare time I had woven two more blankets, which Archer took right over to Carter Pierce's store to pay down some of our credit. I was really pleased to be a contributing family member at last."

I was sure that Hewn must be getting tired of my rambling—he was not ordinarily much for small talk—but he persisted in asking questions and stirring up recollections, not all of them unpleasant.

"Ermine says you've always been a vegetarian, even after leaving the orphanage. Out in that country, that must have left you with few alternatives."

"That's for sure," I agreed. "At first it was just millet and sweetpotatoes with occasional crowder peas or limas. I like all those things but it soon got awfully monotonous, especially compared to the variety I was used to at the orphanage."

I remembered how desperate I had been to broaden my diet. Out along the riverbank, I found some wild chicory growing. I dug up the roots and kept them in the yam cellar. In midwinter, I brought them out and forced a bunch of nice blanched salad greens. There were three old pecan trees out behind the pigsty, and I could hardly believe they weren't being used. But to Archer, "crops" meant "cash crops"; and when it was potato-digging time, nothing else mattered, so the pecans went to the pigs. I gathered up a lot of them myself and brought them to the table, all shelled out. Everyone enjoyed them but considered them an extravagance.

I also went through the sweetpotato vines and pinched off some tender young leaves for boiling greens. Archer had never realized that sweetpotato greens were good eating, despite growing them his entire life. I shared all these things with the family, and they were appreciative, but when I asked Archer if I might use a tiny plot for a kitchen garden, he rejected the idea out of hand. "We need every square foot for crops—haven't enough as it is. Such fancy vittles is a luxury we can't afford regularly." It was futile to remind him that he was losing money on the sweetpotatoes and the hogs, whereas at least the greens and nuts were better than anything our neighbours had to eat. Melody also cajoled him, but he was adamant.

Then a couple days later, Jasper Gates rode by to discuss business. Now he owned the bottomlands downriver from us where he raised cotton. But between that and our place lay another small irregular field, about three acres, which he leased to us. On it we grew sweetpotatoes, most of which he bought back to feed his bucs. Shrewd businessman that he was, Jasper always squeezed as much rent as he could from Archer then dickered him down to rock-bottom on the sweetpotatoes. This day, the value of that land was up for discussion again, but Jasper's approach was different.

"Say there, Seekings. I've reconsidered about that end lot. I guess I want eight falcons twenty for it next year."

Archer just stood aghast. "But, sir," he sputtered. "I'm already paying you six and forty-five. Why, you'll ruin—"

"No, no, hold your horses, damn it. I'm not talking about per acre, I mean for the piece. That's my best offer—take it or leave it."

His tough talk was plain irony. Before he could reconsider, Archer shot back, "I'll take it!"

"I should think," mumbled Jasper. "By the way, what is this I hear about the boy wanting to make a garden?"

"Oh, well, you know how kids take up fool notions, as if we had any space to—"

"Well, I can't see any problem with that, can you?"

"Uh . . . no, of course . . . not. No problem . . . He'll just have to . . ."

"Doesn't seem like he ought to need too much space—how big did you have in mind, boy?" I hardly knew what to answer. I couldn't imagine how he knew anything about the matter, much less why he should care about it.

"I don't know, sir. I suppose I was thinking about four or five rods."

"That's all? Why, there ought to be that much to spare in the end lot, right, Seekings?"

"Oh yes . . . yes, indeed, sir. All he needs, sir . . . no reason why . . . not."

"Damn right!" confirmed Gates, and without further discussion, he jerked his horse's head toward town and galloped off, leaving Archer staring slack-jawed after him.

*   *   *   *   *   *   *

"Well, I'm sure you've heard more than you want to about all that," I said shyly as we crossed the Lightning Knoll road and headed back up-island.

"Not at all," rejoined Hewn. "You're just getting to the most interesting part. Do please tell me more about this garden enterprise of yours."

The way he said "enterprise" gave me an inkling of why he found my story so interesting. I couldn't quite put my finger on it, but I continued anyways.

"Well, Archer kept his word, all right, not that Mr. Gates left him much choice. And anyway, he had no cause to begrudge the loss of land. My allotted space was in a long, narrow corner where two property fences converged at an acute angle. The shape made it difficult to plough without denying the mule room to turn. Because of that, much of the ground was fallow and weed choked. Archer was gaining a lot and sacrificing little—even he admitted that."

I started on the project at once, even though warm weather was still weeks away. I had promised not to neglect my usual work, so I only managed to spare an hour or so each day. I knew better than to even ask for any pig manure, but I could compost the weeds with some river mud and last fall's pecan leaves to supply at least some fertility. I really had a pretty vague idea of what I was doing. You see, I could only act out what I remembered from the orphanage garden, and that was spotty at best. I generally had no idea why I was doing the things I did, but I kept doggedly at it, and after a couple weeks, I had prepared a patch nearly three rods square.

Meanwhile, I wondered what I was going to plant in it. Though Umberlands is farming country, it's not really gardening country. Very few people in our area keep subsistence gardens, and seed is not easy to come by. What is available is usually expensive and of dubious quality. I remembered the marvelous assortment of superior vegetable varieties we had grown at the orphanage. I wrote a letter to Faring, knowing he would share a bit with me. The problem was that I couldn't mail it. Besides, there being no public mail system, I had no money for a courier. I couldn't expect help from Archer who resented any contact I had with Stewards, especially Faring. So I held onto the letter, waiting for a chance.

There was a dark-skinned fellow, a notions-and-oddment peddler named Sylvan Brackenbush, who came through town every week. He and his family were refugees from the fighting in Upper Tupelo, and somehow they had ended up in West Umberlands. Of course, he could not own property, but he and his brothers operated a network of peddling routes, dealing in miscellaneous small goods. Most folks, even his customers, tended to abuse him because of his colour; but that was not how I was raised, and we became casual friends. One day, after trading a few sewing needles for some of Melody's duck eggs, he pulled up beside the garden where I was working.

"Well, Yaro, my buddy, it seems you have some work ahead of you."

I explained about my project and mentioned the problem of contacting Faring.

"Well now, that's beyond my territory, but if you give me that letter, I can see that someone will deliver it to your friend."

"Oh thanks, Sylvan, but I don't have the price."

"But you will have, once this garden gets going. I haven't had any exciting food since we moved here. What say, maybe a quarter-falcon's worth of this summer's crop, my selection?"

"That's a real fair deal, if you don't mind waiting."

"Knowing you, I consider it as good as on my table. Now give me that letter."

A couple weeks passed with no word from Sylvan, and I feared that my letter had gone astray. The soil was warming up, and I knew that I must start seeds soon to have well-established plants before the dry heat of summer. I hauled water for my compost pile and scrounged sticks and twine for trellising, but I began to fear that it was all for nothing. Then one evening, I heard the rattling of Sylvan's cart on the deep rutted road. With a wide grin he, handed down a large parcel.

"It's a lot heftier than I expected, Yaro. I probably should have asked for a half-falcon's worth."

"A half-falcon it is Sylvan. What's your preference?"

"Tomatoes and collards, but I suppose it depends on what's in there," he said, pointing to the package.

There was indeed collard seed and three types of tomato and so much more. Cuttings of grapes, scuppernong, even a couple of ball-rooted figs and persimmons. And a mulberry seedling from under the big tree by the wall where Faring and I often sat. Best of all there was a letter with news from everyone. It was warm and upbeat; the tone was meant to cheer me up rather than rekindle my longing for the place, but all in vain. As I read and reread the page, my tears spattered on it until it was barely legible. They said Mica, who was fifteen when I left, had been draughted and was serving with the occupation forces in Upper Tupelo. That was a relief; much safer than fighting guerillas in the Coquinas. Since my departure, there were also two new arrivals at the orphanage, their family a casualty of the uprising.

I hurriedly got the seeds in the ground. The woody cuttings were already rooted, so I planted them directly, setting them deep in the newly worked soil. I knew to place the woody perennial crops along the rail fence where in future years *they would give a light shade, protecting the garden, and so the vines could climb along the fence.*

That year, we had heavy spring rains and the newly sown garden became a swamp. The nearby Possum River went on a rampage, rising overnight to a coffee-hued torrent that clawed at the banks. Luckily, the flooding did not reach my garden, nor did the rain wash out much seed. When the water receded just as quickly as it had come, everything was deliciously moist, indeed muddy, but I knew those conditions wouldn't last. Soon summer heat and drought would parch the tender seedlings unless I did something to protect the soil. Leaves or hay were too scarce, but at the orphanage, we sometimes used flat stones as a groundcover.

About a mile away, there was an old quarry dug into a low, ledgy ridge that paralleled the river. It was mostly sandstone with alternating layers of shale, which had exfoliated in large thin sheets. All the good, thick pieces of sandstone had been removed over the years—it could be seen in most of the buildings in town—but heaps of the shale waste lay scattered about for the taking. Archer wouldn't spare me the pony and cart, so I made daily treks to the quarry with the wheelbarrow, returning with as many thin slabs as I could push. Bit by bit, day by day, yard by yard, the mulched portion of the garden expanded like a mosaic blanket spread over the earth. Between the slabs I planted the most drought-prone crops: groundcherries, spinach, and collards. I couldn't cover the entire area that year, but I planted most of it with okra, chard, tomatoes, and pole beans. I really didn't want to waste any available space.

"And how did that work out?" interrupted Hewn.

"I was lucky that year. We had several showers during the summer—not at all usual. By midseason, when things were back to normal, I had most of the garden mulched.

"Of course, it was a great year for weeds as well." I added. "Kudzu and thistles poked up through every crack in the mulch, right where crop plants were supposed to be. It made weeding really tricky."

I reflected a moment as we walked, then volunteered, "There's another part of the story you probably don't want to hear."

"Sure I do. Continue."

"Might make you sick."

"I've a strong stomach."

"Well then, ordinarily I enjoyed my daily walk. It was tiring at the end of the day, but the air was still nice from the rains, and the road, though rutted, was not yet hard and dusty. On the ridge not far from the quarry stood a signal tower, kind of like you have here, except it was only for police use. Well, one evening I came over the rise and saw the most ghastly thing—bodies hanging from the tower frame. Apparently, they were rebel prisoners executed earlier that day. None looked like local men to me, although with their purple faces and sagging bodies, it was hard to be sure. Executions are usually done at the courthouse over in Shoatmart, but I guess they wanted to spread the horror around as much as they could to keep everyone in line. There are no gallows in Dryford so I guess they improvised by using the tower. I puked up all my supper right on the road—it was so gruesome. I've seen dead bodies since then, but hardly anything has affected me quite like that."

We didn't say anymore until we got back to the house.

Chapter 17

It seems to me that one thing all Esperians share is a love of stories. Their own stories, foreign stories, long epics, or short vignettes, stories with a moral, stories with a punch line, tearjerkers, cliff-hangers, tall tales and history. They love to tell them, to hear them, to discuss and dispute them, and they love to memorize and criticize them. Wasn't it Shiningsea who said, "All stories are stories of life, indeed stories are life"? And she should know.

Stories are how we share experiences, and I suppose the most interesting stories are those about experiences alien to our own. At least that's my explanation for why so many of the people I met showed such keen interest in my adventures. Of course, it helped that everyone was very concerned about events in Anagaia, particularly at that time, so any firsthand information was well received.

My own feelings about this were a bit mixed. I had always been a rather private person, if only in self-defense, and was not wholly at ease telling others about such intensely personal events. On the other hand, I felt a real need to recount my past, if only to make it real to myself. My own sanity demanded some evidence that I was not born on the *Minkey* as it entered Harking Bay; that I had a life, an existence long before then; that I had a home, a family, and friends; that there was a place where Yaro Seekings was well-known. And so I was generally willing to share my stories with all comers.

Hewn was an especially attentive listener. Of course, he understood better than others the context of my story; he had lived there long himself and knew many things about Anagaia that I did not. He had been intimate with the very centres of power. Yet he had not been down there for several years, and his acquaintance with the provinces was superficial, which he tried to remedy by interrogating me on every possible occasion. He often showed the most interest in things which seemed of little consequence.

"So you continued with your garden project beyond that first year?"

"Oh, I certainly did. It became very important to me, a little piece of my life over which I had some control."

"And did Archer come to appreciate your efforts."

"I guess so, although he wasn't awfully gracious about it. That was just his way. But the family really enjoyed the variety of stuff I brought to the table. Archer did let me slightly enlarge the garden area after the first year, but he always begrudged me the time it took to care for it."

"I suppose you must have had more than you could use of some things. Did you sell anything?"

"Yes, it seemed there was always a surplus of tomatoes and greens. I sold some to the village store. Carter Pierce, the former constable, ran it for a short while until he had a stroke. Then it was taken over by Grandville Chanter. He was a ne'er-do-well relative of Lord Shackleford's wife. I guess she set him up in storekeeping to keep him out of trouble. I used to sell my blankets to him as well as my produce."

"What about the Palmettoan peddler you mentioned?"

"Sylvan Brackenbush? Yes, I sold to him too. He bought both produce and blankets from me, but I'm afraid that it brought him trouble."

"How so?"

"Well, the first time I sold him something, he brought out his scales and weighed it all. I told him the price per pound, and he figured it up. It seemed like quite a lot compared to what I got at the store, and I said so to Sylvan. He winked at me and said, 'That's because I don't sell no magnets.'"

"Magnets?" I blinked in confusion. "What are you talking about, Sylvan?"

"Well now, don't mention where you heard it, but the next time you are in that store, buying or selling something, you just watch his hands real careful. You'll see what I mean."

Next time I had occasion to be at the store I watched discretely as Grandville waited on another customer. Sure enough, when he went from selling to buying, his hands slid deftly from one weigh pan to the other. And when I peeked underneath, I could see several magnets clinging to the bottom of one. I left the store very angry, but when I suggested to Archer that we should expose the fraud, he was adamant. "No, sir, you just mind your own business. We don't need to cross up that family." But Archer obviously wasn't going to continue being cheated himself, so he took to driving over to Shoatmart whenever he had goods that needed weighing. Melody and I told a few of our friends, and as word got around about the crooked scales, others took to making the inconvenient drive to Shoatmart. It was only a matter of time before someone got the idea of having Sylvan pick up things for them. Of course, with his peddler's markup, there was probably little savings, but I guess people figured that if Grandville was stooping that low, who knew what other ways he was cheating them? The store had a sudden drop in business.

We never told how we knew about the scam; but one week, Sylvan failed to show up and then the next. After a while, a rumour circulated that a "local citizen" had denounced Sylvan Brackenbush as a gunrunner for the Amanita. Friends of mine, people who would know, said that was a lot of bunk, that Sylvan's only offense was talking about magnets.

I was expecting Hewn to ask me the question that I thought would be obvious at this point, about my own links to the Amanita brotherhood. Instead he asked me something that seemed totally irrelevant. "Tell me, were there any Steward institutions anywhere in that area, I mean closer than the orphanage?"

"Well, not that I heard of, but that doesn't mean a lot. I didn't get around all that much."

"So you had no regular contact with Esperians?"

"No, not at all. On occasion, one heard about swarthy travelers with beards and long hair passing through the area. But Dryford was off the Imperial Highway, and foreigners were very rare"

Upon reflection, I added, "There were a couple of fellows once, when I was sixteen. Nice guys." And I proceeded to tell Hewn about my meeting with the Esperian surveyors.

I was using the early morning to catch up in my garden before starting work in the yam field. I saw the two strangers moving slowly across the field, toward the riverbank. One had a curious instrument on a tripod, and the other stood a ways off with a tall striped pole. The nearest one saw me staring at them and called out in good Anagaian, "Hello there! We're doing no harm. Just following the course of the Possum River."

I knew less than ten words in Esperian, and I used half of them to greet the men then reassured them in my own language that their trespassing was not resented. I walked over to them and asked politely what they were doing.

"We've contracted with your government to survey this part of the Possum River valley. It's one of the missing quadrangles, you know."

"No, I don't know. What are quadrangles, and why are they missing?"

"Well, you see, this area was all mapped out quite precisely by the Ancients. During the Calamities, our ancestors collected thousands of maps in the Archives, but many of them were lost or destroyed. Our job is to resurvey those areas as accurately as we can. Of course, we don't have all the technical resources the Ancients had, but we can do far better than the crude charts used by the Olotal's officials."

"Where is this Archive you mention?"

"In the Sanctuary Mountains, back home, there are these caves—tunnels, actually—where the early Stewards hid out. Later, they used the caves to store books that they retrieved from the ruins of their enemies. I'm surprised you don't know about them since you've apparently been there."

"Been where? Esperia? Heck no, I've never set foot out of Umberlands."

"How curious. You greeted us in very proper form—I thought I even detected a trace of Laughingwater accent."

"That's about all the words I know in your language, but I've heard them often enough. You see, I was raised by Stewards in an orphanage way east of here."

The fellow gave a start and said, "Ohhh . . . Why then, you must be Yaro."

It was my turn to do a double take. "Yes, but how . . . ?"

"We were at the Cleftridge facility ourselves, just two weeks ago. They gave us a letter for you. We left it at the village store since we didn't expect to meet you."

I wanted very much to chat with the surveyors, but the second man interrupted. "I think that fellow is calling to you."

Looking back at the barn I saw Archer shouting and gesturing crossly for me to come. When I reached him, he sputtered.

"I said you could work awhile in your garden—that doesn't mean lollygagging with every stranger that comes traipsing by! Who were they anyway?"

"Esperians, making maps for the government."

"All the more reason to stay a-shed of them. Troublemakers, the lot. Those half niggers have messed up your head enough as it is already."

I didn't try to argue with him, but first chance I had to slip away, I called by the store for my letter. It was meant to be cheerful and newsy, but it filled me with sad longing. Two new children there. Veerio had suffered a heart attack and been sent back to Esperia. Bracken now head Keeper of the Orphanage. I was baffled by a cryptic note penciled on the inside of the envelope flap: "B.B.gone." Of course it referred to my old pal Boon Blotch, but how was he gone? If he had been snatched up by one of the press gangs, why couldn't they simply say so. There was no need for secrecy about being in the army. Something was clearly wrong about it all, and no one dared to tell me plainly. And what about his little brother, Kit, who was so completely dependent on Boon? There was no way to find out what had become of them.

We walked in silence for a while. Hewn could be brusque at times, but he was not insensitive, and he understood my painful thoughts. After a few minutes, he asked, "And what about yourself? How did you avoid becoming cannon fodder for the Olotal's latest 'final assault' on Grand Coquina?"

"Not by any resourcefulness of my own, certainly. Although Archer Seekings was technically a landowner, the best that would have gotten me would be a minor commission, not an exemption. I never knew why I always got passed over, until about a year ago, when it got around that Fawn and I were seeing each other. I heard that Lord Shackelford pointedly reminded the local CADS agent that I was eligible for the draught. He ordered me to report to his office, but when I showed up, he said to forget about it and go home. Evidently, Jasper Gates had objected that his plantation could not function well without my services (weekly weeding in his wife's flower garden?). Anyway, Agent Longwood hinted that Shackleford was dropping the matter, rather than risk an unseemly public squabble between landowners. But it certainly made me wonder why Jasper would stick his head out so far for such a nobody as me."

Chapter 18

For the next several days, an intense cold snap set in, freezing every freshwater surface into a hard black sheet which thickened with each passing night.

On the last morning of the Esperian week, I joined some of the others for a meeting at the bannerhouse. In most other societies, such a meeting could be called a" religious service"; however, the term seemed incongruous for a largely atheistic society. Stewards themselves have no problem with the label *religious*, but the word means something rather different for them. In fact, they use lots of words that seemed strangely out of place to me. It took me awhile to get used to hearing words like *holy, sacred, blessed*, etc., bandied about by these atheists with no less piety than any devout believer. On the other hand, I never heard anyone use the word *spiritual*, which is far as I know is untranslatable into Esperian.

I had attended a few temple services in Dryford, usually at Seekings' insistence, so I had some basis for comparison. In both cases, a group of people (called a congregation) gathered in a large building to sing hymns (yes, the Stewards call them that too) and to hear readings from the Holy Scriptures (the same Scriptures, for the most part). Someone called a preacher (in both societies, although Esperians usually refer to theirs as the Keeper of the Vision) delivers a moralistic scripture-based speech, which Anagaians call a sermon, whereas Stewards usually call it a commentary. Thus far, there are surprising parallels; but beyond that, the similarity ends. At the Steward meeting, there is nothing called prayer; actually, Esperian does have a word which derives from that, but it connotes something much more active than closing one's eyes and pretended to talk to someone.

This was a sizable gathering, considering it was not a high holiday, and the attention level seemed high for such a lengthy commentary. When it was over, many people lingered to discuss it at even greater length. I noticed that people asked many questions of Orris, the elderly Keeper of the Vision; there were even some arguments. Orris seemed to take no offense at them; he even solicited comments from those he knew to have dissenting opinions. At times it became quite animated, and I wished I could understand more of it. What I could understand was that this was part of the consensus-building process of which Hewn had spoken. Orris had propounded a position and was now eliciting the feedback, which he would relay to the Council. If any kind of conclusion were to come out of this, it would only be after many such two-way discussions as were happening today. But I was curious to know what the particular issue was.

"Window glass?"

"Well, basically yes. I mean, there was the usual statement of broad principles, but when it came down to specifics, that was the main topic. Wouldn't you say so, Myrica?"

We were just passing the tidal dam below the wrackplant. The current was passing unfettered through the open sluice where even the mill wheel was disengaged so that it too might observe the weekly holiday. Marten and his second cousin and I were ahead of the others.

"Yes," agreed Myrica. "But I didn't really get anything new out of it. The Keepers of the Vision are just trying to reaffirm what they've already established via the Blood Laws, the Vine Laws, the Nest Laws, and so on. Nearly everyone accepts their position, at least around here. It's just that they're trying to push for concensus before the technology is in place while some object that it should be the other way around. That's what most of the arguing during the greeting time was about."

"But none of that makes any sense to me," I complained. "Why didn't he just talk about religion?"

"He did," insisted Marten. "Religion and nothing else."

"How so?"

"Well, you see, the Scriptures have a lot to say about this problem. However, that's not the passage that ordinarily would be read today. Orris added it on because it's more relevant to what's happening in Council now. It will automatically come up again next summer. That's when the Slave Laws are *supposed* to be read, and of course, you can't just talk about jubilees and ear piercing without bringing up window glass—"

"Wait a minute, wait a minute,not a word you've said so far makes any sense to me. Are you saying the Scriptures have laws about slavery?"

"But of course. Don't the priests in Anagaia talk about them?"

"I don't think so. Our local priest always said most of that old stuff didn't apply anymore."

"Well, of course. None of it applies if you don't want it to."

"But look here, what's the point of bringing slavery into this? It is been illegal everywhere since before the Calamities."

"Not here, it isn't," remarked Marten quietly.

I stared at him aghast. "What?! You're joking. There are no slaves here."

"Of course there aren't. But the laws still exist."

"Meaningless laws, you mean."

"Not meaningless to us. If you study those ancient laws, you'll notice that they never did condone slavery, but rather put restraints on an evil of the day. If you carry those restraints to their logical conclusion, then slavery becomes untenable."

"So they do abolish slavery then."

"In effect, yes, but technically, not."

"Then why bother with the charade? Why not just say it's forbidden and be done with it?"

Myrica inserted, "I remember Grandma saying something about that once, in another context. How did she put it? 'If you close the book on it, you abandon a line of reasoning, which may be useful later.' Or something like that. She's right behind us, so you can ask for yourself, but that's the gist of it."

"You see, Yaro, we never discard anything. Whether it's a cracked iron pot or an antiquated law, we recycle it."

"But what use can that law possibly have?"

"The Slave Laws? Why plenty, in recent years. You see, every arrangement between employer and employee is some lesser degree of the master-slave relationship, so every principal can be applied to a less extreme situation. I suppose the opposite extreme is a mutually advantageous partnership of free will, and that's what the Slaves Laws point toward. But after all, the distinction between slavery and worker exploitation is often blurry, and nothing shows that better than the Anagaian Contract System. Now Anagaia, as you say, explicitly forbids the institution of slavery, yet where would you rather be an employee—there or here?"

"Hmmm" was the most I could say at first. There certainly was nothing to argue with there. "So get back to window glass. What's the connexion?"

"That's what Orris was trying to explain today. He was pointing out that the glass workers as well as the coal miners who supply their fuel are all abused, and we, by being a market for that glass, are also culpable for their ill-treatment. Okay now, Anagaians use a lot of coal to make glass, and of course, the colliery owners wouldn't dream of accepting responsibility for their workers' health. It's the Contract System again. No worker would sign those contracts if he had any choice. And that's close to a definition of slavery."

"Yes," I replied. "I know you're right about that. A fellow in our village came back with a crippled leg from a cave-in. He said there wasn't enough timber shoring up the tunnel, but he wasn't compensated for his loss. In fact, it happened in midweek and because his injury kept him from finishing the week, he had to forfeit that part of his pay which he'd already earned. Of course, he couldn't read and didn't know that was in the contract. And yet "—I reflected—" for all that, I myself was considering going up to work in those same mines. As you said, there wasn't too much choice. But look, if it was out of my control, how much can anyone up here do about it?"

"That's the question, isn't it? I'm sure I don't know either, but I expect we'll be hearing more about it soon. See who's coming."

Several rods behind us, Hewn and Ermine were joined by a middle-aged woman who had sat near us at the meeting. Her name was Candle, and as it turned out, she had been invited to take lunch with us at Stonesthrow. Marten mentioned that she lived at Rosearbor, a stead at the north end of the island, and that she was a member of the VFC.

I found myself seated across from her at the table, and upon being introduced, I promptly asked her what VFC stood for. Her Anagaian, though far better than my Esperian, left much to be desired, but Ermine helped to fill in our deficiencies.

"This stands for Vision Fulfillment Commission. You know Council of Keepers of the Vision, yes?" I said I had heard of it. "Well, you see, these people basically are scholars, philosophers, you know, maybe something like high priests in your country. They read Holy Laws, tell us what they think it should look like today, you see. But they cannot command, that is, they cannot force from their selves. Because they lead us, but their power comes from us, you see, so they must make—what is his word, Ermine?"

"I think you mean *consensus*."

"Ah, just so. They must help make consensus, which means before they can tell us, they must also listen. Anyway, when they have made consensus, they . . . what is the word? . . . *Propound*, yes, they propound the law, which of course is really their interpretation of the law. Of course they can propound laws at any time, but unless they first make consensus, they just look foolish because too many people ignore them, you understand?"

In fact, I understood little of what she said, not so much because of the language as because I did not yet understand how Esperian politics worked. But I felt I could get clarification of that later on from Hewn or Ermine. So I asked her exactly what it was this commission did.

"Ah yes, now we come to that, good. You see, once there is the idea of what the law is, we still have the question of . . . Ermine, what means? . . . Yes, *implementation*. How do you put this law or policy into action? Especially since the law usually ends up in the form of, not a simple command but a group of regulations. Also, after a time we must, how do you say, *monitor* the progress of this idea, to see if it is having the desired effect. You might say the Keepers of the Vision are the broad thinkers while our job is to look at the details."

"So for example, would you deal with something like window glass?"

"Aha, so you do see," she laughed. "Yes, yes, yes, now that is right in our way. Then you know something about that, although you are a new immigrant?"

"Not really, that's why I'm asking. What is it all about?"

"Well, I will try to explain. You know why we are concerned about glass from Tramont?"

"Not specifically, but I can well imagine why you might be concerned about any Anagaian product."

"Not just any—some products we wish to encourage, no matter what. But this glassmaking, it is one of the worst abusers of contract labour—you know, you call them bucs—and on top of that, they burn so much coal with no attention to the air and water in those communities."

"But I know you have selective boycotts on Anagaian cotton for similar reasons. Why don't you just boycott glass as well?"

"There it is, ah yes, that is exactly the point!" she exclaimed, clapping her hands. "It is our own fault, yes. For cotton, we have several things we can do. We have developed many—how do you say?—*alternative* fibres of our own: flax, hemp, bast, nettles, on and on. Also we have some other cotton suppliers, like Palmetto. And of course, we can simply cut back our use, if we are careful. In short, you see, we can manage all right without them."

"But glass?"

"With glass it's different. We depend on that glass. We are recycling, but it is not enough. Most of our own sand is not pure enough, okay for jars and such, but not windows. People are searching for better deposits, but so far, not enough is found. We can cut back on use, but that makes other problems. If stead windows aren't all double, we burn much more wood from our forests, and that's against other policies. If we stop building greenhouses, some areas become less self-reliant for food. All our solutions don't . . . how do you say? . . . add up to one. Here is a case where the Vine Laws should be supporting the Blood Laws and the Slave Laws, but as a society, we have not acted enough to fulfill our Vision, and now we have this problem."

"Hmmm," I mused. "I do remember on the ship coming north, we carried a lot of glass." Then I had a sudden thought. "But there was also a lot of cotton onboard. I didn't think anything about it at the time but how was that possible?"

"That would be certified cotton," explained Hewn from down the table. "There are a very few plantations in Hither Anagaia, which we have specially certified to grow cotton for us. We set the standards for how they treat their labourers and their soil. We pay them enough to make it worth their trouble while their neighbours struggle to market theirs at all. It is limited though, because it only works near our missions, where there is someone on the spot to monitor compliance."

"And a similar arrangement wouldn't work for glass?"

"We've tried, but the owners of the coal mines and glassworks have blocked us. It all boils down to our options, as Candle says. The cotton growers know we can get along without their cotton, so we have some leverage, but the glassmakers have us up against the wall, so they're not very cooperative. Their collieries continue to be deathtraps, and they refuse to use even the most basic pollution-control technology."

Everything they were saying rang true, I realized. I didn't know squat about the glass industry, but I did know that Anagaia was not a place where you could count on any goodwill from an employer toward his workers, or vice versa. Although I knew the present company were far better informed than I on such matters, I couldn't resist offering my own opinion:

"You're better off not to depend on anything Anagaian, regardless of who grows it or how it's made. You cannot trust anyone there, not the government, not the landowners, not even the peasants, and I am one of those. Keep looking for cleaner sand—that's your only solution."

What was getting into me? I wondered as the others stared thoughtfully in my direction. Only a few months before, I wouldn't have dreamed of blurting out such bullish opinions. Oh sure, Dr.Borestone and I used to have our chats, but we both knew they were no more than that. Here I was, presuming to advise policy makers, experts in their field. Although they listened politely, I felt suddenly embarrassed, not at anything I'd said, but at the unwonted forwardness of someone I barely recognized as myself. As soon as I could gracefully do so, I excused myself and went for a walk.

Chapter 19

The windmill stood idle behind me. The shaft was unpinned, and the turbines were locked open to dump the wind, which had to content itself with whistling shrilly through the louvres.

I had come to be alone, to sort out my thoughts. There had been so many thoughts in the past few days. They all seemed to go together, but it was hard to make the connexion. I was especially puzzled about myself. I actually pulled off my glove to stare at my hands in the bright light. Yes, the lines and whorls were in the same familiar pattern. The pale scar on my left thumb reminded me of the scorching day long ago when I had slipped with the grain sickle. Yes, it was still me, Yaro Seekings, the young peasant from Dryford. All that life had really been mine. The fact that I now found myself in this baffling northern land could not change all that. Yet it was me that was changed, not just the landscape and the people. Where was that reticent fellow who always kept his own counsel? And where had this outspoken immigrant come from? I had to wonder if even my steadmates recognized me as the shy refugee who had stepped off the *Minkey* only weeks before.

A fresher wind kicked up new whitecaps on Harking Bay as a pair of herring gulls wheeled overhead. It's not that I've changed at all, I reflected. It's more like I've always been waiting inside myself. The same self, but one who could only ripen—is that the word?—could only *ripen* under the right conditions. Even now it might be premature to burst forth until I understood my new habitat better. Yet I could feel myself expanding, stretching against the old skin. All my life I had been carried along by currents; what was different now was that I could do more than just tread water. I could actually swim in a direction of my own choosing, perhaps even—what conceit!—perhaps even have some slight influence on the current itself. My inner thoughts were like the bay breeze in my face, bracing yet ever shifting, and I sat for quite awhile, trying to sniff out the direction of the wind.

"Do you mind if I sit here too?" I was startled by the voice over my shoulder. A few moments earlier, I would have minded very much, busy as I was with making my own acquaintance. But for now anyway, I seem to have figured out all I could alone, and I was not averse to company. Least of all Myrica's, for it was she who now sought out the hard bench beside me.

"Not at all," I replied, sliding over to make more room. "It's the only warm spot up here. Were you looking for me?"

"Not really, although I knew you'd gone this way. I just felt like a walk myself. I always come up here for the view. We don't have anything like this at home."

She gestured off toward the southeast where Telling Island sprawled in the bay. It was the next largest of the Randoms, but it lay low and nearly level, with no towering headlands comparable to that upon which we sat.

"So where is your home? Can we see it from here?"

"Hmm . . . let's see, no, not quite. It's there, just inshore from that second cove. The trees hide it from here."

"It's not that building whose roof we can just see?"

"No, it's just beyond that. What you're seeing isn't a steadhouse. It's my factory."

"Your factory? You mean you own a factory?"

"No, no, I should say 'our factory'. All I meant is I'm the steward of it."

"Really!" I exclaimed, no less impressed. "It looks pretty big."

"Yes, but it's mostly materials storage and curing trays. Only six of us operate it, depending on the season."

"And what do you make there?"

"Gaskets, mostly, for canning jars. Do you see that grove of trees just beyond the building?"

"You mean, away from the shore?"

"Yes, those. They're yukomnya, or milk-sap trees."

"Ah yes, I've seen some down at our place. At Stonesthrow we use the latex to impregnate the canvas raincoats we sell. How do you make jar rings?"

"Well, we combine the latex with sunflower pith and tow fibre, then shape it under heat and pressure into rings. The jar rings are our main product, but sometimes we do special orders for other factories—for example, pump washers and shoe soles and bottle stoppers."

"Wow! And do you sell them all over the country?"

"Some, but mostly here within the fair. Other fairs have their own factories, in accordance with the Vine Laws. We do sell some of our surplus latex inland where the milk-sap trees aren't hardy enough. There's a strong demand for the products, and it pays very well."

"But that's something I don't understand. When I work in the stone yard, for example, I'm expected to turn all my pay over to Ermine. Of course that's only fair, since the stead is going to a lot of expense on my account. But in your case, you must be earning an income much greater than what you yourself are consuming."

"Why, I should hope so."

"Yet you don't get to keep any of it."

"What would be the point of that?"

"To spend on something you want."

"What would I want that I don't already have?"

"Surely there must be something you'd like that's not for the whole stead, but just yourself."

"Then I would ask for it."

"And what if they don't think you need it?"

"No one is likely to deny me anything reasonable. For one thing, they may want something for themselves someday and wouldn't want to be denied either."

"Okay, but don't some people abuse that and make unreasonable demands? I'm not talking about yourself now, I'm just curious about how things work here."

"Sure, some people abuse their fellows. I guess that's human nature."

"Then what keeps it from getting out of control? Because from what I've seen, it works perfectly well, and I wonder how."

"Well, it doesn't work perfectly well. Nothing does here, and I suppose it doesn't anywhere else either. Most people want to be known as supporters of their group, not as parasites. But of course, when someone demands more than they ought, or contributes less than they can, they dishonour themselves, that's all."

"That's all?! You mean you do all that extra work and bring in all that income, just to get honour?"

"I guess I'm the one who's confused. What else would I do it for? In your country, why do some people make a special effort?"

"Why, to get ahead, of course."

"Ahead of what?"

"Ahead of whom, you mean. Everyone else, that's whom."

"I guess that makes sense, sort of. But when you earn more than everyone else, what would you do with that?"

"Why, spend it on yourself, unless you are generous and choose to share it."

"What is that word, *generous*?"

"Yeah, you know, *generous*. I don't know the Esperian word for that yet."

"I'm not sure there is any."

"Oh sure, there has to be. It means 'not selfish.'"

"You mean, you think it is wrong to be selfish?"

"Who doesn't? I mean, people are often selfish,though no one says it's a good thing."

"Hmmm . . . I think there's some problem with these words of yours. I'll have to ask Grandmother to explain."

The conversation did indeed seem to be bogging down in linguistic quagmires, so I let it drop for the time. We sat quietly, watching a gull struggling to eviscerate a sea urchin he had just scavenged. Immediately, a dozen others swooped in to contest his prize. They becked and mewled raucously for several seconds, until a couple of them managed to snatch some loose bits and flew away with success in their beaks.

"I hope I didn't offend anyone by leaving so quickly."

"Not at all. I know they're eager to hear the opinions of someone with a different perspective. Candle says that sometimes policy makers lose sight of the very people on whose behalf they claim to be acting."

"Oh say, speaking of Candle, maybe you can explain something. When I was taking leave of her, she said something curious in Anagaian . . . now how did it go? . . . 'may you dwell in the Larger House.' Now what was that all about?"

"But you know. You say that yourself several times a day."

"How so?"

"When you greet anyone in Esperian or leave them or wish them good luck, for that matter, the idiomatic expression you have learned to use—well, if you take it apart, literally, it means 'may you dwell in the Larger House.' She was merely returning your courtesy, although I suppose it doesn't translate too well."

"But what does it mean?"

"Oh, I assumed you knew already, and I guess she did too. It's just something that every Steward takes for granted. I'll try to explain it, but I'm not sure . . . ah, I think it's coming to me now. Okay, you know that word you used a minute ago: what was it—*generous*? So let's say you go buy a new coat. Do you call that *generous*?"

"Of course not, if it's for yourself."

"Selfish, then?"

"Not really, not if you need a new coat."

"Then let's say you have a hundred gold sceptres to spare, and your community is building a library. If you give them that money, is that what you mean by *generous*?"

"Yes, I certainly call that generous."

"But you said buying the coat was not generous."

"Of course not; you're just supplying your own needs."

"But don't you think the library will supply your needs?"

"Well, I suppose so, if you use it enough."

"No, no, I mean even if you never enter the door. It will be a general benefit to the community, and you are part of the community. At least as we look at it, either one—the coat or the library—is a *selfish* expense, but the library is *selfish* at a higher level. I think that's the difference in our ideas. It seems that if you work toward something which is beyond your own immediate personal needs, you say that it is not *selfish*—it is *generous*. But to our thinking, no one does anything which doesn't fulfill themselves somehow, unless they are terribly perverse. It's only a question of whether the need is an immediate demand of the creature—and those needs must be fulfilled first!—or whether we have moved on to some higher level of self-fulfillment. That—the higher levels of self-fulfillment—is what we mean by the 'Larger House.'"

As I listened to Myrica talking, I couldn't help thinking how much I envied her. This country, this civilization that I had come to admire so much, was clearly the product of a vision in the minds and lives of its people. Now I was trying to make that vision my own, and it was difficult. But for Myrica, like everyone else here, it was as natural as wearing her own skin. She was born with it, and it took no conscious effort to fit into it. For me, on the other hand, it was like a garment which I had long admired, but now that I was allowed to put it on, I found I had little idea of where to stick my head or my hands.

Our conversation tapered off to small talk as we sat, soaking up the meagre warmth of our protected niche. The entire expanse of Harking Bay, from Runaground across to Covey's Sleeve, was empty of any sails, quite unlike any other day of the week. The wind-whipped waves crashed relentlessly against the unforgiving cliff-base below us, leaving a glisten of rime-ice on the granite face. Gulls continued to wheel about the windmill tower. We both watched them for a while without saying anything. Myrica was the first to pick up a new thread of conversation.

"What's it like there?"

"Where?"

"Anagaia, or rather Umberlands. I've heard a lot about Hither Anagaia, since Mama spent her teen years there when Grandma and Grandpa were at the embassy, but I've never met anyone from west of the Foxfires. Can you describe it for me? Like the land, how does it look?"

"Dry. More than anything else, dry. Too dry for trees to grow. You can only grow crops near the rivers, where you can irrigate. Elsewhere, it's mostly scrubby grazing land."

"Are you saying there are no forests there?"

"Nothing like around here. In the hills, there are brushy patches where folks gather sticks to sell for firewood, but never anything big enough to need splitting. I've heard folks say there used to be forests, though, but that was centuries ago. Now it's mostly mesquite and cottonwood, things that only used to grow much farther west."

"What's a city like? Mama has tried to describe it, but I can't picture it."

"I had never seen a city myself until my last few weeks there, when I was hiding out in New Chalice. My home was near a tiny village on the Possum River. I can't compare it with anything you know. Most of the people there have either too much or not enough—mostly not enough. People don't corporate much, even when they might all profit from pulling together. None of that 'Larger House' stuff. You used a library as an example—well, I've never heard of a public library in all of Umberlands. It's just not like here."

"So you lived in a village. That's sort of like a banner, isn't it?"

"Not much," I explained, remembering the time Wren had tried to explain it all to me. "Most of the folks are clustered in one little place, while the rest are scattered far apart. Not much community life happens in the villages. If you want to find a museum, for example, or a sports arena or a concert hall—or a decent job, for that matter—you have to go to the cities where everything is concentrated. Even though the cities are very crowded—more than you can ever imagine—the overall population density is much less than here because the countryside is so empty compared to here."

"And your stead? How many lived there?"

"No steads there. Only small houses with a single nuclear family in each one. There was just Archer, Melody, and me—Mrs. Seekings died a few years ago."

"Archer? That's your father?"

"Adopted father," I corrected hastily. "The only thing that seemed like a real family was Melody, my adopted sister. I don't know my birth father. The closest thing I have to a father figure is Faring, my mentor at the orphanage.

"I do have this, though," I carefully reached into my pocket for the little wallet I always kept with me. I guess I'd forgotten that Myrica had already seen my mother's note, and she was too tactful to remind me. I suppose it made me feel that I had roots like anybody else; a homeland, a heritage.

"And what's that, if I'm not being too nosy?" A piece of broken pottery lay in my palm where it had slid out with the note.

"It's a friendship token. See on this side—that's my name in Anagaian script. On that side, those scratches—that says *Boon Blotch*. He was my chum at the orphanage before I was taken away. We were close friends, although he wasn't always easy to get along with. I'm worried about him."

"Oh? What happened to him?"

"That's just it, I have no idea. He disappeared from the orphanage, probably with his younger brother. I never could find out what became of them, but I'm sure they're in trouble, if they're even alive."

Myrica's eyes widened as I mentioned this, and I realized I was telling her about life as she did not know it.

"Excuse me, I didn't mean to shock you."

"No, no, I wanted to hear about it. We hear awful reports from down there, but it always seems so distant. Never anyone I know. So what happened to you, after you left your adopted home? I heard something about your being blamed for something you didn't do."

And so I told her everything she wanted to hear, and a good bit more, no doubt. I told her about my wealthy friend, Jasper Gates, and how we had quarreled when he refused to let me marry his daughter. About how I had arrived at the irrigation well to find his body lying at the bottom with a crushed skull. About my trial and banishment, about languishing on the hot plains without food or water. About finding my mother, only in time to bury her. About sneaking through the mountains with the Old Cougar and his drug-running kinsmen, and watching Fester Gilding ambushed for his opium. About hiding out in a cemetery in New Chalice, and finally fleeing the country aboard the *Minkey*. It was painful to recall it all, and Myrica sensed that.

"I never imagined . . . I, I never meant to put you through all that."

"I wanted to tell it," I reassured her. "Ever since the hearing, everyone at Stonesthrow seems to consider it a closed case, but I still want to tell everybody that I didn't kill Jasper Gates. He was my friend, and I don't know why he rejected me, but I didn't kill him."

I was shuddering from more than the cold. Myrica put her hand on mine consolingly. I appreciated the gesture, though it made it harder to hold back tears.

We talked awhile about other matters. About Lord Amberson and his newly refurbished yacht. About the creaking sounds in the frame behind us that held the solar reflectors. About the cold in general.

"Hey, have you seen the #6 Guillamot Quarry since last week? The pool is frozen at least three inches deep and crystal clear. There hasn't been any snow to speak of yet, and it's smooth and bare. Some of us are having a skating party there tonight—you should come along!"

The way she phrased that made it easy for me to accept. It wasn't like I was to be her escort. Ever since leaving Dryford, something in my situation made me feel nervous in female company, even while I yearned for it. Still, an outing to a quarry seemed to present no complications.

The only problem was that I had not the slightest understanding of the Esperian verb "to skate"; we hadn't covered that yet. No one had ever informed me that these generally reasonable people would strap blades onto the soles of their boots and go careening at breakneck speeds across frozen ponds. But I had a lot to learn, so I went home and borrowed a pair of skates for the occasion.

Chapter 20

The #6 Guillamot Quarry had been worked out for many years and was now flooded with surface water. In its chill granite basin, the pond froze early to a safe thickness. On three sides, the high quarry walls reached up to block the wind while the fourth side opened northward to give us a striking panorama of Galeslee Strait and the Beacon Hills. Seen through the subzero atmosphere, the stars really did seem to sparkle, and oh how many stars there were! The entire Milky Way seemed to pulse like a living flashing stream. I had never seen such a celestial display; the dusty skies of my native Umberlands were more conducive to grand sunsets.

On the granite-rimmed shore of the rink, a small bonfire was kindled after sundown for the warming of hands and toes. For a few minutes, I watched as dozens of figures in quilted clothes glided and swooped across the pond's congealed surface. They seem to do it so effortlessly, and Myrica was among the best. I strapped on my borrowed pair and ventured timidly onto the hard ice. I hadn't told Ermine about this—my knee was pretty well healed up by now, but I knew she would fret about it. In no time at all, I could see why. My feet flew into the air and I hit the ground—or rather ice—more suddenly than I would've thought possible. It might have smarted worse if Myrica hadn't had the forethought to tie a padded belt around my backside. She and others helped me to my feet, and I tried again and again. Still, my derrière continued to make regular acquaintance with the uncompromising ice. After one fall, I muttered aloud, "Just like everything else here, it's so easy for the rest of them. I'll never get the hang of it!" But others gave me tips, showing me how to lean just a bit ahead of my skates, but not too far, and how to push back with one foot at an angle and not locking my knees. Indeed, I did catch on, and before very long I was scooting around by myself, often off-balance, but standing more than falling. I did not have the flowing grace that most of the others had—nor have I ever gotten that—but I could at least stay upright, sculling along with some degree of confidence, as Myrica applauded my progress.

People found all kinds of ways to get around on the glassy rink. Some glided forwards, other backwards while a few spun around in tight circles. Several people formed a chain, holding hands and whipping around until the end one would let go and fly off like a cannonball. Couples promenaded around the rink arm in arm, starlight flashing off their skate blades. I kept to the edges of the group, not antisocial but unsure of my ability.

At one point, Myrica glided up behind me, taking my mittened hand in hers. It was only a friendly effort to draw me in with the others, but before thinking, I yanked my hand back so hastily as to convey something I did not mean. She graciously withdrew her hand and glided on, seeming to take no offense, but I knew she had interpreted my gesture in the obvious way—the wrong way. I saw her skate over to the edge and step ashore next to the bonfire. She was the only one there at the moment and seemed to be merely warming her fingers by the blaze, but I knew better. I also knew I must act immediately to rectify my rude behavior. I skated over to the edge of the shelf where she stood and reached over to take her hand.

"My mind was on something else," I apologize weakly.

She smiled lightly as if to dismiss the notion that she might have been hurt, and taking my hand again, she stepped back onto the ice. I could tell she was a little confused at my apparent vacillation, but what could I tell her? How could she understand that the turmoil within me had nothing to do with her?

I liked Myrica; I liked her very much. However, I was uneasy about showing too much affection, lest she misunderstand my intentions. That would be easy to do, after all. From the viewpoint of those around me, I was unattached, available. Even those who knew that I had a fiancée back in Umberlands—and I made no secret of it—could not be expected to take that too seriously. They all knew as well as I did that I could never go back to Fawn again, nor could she come to me. Like it or not, it was over, but knowing that and accepting it were two different things.

This was, after all, not the first time I had been suddenly uprooted. As a child, I had been torn away from my orphanage home. Now, as then, I had arrived at my new home with few possessions, but an awful lot of baggage.

*   *   *   *   *   *   *

One morning, I woke to find what I had most dreaded ever since coming here. I sat up in bed, hearing the sound of a silence so deep in seemed to engulf the whole stead. I crept over to the window and pulled back the heavy window quilts. It was probably after dawn, but you could see nothing of the horizon. Only the near edge of the yard and the windowsill at my chin revealed what was happening. A thick white blanket covered the ground, and flakes were piling into every little ledge of the window sash. In the road out front, I could barely hear some people tramping by, their footfalls all but annihilated by the swirling gauze curtains of snow.

You may well be amused at my apprehension, but where I came from, this simply did not happen. Oh, we saw snow, to be sure, though not every winter. And when we did, it was never more than a couple inches, which disappeared in a few days. But we heard awful stories about the horrific snows of Esperia and Concordia where the accumulation was measured in feet. We could not imagine how anyone could survive in such conditions, yet here I was, seeing it for myself. Burnet and Marten were stirring too, and they seemed to view it with little concern, even pleasure.

Marten murmured drowsily, "The rolling team has just passed without stopping. They must still be fresh. Maybe we'll have time for a bit of breakfast before they need a relay. It will be a while before they come back across on the other lane.

We shuffled downstairs to the dining hall where the others were already drifting in. Dawn and Freeheart were on breakfast duty that week, so they had been up for an hour or more already, stoking up the fires and preparing food. I had not yet adjusted to the Esperian idea of breakfast: thick corn-and-chestnut porridge with dried blueberries, oatcakes slathered with oliveberry sauce, and dry-fried potatoes with sauerkraut. Nevertheless, lean as I was from my recent deprivations, I do believe I did justice to it.

"Say, Yaro," mumbled Marten between mouthfuls. "Are you going to join us on the roller this morning?"

"Sure," I replied gamely. I hadn't the slightest idea what he was talking about, but I wanted to be included in whatever was happening.

"I wonder," interrupted Ermine. "You're much improved, I admit, but are you sure your knee is up to it?"

I was going to tell her about my recent skating adventure, but before I could respond, Marten interjected that I could be a fifth puller—an extra. If I tired out, I could just drop off or be replaced at the next stead. She agreed, and we both bolted down the rest of our food and snatched our coats and boots, to be ready when the crew passed again. Sure enough, we soon heard a faint jingling of bells out in the front yard and several voices yelled out "Relay!" We raced out to join them, four people standing huddled against the blustery weather. Behind them lay a strange piece of equipment, essentially a huge wooden drum about six feet long and perhaps three feet in diameter. It was fairly light, but it had a rack on top to hold additional weights when needed. Along the lower back side of the cylinder, a sharp-edged wooden board was set close to the drum surface so that any snow which tried to stick to the roller would be knocked off before it could build up. From each end of the axle, a shaft came forward to join in front, forming a single long shaft by which it was drawn.

Only in the island's dooryards was the snow actually shovelled away. Elsewhere it was simply beaten down by these large rollers to stay packed until spring. The standard crew was four, but when more hands were available, they simply grabbed a short tow rope at the fore-end of the drawbar. I took that position to begin with. One of the previous crew yielded his place to Marten and headed home to a warm breakfast.

The snow was only three or four inches deep, and it packed down easily with the first pass. Sometimes there were spots where it drifted and gave more resistance. It became obvious why we were doing this now instead of waiting for the storm to end, which it gave no sign of doing. It was much easier to roll the same roads twice or more than to try to get through it once it became deeper. Every so often, when someone had taken their turn or was tired, we would pause in front of the next stead and yell "Relay!" Usually, we were more or less expected, and someone would come out to relieve one of us. If not, we would try again at the next stead. Thus the team was constantly rotating.

When we passed Rosearbor, Marten was ready to quit, but I stayed on. Not that I wasn't tired too, but I felt exhilarated by the cold and the company. Even if I couldn't speak their language well, the feeling of belonging to a team was gratifying. I didn't know any of them, and our swathed faces made it hard to recognize each other anyway. On and on we tramped, stopping a couple times for relays, until I was the only one left of the original crew. At Straitside we were joined by Citrine, a close friend of Burnet's. I was a little surprised to see a woman on the crew, although she was certainly rugged enough for the job. Only then did it occur to me to glance around at the other team members. Above the wrapped scarves I detected three pairs of decidedly feminine eyes. As Citrine thrust an arm into the harness, I smiled at myself for being the only one who saw anything noteworthy in the situation.

When we crossed the intersection of the Towers Road, I saw Burnet standing there. He asked if he might relieve me as the household were growing concerned for my well-being. Although I assured him I was fine, I gratefully surrendered my position to him and watched them pad off into the snow with the soft creaking of the roller at their heels. Elsewhere on the island, other teams were doing the same, so that by the time the storm ended, most of the roads would already be passable. The hardpacked snow would support anyone on foot or skis and made going easier for the pungs and pedisleds, which were the usual means of winter transport.

When I arrived back at the steadhouse, winded and calfsore, I was pleased to find that my rolling time was noted on a "service board," which would be credited toward Stonesthrow's taxes. By now, I realize that since our basic tithe was already accounted for, whatever labour we did on the roads was technically a "freewill offering." That meant I hadn't really saved us anything, but rather had garnered a bit more "honour" or "prestige" for myself and the household. Although I hadn't quite gotten used to the idea, it did please me to know that everyone else valued my contribution, however that value was expressed.

Chapter 21

One morning late in the week, I stood at the door of an office in the Alga bannerhouse. I'd come there thrice already that week without luck. It was the Keeper of the Vision I sought, and he was obviously a very busy fellow. He often dropped by Stonesthrow to discuss some issue with this one or that, sometimes even with me, but now that I was looking for him, he was never about. I suppose it hadn't occurred to me that he might spend as much time at *all* the steads on the island, sharing opinions with all of them too. His assistant was usually there, and I'm sure I could have talked to her instead, but she seemed like more of a "doing" sort, and right now I preferred a "wise old philosopher" type.

"You're in luck, this time, Yaro," she greeted me. "His leg is bothering him, so I'm going rounds today. Go right in."

The Keeper of the Vision was hunkered over a small heater stove, behind a desk full of books and papers heaped in some order only he could discern. He was severely crippled on one side; they say he served a missionary stint in Anagaia and contracted polio there. He was now in his late sixties with a thick mane of steel gray hair and a beard gone nearly white. Despite his atheism, he was probably the closest counterpart one could find here to the village priest of Dryford.

"Sit down, my friend, make yourself comfortable, as I'm trying to. I feel this chill awfully, you know." He drew a second shawl over his shoulders.

"I need to talk with you. It might take a while—do you have the time?"

"In about twenty minutes, I have to attend a planning session in the auditorium. Until then, I'm at your disposal. Spill it."

"The Vision," I blurted out. "What is it?"

"Oh, great wonders! That's no quick little chat now, is it?"

"I realize you can't tell me all about it, but I just want to understand what it is. Hewn urges me to just wait and put the pieces together as I see them, but I'm frustrated trying to figure it out by myself. If I see the 'big picture,' surely I'll be better able to see how the pieces fit."

"Yes, yes, of course. I expect Hewn feels you won't be able to recognize the 'big picture' because it's so . . . well, so taken for granted. He's probably right too, you know.

There's no need to bother yourself over abstractions. Still, what kind of a vision-keeper would I be to discourage anyone from searching in their own way? Since you insist, let's have a go at it."

Then instead of talking, he simply huddled back in his chair and stared pensively at the stove for several moments as if he might absorb some of its warmth through his eyes.

"First, you need to know that people often mean different things when they speak of 'the Vision.' For example, the details of our country and society: the way it looks, the way it works. But I think what you're after is bigger than that. It's what we call the 'mythic vision.'"

"Yes, yes, you're right. That is what I'm after."

"Well now, to understand the Steward Vision, you must understand the opposing vision."

"You mean, the Anagaian vision?"

"For example. Do you know what that vision is?"

"Not really. I wouldn't even know there was such a thing, except there was a man in our village, Dr. Borestone, who tried to explain something to me that he barely understood himself. He had lived in Esperia, you see. He did talk about something called a mythic vision and said both Esperia and Anagaia had one, but they were conflicting visions—he wasn't sure just how."

"There you have it. You see, Yaro, this mythic vision stuff is all about how man views his world and his own place in it."

"But that's awfully general, isn't it? How *do* we view it, and how do we differ about that?"

"Well, let me just tell you a bit about how I view it, and we'll go from there. It may not sound like much, but here goes: to begin with, I see the world as a very large place. Life—all life—is merely a tiny dimension of it, a messy bit of scum on the surface of a huge and otherwise tidy rock. Mankind is merely a minuscule feature of that great web we call life. Indeed there's no particular reason to assume that man is at the centre of that web any more than any other life form, or indeed that there *is* any centre. Okay, so far?"

"I guess so. I mean, what is there to dispute?"

"Quite. Now we call this all a creation, and this creation is a great experiment, and all humanity is just one of countless experiments. By the way, the outcome of all these experiments is by no means a foregone conclusion. Creation itself is not a done deal, but an ongoing adventure which, for all we know, may never have had a beginning, and may never end.

"Furthermore, this world I see is basically a nice place, despite what we see as flaws. Nature is on man's side, insofar as he is on nature's side. Even the fact that it requires a constant struggle to survive is not an evil because that struggle makes man a better creature, and the world a better place. I could go into more detail, but what do you think of it so far?"

"It all sounds reasonable enough. Like you say, we take it pretty much for granted. Where's the controversy?"

"Well, now let me describe another vision, and you look at it through the lens of your Anagaian experience: man is the centrepiece of creation, the pinnacle of life's linear development. The earth was created as a home for man, everything is there for his enjoyment. Nevertheless, the world is basically not nice, it is a threat to man. There are weeds and thorns, diseases and predators. Nature is wild and chaotic. Mankind must bring order to it, he must subdue it. If he fails, if the wall of civilization is once breached, the forces of nature will overwhelm him. It is man against everything else. The problem is: by his very triumph, man must destroy the very base on which he stands, so ultimately he must lose this struggle. Fortunately, none of this really matters since there will always be another more perfect world awaiting man, another continent, another planet, another paradise where with no effort on our part, a static perfection will prevail, a world where nothing will evolve or need to."

He looked at me expectantly.

"It's exactly opposite the first vision," I acknowledged. "Yet I have to admit much of it sounds just as reasonable. I suppose all of it would, if I had been raised in the Anagaian religion."

"A good point: aspects of our vision occasionally pop up in Anagaian life and vice versa. Here's a tiny example: as you know, there are holy shrines scattered throughout Anagaia. These often consist of little groves of trees which are associated with some miracle or other. Probably the greatest miracle is that these groves are allowed to exist at all, in a land where trees rarely reach six inches in diameter before feeling the fuel-sellers' axe. This holding of forests sacred is a very old thing indeed. And it stands in defiance of the whole modern notion that forests are dark and dangerous places, better cleared and civilized."

"Okay, I think I see. So here are two ways of looking at the world, very different and yet both kind of fit the facts. But so what? I mean, can you clarify how this affects whether people cut trees or leave them? I mean, aren't they basically just stories?"

"They are indeed 'just stories,' but consider this: bound up in every story is a blueprint, a plan, a map—or shall we say, a vision? A story may seem to simply tell how things are, but it also implies who *we* are, what we've done, and where we think we're headed. To use your example, if a people's mythic vision places themselves at the centre and apex of creation, then they will see trees as existing only for their own use, and they will cut them down to the very last tree if it suits them. And furthermore, they will make a virtue of it: it's the will of God or manifest destiny or something."

"So do I understand you right? We are acting out our story, but if we have the wrong story, we'll act badly?"

"Well put! So what do you need me for? You've figured it out yourself."

"But only so far. I learned that much from my friend Dr. Borestone, but that's about as far as he could take me. Clearly there's more to it. For example, how did that story—that vision—come about in the first place?"

"In just the opposite way, I suppose: people were acting a certain way, and the story, or stories, they told began to reflect that reality. Sort of like the oak and the acorn, isn't it?"

"Actually, that's the very analogy Hewn used."

"You see, Yaro, these are the very questions we vision-keepers are always addressing. It's not hypothetical—the implications are quite real. Many of us believe that those two visions we discussed are not really distinct and exclusive. You yourself just said they both make sense when you look at them from the right vantage. Therefore, we Stewards must be diligent that harmful elements of Anagaia's mythic vision do not subtly permeate our culture. It could be disastrous."

"Then you admit that it is possible—for one mythic vision to replace another, by conversion or subversion or whatever."

"Well, I assume so, though I can't imagine just how it would happen. You see, mythic visions tend to be very conservative and self-propagating. Still, we do see these minor crossovers all the time, and we do know of at least two instances when the mythic vision changed radically."

"How? When?"

"Well, you see, I'm treating all these visions as if they are only two because although societies differ vastly in their religions and lifeways, Anagaia, Palmetto, Borealia, the Coquinas, and most of the others all share the underlying assumption of unsustainability. Likewise, all the Steward nations share a vision of sustainability, in common with the ancient hunter-gatherers, despite our enormous differences. With the exception of Stewards, probably not one individual in one million is aware of that common tradition—it is too deeply assumed to need discussion.

"There is reason to believe that the sustainable mythic vision was once the vision of all human societies, perhaps for millions of years. But several thousand years ago—yesterday really—a new mythic vision arose based on unsustainability, and it grew to encompass most, but not quite all, of humanity."

"How did it grow?" I asked eagerly.

"Again, I don't know, but I suppose by the very fact that such societies are unsustainable. They cannot accept limits or boundaries for themselves, so as their resources are exhausted, they must conquer their neighbours or perish. Over time, as their technologies allowed, these folks subdued or annihilated all the others, so eventually their vision—the story of unsustainability—became everybody's vision, or very nearly everybody."

"The only exception being the Stewards?"

"Not the only exception: there are believed to be pockets of what we call Old Story people left in the tropical rain forests beyond the Coquina Sea, still living much as they have for countless millennia."

"Oh, that's right." I remembered, thinking of stories Hewn had told me of primitive peoples, living in the jungles as they have for ages. "But Hewn said the Stewards aren't descended from them."

"That's correct. What we Stewards call the Vision began mere centuries ago, during the Calamitous Times. After all, our ancestors came out of the same pre-Calamities civilization as did Anagaia and the others, but they chose to go a different route, to retell the sustainable story, to live the sustainable vision.

"Of course, our lifestyle, our material culture, is nothing like that of those tropical forest dwellers I mentioned—nor do we need to be like them. After all, their societies weren't utopias either. They could be pretty nasty, and most important, they were defenseless against the New Story peoples. If we wish to protect ourselves and our land from New Story invaders, we must have a different population using different technology, and so forth. At the same time, if we want to protect the land from ourselves, we must also retain the essential parts of the Old Story, and that's what we try to do.

"That is our particular Vision, Yaro. There is nothing ultimate about it—it is merely one way, the way we've worked out so far of living sustainably on earth because, you see, insofar as our society is sustainable, we can keep on making mistakes—as we surely do—and trying again and again to get it right. That's the nature of evolution, that's the nature of *life*. Unsustainable societies don't have that leeway—regardless of whatever else they may do right, they are doomed."

At this point, there was a light rap at the door.

"And now, I must tend to other matters. We can talk more about this later, but keep this in mind: we act out a vision, yet that Vision is merely a manifestation of our lives. Does the oak make the acorn, or does the acorn make the oak? Perhaps it makes no difference, unless you're trying to find some point at which to influence the process, then it may be all-important."

As I returned home, I thought about all he'd said, and of all the new questions his answers had begot: how did the first Old Story people turned into New Story people? How and why had the early Stewards gone about consciously changing their own mythic vision? Was it possible to convert another society to your own mythic vision, especially if they were already antagonistic to you? However elusive the answers might be, it felt encouraging to think that I was at least beginning to frame my questions more clearly.

Chapter 22

1/2/48: This is my diary, which Hewn says I must keep. I am learning to write Mok script, and I now know a lot of Mok words, so he says I should practice. He says it will help me in other ways too. Each day he will correct my grammar and spelling. The script is very difficult, but the grammar and pronunciation are very regular and logical. I must often use a dictionary. Anyway, this is it.

Yesterday was my birthday. At least I have always treated it as my birthday, though I don't know exactly. No one here makes much of birthdays. I think it is considered poor taste. However, for *my* birthday, the whole island celebrated. The whole country celebrated. That is because my birthday is also Esperian New Year's, the shortest day of the year! The whole house was decorated with evergreen boughs, straw snowflakes, and other ornaments. On New Year's Eve, all the lamps were blown out, leaving only a little candle burning on the main table. In the near dark, Ermine recited an ancient legend, after which little Thistle began singing, all alone. The words were from Ermine's story turned into a round. At first, her lone voice sounded almost lost in the big house, but slowly others joined in until it was like a whole chorus, going on and on. Meanwhile, someone used the candle to light several others, and so on until every lamp and candle in the house was lit. Esperians are usually very careful not to waste lamp fuel, but not last night. The whole house was incredibly bright and full of loud sweet music. We stayed up all night and kept the lights burning. Some candles had to be replaced. Down at the bannerhouse, someone kept ringing the bell. Even up at our house, it kept people awake, if they weren't already. In the morning we ate "moose ears": pastries stuffed with sauerkraut, garlic, and other things. They were very spicy. We also had all kinds of cakes and sweet biscuits. My favourite are called snowflakes. They are thin sweet oat wafers stamped with snowflake patterns. We toasted the New Year with currant juice, very clear and tangy. After dinner on New Year's Day, there was a big meeting of the household, at which everyone was present. Even Tilia and Fulmar came home for the day. The meeting was very important, but I still haven't figured it out. It's all very complicated.

As I reread that entry today, my reaction is still that it's "all very complicated." However, I have come to understand the process enough to describe it more clearly. New Year's Day is also called Reckoning Day. What that means is that every stead holds its annual business meeting. (That is why Tilia and Briar were both there: since all business is consensual, everyone's presence is required). Of course, every stead holds weekly household meetings, where day-to-day issues are worked out, so the annual "reckoning" tends to be more of a general stock-taking. I was invited to attend, even though as a sojourner I had no decision-making rights.

Despite the considerable progress I had made in the Mok language, it was hard for me to follow the details. It consisted largely of individuals reporting on the income from their various activities and suggestions for how the budget should be adjusted. I was intrigued to discover that the word *spend* has a quite different meaning here. Although part of the Mok lexicon, it has the clear connotation of *exhaustion*, or being completely used up, even wasted. In most of the instances where Anagaians use the word *spend*, an Esperian says *invest*. Even when talking of buying a toothbrush, for example, the Esperian *invests* in one, with the clear implication that some return is expected. Most curiously, it seemed to me, the Esperian word *investment* is also used for what Anagaians would call *charities*.

There was a little discussion about a small sum for the purchase of supplemental firewood. I sensed some embarrassment at the need to discuss the matter at all since it was a blatant violation of the Vine Laws, but Ermine reminded us that it was an improvement on the previous year. The red maple planting on Inner Cabbage Island had yielded its first crop of thinnings, which amounted to a half cord of pole wood. Hewn remarked that whereas we might be self-sufficient for firewood in a few years, we have much further to go with grain. That made me feel a little awkward since the food shortfall was aggravated by my presence there, whereas I had no impact on the fuel consumption.

Alaria was pleased to announce that the new line of push brooms we were making had sold very well in the past year, and prospects for '49 were even brighter since we had begun to export them to Borealia.

One particular discussion aroused my interest, only because it gave me some insight into how economic decisions were made. Freeheart proposed that the stead should purchase a new bicycle. We already had three, but he pointed out that several stead members had frequent business in other banners. A fourth bicycle would save valuable travel time, since one of the present ones was often needed by Hewn to get to his meetings. There didn't seem to be any disagreement on that, but there were two concerns. One was *image*: would other steads get the impression that Stonesthrow was living it up while the mainland was subsidizing long-range development on Alga?

Freeheart's mother argued that anyone would admit that a bicycle was a tool, not a luxury. Although everyone agreed, I was intrigued to see how seriously people treated the question. Everyone was very concerned about Stonesthrow's "honour."

The other concern was the cost. An Esperian bicycle, even a basic single-speed model, is a finely crafted machine and a major investment for a household of only fifteen workers. It wasn't so much a question of affording it—Stonesthrow was rich, after all. But most of that wealth was committed in one way or another, so a purchase like that meant budgeting less for something else. Someone suggested reducing our pledge to the Alternatives R&D projects, and Hewn nearly went through the roof.

"We mustn't do that! Those projects need every bit of funding they get right now, especially the Fibres Division. You have no idea how urgent their work is. We've already committed ourselves to the boycott, but it will boomerang on us if we don't provide ourselves with more options. If it comes down to that, I'll walk wherever I have to go."

Put in that perspective, the suggestion was instantly dropped. Someone else suggested that since we hadn't requested any reimbursement from the Refuge Fund for my expenses, we might apply for that, which would offset much of the bicycle's cost. But Ermine argued that it really wouldn't be fair, since my work nearly balanced my expenses. I doubted that, but no one made any objection.

Finally, Marten suggested, "Why don't we purchase half a bicycle? Highshore is in exactly the same situation. Perhaps the two steads could co-own a bicycle since we are so close. I should think we could make up that amount from the increase income from the brush-shop."

"Well, we mustn't go spending money we *expect* to make," cautioned Ermine. "I suggest that we wait until Banner Day and see how finances are going then. In the meantime, we can sound out Highshore on the idea. What do you all think?"

There was a unanimous approval, or at least no objection, so the meeting moved on to other issues. A lot of routine matters were brought up and decided upon. Ermine reminded us that Alga's small subsidy of the Sundew Canal project would end that year as the work neared completion. The banner would need to decide how to reinvest the freed funds, and did we have any suggestions she could take to the Banner-Reckoning? Teal made a recommendation, which the others heartily seconded. It didn't make much sense to me, and I thought I must've misunderstood. Later I asked Ermine about it.

"A technical school in Tramont? But how can you call that an investment? It's not even in the country!"

"No, of course not. One also has foreign investments."

"But it's a charity, not an investment. I mean, when you spend money on a bicycle, you have a bicycle."

"Quite true. And when we invest money in a school, we have much more than a school."

"Perhaps if you're talking about philanthropy, but I thought you were looking for business investments."

"Business indeed. May I remind you, Yaro, that we don't even have a word for philanthropy in our language. Philanthropy, charity, altruism—the reason you're having to resort to Anagaian words is because those are Anagaian ideas. We don't have any truck with them here. And besides, we don't throw our money down rat holes—we expect a good return from it."

"But what do you get in return for a school in a foreign country?"

"Many things. A better trade partner, for one. Backward, ignorant people do not produce valuable goods, nor can they afford to buy ours. Moreover, miserable peasants are not safe to have as neighbours. They will rise up one day and take control over their own lives, and when that happens, let them remember us as friends who helped them to better their lives. Helping them is neither idealistic nor cynical—it's just good business. Admittedly, it's a very long-term investment, but when you dwell in the Larger House, you can afford that."

The remainder of the first week was very hectic as it is every year. That is the time when many organizations—and there are scads of them—hold their annual meetings. They choose leaders, set budgets, and plan programmes for the newly arrived year. A disproportionate number of those gatherings are held at Alga, due in part to the concerted efforts of community leaders like Hewn to entice them. Promoting the sterile but scenic island as one of the nation's main conference centres is a clever strategy for attracting wealth to a place where wealth does not naturally sprout from the ground. In particular, several of those steads closest to the landing derive a fair chunk of their income from housing and catering to the many attenders. Despite the best efforts of everyone, it is a chaotic business. On any given day of that week (and spilling over into the next), the island's population is more than doubled. Extra boats are pressed into service, shuttling visitors across Galeslee Strait. Steads set up extra cots in every available corner to accommodate the visitors. As varied as they are, all these groups are perceived as serving one common purpose, as Hewn explained to me late one evening.

"They all fulfill the Cutoff Laws."

"The Cutoff Laws? Now I've never heard of that one before. What's it all about?"

Hewn had just returned from an all-day session of the Random Islands Resource Development Commission and clearly wasn't in a mood to elaborate just then. Instead, he simply wagged his hand and yawned.

"At breakfast, perhaps."

Next morning over chestnut cakes and caragana sausage, I held him to his word.

"Like most of our laws," he began, "it starts off with a basic statement, and we proceed to wring everything we can out of it. 'Don't cut yourself off from the people'—it sounds simple enough, doesn't it? Yet it is rendered meaningless if the people cut *you* off, even if it's only by neglecting the kinds of connexions that should unite us.

"Consider this: ours is a culture which tends to favour collectivism over individualism. Now throughout human history, the only examples I know which combine communalism with a consensual government are tribal societies: hunter-gatherers. In some ways, they

130

are our model for our own society, yet unlike them, we are a technologically complex society with over six million members. We cannot all simply sit around a campfire and hash out our collective business. It is not enough to decide to have consensus, we must forge consensus. Now forging implies a lot of heat and a lot of sparks, yet it results in a unified strength of composition, which you don't get by simply pouring molten material into preshaped molds."

"So what has that to do with the Society for Invertebrate Studies, just for example, or the Paragon Pipers Band?" I asked, still puzzled.

"I'm getting there. Would you please pass me the maple syrup? Thank you. Now, it's hard enough to achieve unity in any culture, but it's even harder if you have elements of your society isolated by geography, educational barriers, economic disparity, and so forth. Under the best conditions, painful disagreements will arise, but we can do some things to keep everyone in the 'tribe' and working harmoniously. We can promote dialogue. How? At the very least, we can keep the roads passable, the ferries running, the towers signaling, the books and newspapers printing. And yes, we can keep the groups meeting, in whatever form and for whatever purpose they choose. Whenever someone from Portage Fair gets talking with someone from Goosegrass or Bluemeadow, they are putting another stitch in the fabric of our civic culture. It is not dissidence that weakens a society so much as stifled dissidence. The radicals who yell out their opinions at the fairgrounds are not to be feared. It is the folks who sulk off in their remote and impoverished corners, muttering against the group in the centre from whom they feel estranged. We must go to any lengths to prevent that situation from developing."

"So what does the government due to encourage such groups?"

"I never said it does anything. In fact, it doesn't have to. After all, most of those organizations are spontaneous creations of the people in their steads, and they are sustained by their own enthusiasm. I'm just saying that these groups are seen as a critical feature in fulfilling the Cutoff Laws. Now you had better get your own breakfast eaten because Marten says he wants to work on your geometry early, before he leaves for the beekeepers' meeting."

Chapter 23

1/12/48: Sixth-day. Continued clear but cold and windy, snow last night. Great weather for jobs needing windmill. Slept late after working so hard at cutting firewood yesterday. Marten didn't wake me, though I asked him. Soyburgers and kasha for breakfast. Did my language lesson with E then math with M. Friends of Elan came from Limpet to visit. Limpet is across the Bay; you can see it from Gannett Head on very clear days. Dinner was barley with rocambole, turnips, and fava beans. So many new foods here—never heard of such variety!

After dinner, I went over to the stone yards to cut grooves in grinding burrs. Grebe has taught me how to lay out the curves on the stone face and how to chisel them out evenly. I practiced a lot on the scrap stone, but now I can do it on the real stuff. I love to work there, or anywhere I can be around people, but Hewn wishes for me to focus on my studies more. He is right, of course, and I enjoy that too.

No one here really understands what it is to be rejected and friendless. I think it's hard to be an outsider here, even if one wanted to be, which I certainly don't.

I wonder if my banishment will ever really take its mark from me. Do you know how many culverts there are between here and the ferry dock? Or which ones are large enough for a person to sleep in? Or have you noticed which gardens are nearest the road and farthest from the houses? All these things are irrelevant to anybody else here. Someday, I will lose the urge to hide extra crackers under my bed. Someday, I'll be able to peer down any well without dreading what I'll see. Someday, but not yet.

For supper, we had a sort of pudding made from sweet acorn meal and some grain I never heard of before. It was topped with gooseberry sauce, which is put up in clay pots sealed with beeswax. It was delicious.

Our company is staying overnight, which is great fun. I can understand a bit of what people are saying, if they don't talk too fast. Also, I've put on a lot of weight.

*   *   *   *   *   *   *

In many respects, I was making great progress during that winter at Alga. My health was completely regained; in fact, it had never been better. My knee was perfectly mended, though with a permanent scar. I had put on weight and probably would have grown chubby, except that the Esperian diet and lifestyle tend to build more sinew than fat. I had enough work to keep me fit and enough study to keep me inspired.

My studies were a particular source of satisfaction. There were enormous gaps in my learning, and I was hungry to fill them, the more so since my new environment offered so much scope for using that learning. I was particularly diligent in my language studies. Though my mental capacities are by no means prodigious, I had unbounded motivation. Mastering a foreign language can take years of patient study, yet in a few months, I had obtained enough skill in Mok to follow some of what was happening around me. I was learning many words in Mok which I never even knew in my native Anagaian, so that my conversations could now be more nuanced and abstract. I revelled in the new vocabulary, swallowing whole columns in an evening. I often tried out new acquisitions on my steadmates and winced at their smiles when I would say something like "That is perfectly amicable with me."

My linguistic successes enabled me to widen my circle of friends. Although at first it seemed as though half the people on Alga were fluent in Anagaian, I soon found it was not so, especially away from Stonesthrow. Now that I was free to go anywhere, I made the acquaintance of a couple of people over on Carry's Neck, which was only a half-mile row across the Strait. I even took a ferry trip over to Goosegrass with Myrica once, to deliver a shipment of pump-washers. While there, she pointed out the place where her great-great-grandfather had lived (who was also Dawn's great grandfather). That was over a hundred years ago, and I marveled that anyone would know so much about their ancestors, especially when they inherited nothing from them—not even a surname. Yet Esperians in general are very mindful of their connexions and of their stories.

I struck up friendships with several young women, but I was always very careful to avoid expectations I could not fulfill. I hated trying to explain things which didn't make any sense to me either. In many ways, things were going better for me than ever in my life, but I still had three major concerns which were unresolved. One was my continuing ambivalence toward Fawn. That would seem to be a moot point, but I still felt bound by powerful strings. Perhaps if the separation had been more gradual, I would have adjusted better, but it was not. The last time I had looked into her eyes, she was my sweetheart, my fiancée. A day later, I was an accused prisoner, doomed never to see her young face again. Maybe it was absurd, but I couldn't close that door that easily.

My second great concern was what I will call my *purpose*, for want of a better term. In Anagaia, one never thought about one's purpose; one thought of surviving or, if possible, of getting rich. In truth, most young Stewards probably do not dwell on their "purpose" either because it is taken for granted. But I could not take it for granted. I needed to have a clear and explicit sense of it. It was not that I had some grand notion of myself becoming a famous leader or anything, but it really did seem possible that because of my unique position as an immigrant, I might make some small but unique contribution. Contribution to what? I was not even sure of that, though I sensed that to accomplish anything at all, I must first understand myself and the world around me.

My third great concern was finding a home, a permanent place where I could strike root. I knew by spring I needed to move out to make room for Fulmar. True, I could return in late fall, but I didn't wish to spend my life doing that. Ermine's statement that no vacancies were expected soon might seem strange in a household with six members over seventy, yet except for Discern, everyone seemed sound-bodied and likely to be around for a good while.

Even were it an option, I realized it wasn't the place I wanted to stay indefinitely. Although the seacoast was an exciting and delightful place to be, it wasn't "in my blood." Nor frankly were broad plains—I had seemed too much of those. I suppose it was something from my happy early childhood at Cleftridge that made me feel drawn to the wooded hills; in any case, it was to such a place that my fantasy pointed.

If I were going to find that ideal stead, I would need to travel a good bit. The idea appealed to me enormously, and it shouldn't be that hard; due to the Cutoff Laws and the Refuge Laws, it was a safe and easy country to travel in. Although there were no horses, there were bicycles, and things here were compact. One could walk across the entire nation in less than two weeks. I was reluctant to travel at Stonesthrow's expense, however willing they might be. Everyone had done so much for me already—if I must travel, I wanted to find some way to do it that would not be burdensome to others. I still had a few months before I had to do anything, but it was very much on my mind.

As if my studies and my work at the stone yard and other enterprises were not quite enough to occupy my time during this first winter, I took up another activity: drawing. Teal was a very accomplished artist, and I greatly admired his skill at depicting scenes around the island. I've read how the Ancients had a way that even nonartists could make instantaneous images of real-life things and even print many copies, but I doubt that any of them were more accurate than Teal's pictures. He specialized in oil painting but was also very good at pencil drawing, and I prevailed on him to teach me how. Well, I never really learned how, at least I'm nowhere near as good as he—but I picked up a lot of pointers about perspective and shading and form. And whenever I had a spare moment—not that often, it seemed—I would walk about the island and try to graphically record things I had described in my diary. I've saved some of them and included a few here, when it seems useful.

Chapter 24

Since early childhood, I had a habit of holding back from group activities until I had observed them at length and figured out everything about them. But since coming to Esperia, I often found myself doing just the opposite: jumping in with both feet, on the assumption that whatever it was, it must be a great idea, and I would understand it better as I went along.

Exactly six weeks into the Esperian year, I found myself up in the woodlot behind the orchard, helping with a curious project. Elan and Burnet and some of the others were thinning out some young fir trees and dragging them to a small clearing. There we lopped off most of the green boughs and fastened the poles together to form a lean-to of the crudest sort. Then we wove the boughs among the poles until all but the front side was loosely enclosed. Snow was thrown up against the walls on the outside, and still more boughs were piled on the roof. It was not the least bit rainproof, but there was no risk of rain at this coldest time of year. Finally, I just had to ask what we were going to do with the flimsy structure.

"Sleep in it," replied little Thistle.

"When?" I asked nervously.

"Tonight, of course. Tomorrow is Squirrel Folk Day."

"You've got to be joking! It's way below freezing now. And what on earth is Squirrel Folk Day?"

"She's not joking," insisted Elan. "A bunch of us always sleep in the bough hut the night before Squirrel Folk Day. That's what the kids call it, its proper name is Deliverance Day. It commemorates an event from the Calamitous Times. Our ancestors came awfully close to being wiped out altogether, and Deliverance Day is sort of a ritual reenactment of their trials and triumphs. Actually, it's a lot of fun."

"Fun? How can you even survive, let alone have fun?"

"It's all in the preparation. Come, help me haul another load of boughs. The more of them you have between you and the ground, the better you'll sleep."

When I learned that even Hewn and Ermine were planning to sleep out there, I figured they must know what they were doing. I also realized that this must be a pretty important occasion since Esperians, and especially Algans, do not consume trees, even fir thinnings, without good cause. Elan explained that the huts were rebuilt from scratch each year and, in spring, torn down for fuel to boil maple sap.

Sure enough, toward dark, a few other steadmates came up, loaded with quilts and pillows and supper. A bonfire was kindled from the dry lower branches, and we roasted apples and chestnuts and spiced dough held on long sharp sticks. The night air was as crisp as new linen and colder than arrogance, but we did indeed have a wonderful time, huddled down under the boughs with scarves over our noses and heaps of quilts over all. The softwood coals soon died down, but we were warmth for each other. Songs and stories and jokes burst forth from muffled lips. In time, the boisterous giggling subsided and was overcome by the crackling silence of the forest. I don't remember finally falling asleep, but when I was disturbed by someone stepping out to pee, I sat up and peered out at the weakening darkness. A few others were in varied stages of wakefulness, but no one ventured to leave our communal cocoon. Finally, just as dawn crept up over Cape Arrival, the other Dawn—Marten's mother—climbed out of our nest and quickly lit a pile of twigs before scurrying back under the covers. Minutes later, others braved the cold to toss on larger sticks, and soon we were all crowding around the pitchy smoky blaze, trying to warm our backsides before the front sides got cold again. We weren't very successful, however, and soon we were all stampeding toward the house, which fortunately was only a couple hundred yards away. There, our less-adventurous steadmates had hot mint brewed for us and breakfast soon to follow. Later in the day, however, the entire household traipsed back up to the hut for something called Juniper's Feast.

I learned there are four elements to the celebration, and we had already fulfilled one of them by building and sleeping in the hut. Custom doesn't absolutely demand that—it just says "staying in them"—and everyone satisfied that by crowding into the hut for the "feast." The second element is the retelling of the "Legend of Juniper," which recounts the events we were commemorating. I give the story here in its entirety, as it offers not only a vignette from a poorly documented period in Steward history, but it also points out clearly the origins of certain features of Esperian culture. Its authorship is uncertain. Although tradition ascribes it to the poet Shiningsea, there are some indications of later additions.

The Legend of Juniper

> When you prosper and are at peace, do not forget. When you dwell in stout houses and feel the warmth of your own hearths, do not forget. When your barns and cellars are full, and you sow and reap in abundance, do not forget. Do not forget that it was not always this way. For your present security was bought at a great price, and your comfort was paid for in suffering. Listen well, then, to my words, all you sons and daughters of the Covenant. Hear what I tell you, lest you take these things for granted.

In the time of our ancestors, it came about that a great calamity befell all the world. The foolishness of men prevailed over their wisdom, and all was chaos and strife. Now there arose a people who chose to be Stewards of the Earth rather than be masters of their fellow men. To that end, they drew apart in order not to partake in the folly of others. But the lords of the nations would not permit it. They would rule over all men or else destroy them. Therefore the Stewards fled into the mountains and wild places to bide there until the evil times should pass. Even there did their enemies pursue them. Though the Stewards hid in caves and planted gardens in secret places, still their foes sought them out. The skyships of the warlords destroyed their homes and crops. Many were dead, and the remnant were in sore distress.

Then came winter, and there was neither shelter nor food. Grievous was the plight of the small bands of Stewards who wandered about the land. Their grain was gone, and amid the deep snows was nothing to be found for them to eat.

Now there was among them a young girl who was called Juniper. She was deaf to the voices of people, having been in the caves when the skyships hurled their fire. Yet it was said of her that she could hear clearly the voices of wild animals, and that she alone could understand their meaning.

It happened that as the Stewards were huddled in their bough huts to await death, there came to Juniper a sound of voices calling to her. Leaving the others, the child walked toward the sound. The people called after her: "Juniper, do not stray into the forest, or you will get lost!" But she could not hear them. And someone said, "Why should we stop her? We are all lost. If she dies from the cold. It will be easier for her than for us." Yet another said, "She has gone to join her parents," for both her parents had already died in the caves.

So the girl Juniper wandered far into the forest. She did not know whither she was going but only followed the sound of the voices. The snow was deep around her, and she fell many times. She was very tired and would have lain down to sleep her last sleep. But hearing a voice again, she opened her eyes and saw a squirrel nearby on the limb of a great linden tree.

"Why do you scold me?" she answered. "I am without mother or father, and my people are dying. I myself am hungry and cold and can go no farther."

But again the squirrel chided her, and she saw him disappear as though into the air.

"Where has he gone?" The child wondered in amazement. She arose and went to the tree and saw that it was hollow. A crack was in its side, and being small, she could enter therein. She said to herself, "This is good. There is no wind here, and the squirrelfolk have lined the hole with soft thistledown so I am quite warm. I will not go back. I will stay here and die."

She felt sharp things beneath her feet and found that they were broken nut shells. Reaching around her, she found nuts and seeds of many kinds—butternuts and hazels and beeches and acorns and maple seeds—every opening was filled with them. Juniper ate some of them, and her eyes began to brighten, and she ceased to feel cold. When she had eaten her fill, she closed her eyes and fell asleep. Yet it was not the sleep of death, but the sleep of contentment.

When she finally awoke, it was morning and she ate more of the seeds. Then she bethought herself, "This is not right. I cannot stay here. I shall go back to my people and tell them what I have found."

So she filled her pockets with seeds and nuts and retraced her steps to where her people languished in their bough huts. When they saw her, they cried out, "It is little Juniper, come back to us alive! She has been all night in the frozen forest, yet she looks better than when she left us. How can this be?"

They made signs to her, and she answered them, "I found shelter in the home of the squirrelfolk, and I was warmer than any of you. I ate at their table. I ate until I was full. Just see here!" When they saw what she had brought, they were filled with wonder.

"Come with me to the squirrelfolk tree!" she said. There is much more there. Come and eat and live!"

They followed her back to the hollow tree and saw that it was as she said. They gathered seeds from the hollow trunk and from many other hollow trees that stood around there, several bushels in all. As they were taking away the seeds to their camp, Juniper heard voices again, and she bade the people wait.

"It is the squirrelfolk. They are saying, 'Shame, o humans! Would you take away all our food and leave us to perish? Is it the way of the Stewards, to plunder the helpless who have shared with you? For we are also the children of Earth."

But the people answered, "We are starving! Are we to leave this food which would save us?"

And Juniper answered them, "It need not be thus. The squirrelfolk always store much more than they need. Therefore let us leave a portion behind for them. To every place where we remove food, let a portion be returned to it, that the squirrelfolk may live and bless us."

The people heeded the words of Juniper, for it was she who listened to the squirrelfolk and she who found the food which saved them. They sustained themselves on the stores of the squirrelfolk until the winter was past.

In time the skyships ceased to return and hurl their fire on the Stewards. For the power of their enemies turned to dust as their own world fell into ruin. When next they invaded the lands of the Stewards, it was with sticks and stones and then not at all as darkness filled their own lands.

The Stewards built anew their homes and planted crops and ate them. And they spread out through all the hill country until they were a secure and prosperous nation. But they never forgot the story of Juniper and the squirrelfolk. To this day, the Stewards honour them by building bough huts in the forest and staying in them. And every winter, on the Feast of Juniper, the children take seeds and other food to share with the squirrelfolk, to thank them for their great gift of long ago.

Following this was the third element: the Feast of Juniper. To celebrate this properly requires the services of a preadolescent girl to portray Juniper. Her duties are simple enough: she first takes a basket of biscuits which are made wholly from tree foods, like chestnuts, hazels, pine nuts, and leached acorns sweetened with maple syrup or pear juice and dried berries. She hands one to each celebrant in turn, then she does the same with cups of juice (some prefer red currant juice because currants grow in the forest, whereas others opt for cider since apples grow on trees, not bushes. I am wholly without opinions on the subject). Only when all have been served and Juniper invites them to partake does everyone eat. After that, anyone may help themselves, but before then, no one may reach for a biscuit—they must receive the first one directly from Juniper's hand—they must be beholden to Juniper.

We were lucky to have Thistle, who played the part superbly, but there are some steads which do not have a suitable child. They usually arranged to "borrow" someone from a neighbouring stead. I've heard of girls who officiate at one feast then promptly leave to do the honours at the neighbours'. They are doted on a good bit, and it's a rare little girl who doesn't spend the day with a swelled head.

The final element of the ritual is the placing of food for the squirrelfolk. Usually field corn or acorns are put out on stumps or feeding trays, which have been set up in the area. Ermine reminded us all that according to the story, we were not merely giving the squirrelfolk a handout, but returning a portion of what was rightly theirs to begin with.

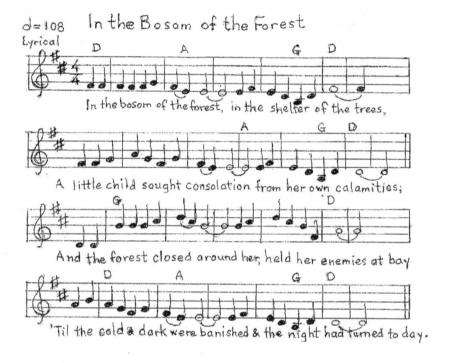

In the Bosom of the Forest

In the bosom of the forest, in the shelter of the trees,

A little child sought consolation from her own calamities;

And the forest closed around her, held her enemies at bay

'Til the cold & dark were banished & the night had turned to day.

When the voices of her people
   Were cold silence in her ears,
T'was the creatures of the forest
   Came to drive away her tears.
In the throes of desolation
   She found solace and release
In the bosom of the forest,
   In the shelter of the trees.

Chapter 25

2/19/48:. I feel like I am getting a better grasp of what life is like here and how things work—at least some of the details. I've been keeping notes on those details, in hopes that they will help me figure out the big picture. Here are some of my observations to date, not very well organized, I'm afraid. I'll start with food.

As everyone knows, the Esperians do not eat foods of animal origin, which they consider too inefficient and unwholesome. Unless one counts honey (which is a source of controversy for some). They further prefer foods whose production does not require tilling the soil. It is a rare meal which does not include some tree foods as a central ingredient. Certainly the most ubiquitous item is the chestnut, which is used in several forms: fresh, roasted, dried, or ground into meal. They accompany grains in porridge, and they are baked in casseroles with vegetables and herbs. Puddings and sweet-cakes usually contain a quantity of chestnut meal. Every stead uses many bushels of the sweet starchy kernels per year. They are extremely important in the diet despite the constant attention needed to keep the blight-prone trees healthy.

Second only to chestnuts are the acorns, which are likewise grown in nearly every corner of the nation. They are leached in cold-flowing streams to remove the bitter tannins. The most commonly used type is the bur oak. Acorns are often used to make a sort of dark steamed bread.

Hazelnuts are also grown and used in abundance. Every stead has a cracking machine through which the dehusked nuts are fed to break and separate the shells. They have a rich oily kernel from which are made a variety of foods, including a buttery spread.

Pine nuts are also widely grown and butternuts, but the latter are difficult to crack and are eaten more as a "special treat."

They also have a kind of dried pea here which grows on a woody shrub. I remember seeing these growing in Umberlands as a child, but those were only eaten by wild birds, whereas here they have been improved by centuries of breeding and selection.

People here seem to eat a remarkable amount of fruit; the evening meal usually consists of fruit with some form of grain or chestnuts. Some of the fruits are familiar to me, but many are not. There are elders and sarvisberries and a curious fruit which looks like a crab apple with acne. Ermine says most of our fruits would grow as well or better farther south, yet I've never seen many of them in Anagaia where fruit is regarded as a luxury.

Esperian cuisine also features several foods which are not tree crops, but are likewise grown under constant mulch. One of these is the terrasol, a lumpy-looking tuber of the sunflower family. It is used as a vegetable and also as a dried meal (much like chestnuts). The tubers are also fermented to produce alcohol for lamp fluid, and the stalks are a source of textile fibre for industrial purposes. Indeed, terrasols are so important in the material culture of the nation that the blossom is a common decorative motif, appearing on rugs, pots, even on the national flag.

I've learned that *Steward* has a kind of double meaning here. Of course, any member of the Covenant is called a Steward (whether Esperian, Concordian, Bisonian, etc.). But it also refers to an individual with a specific responsibility, such as the steward of the wood box. These stewardships are large and small; indeed there are an infinite number of unspoken or informal stewardships which are often taken for granted. An obvious example: everyone is a steward of their own personal possessions. I've not yet figured out just what all the formal stewardships are, but I've been writing down what I can, and this is what I've figured out so far:

The person who is responsible for the entire household, its possessions and enterprises, is the stead steward, which is Ermine. That is certainly not to say that she does most of the work herself—that's not what is expected of a steward. She has a clear head for administrating a complex operation. She politely asks you to do this or that and make sure you follow through on it. That itself is no small job, considering that a stead is not only a communal residence, but an intricate agricultural and industrial enterprise whose varied needs and interests call for a great attention to detail. It is a huge responsibility and a big honour, but neither is too great for Ermine.

As if overseeing the general affairs of the whole stead were not enough work, Ermine is also kitchen steward. That too is a demanding set of responsibilities, but fortunately, everyone is always eager to help her.

There is a fuel steward, responsible for supplies of firewood and lamp fluid and candles—that's Marten. Tilia is steward of food supply; she makes sure the pantry and cellar are kept stocked and notifies Ermine of shortages or surpluses so menus can be planned accordingly. The clothing steward (which is Corolla) makes certain that everyone has adequate clothing and that everything is kept mended and laundered. The housekeeping steward is Vervain. There is the maintenance steward (Freeheart), and he also has numerous duties away from the house (he is a very hard worker), so he ends up doing too much of it himself. He is greatly admired for his efforts, but it leaves him little time for leisure, which he doesn't seem to mind.

Separate from the house, the woodlot steward is Dawn, where her son Marten is hive steward, and her husband Freeheart is equipment steward. Dawn also serves as crop steward, another formidable responsibility, but unlike her husband, she knows how to delegate work.

Besides these responsibilities, Stonesthrow has three wholly owned enterprises, each with its own stewards: the broom-and-brush factory (Alaria), the candle shop (Elan), and the rainwear shop (Corolla).

Even this does not begin to show the whole picture because several steadmates hold stewardships at the joint enterprises or in banner affairs. For example, I know Vervain is steward of something over at one of the chemical plants, and Burnet is also banner steward of winter roads.

As a temporary resident, I have only minor short-term duties, as when Marten asked me to be steward of the laundry-room woodbox. Even Discern has his honourable duties, which he discharges from his wheelchair. He is steward of the stories, which may sound dismissive to anyone who doesn't understand how much Esperians treasure a well-told tale.

Funny—as I write this, I realize that the only stead member having no formal stewardship at all is Hewn, yet hardly anyone comes and goes more than that "retired" diplomat. I guess that's why: his schedule is so irregular and he is always having to run around to meetings elsewhere. He certainly makes himself useful, whether at the wrackplant or the stone yard or teaching me.

By the way, I've noticed that nobody ever actually seeks to be made a steward. The very sort of person who would do that is the sort who would probably be passed over. For example, I remember how on Reckoning Day, Ermine expressed her readiness to be replaced by someone else more competent. Everyone reassured her that there *is* no one more competent and urged her to continue in the position. I can already see a good reason for her doing that: since no individual really has any power to coerce, if you don't have a clear mandate, you simply cannot function; and to fail at a stewardship is vastly more shameful than never having been steward at all.

The waresroom is such a curious and distinctive feature of every stead that it would be well to describe it here. In a society which relies so heavily on barter, I can't imagine how they could manage without it. It is often merely a very large closet, but it is invariably crammed beyond capacity. Only the most diligent supply steward manages to keep it well-organized, and it's no wonder since the contents are extremely diverse and constantly changing. Tacked on the inside of the door is the ubiquitous inventory sheet, decipherable only by the steward, if anyone. One typically finds an odd assemblage of household wares: cooking utensils, writing paper, mica panes for the stoves, matches, soap, assorted hardware. Then there are always a few of those awkward-to-store and seldom-called-for items that inspire comments like: "I trust you didn't pay too much for that!" There are often ingenious systems of shelves and racks, clever attempts to keep everything logically and visibly arranged. Utterly futile. There really are a dozen candles left in that gross box, but you'll never know it unless you push aside that stack of quilts. Or check the inventory list, but that's no good; they've been crossed out so often by earlier removals that you can't read it anyway.

I exaggerate, of course. The waresroom is a constant source of handy items—if not for steadmates, then perhaps for an inquiring neighbour. Every bannerhouse has its own waresroom too, or several, often in separate buildings. The contents are mostly items sent in by steads in payment of taxes.

I mention the waresroom because it is, I believe, emblematic of everything good and bad in the Esperian trade system. The dependence on barter and nonstandard currencies is bizarre. It seems calculated to frustrate commerce and enforce the Vine Laws. Anywhere else, such a patently cumbersome system would strangle any markets, yet the reader doesn't need me to describe what a formidable trade partner Esperia is. Indeed, Marten suggested to me that part of the reason Esperian export goods command such good prices—aside from their quality—is that the makers are not absolutely bound to sell them.

2/23/48: Snowing most of the day. I did a stint on the rolling crew this morning and an hour laying out grooves at the stone shop, but otherwise stayed indoors and studied. I've been learning so many new things about Esperia that I can hardly keep it all straight, so I'm putting it down before I forget.

Thanks to Marten, I finally understand how the Esperian calendar works: there are thirteen months, beginning on the winter solstice—my birthday; all the months have twenty-eight days, except the last, which has twenty-nine, or on leap years, thirty. Therefore the summer solstice, or Banner Day, falls on 7/14, the spring equinox is 4/7, the autumnal equinox is 10/21, and Deliverance Day is on 2/15. Understanding it is one thing; adjusting to it may be another.

Marten also told me this—now this is amazing: the government here does not mint coins. Get that? There is no such thing as Esperian currency! He just says "It's not something they do"—as if that explains it all. The weird thing is that they do use every *other* kind of currency. I've seen Anagaian falcons and bullheads here as well as Coquinese conches and marlins, and Palmettoan torches and Borealian quarter-Shields. The other day, Elan even showed me a silver decade from the Prairie Federation—however did that end up here? Nevertheless, they are all circulated freely here, at whatever the prevailing value is. Because of that, Marten says I need to know the different denominations, even though their relation to other national currencies is always in flux.

There is a household income tax paid by the stead to the banner. This is fixed by law at 10 percent, and cannot be increased, but Marten says that number is totally irrelevant since no stead would dream of paying that little; the community would immediately try to offer *them* financial assistance, and that would be too humiliating. Of course, in a barter economy, that means you owe 10 percent of your wheat, 10 percent of your zucchini, etc. That might not be very useful to the banner, but the tax steward has the option of crediting any commodity at its value to the banner. Therefore if Stonesthrow insisted on paying all its taxes in salt, for example, they might find it advantageous to trade the salt elsewhere and pay the banner in something it needs or values more, such as bridge-repair labour. Most Esperians don't appear to have any great problem with "big government"; they only care that it be efficient and accountable. The key here seems to be "consensus": since government at any level cannot force compliance with its will, it must first convince its citizens of the desirability of some policy or action. If they don't wish to support it, they won't. Therefore, in effect, the government is not demanding obedience; it is requesting assistance. Does it get it? Incredibly, nobody here even contemplates cheating on their tax-obligations— "they would dishonour themselves"; and believe me, no one here takes that lightly. There is, it seems, almost a competition to exceed others in support of "the tribe." Payments are posted publicly, and people really look to see how much their neighbours overpaid, raising their eyebrows when some less-endowed household is particularly forthcoming (I now understand that the word *generous* is not really appropriate). They get many things for their taxes, not the least of which is that they hold their heads high. There is no prestige in poverty; people work hard to get rich, but for one central purpose: to pay rent in the Larger House.

The banner in turn pays at least 10 percent of its tax revenue to the national government (fairs do not figure in this) to support its functions. Again, people invariably give much beyond the required minimum, although both banners and steads often withhold part of that extra (freewill offering) from the general revenue because they may wish to make a greater or lesser priority of supporting a particular programme. For example, when Alga had an increase in revenue, a group of banner folk, led by Hewn, lobbied for the new funds to be remitted directly to the Alternative Fibres Project rather than to the general appropriation for the Vision Fulfillment Council. That is perfectly legal and acceptable. Of course, if many people did that, the Council would get the idea that it ought to revise its budget.

By the way, many foreigners believe that the national capital of Esperia is Goosegrass, but this is not so. In fact, the centre of national government is wherever the legislature (and the VFC) is currently meeting. This rotates yearly from one fairbanner to the next. Therefore Goosegrass (for example) is the government seat only once in every eighteen years. Of course, this would be impractical if the government were as centralized at the top level as it is in most nations, but in fact, its functions are relatively few. During the seventeen years when those buildings are *not* the government seat, their office spaces and assembly halls are appropriated by the fairbanner for other uses. However, the foreign consulates *are* permanently located in a few large buildings at the Goosegrass Fair, which gives many foreigners the false impression that this is the "capital city." No wonder they are unimpressed!

2/26/48: Very cold and cloudy today; more snow. I'm surprised to find that the fabled Esperian winter is not half as uncomfortable as I feared. I guess it's partly because I have such warm clothes. I still have Wren's fall coat, but I've since borrowed a long heavy quilted coat, and I'm making a new one of my own so I can return both. Esperians don't use wool, but I have thick quilted boot-liners in lieu of socks and flannel-lined canvas gloves with rubberized palms so they last longer. I find I can enjoy working outdoors in weather that would have Umberlanders huddled around their little fires all day. And that's another thing: the houses are all so thick-walled and tight that they are cozy even in the nastiest blizzard. At first it seemed to me that it took a lot of fuel to heat this large house, as indeed it does, but then I realized that it is warming eighteen people. In Dryford, we used about half as much fuel, but it served for only three or four people, and we were still cold.

I've been learning to use skis. Snowshoes are simpler and great for working in the woods when the snow is deep, but when you really need to cover some miles in a hurry, skiing is the thing. The roads here are all hard rolled, and you can skim along as if on horseback.

I memorized thirty new words this morning—mostly verbs. I'm getting so I can say more complicated ideas now without recourse to the dictionary (yes, I had to look up *recourse*). Mok is a very expressive language, and I want to be able to speak it like a native, no matter how much work it takes.

I've noticed that no one ever curses around here. I mean, even low-minded people (and there are such, believe me) just never swear. That's not to say that folks never use banal expressions—in fact, they can be pretty colourful—but I've never heard any of the kinds of oaths that are used by people elsewhere. It took me awhile to figure out that these are not prudish folks, rather it is because they are all atheists, born and raised among other atheists! What satisfaction could they possibly derive from consigning someone to eternal flames or calling down the wrath of some exalted being? Given their perspective, cursing must be a hollow experience since only a true believer can evince a gut-felt blasphemy.

Yesterday, I did something which is hardly remarkable for anyone here, but it's certainly a first for me: I joined an organization. Back in Umberlands, there's only one "organization" you could join, and you might be hanged for doing so. What I joined, however, is not the Amanita Brotherhood, but the Bluemeadow Archaeological Society. I joined it for a couple reasons: I'm really eager to widen my circle of friends, especially off the island. Other folks here seem to have connexions all over the place: relatives, acquaintances, colleagues, business associates. I too need to have more varied contacts if I'm ever to find a permanent place that suits me, and joining an organization seems like an obvious starting point. And, oh yes, I also happen to be very interested in archaeology just now.

I've always noticed that Esperians wear no jewelry or cosmetics, and their clothes are generally not very colourful. If you ask anyone about this, you're apt to get some scriptural passage as an explanation, but that doesn't wash too well with me when you consider how they recycle the Scriptures so freely to suit their own purpose. This is what I think I've figured out (it seems I have to figure it all out by myself since no one can explain what everyone takes for granted): because of the strong emphasis on the common, or "tribal" interest, some things that smack of individualism tend to get repressed. Not by any blatant or intentional effort, but simply by lack of reinforcement. Anyone who pays great attention to their own appearance would, I imagine, be viewed as superficial or self-centred. Now there is certainly no law here against superficiality or self-centredness, but one certainly wouldn't garner much esteem for such "Smaller

House" attitudes, and esteem is what it's all about here. I mean, even though plenty of people *are* superficial and only pay lip service to the Larger House ideal, it is nevertheless the shared ideal, and even the lip service tends to strengthen it. To support my theory, I would point out the lovely flower gardens around every steadhouse, and even more, the careful decoration of bannerhouses. It seems the higher or broader the level of "self-interest," the more effort is lavished on it.

Considering how many rules and regulations there are here, I wonder that there's so little formal structure for enforcement. I mean, there are no police as such, but there is a remarkable degree of self-policing. Hewn says it's because of the consensual government. The people themselves will enforce laws they consider their own. The Council can "make" laws, but laws are "enacted" only by being observed, that is to say, if people observe them. Here, if you flout a law, you won't be formally arrested, but you will incur the disapproval and rejection of your peers, which for these people is a far more potent sanction than fines or jail. By the way, there is no capital punishment here. Hewn explained that although the Scriptures say that certain crimes are deserving of the death penalty, they also make it impossible to carry that out.

Another institution I learned about recently is the Bee-Free movement. They are a group which opposes the keeping of bees or at least the use of their products. Part of their argument is that it is not really vegan to eat honey, which they call things like bee-spit and bee-puke, although it is neither. Marten says the counterargument is that the compelling reasons for being vegan don't apply very well to beekeeping. You don't have to kill or castrate the bees or their young to keep the supply coming. They don't occupy space or consume resources that could otherwise be used more efficiently, whereas you have to "bleed" maple trees and burn fuel to make syrup. Of course, Marten is himself a beekeeper. He did point out that honey is not the most important product produced by bees. There are several alternative sources of sweetening, like maples, malted grain, and sugar beets; but there are few alternatives for wax and propolis. He says many beekeepers feed back a lot of the honey crop to induce the bees to make more comb and thus more wax.

No doubt there are stronger arguments against beekeeping; after all, I've never really talked to one of the opponents, so I should not speak dismissively of their concerns. I bring it up mainly to emphasize that all is not smiles and nods here.

There are definitely people, even here on Alga, who are dissatisfied with the way some things are; and if they were to get their way, presumably the others would be dissatisfied. The fabric of Esperian society is not free of snags, but somehow they don't seem to weaken the overall strength of the cloth.

I keep wondering about this concensus thing that seems to hold things together. I guess any society relies somewhat on concensus, but here, everything seems to really hinge on it. What I can't figure out is how it came into being in the first place, and how so many millions of people could agree on so much that is so important to how they operate. Because in fact they do—no matter how they point out all the dissent and controversy among them. That's also true, but through it all run a very strong thread—no, a mighty cable—that splices them all together, not seamlessly, but powerfully. Marten reminded me that the Stewards (and especially the Esperians) have a very narrow common origin. A small group of individuals—some say a few hundred—comprised the bands of early Stewards. And far fewer of those—maybe dozens—actually survived the Calamities to contribute ideas and values to the nascent culture. Moreover, there has never been any significant influx of newcomers to dilute those original values. It has all grown out of that founding core group. But of course, that says nothing about the lack of conflicting core values arising spontaneously over time. When I discussed this with Orris, he suggested that there is such a thing as "herd philosophy." That means that when the vast majority of a population accepts something, the rest tend to go along even if it defies logic or is against their own self-interest. Whatever may be the great, or abstract truth, shared or communal "truths" will trump anything else, at least as long as it seems to be working.

2/28/48: It seems truly amazing that I could have been raised by people from here and yet know so little about them and their country. Now that I am learning about them, a lot of things I never understood before begin to make sense.

I've just learned about something called the Non-Combustion Movement. Actually *movement* is a pretty weird word for it because unlike the Bee-Free Movement, it's not really some bunch of grassroots activists. It's a totally mainstream thing; in fact, it's sort of a government agency. One of its main objectives is to preserve the forests or more precisely, to maintain the ratio of forests to cleared land. Since Esperia has no coal deposits, that means controlling the amount of wood and charcoal consumed for fuel. However, Marten said that even if they had lots of coal, they'd be reluctant to burn it for fear of releasing too much carbon. I asked him what was the problem with that, and he wasn't so clear on it himself, except he knew it was a big problem at the time of the Calamities, maybe even *was* one of the Calamities.

These folks are like that: just tell them the Ancients did such and such, and they'll want nothing to do with it. They really despise that civilization, just as much as Anagaians emulate it.

Anyway, what this Non-Combustion thing means is that they're set on not burning anything they don't have to burn and getting the most efficiency out of what they *do* burn. For example, the kind of furnace we have at Stonesthrow is common throughout the country. It has channels, or flues winding through a great mass of masonry, which acts as a heat sink. This method of heating gets the most warmth out of the wood, while no soot goes up the chimney.

Since metals, glass, and ceramics entail lots of fuel in their production and recycling, their use is avoided when something like wood or stone will suffice.

Also they are fanatic about fuel efficiency generally. Every kiln steward or foundry worker is alert for any innovation that will save even a scoop of charcoal. For this reason, many industries use parabolic reflectors to preheat components for the furnace, and most factory fires are carbureted for cleaner combustion.

There is something here that doesn't make sense to me; at least it doesn't seem to fit the usual laws of economics. Wood is relatively expensive here, yet it is very

148

plentiful. Unlike Borealia, Esperians are not eager to export as much wood as Anagaia would like to buy. They refuse to sell raw logs but only milled lumber or better yet, manufactured wood products. Borealia, for its part, has long been exporting logs as fast as they could cut them, so that they now have neither the quantity nor the quality of wood that Esperia has. Yet they continue to sell cheap because they must have the foreign exchange. I just don't understand it.

Chapter 26

When I had first arrived in Esperia, every article of clothing I wore was borrowed from someone. Gradually, I had acquired clothes that were my own, beginning with waterproof boots and quilted socks. Then Corolla had taught me how to use the treadle sewing machine and had helped me to make a few shirts. The linen was made right on the island from locally grown flax. There was a small seasonal textile "mill" down on the shore where the force of the tides served to power the bobbins and looms. It was designed only to provide cloth for the island's own needs, but it did that quite nicely. All I had to do was cut out the pieces and stitch them together. The only remaining project was my coat, a loose quilted garment that pulled over my head. That did not go quite so fast, what with all the cattail batting and hand-sewn seams, and it was the week after Deliverance Day before I finished. I now thought about Wren, whose fall coat I had still not returned. I hadn't seen him since the *Minkey*, although he promised to come visit. He had written twice though, saying that he meant to come but was preoccupied with a special project he was working on. Therefore I took it into my head to go visit him at Longlogan so I could return the coat and impress him with my Mok. When I suggested my idea at supper, everyone seemed to approve. No one mentioned the obvious alternative of simply mailing it to him on the ferry, which would cost a trifle and save lots of my time. Ermine simply asked, "Will you go tomorrow? Marten will want to know if you're not having a math lesson."

"Well, no . . . at least, I thought I'd wait until the first of the week so I can finish the pair of grindstones I'm working on in the shop. They are on order from the grist-mill over at Covey's Sleeve, and I thought I'd deliver them on the way, to save shipping costs."

"Oh, so you won't be taking the ferry?"

"If it's all right with everyone, I thought I'd take the overland route through the Beacon Hills so I can see more new territory. It shouldn't take much longer since I won't have to deal with all the ferry stops."

"Sounds like a good idea to me. Be sure to take a map along so you won't get lost. You should be able to catch a ride over to Covey's on the mail boat."

So it happened that I greeted the dawn of the next week, sitting in the bow of the midcoast mail as its tacked eastward across Compass Cove. My skis lay against the gunnels, and my new-made pair of millstones sat solidly crated on the deck under my seat. I was justly proud of them, my first complete project in stone working. I did not have to pay shipping on them since the mailman did not have to unload or deliver them. We dropped off a bag of mail and some parcels at a pier on the north tip of Telling and picked up a second passenger, who was going to Rose Point, on the mainland. After dropping her off, the mail boat headed up Covey's Sleeve, a long narrow tongue of the sea which was flanked by low granite cliffs for most of its length. At its upper extremity, the ledges tapered to nothing, amid a broad salt marsh extending inland. Here, surrounded by mud flats and reeds, stood Covey's Landing.

After delivering my two crates, I started up the Beacon Hills road, aware of a feeling I had not experienced for many years, if ever. It was a feeling not so much of independence as of unaccountability. For the next day or two, I was free to go wherever I wanted, to do whatever I wished. The only fixed point on my itinerary was Longlogan, but how I got there and back was wholly at my discretion. You must understand that in my native Umberlands, one may not leave one's district without official papers, which even specify route of travel and expected time of arrival. It is supposed to prevent banditry, which it completely fails to do, but it does give the police tight control over people's movements. Therefore I now felt more than free; I could now fly. I had a map, a lunch, and a little time all my own—the Olotal could claim no more. I also had something which I'd never before possessed: a sort of boldness to approach strangers, with the assumption they might not be hostile. In Anagaia, it just wasn't done; one minded one's own business. I found myself being downright outgoing, if not by their standards, surely by my own.

Throughout my journey, I encountered plenty of people on nearly every road. I got many curious stares but always warm greetings, and often in my own language! Most were on foot or on skis, although a few rode curious conveyances called pedisleds. A pedisled is somewhat like a bicycle with a ski instead of a front wheel and a pair of belted half-tracks replacing the rear wheel (the more modern ones are convertible into bicycles for summer use). They can be rather treacherous to handle, and I learned to give them a wide berth.

I made very good time at first, skimming over the hard-rolled roads on my well-waxed skis. There were so many possible routes to choose. I opted for one road which sidled up across the shoulder of one of the Beacon Hills. Even under the deep snows, I could see that the land was all terraced and walled as on the island. Here on the mainland, the most noticeable difference was the larger size of the woodlots—certainly these people were not importing firewood in violation of the Staples Rule. But like Alga, these woodlots were all highly managed, every tree pruned and thinned, some of them in carefully spaced rows of alternating species. Everything had an orderly look. Almost everything.

The one exception was so dramatic that I could hardly believe my eyes. Here was a stead yard, then a hayfield, above that an orchard—suddenly it all stopped. Beyond was a stone wall, and on the other side woods, but not at all like the woods elsewhere. No orderly rows, no sign of planting or thinning, no access lanes for harvesting mature trees. And there certainly were mature trees. Some huge giants were broken over from age and lay toppled amid their own crushed limbs. I was puzzled. People on Alga were grinding up rocks to gain a few more acres of precious growing space, yet I saw one fallen ash tree which could have supplied a fourth of Stonesthrow's fuel needs for the whole winter. I say "could have" because the trunk was obviously decayed now, rows of dried rainbow conks jutting out of the snow-encrusted bark. I looked out across the Strait. I could probably see my dormitory window at Stonesthrow since I had often stood in the window, looking over at these hills. What a waste of wood, I thought, within sight of the place where people needed it so much.

I had to admit, though, this unkempt forest had a certain savage beauty of its own. There was a seemingly chaotic hodgepodge of ages and species. A dense spinney of firs poked up around the rotten carcass of the ash tree. Some trunks were over three feet in diameter, with no indication that the pruning saw had ever seen use there. An enormous hemlock snag, apparently killed by lightning, had never been removed, but its topmost branch stubs cradled a large osprey nest.

I could only remember seeing anything like this place once before, and it wasn't in Esperia. During my banishment, I had once passed an area of several thousand acres much like this one where no trees had been cut (ever it seemed) although closely cropped pasture came right up to the edge of it. There were signs which identified it as the Accursed Lands, a region where in Ancient Times, some catastrophic accident had occurred, which had poisoned the land for all time. But there were no such signs here. Indeed, I saw several places where snowshoe tracks went into the forest and came out again. Nothing indicated that this place had any evil associations, yet it was plainly considered special. The intense domestication of the stead lands on one side of the wall contrasted so starkly with the utter abandonment of the wilderness on the other side that it was perfectly clear that the boundary, the wall itself, was a powerful symbol of something. But of what? I stowed the question away with others for my return home.

For almost three miles, the road continued alongside the old-growth forest, which was shown on my map as a crosshatched area marked simply SG. A mile or so beyond that, my route joined a small brook with a curious name of Sacred Rill. At least I found it curious that a people whose language had no word for *spiritual* would give such a pious moniker to a mere watercourse. Just past the Beacon bannerhouse, the road became suddenly steeper. The map showed it crossing over just below the peak and continuing down the opposite side to Bergamot Brook. I assumed it must be kept open since there was a signal tower on top. That tower, in fact, was my reason for choosing that route: it was the same tower that had relayed the news of my arrival to the people at Stonesthrow. It was a curiosity to me. A similar tower had been built near my village in Umberlands, soon after the Amanita Uprising (I had never realized that the technology had been imported from Esperia.) One would approach it only with great caution, if at all. It was a CADS installation; and unauthorized persons displaying interest in it were liable to the suspect, at best. Here, I was assured, one might inspect the tower with perfect impunity; so upon reaching the summit, I mustered my best Mok and hailed the occupants. In a moment, a trapdoor opened in the tower floor and a voice floated down.

"What'll you have?"

"Just looking around. I always wondered how these things worked. Is it all right?"

"Sure. Come on up!"

"Wha . . . ? You mean, up there? Can I really?"

"Just watch your step—some of those treads are icy."

Eagerly, I kicked off my skis, and I climbed up the many steps which spiralled up the inside of the tower's legs. I counted them, sixty in all, much more than what was needed to get above the stunted spruces that carpeted the crest of the hill. At the top, I swung up through the trapdoor into a small cabin that was fairly warm, considering the weather and its exposed position. Glass windows on all sides looked down on a dazzling winterscape of sea and land. Before noting all of this, however, I made acquaintance with the signal crew, a team of two women and two men. They comprised one of the six-hour shifts, which operated the system round the clock. They were at a brief lull in their signaling work and so had time to explain things to me, which they did most willingly. But first, one of them asked me a question which I thought rather queer.

"Were you sent by the Brotherhood?" I was baffled. I only knew of one Brotherhood, and what would this fellow know about that?

"Why, no. What you mean?"

"Oh, nothing. Just curious."

Another team member hastened to direct my attention to the centre of the room, where stood a very large version of the solar reflector I had watched Wren use aboard the *Minkey*. This one used a combination of parabolic mirrors and polarizing lenses to concentrate and direct a powerful light beam in whatever direction they chose. Actually, there were two beams, aiming east and west. At intervals, they would be turned north and south. Also, the team I described was actually two teams, each pair facing in either direction. They explained that the entire system was laid out in a grid with each tower located on the most prominent site in its neighbourhood. For one hour, signals would be flashed east and west, then north and south for an hour. For example, the person receiving from the west would write down each message as fast as it came in. Each time a page was filled, he or she would pass it to the transmitter, who would flash it onward to the east. While this was happening, the other team would be receiving and transmitting in the opposite direction, from east to west. Each unit, or item, of a message was introduced with a routing code, which also indicated whether a message was "prime-line," "all-system," "single-receiver," etc. Whenever there was transmitting time available during a given "slot," personal messages could also be relayed, for a fee; however, unless the message were urgent, mail was much cheaper.

At nighttime, the solar reflector was replaced by a powerful carbide lamp. During foggy or stormy weather, the system was essentially useless, and communications piled up until conditions improved.

This is how Esperians get most of their news. Each receiver would sort out the news items relevant to that area, and they would be printed each day on large sheets of cheap paper, which were tacked up at the bannerhouse for all to see or to be circulated around from stead to stead. Each week's news sheets would be taken down, de-inked, and recycled again and again.

Soon the signaling cycle picked up again, and I had to watch quietly as shutters slid and typewriters clacked and telescopes squinted at the horizon in search of the nation's news. Letting myself out the floor-hatch, I redonned my skis at the bottom and wended my way down the north side of the hill toward the Bergamots.

Because of my meandering itinerary and frequent stops, it was after dark when I arrived at Longlogan. Fortunately, Wren's home, Pierstead, was easy to find, close by the bannerhouse. It stood on a narrow neck of land between the Bluemeadow River and a body of water called the Long Logan. When I got there, Wren had just arrived himself. I greeted him with effusive warmth, which seemed to embarrass him—I believe he hadn't told his steadmates much about his role in rescuing me. I tried to, but he brushed it off.

"Have you had supper yet?"

"No. I carried my lunch, but I was invited to a stead on the way, so it's still in my bag. Is it all right if I stay here tonight?"

"Oh, but you must. I have something to show you, but it's too dark now. Let's get a bite to eat and join the others in the meeting room—I think there's a programme tonight."

If Pierstead was anything like Stonesthrow, there certainly would be a programme. Hardly an evening passed without some sort of planned event. Of course, not every stead had a Hewn to orchestrate such a full schedule, but the folks at Pierstead were not ones to "sit in the dark" either. As it happened, there was a neighbourhood chorus performing music of the Coquinese Islands. They were pretty good, and the company was jolly, but I was bushed from skiing almost twenty miles over wintry roads. When Wren finally led the way to the men's dormitory, I had no trouble falling asleep the moment I lay down.

Next morning, Wren showed me around the steadhouse, which was much like Stonesthrow in layout, but considerably larger. Like other steads I had visited, they had their own assortment of cooperative enterprises, including a small foundry which made cast-iron pots and stove doors from recycled scrap. They also cut ice in a really big way, mostly for export to the Coquinas and the Palmetto Republic. Although the Long Logan was essentially a narrow estuary formed where Longlogan Brook joined the Bluemeadow, the two waters were separated by a long stone causeway, which made the Logan flow over a spillway. This not only made a source of power for a sawmill and planing mill, but it also kept the waters of the Logan fresh while the Bluemeadow at this point was mixed with tidewater. The Logan, therefore, froze deep and clear; and its hard black ice was cut and stored in sheds along the bank, packed between layers of sawdust from the mill.

As we walked around, Wren asked a lot of questions about what I was doing on Alga, and my plans for the future. I told him as best I could, but explained that there was still uncertainty as to where I would end up.

"And what about you?" I asked. "I suppose you'll be going back south on the *Minkey*?"

"No. That was just something I did once. I wanted to see the world. I may go to sea again someday, but for now, I'll go back to working on a tramp."

"A what?"

"A tramp-boat. Come on, I'll show you."

Wren led the way down a narrow ramplike road that came out by a string of long low sheds, which lined the water's edge. Inside one of them, we stood on a platform overlooking a number of curious little boats. The near ones were about forty-five feet long, the farther ones about thirty. They were shaped much like the long shallow serving trays I had seen at the brass-beaters' shops in New Chalice's Smith's Quarter. Each boat rested on a heavy wooden carriage riding on wooden rails, which sloped down into the water. As we descended the stairs, our footfalls echoed noisily in the cavernous frame building, and our voices bounced mockingly off the split-shake roof.

"Our stead and a few others are in the boat business," Wren explained as we picked our way over each set of rails in turn. "We build them to sell, and we also operate them. These larger ones are called line traders. Most are sold outright to large enterprises. This one here is leased by a furniture manufacturer. Like the others, it's in here for new caulking and paint. The other one is co-owned by a brickyard and a shingle mill. They are at opposite ends of the valley—it goes out with bricks and comes back with shingles. Line traders typically carry a single cargo, from point to point, as they fill orders. Very efficient, very profitable, very boring."

We moved a few feet farther to where a couple of smaller boats sat in the process of being refitted.

"Now these," and his hushed voice assumed a tone of near-reverence. "These are tramp-traders. They don't carry anywhere near as much as the liners, but they're designed to float in a minimum of water. They can maneuver in the tightest canals and get into places where nothing else can."

"And what do they carry?"

"Anything and everything. A little of this and that. And they don't have a fixed itinerary but go wherever there's a chance of trading. That's why they're called tramps. And believe me, these are the wave of the future. Most of the new canals being built nowadays are smaller shallow links to remoter areas, which until now have had only overland transport. Because of recent interpretations of the Cutoff Laws, the emphasis is on more small-scale infrastructure, and these boats are tailor-made for that."

"So you'll make a lot more profit from them, eh?"

"We can make a profit from either kind of boat, but these will be of growing use to the nation, I'm expecting, and of course, that will bring us greater honour. Quite literally, these pick up where the liners leave off. A lot of people in our banner work on these. I was on the *Dawn-Greeter* with my older brother for two years before signing on with the *Minkey*."

"And you'll be going back with him this year?"

Wren gave a conspiratorial wink and gestured for me to follow. At the very end of the shed, hidden by all the other craft, sat a smaller-yet version of the wide-bottomed boats. It was obviously brand new, still smelling of planed larch and tarred caulking. The glistening yellow paint was tacky. Over the wide-angled bow a splashboard was fresh lettered with the words *Come-What-May*.

"Isn't she a beauty?" Wren murmured, and he began ticking off her virtues as he might a beautiful woman. "Absolutely state-of-the-art hull design. Minimal thickness. Highest ratio of capacity-to-displacement."

"What does all that mean?"

"Mean? Why, it means she can float on a damp sponge while carrying two and a half tons of cargo. And with only six feet five inches of beam, it means she can squeeze up a lot of the stead canals which are only built for bantam-scows. Yaro, this is the cutting edge of boatbuilding technology."

"I get the feeling that's not the only reason for your excitement. Is this the boat you're going to be working on?"

"More than that. I've been assigned as steward."

I realized that although Wren was trying to appear modest, he was inwardly bursting with pride. And no wonder; to be put in charge of an experimental craft like this after only two years experience must mean a great deal.

"That's quite an honour, Wren. You must have acquitted yourself very well on the *Dawn-Greeter*."

"I guess they were satisfied. But this will take more skill. To make the most of its special advantages will require a wholly different strategy, different routes, creative cargo management. I only hope I'm up to it."

"I'm sure you will be. You've obviously been giving it a lot of thought. You must be really looking forward to it."

"I guess I am too. And what about you?"

"What do you mean, what about me?"

"I mean, will you join me?"

"Join you . . . on the . . . are you serious?"

"Never more so. As boat steward, I get to select my crew. It takes two, usually three, to handle one of these. My cousin should be available to join us, but most of the guys around here are already booked on other boats. I know you've been wanting to see more of the country. Believe me, there's no better way."

"Yes, yes, I know. But . . . of course, I'll go with you."

"Well, you must ask your steadfolk first."

"Whatever for?"

"They're your stead, Yaro, until you find another one. You may need to return there in the winter. After all, we won't be on the water all year round."

"Yes, of course, that's not how I meant it. I mean, why should they object, since they need me out of there anyway?"

"I doubt very much they will object, especially since you would be earning them a lot of income, more than if you were there. But remember: never sever your connexion with a stead until you've established a new one. For now, it is Stonesthrow that certifies your right to be in the country. If you are sick or in trouble, they are the ones who will help you."

"Yes, certainly. I know you are right. So assuming they agree, when do we leave?"

"On the twentieth day of the Fourth Moon, in the third week of spring. That's a full week before the others usually leave, but I want to get into the upper streams as soon as the ice is out. In every valley where we are the first to arrive, we'll make the best deals. I predict we'll make as much in that first week as in the next month, if we can just get through. The *Come-What-May* will help us do that."

I can hardly describe the elation I felt at the prospect of traveling around the country while gainfully employed. Wren explained that instead of wages, I would be paid a share of the profits, mostly in barter goods, so that Stonesthrow became, in effect, a partner in the venture. A minor partner, of course, since Pierstead provided the boat and two thirds of the crew. On the other hand, we would emphasize Alga's products in the cargo, further enhancing Stonesthrow's profits.

I realized that none of my wages, whatever form they took, would belong to me personally, but by now I had come to accept that completely. I understood and appreciated the value of what I was receiving instead. Not only security, but that feeling of which Myrica had spoken, of being an esteemed contributor to the household. Furthermore, it also occurred to me that whenever I came to seek membership at the stead of my choosing, it couldn't hurt that I had already proven myself a valuable steadmate elsewhere.

*　　*　　*　　*　　*　　*　　*

The very next morning I thought to ask Hewn about the enigmatic forest I had passed. I could have asked Wren or the signal crew or anyone else, but I had a feeling I would get a more thorough explanation from the old ambassador.

"Oh yes. You must have passed the Beacon Hills Forest. It's a small unit of the Sacred Groves."

"Small, my word, it must be thousands of acres!"

"Tens of thousands, but that's pretty small compared to the main block up north of the Sanctuary Mountains."

"But it looked so wild and . . . and daunting."

"It's not necessarily meant to look daunting, but wild, yes—that's the idea."

"Yet the woods around it all looked so kempt and orderly."

"Whose notion of orderly? Our notion, Yaro, based on human priorities. The Sacred Groves are based on other priorities: their own. They have a perfect orderliness which serves the needs of many others."

"Like whom?"

"Everything that's there: deer and salamanders and ferns and skunks and worms and mushrooms. They're all nurtured by that old-forest habitat."

"Great, but what about people? There's an incredible amount of dead wood lying around, rotting, which you could use here."

"What about people, you ask? Well, take a look at this map, Yaro, and see all the areas that are *not* crosshatched. These lands are *all* about people. We've modified our habitat greatly, to suit our own needs, but while we've strived to maintain balance and diversity, it is decidedly *not* natural. It is too . . . how did you say? . . . 'kempt.'"

"I guess I see what you mean. Still, I don't see why people couldn't take away some of those trees that are already dead. Would that upset the whole thing?"

"Probably not. After all, the size of that tract is not based on some mystical number—we could even clear a few more acres for cropland without devastating the whole preserve. But just where would you stop? We have to draw a stark line somewhere, however arbitrarily, and stick with it."

"So are people allowed to enter the Sacred Groves?"

"Most certainly. But just as that wall marks the exact limits of the preserve, so there are strict rules regarding what you may do there. For example, don't you ever, under any circumstances, try to kindle a campfire there—never mind that they are periodically swept by lightning-struck fires."

"And what else?"

"If you are in the Groves and you come across some berries or nuts or something, feel free to stuff your face. But don't even think of putting a single one in a basket to take home. Let's see: no wheeled vehicles, not even a wheelbarrow. No cutting trees or peeling bark, of course. There are others I can't remember offhand, but you mustn't enter the Sacred Groves without first learning the rules. They are some of the strongest taboos in our society."

Chapter 27

Cracks began to show in winter's stony face. Everything still froze solid at night, but there were days when one hardly needed a coat to work outdoors. As the lengthening daylight hours began to stir the trees to life, some people on the island set about tapping the sugar maples, but my mind was on more than boiling down syrup. Every morning, I watched the floating masses of ice drifting in the bay, and I knew that they heralded the beginning of spring breakup on the Bluemeadow. Other rivers would soon open, and it would be time for the *Come-What-May* to set off on her wanderings, and me with her.

As the longed-for day approached, my eagerness became almost insufferable, for myself and others too, I'm afraid. At Hewn's suggestion, I spent less time at the stone yard, and more time on my lessons. I did my best to concentrate on math and science, but I was easily distracted. I continued to make good progress in Mok—no one had to remind me how useful that would be. But mostly I liked to stare at the map on the meeting room wall. I had already committed much of it to memory, yet my eyes struggled to pry behind the lines and dots, to see the actual places themselves.

Only a week before our scheduled departure, a glitch threatened to delay the whole venture. A message arrived from Wren, saying his cousin had injured his wrist in a boatyard mishap and wouldn't be able to join us, at least for several weeks. All the other boatmen he knew were already engaged by then. Wren thought it unlikely that two of us could manage *Come-What-May* by ourselves.

I had hardly finished reading the letter before I was hurrying upstairs to the broom-shop. I entered to find Marten and Alaria, trimming square the straw on a batch of recently made push brooms. I got right to the point.

"Marten, you know that trade survey you were considering volunteering for this year?"

"Yeah, I was toying with the idea, but I haven't thought much more about it."

"Well, start thinking."

"Why, what's up?"

"The boat I told you about, the *Come-What-May*. It's leaving the first of next week, with Wren and me and one more. Are you coming?"

"Me?! On a tramp-trader? You're kidding. I'm not cut out for that kind of stuff."

"And why not? You're hardworking and rugged enough. You're just not adventuresome, but that can change."

"I don't know, that's a pretty unsettled sort of life. Still, I do see what you're getting at. A more perfect opportunity for collecting commercial data would be hard to imagine. The tramps go everywhere and deal in everything."

"Yes, and you'd be threshing two sheaves with one flail. While compiling your lists, you'd be earning income for Stonesthrow and honour for yourself."

"I have to admit, it's an interesting proposition. But that's awfully short notice—only a few days. I promised Alaria I'd help out here this week, to finish these brooms before the fairs start up. And I still haven't submitted the fuel-consumption tables for Alga yet."

"I'll tell you what: you go work on your numbers, and I'll take your place here. I've gotten behind in my math and science, but you could help me with those as we travel."

"I suppose so. But I'll have to get the household's permission first. I think everyone will agree. I wonder if Burnet will take back the hive stewardship for a few months."

"Stead meeting is tonight. We can bring it all up then. Meanwhile, I'll check with Wren, but hopefully he'll go for it."

*　　*　　*　　*　　*　　*　　*

The new week broke warm and lowery. An occasional spitting of rain helped to dissolve the shrouds of cold fog that rose off the crumbling snowbanks. It was barely light as we stood on the pier at Carillons, helping Wren load cargo onto *Come-What-May*. He had single-handedly brought the empty boat down from Longlogan a few days earlier, and already several hundred pounds of crockery, glass, and imported figs were loaded on. Also on the pier was the tarp-covered pile of goods from Alga, which Elan and I had brought over during the week. It had taken two trips on the *River Harp*, but at last we had gathered an assortment of island goods, which we hoped would be in demand inland. Wren approved of our selection: salt, bay wax, rainwear, brooms and brushes, rose hip purée, sea vegetables, matches, gelatin, iodine and other chemicals, candles, and grindstones. Wren complained that the grindstones had an unfavourable weight-to-value ratio, but hastily added that the same could be said of his crockery; and whereas good crockery could be gotten anywhere, our Alga burrstones were famous for their fine-grained toughness. We also brought along a consignment of pump-washers and canning-jar rings plus assorted books from Telling.

Since I had last seen *Come-What-May* on the ways at Pierstead, its builders had added some finishing touches. A bright red stripe circled the hull just below the gunnels. A "dingle," or canopy, had been added in the middle, consisting of a few bent hoops with a waterproof mat stretched across. Like other tramp-boats, there was a public service notice printed on the canopy, designed to be read by people on the banks or bridges. Our canopy read, "Have you flossed today?" The dingle was meant for sleeping quarters, but the three of us could barely lie comfortably in it, even if it were not crammed with merchandise. Forward of that was a set of weatherproof lockers with assorted drawers and compartments for miscellaneous items. The central canopy had rolled up canvas extensions, which could be stretched fore and aft to protect our wares in heavy rain, though of course we couldn't operate the boat with it in place. There was no deck as such; we stood on a reinforcing slat-grid on the inside of the hull with cargo arranged upon pallets.

Somehow the boat looked even smaller as it floated precariously low in the slush-littered water. We stowed the cargo with careful attention to balancing the weight. Wren had a great knack for consolidating stuff: larger crocks had smaller crocks nested inside, and the smaller crocks filled with sacks of salt or boxes of matches. Wren said we would soon diversify our merchandise, though it seemed to me we had quite an assortment already. Eventually, we had everything arranged to Wren's satisfaction, and we pushed off.

A tramp-boat uses neither sail nor oars as a regular thing. It is normally propelled by poling, but the lower Bluemeadow at flood stage is too deep for that, so we used a "thruster," one of those bellowslike devices such as are used to drive the ferries. Ours was simply an attachment, one of several devices which could be fastened onto the versatile twelve-foot poles. This was mounted in a single oarlock near the stern and pushed and pulled manually. It was a slow business just crossing the Bluemeadow, and there was a constant risk of damaging the thruster on half-submerged chunks of ice. Near the west bank, we were able to proceed upriver using both poles and the thruster. It was a struggle to make headway in the strong current. After Longlogan, it became much harder yet as the tide no longer favoured us. We continued to hug the shore, not only so our poles could reach bottom, but also because the current was weakest there. Indeed there was a slight counter-eddy, which helped a bit; but for the same reason, that zone was choked with broken ice washing down from the upper valleys. This threatened at times to stave in the boat's light hull, but we had another weapon against that. Each pole had a threaded brass fitting on the end, and to the two poles which were not equipped with a thruster, we attached a forged piece which had both pike-point and hook. With this tool, we could fend off ice or other flotsam which might be a menace.

It was grueling work with nary a break, lest the boat be swept back and we lose what we had gained. Once in a while, we'd lodge the stern against some projection on the bank and hold it there with the poles while we caught a moment's rest, but mostly we just toiled upriver, slowly gaining on the current. Our arms and shoulders were exhausted, and Marten and I began to wonder if we had signed on for too much. Wren assured us that it was only because he had insisted on rushing the season, and it would be much easier once we reached the smaller streams that were *Come-What-May*'s true element.

After a long morning of struggle, we finally nosed the *Come-What-May* up to the floating wharf at Bluemeadow Fair, which was just opening for the season. The fairgrounds were still muddy and slushy in places, and Wren said it was not in full swing yet, although it seemed pretty busy to me. The booths and tables had been open since early morning, but we were not there for the market itself. We merely had an errand to run. A shipper from Fairhaven needed a case of window glass delivered to a trader at the fair. It was Tramontese glass from the same shipment we had brought in on the *Minkey* last fall. The glass was preordered and had been sitting in a warehouse at Fairhaven all winter, waiting for the ice to break up. There was no bargaining to bother about, just a simple delivery.

At the floating dock, I noticed a tram or railway, which carried traders' wares up the steep slippery bank to the fairgrounds; when you pulled a clutch lever, it actuated a cable pulley, which was driven by a waterwheel at the riverside.

"This should only take a few minutes, but we might as well enjoy a hot meal while we are here. Why don't you guys go over to the caterers and I'll join you there later?"

As we headed toward the covered food tables, Marten said, "I have to relieve myself. You go ahead, Yaro, and I'll meet you."

Lines of fairgoers were already forming at the various tables. I had a pocketful of small change for such expenses: a hodgepodge of Anagaian bullheads, Borealian quarters, and Coquinese palms, but not a single Esperian piece. I had already learned that any foreign currency would be readily accepted, so I approached the caterers' pavilion with confidence. It was impressive, this buffet of various hot dishes, tastefully arranged on long plank tables. I could not recognize half the things I saw there, but they looked and smelled delicious. What was not at all clear to me was how much the various items cost; none were marked. Barely noticeable beside each serving dish was a small scrap of reed-matting with a few Anagaian bullheads. They lay there as if forgotten, with no care lest they be stolen. There were few people tending the table, only a couple of older men washing dishes in a large steaming tub and a younger woman who stood behind the table, holding a wooden plate as if to serve me. I pointed to a large casserole and asked, "That looks good; what's in it?"

"That's Runaground stew with barley dumplings. It has sauerkraut with red beans and tomatoes. It's a bit peppery, if you like that sort of thing."

"And how much does it cost?"

For an instant the woman looked flustered, as though I had asked her a deeply private secret. Then she smiled, rather wanly it seemed, and replied, "It doesn't cost anything. It's free."

"Really?! But what about all these other things?"

"They're also free. Everything here is free."

"How marvellous!" I exclaimed. Wren must have misunderstood when he handed me lunch money. With no pecuniary restraints to my appetite, I proceeded down the table, asking for a portion of everything that looked good to me, and indeed almost everything did. The serving woman, who at first seemed nervous, now seemed to repress a giggle as she piled my plate higher. Handing it to me at the end, she offered, "I hope you enjoy it all. Now don't waste any, and let me know if you want seconds."

I was just walking away with my feast in hand when Marten appeared at my side.

"Well, I see you've already got quite a platter full. I'll grab something and be right with you. You've already paid for yours, I guess."

"No, it's all free here. I asked her and she said 'no charge.' Really."

"Of course, we have to pay. Let me see what you took."

"No no, I mean it. She said 'no charge.'"

"Of course she said 'no charge'—what did you expect? You go ahead, I'll just add it on to mine."

But I couldn't go ahead; I was too confused and embarrassed. I watched as Marten went down the table, requesting a few items. At the end, he did some mental calculating and dropped an assortment of foreign coins into a wooden bowl with others, along with a small bag of salt. The woman smiled at him, bade him a good nooning as she had me. As we walked over to the covered eating tables, I couldn't help grumbling; I felt almost humiliated. "Why wouldn't she accept payment from me? Does she think I'm some beggar?"

"She didn't refuse payment. You apparently made the mistake of asking the price."

"Why was that a mistake? How else was I supposed to know?"

"Sit down and I'll explain. Here's a spoon—you forgot to pick one up. You see, we have a law here, or a custom, or whatever you want to call it. No one may deny anyone else a meal, or a night's lodging either. It's just something one doesn't charge for. But then there are situations like this: the banner of Bluemeadow sponsors the fair, and they charge fees for the stalls and the tram and other services. Except meals—they may not properly charge for that. Yet we don't want them to do it for nothing—they couldn't continue it. So we give them 'gifts' of a suggested amount—those coins tell us what their costs are, not what they demand. We can pay more if we want to or less if we have to, but we know that if we want them to keep doing it, we need to make it worth their while."

"But what if some people cheat them?"

"They would only bring dishonour on themselves, and no Steward would want that. It more often happens the other way: when someone particularly enjoys a dish, they put in extra even though it's not expected. I admit it's sort of a charade, but it works perfectly well for us—it's only outsiders who have trouble with it."

I winced at that word. I was trying so hard to become an insider, yet it was so difficult sometimes. At least I now understood one more rule of the game. I also understood why my steadmates never traveled anywhere without carrying small gifts. No one would ever ask for them, even from total strangers, yet to neglect them when one was able would be considered poor etiquette.

*   *   *   *   *   *   *

I would have liked nothing better than to see more of the Bluemeadow Fair. From our table, I could see the hubbub of buying and bartering all over the broad and level fairgrounds, but Wren was determined that we should hurry along.

The weather was fickle, offering frequent promises of clearing then socking us back in with a cold drizzle. Even when it was clear, thin sheets of fog continued to cling to the river's surface, veiling the grinding blocks of ice which spawned them.

In our zeal to crowd on cargo, we had left ourselves little freeboard above the racing current. *Come-What-May* was certainly a state-of-the-art craft, but her strength was in shallow water with lighter loads, and Wren acknowledged he had to adjust his thinking. Marten nearly panicked when he noticed the water lapping above the red line on our hull, and I tried to stifle my own nervousness. Things improved somewhat when we stopped at Witty Moor's where we made our first deal: two hundred pounds of caustic soda to a paper mill. Even though our pay included a few cases of writing paper, it was a net loss in weight. Then at Ironwood, we rented a compartment in a depot where we left over half of our salt and several other heavy items to be reloaded later. After that, we rode noticeably higher in the water.

In some places where the current was unmanageably swift, one would find a tram-cable powered by waterwheels mounted on the bank or on artificial islands in midstream. These wheels turned slowly but inexorably as the river surged past their buckets. We would hook onto the lower end of the looped cable and let ourselves be towed upstream by the power of the very current that was opposing us. As we neared the next island and its pulley, we could snap a second leadline onto the new section of cable before the slack was lost. One had to be quick about it though because the pulley had a derailing shoe, a mechanical device which automatically unhitched us before our leadline could get tangled in the pulley. If we were derailed before rehooking the bypass line, we would find ourselves being swept downstream, stern first, trying to grab the cable again. It did save a lot of back strain, though, since the only work we had to do was keeping the boat headed right and being ready for transfers.

The "blue meadows" from which the entire valley takes its name were only found in the lower sections of the river, where the silver-blue clay coated the salt grass at high tide. Farther upstream, we found ourselves between high banks of gravel, which sloped down steeply to the water's edge. They looked as though they might slide down on us, were it not for the dense willows and other vegetation, which anchored the gravel in place.

After leaving Ironwood, we entered the mouth of the Broadlea River, turning our bow westward into a stretch of water that seemed wilder and rougher than anything yet. I think it only seemed that way because the day was late and our unconditioned muscles were rebelling. At least there was little floating ice to contend with, and the bottom was shallower, meaning that the rushing water was less wont to snatch our poles from our grips. It was our usual suppertime, but Wren insisted we must not rest yet.

"Once we get into Trice Canal, we can take it easier," he promised. "I want to get there while the lock-keeper is on duty. If we're going to be in Broadlea when the fair starts, we should be at least as far as Echo Brook by tomorrow night, and we'll need to make a few stops on the way."

"What's so important about the fair?" asked Marten. "I thought you said our specialty was getting to hard-to-reach places."

"So it will be. But we need to diversify our cargo more before getting to them."

After a mile or so of struggling upstream like a broody salmon, we saw an appalling sight before us. Between the high gravel banks, a long and formidable rapids plunged headlong toward us, stumbling between gigantic boulders that churned the melt-swollen freshet into angry froth. It was clear we weren't going to fight our way up through that, but we poled over to the bank on our left where we saw what looked like a brook entrance. It emerged from a sort of artificial canyon walled by great stone slabs. I had never seen such a place, and I felt nervous as two massive wooden gates began to close behind us, blocking off our return in that direction.

"Don't worry," Wren assured me, noticing my agitation. "It's only a lock. The lock-keeper is about to bring us up."

"Bring us up where?"

"You'll see. Watch."

Watch I did as a jet of water began to spurt in from a large pipe in the stone wall, just above the waterline. There was a second closed gate in front of us, and we were now floating there between them like a cork in a washtub. As the water rushed in, drowning its own entrance, we floated ever higher until both gates were nearly underwater, and we were now at least ten feet higher than when we began. On the bank we could see the lock-keeper turning a shutoff valve to close the great pipe, then he began pushing against the small end of a forty-foot-long spruce beam, whose other end was part of the upper lock gate. No longer pinned by the force of unequal water levels, the gate very slowly opened its heavy-timbered door upstream. This allowed us to exit easily into a long narrow body of water, almost without current. It was, I soon learned, the Trice Canal, a man-made channel nearly two miles long that gouged its way straight across the valley floor, skirting Trice Rips and its dangerous rocks. It seemed a bit absurd to have all that shuffling of wood and water just for one tiny boat, but Wren informed me that at most times, we would have had to crowd in with several other boats, who would be raised up at the same time.

Now that we were safely in the Canal, Wren was more relaxed. We tied up to a willow that overhung the water and crawled into the tiny hovel to change into dry clothes. It had drizzled off and on all day, and we were pretty well soaked. It wouldn't be easy to find dry cooking wood even if we had wanted to wait that long. Still I wasn't looking forward to a cold meal, but Wren had already solved that problem in a simple yet elegant way. From the storage compartment under our beds, he pulled a box wrapped in blankets. It held a large crock packed in dry shavings. The savoury runner bean stew inside was only slightly cooler than when he had packed it in there that morning. We made short work of it as well as the fresh bread, which our own steadmates had thoughtfully put in for us. Although it was barely dark when we finished, Marten and I could think of nothing more pleasing than slipping under our covers—I can hardly call it a bed—and dropping off. Wren, amazingly, had a bit of restless energy left, and he reached into the shallow locker space under our bedding and pulled out his dulcitar. I had heard him play it aboard *Minkey,* and I knew we were in for a treat. As he plucked away at a bittersweet love song, Marten and I drifted off into a deep and well-earned slumber.

Chapter 28

Morning dawned chilly, but at least it wasn't raining. A damp breeze kept the wrung-out clouds tumbling ahead of it, opening up scattered rifts which gradually organized themselves into larger swatches of blue. Wren was already up and on the bank. He was crouched over a tiny bronze grill, roasting hoecakes and tempeh steaks over some charcoal he had bought from the lock-keeper. After rolling up my bedding and washing up in a basin, I went ashore. Wren didn't need my help, so I walked over to view the rapids from above. Marten was already standing there, hypnotized by the sweeping torrent. It was so savagely powerful. Of course, the lock behind us was also powerful, but in a gentler way. After all, it had lifted us almost daintily past the thundering waters that would have pounded us into splinters. Shaking my head in wonder, I shouted over the din, "That thing over there wasn't built in a year, I'll bet!"

"Certainly not," agreed Marten. "This one is very old—I'm not sure when it was built—but there is a similar one, the Sundew Canal, being built right now. It's due for completion this fall, but it has been under construction for the past six years."

"Incredible! It must have cost many fortunes."

"No doubt. But it will make many more."

For some reason, his remarks reminded me of a passing comment Ermine had once made. "When you dwell in the Larger House, you can afford such things."

When we left the Canal for the stream, we again had to work harder. Nevertheless, it was much easier than the mighty Bluemeadow, and we encountered less ice. No longer hemmed in by high gravel banks, we now had frequent views of the broad silty floodplain around us. The shore was dense with willows, most of which were not wild but cultivated for the making of baskets, woven trays, and other such things. Nor were they all one kind; the barks were of different colours and textures, and the flower buds ranged from grey to pink, giving the banks the appearance of a twiggy bouquet. Here we saw occasional flocks of mallards and ruddy ducks. They were the advance wave of migrating birds which were just pushing their way into the winter-rid valley.

Wren rejoiced that we encountered only one other tramp-boat in this section. Tramps pride themselves on being the first afloat each season, just as some gardeners gloat over their early sweet corn or tomatoes. There were some local craft on the water—tiny affairs called bantam-scows—taking advantage of the high water to move cumbersome goods from one stead to another. But we appeared to be the first "outsiders" into the valley.

There was so much to see here, and Wren was the perfect person to see it with. In his two seasons on his brother's boat, the *Dawn-Greeter*, he had learned the lay of the land as well as he knew his workbench back at the boatyard. Every tiny brook was a familiar landmark to him, each weir an old acquaintance. During long winter days of caulking hulls and planing strakes, he and his fellow trampers would talk about the places they had been the previous season. They would exchange information on currents and shallow bars, clearances of bridges, and widths of canals. Where was there always a good demand for hemp rope? And who made the best wheelbarrows? Who was the person to see at that factory, and when were the best weeks to visit that fair with salt? There was actually a guide to help tramps and other tradesfolk. It was called the Nine Fairs Production Inventory, and it listed every stead in every banner in every fair in the region, along with the items they produced for trade. Detailed as it was, no one depended on that alone. After all, it gave no indication of what goods those places were likely to *want*. One simply had to guess at that based on experience and intuition, and of course, it was always changing. Wren had a good nose for such things, there was no denying it.

We made one brief stop during the morning to barter salt and two of the large crocks we had brought from Carillons. It was a small sauerkraut "factory." I use the word loosely, because the *factory* consisted of a single large room in the wing of a steadhouse, very much like the rainwear *factory* at Stonesthrow. Their specialty was a tangy concoction of salted mustard-cabbage, garlic, and hot peppers, which I got to taste. I've since learned to relish it, but my first reaction was tentative at best.

That stead, like so many others in the Calamus area, also made willow baskets. We admired a local design known in the trade as Calamus Split-Rim. It is a wide laundry hamper, and we took several of those in partial payment for the crocks and salt. The value was not equal, and I noticed the woman in charge gave Wren some round metal disks that looked like very large coins. I asked him about it later.

"What country are those from?"

"Right here."

"But I thought Esperia didn't mint coins."

"These aren't coins—they are ingots. These shiny ones are tin, these three are manganese, and this little one is silver."

"It's silver and it's coin shaped. So what's the difference between that and a coin?"

"This is just raw metal. It's made by a private smelter, in no way guaranteed by the government. Its value is totally floating, like any other commodity. There are several items we tend to use like currency here, things like maple sugar, beeswax, salt, lye, essential oils or spices—anything that is convenient to carry and store, and easy to convert. The ingots are like that—at any point, they're likely to be made into something else. For example, if this silver ever goes abroad, it will probably become coins or jewelry. In this country, it is more likely to be turned into conductor plates, but in the meantime, it's handy for making trades even. You'll notice the only thing stamped on that is the symbol for silver and the exact weight. It is worth whatever someone will give us, no more and no less."

"So the government doesn't even try to standardize its value?"

"Nope. The government does some things to regulate the economy, but not in that way. They issue recommendations, which are designed to help us fulfill our Vision. Since it is our Vision, everyone is usually eager to follow their guidance, but as to details like what something is worth, they leave us to hash that out on our own."

"We know our society looks bizarre to others," Marten inserted. "We've been called communists, socialists, laissez-faire capitalists, atheists, and religious fanatics, and in some way or other, they are all true. And just by the way, let me correct something Wren said before. Technically, it's true that Esperia does not mint Esperian money, but we do mint coins for Anagaia."

I just stared with my mouth open, so Wren explained. "That's right. Anagaia mints their own copper bullheads, but every silver falcon and every gold sceptre in circulation since 423 was minted at a banner up in the Tarnish Hills."

"That's hard to imagine," I demurred. "The Onyx Palace is always raging about how perverse and sinister the Stewards are. Surely they would never trust such a sensitive job to foreigners, let alone Esperians."

"Nevertheless, they do," insisted Marten. "For generations, they had been sending loads of gold and silver bullion to a little foundry complex in Painted Post and getting back finished coins which exceed their specifications. Despite whatever propaganda they may feed their own citizenry, the government of Blaze II apparently considers Esperians more trustworthy than any of its own people. They insist that all the dies be kept at Painted Post, and all bullion must be transported on Esperian ships with all Esperian crews. There was probably some onboard the *Minkey* with you." To which Wren nodded knowingly.

There were so many paradoxes about this country, so many absurdities; at times I had the feeling that the whole nation existed for the sole purpose of making a fool of me. These atheists claimed to base their actions, if not their beliefs, on something they themselves called the Holy Scriptures, a mythic text which other nations consider "God-given." Their government did not force people to pay taxes, but only told them what they owed, and everyone then vied with each other to pay several times that. It was strictly forbidden to salute the national flag, or any other for that matter. The people did not use any titles of address, yet I never saw a more universal attitude of mutual respect. Of all those paradoxes, this one seemed the most preposterous: the nation claimed to be founded on a subsistence economy, with commerce playing a "peripheral" role, and that commerce based primarily on barter. Ever since my arrival, and especially since boarding *Come-What-May*, I had seen evidence of a huge surplus of goods, much of it sent to the regional fairs and even for foreign export. Did not the vast Anagaian League, which made no pretense of self-sufficiency, import most of its high-quality manufactured goods from tiny Esperia? And weren't they a major buyer or Anagaian cotton, at least before the boycott? Not a market economy? Were these people kidding themselves? I had questioned Wren narrowly about this, and he insisted that we tramps had a very distorted perspective, being smack in the middle of that "peripheral" commerce and thus unable to see the larger picture.

I remained no less skeptical the following morning when we pulled into the Broadlea landing, just as the fair was getting underway. It appeared much like the fair at Bluemeadow; there was a wide wharf where trading boats like ours tied up. A battery of handcarts, dollies, and wheelbarrows lined the wharf, rentable for a small fee, to move one's wares up to the market grounds. The bank was lower here, so there was no tram of the kind we saw at Bluemeadow. In this part of the Broadlea Valley, the river meandered so much it almost met itself coming and going. Those springbows (or oxbows, as they're called elsewhere) are sometimes cut off by a younger channel or a canal. The fair grounds were situated in such a loop so that it was essentially an island, a large level field only a few feet above the high water. I was told that Broadlea fair sometimes opened a week or two late because of flooding. Today was in fact the first fair of the season—as it had been at Bluemeadow—and although there were only a few boats at the landing, there were plenty of buyers. People had been busy all winter, building up inventories of their own products while using up the goods they needed for themselves. It was therefore a seller's market, for the time being. In the coming weeks, other boats would follow us with more of the same, at lower prices. Our customers realized this, and those who could were inclined to hold out. Nevertheless, we did a brisk trade. It was a great education for me to observe it all. Wren did all the bargaining, and I stood by and presented items which were wanted for examination. Frequently, I would run back to the boat to fetch out something we had not expected to offer there. Marten also observed. He was constantly writing down notes about selections, sources, prevailing prices, quantities offered—this place was a paradise for a Keeper of Numbers. He was especially interested in the reception of certain imported goods we had brought with us. For example, he noted that dried figs and apricots were widely popular, despite the high price; everyone bought some, but always small amounts. Our window glass was a total sellout, even at a high price, and we regretted leaving so much at the Ironwood Depot. No one was holding back, realizing that the commodity might become dearer rather than cheaper as relations with the Empire deteriorated. We sold small amounts of salt and crockery; no one wanted our cast-iron pots. Dulse from the coast was in great demand, and we sold a lot of whisk brooms and scrub brushes, although locally made ones were also being offered.

Wren was a relative newcomer to this trading business, but he was no amateur. He had learned much from his previous stints on the river, while his year on the *Minkey* had broadened his familiarity with foreign imports. And there was so much to learn. It seemed like every deal was an incredibly intricate affair, requiring an up-to-date knowledge of the value of hundreds of different products. Moreover, the emphasis on barter created its own complications. Often one could not close a deal because of uneven exchanges or because of the need to swap goods for which the trade partner had no use. In some cases, we resorted to all sorts of complex arrangements, often involving third or fourth parties, in order to strike a deal that was satisfactory all around.

Bartering did not imply that values were vague. On the contrary, everyone knew precisely what an item was worth, at least to them, and they dickered hard to get that. Although no one would ever intentionally cheat you, everyone had to assume that you know what your stuff was worth.

Wren had a good instinct for what external factors might lean trading more to our advantage. For Stonesthrow's contribution to our initial cargo, he had suggested we emphasize waterproof clothing; these were a sure sell in the showery weeks ahead. Yet his judgment wasn't always perfect: we had loaded on far too many candles. He assumed, reasonably, that people were out of them after the long dark winter, but he neglected to consider that they would not be eager to stock up again until fall.

Rather than haul around eight cases of hard-to-sell candles when the space might be better used, we left most of them in a depot, or warehouse locker, near the Broadlea landing. Every fair banner, and many other riverine banners, had such small storehouses where traders could cache merchandise that might be wanted later. This storehouse, like the one at Ironwood, was a twelve-by-eighteen-foot frame building set up on wooden posts with flared metal collars to deter rodents. Our own compartment was nearly empty, we being the first to arrive that season. There were a few cases of miscellaneous goods stacked in one corner where Wren's brother had left them the previous fall. Since we were all partners in one venture—the *Come-What-May*, the *Dawn-Greeter*, and the *Dew-Treader*—we looked the stuff over and took what goods we thought we could trade to advantage, taking care to leave a tally sheet on the wall, itemizing what we had taken. I was puzzled.

"Who has the other two compartments?"

"I have no idea."

"You mean they might be total strangers?"

"Of course. Why?"

"Well, what's to stop them from taking our stuff?"

"That partition. It clearly separates their stuff from ours."

"Separates maybe, but there is no lock or anything. Nothing to stop them, or anyone else in the world, from barging in here and helping themselves."

"But there is that partition," Marten persisted. "How could they not know it's ours?"

He seemed to assume I was missing Wren's point while I assumed they were both missing mine.

"Sure, they'd know it, but they wouldn't care."

"I see what Yaro means," Wren interpreted. "You see, Marten, it's just not like this in Anagaia. We used to have to post a guard day and night, or people would steal stuff right off the ship."

Marten stared at Wren with incredulity. "But aren't they afraid of dishonouring themselves?"

"No, that's just it, you see. It's all different there."

Marten gave a shake of his head that began with disgust and ended with pity. Obviously, he wasn't used to dealing with people who dwelt in "the Smaller House."

Chapter 29

"How long will it take to fill? It seems like forever!"

"Nonsense. This lock only takes nine minutes in midsummer. It should take even less now."

"Sure, and once we get through this one, we'll have to pole like mad for a quarter mile, only to wait in another lock."

"What are you griping about, Yaro? Look at all the rest you're getting. What's easier than lying here, waiting for a lock to fill?"

"I don't care so much what's easier. I didn't come on this trip for a rest. I want to see the country, and this is so slow."

"I sure don't mind the rest spells," commented Marten, who had been scribbling in his notebooks. "It gives me a chance to organize all my data from yesterday. But what I don't understand, Wren, is why we didn't stop to trade at any of those places we passed. We came right through Seven Oaks and Winterford."

"When you were taking notes yesterday at Broadlea, did you notice anything about the goods?"

"Only that there was an unthinkable variety of them."

"Not really. If you looked into where they came from, as I did, you'd find that most of them originate in the central valley, within fifteen miles of the fair."

"So what does that mean?"

"I think it is because many of the upland areas are still icebound. Those few traders selling wares from the uplands mostly had smaller items, stuff they could carry on their backs or handcarts. Goods from farther downstream were well represented at the fair because anyone can get to them now. The *Serendepity* will probably be along here in a few days, and with their greater capacity, we needn't compete with them. We must find our niche, which is in shallower water. Okay, guys, the ball is up. Let's go push."

Like the vast majority of small locks which dot the countryside, this one was unmanned; we ourselves had to open the lock gate by means of a very long beam which we slowly pushed backward. On the fulcrum-post, a tacked-up notice made me smile. "According to the Pits-and-Parapets Laws, it is forbidden to open the lock gate until the float ball in the indicator tube shows that pressure is equal." In the margin, someone had scribbled the same thought I was thinking, "Who would be silly enough to try?"

"Where did you say that sewing machine is to be delivered?" Marten asked.

"To Phoebe. The bannerhouse, he said, or as near as we can get."

"Is the bannerhouse at Phoebe Landing?"

"There *is* no Phoebe Landing. Flute Brook is supposedly unnavigable at that point, at least by tramps. It is partially canalized, but only for local bantam-scows."

"Those little things can fit in a washtub! How are *we* to get through?"

"Everyone is assuming we can't, but we'll just have to see for ourselves. There's plenty of water now, it's mostly a question of width. Anyway, we'll see what other business can be gotten on the way there. Otherwise I wouldn't have agreed to it."

I should explain that most waterways in Esperia are navigable by design, if not by nature. Any stream of consequence is "canalized," which means its channel is cleared of sandbars, rocks, or other obstacles. Wherever there are impassable rapids or falls, one finds either locks and canals around them or the cable system described earlier, called river trams. Some smaller brooks are literally staircases of water where one essentially goes from lock to lock, rising but a few feet with each step, usually accompanied by a fish-ladder. To say that they are "navigable" is not to say that larger boats may travel on them. Many of these "canals" are hardly more than ditches, less than eight feet wide with no more than a foot of water. They were dug to accommodate "bantam-scows." These crude home-built barges, about four feet wide and only eight or ten feet long, are the butt of trade-boatsmen's jokes, but their aggregate contribution to the national work must not be underestimated. In any case, the fact that a stead was accessible by bantam-scow was small encouragement to us.

Farther upstream, we came to another lock, this one higher than usual, in order to surmount a small waterfall. We obviously were going to have more than a few minutes to wait. Now it was Wren's turn to be impatient.

"Look, I've got an idea. Up on that rise, I can see two steads, close to each other. Can't be over a half-mile away. I'm just going to run up there and see if I can deal. You guys use your time doing some of that tutoring you're supposed to be doing. I'll be back soon."

"But you're not going to take any goods?"

"It's not worth it without any idea of what they'll want. I'll just take along the cargo list."

He must have run both ways and spent little time bargaining because he was back inside twenty minutes before the ball was up. We assumed he'd had no success.

"Plenty of luck," he corrected, panting. "To begin with, they want two of those small pickle crocks, twenty-five pounds of salt, four pounds of dulse, a four-ounce vial of coriander oil, a hundred-foot spool of hemp cable, and a three-inch thrust bearing for their windmill."

"Nice work! Where did you trade for?"

"A keg of pine tar, two wooden clocks—they have a clock factory at the second place—and ten pounds of dried blueberries. The rest they made up in combs and hairbrushes—beautiful lilac wood handles, wait till you see them!"

"What do you mean?" I interrupted. "Aren't we going right back to get the stuff?"

"Not enough time. The ball just came up. Anyway, there's no need. I told them I'd leave their stuff at the lock and someone will pick it up before dark. We'll pick up our stuff on the way back down tonight or tomorrow. I asked them to cover it with a tarp so the clocks will stay dry."

"But how could you?" I objected. "Someone might steal the stuff before they come or steal our stuff before we get back."

They both gave me sympathetic looks that made me feel very much like a foreigner.

"Never mind, I know. They would dishonour themselves."

*   *   *   *   *   *   *

As it turned out, we had plenty of trouble getting the *Come-What-May* all the way to Phoebe. At times, the banks practically scraped the gunnels, and in the shadier sections of water, we sometimes had to chop our way through leftover ice shelves, but at least there was depth and to spare. That might not be the case later in the summer, which was why no one had ever gotten a tramp-boat in that far before. In fact, the water was now so high that we could not get under one bridge without first loading in a bunch of large rocks from the river to make us ride lower in the water. But we had the satisfaction of seeing people's startled looks as the shallow-bottomed tramp pulled up behind their bannerhouse.

In the end, the sewing machine delivery was the very least of our business dealings in that place. The banner had numerous light industries, and much of their production was sent to the fair by handcart, at considerable expense of labour. Realizing what an opportunity we presented to reduce freight costs, they scrambled to make deals with us while the water was high and we were there. One of our best bargains, and theirs, was a lot of hardware from a threaded steel factory. We loaded a couple hundred pounds of bolts, nuts, C-clamps, vise-screws, and such, enough to make us scrape bottom at drier seasons. Needless to say, we dumped the river rocks.

Our business in Phoebe took us so much longer than expected that it was clear we would have to spend the night there. We were prepared to sleep onboard, but the steward of the bannerhouse insisted we be their guests. Several neighbours came over to share our visit, and there was an animated discussion of the possibilities which this new design of boat presented to their banner. Before we went to bed that night, our hosts were already hatching plans for modifying the canal.

"Why, if we're that close to having access," they argued, "it might be well worth widening it a foot or so and maybe even installing a lock and weir to deepen that last half-mile. Just think . . . tramp-boats right here!"

*   *   *   *   *   *   *

I have said relatively little so far about the *Come-What-May* itself. Since this curious boat was my principal home during an important and eventful period of my life, it would be well to give a more detailed description of it. The entire length of the hull was twenty-six feet, four and a half inches while the width was six feet five. The gunnel was parallel with the water all around, but at the bow and stern were splashboards to keep rough water from breaking over the side. The boat seemed awfully fragile for the loads it was meant to carry. Sheathed in two layers of seasoned larch strips and overwrapped with tarred linen canvas, the hull was nowhere over an inch thick. The framing was of strong light spruce, steam-bent into the proper curve. Even more important was the form of the hull, a broad shallow pan shape with nearly parallel sides and a rather blunt point at either end. Bow and stern were basically identical, a frequent advantage in tight canals where one cannot turn around but must pole long distances in reverse.

The *Come-What-May* could float in six inches of water when stripped down, which of course she never was. The actual draught depended completely on the weight of the cargo, but her ratio was more favourable than any other craft afloat at the time. There was a trade-off, nevertheless, and we were ever alert to the need to transload heavy or bulky goods as quickly as possible in preference to compact higher-value merchandise. Among the larger tramps tied up at the fairs or along the main rivers, we were barely noticed; but on the remoter brooks, *Come-What-May* attracted great attention just for being there. In fact it was so common to find no wharf at which to dock and load that we had to improvise a sort of lightweight gangplank for sliding goods onboard. Wren made a careful note of that, along with other modifications that might improve *Come-What-May*'s successors, already on the drawing boards back at Longlogan. We never lost track of the fact that we were a prototype, an effort to push back the parameters of design.

Chapter 30

"It'll be in one of those up there, on that top shelf. There, can you reach it? Don't knock down those other books!"

"Yes, yes, I've got it all right," I assured the old woman as I climbed back down the ladder with the desired volume in hand.

We laid the book on a round oak table in the corner and began thumbing through it. I was in the Winterford Public Library, which is in the bannerhouse, as they usually are. I had chosen this particular library only because it was the closest one at hand when I first got the idea.

"You say this fellow was almost like a father to you, but you haven't seen him for over eight years?"

"Yes, I was taken away. There was nothing we could do."

"Oh, I see. So you hope to write to him?"

"Well, certainly I would try that, but there is little chance of anything reaching him—you don't know the mail there. I just hope to find out where his family lives and perhaps learn something about how he is doing."

"Okay, now, let me see, let me . . . here is the index."

The librarian was an amicable but fussy old lady. Though I am of but moderate height, I overstood her by a head. I had hunted her down at the adjoining stead where she was busily tying pear limbs to an espalier on a high stone wall. When I explained my quest, she had dropped everything as though it were a serious emergency that she alone could tend to, though in fact, any number of people could have shown me the reference book I was needing.

"We're getting closer here. Now, Umberlands . . . let's see: hospital, hospital, hospital, factory, co-op, buyers co-op, school, school, demonstration farm, . . . there are quite a few projects there as you see . . . ah! Here we are . . . orphanages. There are only two in the territory, it seems, and one is the Mid-Umberlands facility in Cleftridge—that's what you wanted, wasn't it?"

"Yes, yes, indeed," I shook her arm with excitement. "That's the very one! So where is he from?"

176

"Patience, my man, patience. As the poet Shiningsea says, 'They make haste who . . .' Well, anyway, let's see who runs that one. Here it is: Laughingwater Foreign Aid Projects, and you'll need this too. Contact: Mallard of Greengate, Otterbank."

Thanking her profusely, I jotted down the information and scurried off to rejoin my crewmates at the landing. As I approached them, I saw another person talking with them on the pier. He walked away before I got there.

"Change of plans," Wren shrugged. "We're going back down to Cinderfield."

"But that's out of our way," I objected. "We were heading over to Bottle Pond."

"And we will yet. We just got a message from the Keepers of the Seed, requesting us to drop by there. Since we are planning to take the canal through to Plum Brook, we may not be back this way for a while."

I had no idea what a Keeper of the Seed was, but I had learned by now that Wren got annoyed by too many questions, so I decided to wait and see. I hadn't long to wait; we only backtracked a mile or so then turned up a small brook called Cobble Branch. At a low bridge, Marten jumped out and hailed a passing cyclist. Following her directions, we tied the boat and walked a half mile to the large stone building whose door sign proclaimed it to be the All-Fairs Phytogenetic Research Institute and Germplasm Repository. It all looked pretty formidable, so I was surprised when we met the director, an affable and jocular woman of middle years. Wren and Marten had only heard about the place, and of course it was totally new to me, so she gave us a brief tour. First, we were shown a deep cellar vault where rack upon rack of moisture-proof chests were stored at a near constant cool temperature. Each of these chests, she explained, held many hundreds of seed samples, representing the whole spectrum of crop species raised by Esperians and even many species which do not grow there. Many of the samples originally came from parts of the world with which Esperians no longer have contact or else those varieties may have become extinct in the place of their origin. The director, whose name was Dace, informed us that before and during the Calamitous Times, there were massive losses in crop genetic diversity, due to shortsighted agricultural policies. I expressed curiosity that they were preserving varieties of crops which Esperians did not even grow.

"Tepary beans, for example, why aren't those preserved in Anagaia?"

"How we wish they were! They could be field-grown there much more cheaply than we can grow them out under glass here. But the Anagaian government isn't interested, although we've offered to help support it. We do have branch facilities in Palmetto and the southern Prairie Federation. But we also maintain backup storage of those here because of the low temperature of our vaults and because of political instability in those countries."

"But why do you even concern yourselves with those crops, since they are not important to you?"

"Not *directly* important to us, but that's dwelling in a rather Small House, isn't it? I mean, it's in our greater self-interest that people in other countries are well fed, and making good seed available helps them to do that for themselves."

As she said that, we entered a large glasshouse where hundreds of trays of seedlings crowded each other for light.

"These here are tomatoes. They look pretty similar at this point, but you should see them later in the field: red fruits, yellow, green, tan, pink, purple, striped, some round and flat, others long like icicles, still others ribbed like a squeezebox! Some have the most exquisite flavours while others are quite inedible."

"Then why would you bother growing those?" I wondered aloud.

Dace collected her thoughts a moment before answering. "These varieties represent the crop-plant legacy of our ancestors, both yours and mine. As Keepers of the Seed, our responsibility is to preserve them, not pass judgment on them. That is for the breeders to do. We merely supply the working material."

"But what's the point of supplying them with worthless material, as you yourself just said?"

"*You* said 'worthless'—I said 'inedible.' You see, the same tomato race that we find unpalatable may also contain the genes for resistance to some newly evolving disease strain. Though useless in of itself, as a parent in a new cross, it may confer the disease resistance to a perfectly delicious new tomato variety. It is amazing what a skilled breeder can do, but only if the raw material is there to work with."

"And where do we come in?" asked Wren, with a growing awareness of time.

"Well, of course, such plant material is not valuable unless it is put to use. Part of this facility is involved in breeding just such new varieties as we discussed, which we release from time to time. In the past, our main vehicle for distribution of improved seed has been the many specialized horticultural clubs, and we shall continue with them. But one of our workers has a relative up at Phoebe, who told us about you and your boat. It occurred to us that you would be an excellent agent for putting these into the proper hands. In particular, we have a lot of varieties which have been specially developed to meet very specific challenges: short cold seasons, poorly drained soils, intransigent disease problems, and so forth. None of these are best suited for general conditions, so it's important that they be matched with the appropriate growers. Since you get into such out-of-the-way places and deal directly with the individual steads, we think you might be able to target them more precisely. Of course, those recipients who find the varieties suit their special needs will naturally propagate the seed for their continued use and hopefully to share with their neighbours."

"Well, of course we'd be delighted to help," declared Wren. "It's only a question of how much seed we can afford, since we are already invested in lots of other cargo."

"Oh, the seed will cost you nothing. Our expenses are covered by the Vision Fulfillment Council. All we require of you is that you take care where you distribute them. Each bag has a detailed description of the variety's traits, to help you decide wisely. You charge whatever you can get, and keep it. If there's something in it for you, you'll be more careful to do it right."

"That's a pretty good deal. We can't lose."

"Nor can we, I think. Now let us know if you run out, and please encourage people to tell us how these do for them."

With that, we were off, each of us pushing a wheelbarrow chock-full of seed crates. We did make a good profit on that seed—as Wren said, how could we lose? Moreover, we had the satisfaction of knowing that many steads were enjoying earlier peppers or larger kohlrabis because of our visit to Cinderfield.

*   *   *   *   *   *   *

As we poled our way up the upper extension of Cedar Stream, we saw several other watercraft, which at least in my mind, put the lie to any claim that Esperia was not a market-based economy. We passed a couple of large line-traders, carrying charcoal or slate tiles from the Talus Hills. At Meremouth, there was a lock that was thirty-two feet long, which made that the end of the line for any larger boats. Only tramps could go beyond there, and we saw plenty of those: the *Intrepid*, the *Ibis*, and the *Bold Balladeer*, the latter two carrying the banner of Longlogan. Wren knew all their crews; in fact, several were his relatives.

There was good reason for all this traffic: by taking the Favour Canal, tramps can connect with the entire Goosegrass Fair, a feat which otherwise involves going all the way down to the Bluemeadow and the sea and thence along Harking Bay and back up the Goosegrass Estuary. Since tramps are not designed to be seaworthy, it also means costly transshipment; so for boats which can squeeze through the Favour, it is the only way to go. A kinswoman of Wren's worked on a tramp-boat that was somewhat larger than *Come-What-May*. They specialized in shuttling cargo from one watershed to the other where the liners could not pass through. That boat was appropriately named the *Liaison*. At the time, they had a contract to haul prefabricated windmill turbines over to Medlar Falls.

I enjoyed reading the various public service notices on their canopies as we passed each other. They ranged from the profound to the mundane, and it was sometimes unclear which were which. For example, one roof exhorted us to "Live Deliberately," while another insisted that "Two Is Enough." I had trouble understanding some of them, such as the cryptic "Castiron Sinks."

Our business was not along the busy Cedar, but on its shallower tributaries where others could not follow. We spent a day haunting the banners of South Groves, and Honeysuckle. The area has several small foundries and glassworks (including the nation's only producer of windowpanes). That is in spite of the fact that there are no iron mines or silica deposits in the Talus Hills. They use only recycled materials: cracked iron pots and shattered bottles are most of their feedstock. They are located there because the steep hills have abundant wood and charcoal, and it is cheaper to haul the raw material than the fuel.

In addition to the Non-Combustion Campaign, there is also something called the Nest Laws, which require all industries to carburate their furnaces with bellows or blowpipes so there is minimal air pollution. Likewise, paper mills and other chemical-using enterprises are forbidden to discharge any waste at all into waterways. One of the results of this stringent law is that all such products are doubly expensive. On the other hand, their closed-cycle processes beget a high level of resource recovery and efficiency, and it is taken for granted that one may safely drink out of any stream or lake in this densely populated country.

We also visited a couple of distilleries—although Stewards are unaccustomed to intoxicating beverages, they produce large amounts of industrial alcohol, mostly for solvents and lamp fluid. One plant distilled aromatic oils for various uses, and we were lucky to obtain a couple gallons of pennyroyal oil. That is a prodigious amount, but during blackfly season, it was impossible to keep enough in stock.

It had seemed to me at the beginning that our cargo was pretty diverse, but by now the *Come-What-May* was truly a floating general store. Wren kept meticulous records of every transaction, crossing some items off the list while adding others on. He would often simply hand the list to a potential customer so they could browse through and pick out something they didn't know to ask for. Yet Wren himself rarely depended on that list for remembering what we had or where it was stowed. He might say, "Will you look in the third drawer down in the portside aft locker? There are some 5/8-inch sleeve bearings there—about five, I think—we sold one last week." He needn't have said "about" or "I think"; he was always exactly right. Of course, we made a profit on every exchange, so we were piling up surpluses of all kinds; the excess which we left at the depots, the foreign coins which were often useful in "making change," and in some cases, promissory notes. In our case, such notes were usually for some commodity which was fairly standard. Although once we did take a note for two cases of blown glassware which weren't ready yet, to be called for on our next trip. It turned out we didn't get back there again, so we swapped the note to the *Dawn-Greeter*, which was heading that way soon. Of course, promissory notes are of limited use when you're constantly moving around and can't judge the quality of the promised items. (I noticed later that notes are far more common in intrabanner commerce. In those cases, labour is a typical commodity; often not only the number of hours are specified, but the name of the labourer and the type of work.)

We never accepted salt for the simple reason that we weren't willing to pay a middleman-added price for something we already had aplenty at factory cost. On the other hand, we never turned down any pearl-ash even though it is produced by hundreds of leachers throughout the country. Dozens of industries use it; if we didn't find any soap makers who would pay our price, we could take any amount back to Alga where it was needed for the manufacture of caustic soda.

Some of the goods we acquired were needed by our own homes. Ermine had sent along a detailed list of things we should watch for and bring back to Stonesthrow as part of our pay. In fact, the list included many items we didn't need ourselves but which she knew were wanted by other Alga steads, and therefore Stonesthrow could use them to settle debts with neighbours.

Despite its inherent awkwardness, this floating-value barter system seems to work perfectly well. No, not perfectly well—nothing in Esperia works perfectly, but it seems to work as well as it is meant to. Goods and services are moved from producer to consumer, debts are honoured, taxes are paid, the nation and its parts are highly self-reliant, and people have a web of connexions—business and other—which bind them into a vitally functioning society.

We visited one machine shop which manufactured steam engines. We didn't buy any since even the smallest ones were too heavy, but we did carry a selection of replacement parts. I was surprised to learn that the larger ones are almost all for export. I remembered that Jasper Gates used a large Esperian engine in one of his gin-sheds. However, I had seen the smaller models in use here, usually to supplement the country's many windmills and waterwheels, when "the blow and the flow" were inadequate and the need for power was immediate. Of course, fuelwood is carefully budgeted in this land, which treasures its forests, but then burning fuel is not the only means of generating steam. Many steads and enterprises had a large parabolic reflector, which focused sunlight on the boiler-tube assembly. These reflectors consisted of large wooden frames, holding hundreds of little mirrors. Each mirror could be individually adjusted to direct the incoming rays onto the desired spot, sort of like a magnifying lens broken into lots of little fragments. Aside from running steam engines and boiling sap or brine, some of the larger arrays produced a beam hot enough for welding.

Chapter 31

The Honeysuckle Manufacturing Company was an impressive establishment, especially to one who only a year earlier had seen but one bicycle in his entire life: Ash Shackleford's plaything. It had been a birthday gift for the pampered brat, and he sped around town for days, showing off and terrorizing pedestrians. But the rutted roads of Dryford were ill-suited for the exotic contrivance, and when a tire needed replacement, the spoiled teen abandoned his expensive toy to hang on a shed wall. An Esperian's cycle is no more a toy than is an Anagaian's horse. When one has to travel overland, one either walks or pedals. They are fine-crafted machines, and the Honeysuckle factory turns out some of the best.

We watched three men making the thick tow-and-fibre "rinds," which cover the thin steel tire-rim. The latex-impregnated rinds give greater traction and cushion the shock on cobbled roads. The factory steward cleaned us out of all our yukomnia stock, although they also produce much of their own rubber. In fact, most of the machined parts were made on the premises or at machine shops in the neighbourhood. The bamboo for the lightweight frames was imported from the Coquina Islands.

Looking at the rows of newly painted bicycles reminded me of Stonesthrow's need for a fourth bicycle. However, it was not on Ermine's list, nor would it be until the household budget was reviewed after Banner Day. Anyway, the kind Stonesthrow required was a general-purpose model, like the Purple Martins we often saw speeding along canal paths, and those were not made here. Honeysuckle makes two specialized designs: the Bumblebee and the Hummingbird. The Hummingbird is an ultralight high-performance vehicle whose two-by-four sprockets give eight wide-ranging gears. They're fairly rare and expensive, used mainly by mail carriers and emergency personnel.

The Bumblebee strictly speaking is not a bicycle, but a tricycle, with a small cart body between the two rear wheels. It is much sturdier and slower—on steep grades it barely crawls while on smooth downhills, it must be braked often to keep control. They're widely used by overland peddlers who cover the areas beyond the reach of streams and canals. If, from an Anagaian perspective, one thinks of the Hummingbird as the vegan's racehorse, then the Bumblebee is a plodding mule.

We had no intention of buying bicycles—they're too great an investment, and anyway, one doesn't go selling bicycles door-to-door. We were interested in spare parts, which were frequently requested. We traded most all of our tin and zinc ingots, which they needed for bronze couplings, and we were happy to unload some scrap iron, which was becoming a nuisance. We gave them an especially good deal on some of the bulky Calamus Split-Rim baskets which had been lashed awkwardly on the dingle-roof. They interfered with every low bridge we passed under, and we were well rid of them, but the advantage was only momentary because Wren got a bright idea. After talking it over, we all agreed we should buy a Bumblebee—not for resale, but as part of *Come-What-May's* own operating equipment in a strategy Wren was just beginning to formulate.

The new plan was this: whenever we reached the upper limits of navigation on a brook, we would load an assortment of light, valuable goods onto the Bumblebee, and one of us would trade his way overland to the next watershed where we would rendezvous at some designated landing. By carrying a copy of the inventory, we could offer the whole range of our cargo to prospective buyers. If the desired item was not on the cycle, we could arrange for the boat to drop it off at the nearest landing.

The plan would greatly increase our effective operating area, but it had drawbacks: it left only two men on board to pole up through strong currents, and it tied *Come-What-May*, albeit loosely, to an itinerary, which is not after all what tramp-traders are all about. And of course, the cyclist would be working in areas already covered by local trike-peddlers who knew the territory better than we did. Nevertheless, we decided that our mandate from *Come-What-May's* owners was to explore possibilities—even risky ones—and this innovation certainly had possibilities.

When we rejoined Cedar Stream, we didn't go back down to the Broadlea, but continued up to Bottle Pond, whence we crossed over via the Wrested Canal into Plum Brook. Here was a perfect opportunity to try out our Bumblebee strategy. To get up Piper Brook, *Come-What-May* would have to go several miles down Plum Brook and then back up Piper Brook, and there was a lot of area between the two that was inaccessible. I lobbied hard for the chance to ride Bumblebee, knowing it would be a rare opportunity to see a different aspect of the country; that is, away from the rivers. Wren had some doubts: although I was reasonably fluent in Mok, I was still a novice at trading. There was no fear that anyone would intentionally cheat me, but without a precise sense of values, I might easily cheat myself. Still, Wren had to stay with the boat, and Marten was not as rugged or adventuresome as I, so I got the job.

* * * * * * *

5/6/48: Today has been really exciting. I'm spending the day at a stead on Stubs Hill. Wren and Marten are over on Piper Brook today, at least that was the plan when they dropped me off the other day at Borage. I've been trading in the banners of Borage, Claypits, Zenith, Followwater, and Stubs. That's a lot of roads pedalled in two and a half days, but I think I've done very well—let's hope the guys agree. I'm to meet them tomorrow evening at Waxen-Amble. I am getting weighted down though; must unload some of these bicycle parts for which there is not enough demand.

The folks here are really friendly. There is a really cute girl here, about seventeen, who's a bit *too* friendly. Well, that's just me, of course—Wren would have no complaint. But they're all nice here, thirty-one people in one household, practically a village under one roof. Nevertheless, they have room for more. Their land is very rich, and the house is huge. They have a nearly enclosed courtyard, and they even have a couple of figs growing in tubs, would you believe? In many ways, it's just like what I'm looking for, but something's not quite right (it isn't the girl either). I'm sure I'll know the right place when I find it.

The last couple days have been a real eye-opener. At last I begin to see what they mean about Esperia not being a market economy. There is just *so* much being done and made here that is for home use or to be bartered with neighbours. For example, food. Very little of our cargo is edible, yet people around here regularly swap food items. They aren't violating the Vine Laws because they produce their own staples even though they swap part of those for other staples. These folks here make a delicious sourdough rye bread, which they share with a neighbouring stead even though they in turn receive steamed acorn bread every Sixth-day afternoon. It's just a custom they have; no one seems to know when it began. This stead also makes a prepared maple-mustard sauce, which is popular all over the banner. Apparently, the Vine Laws don't apply to it.

I presented them with a couple pounds of imported dried peaches as a host-gift. The pantry steward seemed reluctant to accept them until I pointed out that permacrops are exempt from the boycott. It feels good that I'm learning my way around here.

As I was saying, there's a whole network of "exchange relationships" (how can I call it a market?) here that has nothing at all to with middlemen, hard currency, or distant markets. Wren was right: that "commerce" we tramp-traders see is the tip of the iceberg; that river of exports flowing toward Anagaia and other nations is of relatively little consequence to the well-being of the Esperian people. I mean, they're all immensely prosperous from it, but shut it off, and no one will be cold or hungry. But here's the real kicker: because Esperians are less dependent on buying and selling, they can drive a better bargain on either side of the counter. Their pulsing commerce owes its strength to the very fact that it is the *second* tier of a pyramid, the bottom tier being the self-reliance mandated by the Vine Laws.

The roads here are quite an experience, much like those on Alga. There's not much difference between major and minor roads—I suppose that's also due in part to the Vine Laws: with no population centres to connect, no road is less important than the next. They're all very well maintained, which I guess is made easier by the fact that none are over eight feet wide. Most are built of several inches of small stones, often from the adjoining fields. They never wash out or get rutted. Whether bordered by fields or woods, there is nearly always a hedgerow of trees just beyond the ditch. These are typically sugar maples or bur oaks, and their boughs usually intermingle over the road. I really appreciate these tunnels of shade of a hot day like this, just as the shaded brooks make our poling a lot more pleasant.

They have an instrument factory here, and I bought a dulcitar. It cost a pint of mint oil and two wooden ladles. I sure hope Wren approves. I don't know how to judge musical instruments, but he sure does. I miss his playing, echoing across the water. He offered to teach me, but I'd rather learned the fiddle: fewer strings.

I guess I'm really enjoying this overland rambling. It's a welcome change to use my legs more and my arms less. Still, I kind of miss the guys. To bed now.

After we all managed to rendezvous near Waxen-Amble, we cached some more stuff in a depot near Sedges. We stowed a lot of hardware, keeping only a few of everything in the locker, and we replenished our supplies of salt, glass and sea vegetables before heading up Smallage Brook. Here, the going was indeed easier, but other tramps were already there, so we sought the less accessible areas. At Callingforth, we found a small woodworking shop that made wooden bushings for machinery. Wren took all they had in stock, which was less than he wanted. Later, above Fullmeasure Landing, we came to another tiny factory, which turned roller-bearings out of hornbeam. We took all their supply too. It seemed to me we were overstocking on such specialized items, but Wren knew what he was doing. It is difficult for a foreigner to even conceive of how many windmills there are in this country, many in less-than-ideal locations. Every single stead has at least one, and some have several. And that is to say nothing of the waterwheels. There is scarcely a brook in the country which is deemed too small to turn at least an undershot wheel. Esperians are no lovers of inefficient hand labour, especially when they can invent a machine to accomplish the thing easier. However, these mills and machines all have moving parts, which break or wear out. Many of the needed repairs can be fabricated on the spot by a competent craftsperson, but the wooden bearings are a particularly precise bit of work and the bushings are best made of seasoned black locust, which not everyone has on hand when they need it. Our ample selection of both items guaranteed a welcome reception everywhere.

We had traded for maple syrup and sugar at almost every stop. Since everyone in this area made it, there was no market for it, yet we consistently accepted it as payment. Any time we were near one of our depots, we could leave it there for one of our sister tramps to carry down to the coast. Virtually, every stead in the nation boiled some syrup, but many did not make enough for their own needs; and of course, much of it was exported to other countries, which are bereft of the noble maple.

We also continued to trade for river-oats whenever possible. I should explain that a wild-growing form of this grain is found in other countries where it's sometimes called wild rice. However, the name is quite inappropriate for Esperia since it is not rice at all, nor is it wild, having been improved by many centuries of selective breeding. I asked Wren about the Staples Rule regarding grain, and he explained that every stead must grow enough grain to feed themselves. Nothing forbids them from swapping one kind for another, especially something like river-oats, which doesn't grow just everywhere.

Wren had an uncanny capacity for sniffing out potential trades where none was supposed to exist. The printed Production Inventory was a useful guide to a novice like me, but he referred to it only occasionally. For example, at a stead near Echo Brook, we were invited to lunch. We had just unloaded a typewriter, which we knew they wanted. The manufacturer, way back at Borage, had assured us they did, although no one had agreed upon the price. We had bought it directly from the maker to be resold for whatever we could get. Well, none of that was any problem—we could always sell it somewhere.

The customer did indeed want the typewriter and was not quibblesome about the price Wren quoted. The only question was what to accept in trade. We took several sets of woodworking chisels and twelve pairs of canvas work gloves, but it needed a bit more to make up the difference. They offered a couple of cedar kegs, but Wren knew the area had plenty of cooper shops, and we didn't care to carry such bulky low-value items. So we let the matter rest there while we joined them at table. It was a nice meal, but we especially enjoyed the fresh hot bread with a kind of fruit preserve we had never tasted before. Wren asked about it.

"Just our own recipe, a blend of quince and pear. We like the way the tart and sweet flavours go together."

"Me too, and I know lots of others would like it. How much is it per case?"

"Oh, we don't make it to sell. We only put up a few cases each year for ourselves and to share with neighbours."

"Half a case, maybe?"

"Six jars? Well, I suppose . . . could you leave us six empty canning jars as replacements?"

"Certainly, and the typewriter is yours."

*　*　*　*　*　*　*

Not all our business deals involved such serendipity. People often left notices on bulletin boards, especially at river-landings, mentioning specific items they wanted or had for sale. There was a slight element of risk in pursuing those contacts because one sometimes went out of one's way, only to find that the sought-for item had long since been bought or sold, and the individual had neglected to take down the notice.

But occasionally, we would follow down such a lead, and that was how we got to meet Maxim.

At Laurel Landing, near the mouth of Stiles Brook, we noticed a scrawled message on a bulletin board: "Wanted: caustic soda, 10 lbs., see Maxim, Hempstead, Reddlepits."

We were intrigued; a paper factory would be unlikely to want such a small amount, a soap-maker or glassworks would probably require much less. Upon consulting the Production Inventory, the only thing we found that sounded right was the Humps Graphic Supplies Enterprise. The contact was a woman's name, not Maxim. They did list specialty papers among their many products, but we assumed that Maxim of Hempstead was no papermaker since most papermaking begins with making wood into chips, and chipping requires more power than sluggish Furnace Brook was capable of providing. Nevertheless, it just so happened that we had a few cannisters of caustic soda in stock (it's not exactly the sort of thing just anyone carries about with them), and since we had business in that neighbourhood anyway, we resolved to drop in on this Maxim.

The banner of Reddlepits is in the region called the Humps. During the last Ice Age, the retreating glacier had dumped a lot of its leftover rubble on the highlands which separate the Broadlea and Laughingwater valleys. It was a sloppy job, to be sure; gravel and enormous boulders were piled into random-looking hills, most of which dropped off sharply toward the south. Crowded between these jumbled hills, brooks were at a loss for a way out. Some of them in fact went nowhere, forming bogs ringed with dense spruce and cedar and carpeted with cranberries and peat moss. Where the waters did manage to find an exit, they wound around interminably through mats of bog laurel and Borealian tea.

The Humps are mostly clad in acid-loving oaks and pines and poplars. A lot of the poplar cut in the Humps is floated down Furnace Brook on bantam-scows to a paper mill on the Broadlea. That mill, like most Esperian paper mills, is about the size of a very large barn, yet it dwarfed Maxim's mill. For Maxim, when we finally met him at the door of his "factory," turned out to be a papermaker after all, though of an unusual sort. He graciously showed us all around, which didn't take long. The plant was not on any brook at all, but located near the crest of Gaunt Hill where an average-size windmill served to run its single small chipper. When there was a stiff breeze, that is—Maxim had to plan ahead. This voluble fellow was usually the sole worker, although his workshop was part of a larger complex called the Humps Graphics Supplies Enterprise. In one corner stood his pulp digester: 1,500 gallons at most. Another corner held the beater, which turned old linen rags into a fibrous soup, which was blended with the clean wood pulp. Attached to the outside of the building (not another thing could be crammed *inside* of it), a small shed held his entire year's supply of poplar chips, maybe three or four tons. On shelves sat the needed supplies: clay, gypsum, caustic soda, waterlily starch—all in less-than-fifty-pound bags. Maxim explained the small-scale: "We . . . er, I make very special types of paper here. See over there, that kind is draughting vellum used for technical drawings and maps. Now this up here is art paper—has to be very exact quality so paint won't bleed nor chalk smear. I can only make a few thousand sheets a day—no point in having anyone else underfoot."

He also explained why he needed such small amounts of caustic soda. "It takes quite a few pounds to make a strong-enough liquor to cook down the lignin, but once a batch is done, I boil off the water and burn the residue. That way I recover most of the alkali to use over and over. I only need to replace the small amount lost. What you fellows brought will last me another year easily."

Seeing our interest, he showed us around the rest of the compound where the other workers were making sized canvas, oil paints, pencils, coloured chalk and charcoal, all sorts of art supplies. None of these products required a great deal of power. In addition to the windmill, there was an assortment of treadle-powered and hand-cranked machines for cutting, grinding, mixing, etc. With the exception of the chalk, most of the materials—flax, linseed oil, cedar, ochre, basswood charcoal, clay, lily starch, and beeswax—were all available right in the immediate vicinity.

I was especially pleased to see the pencils painted a cheery blue with a red stripe. When I was a child at the Cleftridge Orphanage, we learned to write with pencils exactly like these, furnished by our Esperian sponsors. Seeing the pencils gave me a queer feeling of nostalgia.

I was also interested to see one of his specialty papers, a high-grade pale-green parchment made for export to Anagaia. Maxim said his entire production of that was bought by a nephew of Lord Creston (Ministry of Internal Affairs), who resold most of it to the Bureau of Documents. I had once used just such a sheet to forge a travel document.

After leaving Maxim's, we made a slight detour up Bog Brook where Wren said he wanted to show us something. The water was tea coloured, and the bottom was almost too mucky to push against. There was no detectable current, and as we glided up the undredged channel, the trees closed in over our heads, all but excluding the daylight. Wherever patches of light did manage to pierce the brooding canopy, we saw clumps of pitcher plants and cloudberrries. Cedar trees predominated, and they grew to a diameter I've rarely seen elsewhere. Scattered among them, black spruces also soared upward, their lower branches drooping and festooned with wisps of gray-green lichen. Overall was a peaceful yet gloomy silence that was broken only by the occasional call of a flycatcher in the distance. There were old fallen trees, their moss-clad trunks sprawled on the spongy earth or hung up in a snarl of dead branches. No towpaths, no mill wheels, no steadhouses, no sign of anything civilized, or even human. It was eerie.

"What is this place?" I asked.

"The Quaking Earth Wilderness. It's part of the Sacred Groves."

"Is it this dark throughout?"

"Not at all. Farther upstream, there is a huge area of bald heath. And there's another part I've never seen, over on Pickerel Pond where tall reeds cover dozens of acres."

"Hewn said people are welcome to explore the Sacred Groves as long as they abide by the rules, but that would be impossible here. There are no marked trails, and it looks as if you couldn't step on the bank over there without sinking up to your hips."

"You're right. People are welcome to enter, but the rules do tend to discourage all but the most resolute from penetrating very far.

"How do the rules keep people from penetrating the Groves by water?" I asked as I wielded my pole-hook to pry loose a submerged log that blocked our progress.

"Like that, for example. Don't do that!"

"What? I'm just trying to push this aside so we can get through."

"Not allowed. No building roads. No modifying channels."

"Then how do we . . . ?"

"We don't. This is as far as *Come-What-May* goes. If you wish to explore farther, you need a canoe or something you can drag over that log. And even then, you'll find more obstructions around every bend. This isn't meant to be a canal. Let's go back."

While in Reddlepits, we stopped at a small foundry. The iron they use is exceptional in that it is not recycled but mined from shallow pits of bog-iron. The ore contains manganese as an impurity and it yields a very high-grade steel, which is much in demand for cutting tools. They made the finest scythe blades in all the fair—probably in the whole country—and it would soon be the season when new grass-blades would be in great demand. Apparently, others also had the same idea, for we were lucky to get a dozen blades. When we finally turned *Come-What-May*'s bow downstream, it was too late to reach the Broadlea before dark, so we tied up at a quiet spot under the shadow of Gaunt Hill where we had a splendid view of the tranquil valley floor.

I lay awake, staring at the woven reed canopy over my head and recalling the day's events, or rather its impressions. Everything I saw or heard in my travels seemed to challenge everything I thought I knew before. I could never seem to arrive at an answer that wasn't in fact another question. What an incredibly different country this was, from the grand Vision to the tangible details of everyday life. No wonder foreigners felt so ill at ease here, yet I actually found it all much to my liking. Was that more a reflection of how miserable my life had been in Dryford, or was I just more prepared for it by my upbringing at the orphanage? And was Esperia necessarily unique? If Anagaia planted forests, would the droughts cease? If Umberlands peasants grew more staple foods for their own use, would they be more prosperous than now? If they gave up keeping livestock, would there be enough farmland to go around? If the Empire were converted to a different religion, or no religion, would it make life any better there? What mattered and what didn't? And just how does change—big or small—come about in any society?

Although I was overflowing with such questions, it is hard for the mind to keep toiling when the body is exhausted from a day's tramping. Somewhere in the darkling shadows, I could hear the low skrahunk, skrahunk of a bittern's call, reminding me of a squeaky pump as I slid off to sleep.

Chapter 32

There had been an understanding from the outset that during idle moments, Marten would tutor me in math and science. Although our labours often seemed long and strenuous, there were enforced lulls especially at the canal locks, which were even more frequent in the upstream banners. I relished these mini-lessons, but Marten had a different priority. He was entranced by tales of high adventure, and truth knows, I had plenty. He had never faced a life-threatening crisis himself and was eager to hear all about mine. So on the many occasions when we waited for a lock to fill, we would sometimes do trigonometry and at other times recall harrowing escapes. I guess it was a pleasant change for us both.

On one occasion we were waiting to enter a lock on Wapato Brook, a tiny feeder of Stiles Brook. The lock was only a two-foot rise, but the brook's flow is so small, it took a full twenty minutes to fill the lock, just like the two before it. We were all feeling bored, but Marten was eager to continue an earlier story.

"You were telling us before about how you got over the Foxfires with those opium smugglers, but I was wondering: once you were out of the mountains, weren't they reluctant to let you go? I mean, you knew too much about them."

"Well, the Old Cougar was true to his word, as those mountain folk generally are. I guess by that time, they were all convinced of my story and realized that our secrets were safe with each other. In fact, the Old Cougar went me one further."

A rough brick inn squatted beside the dirt highway, which threaded its way down the valley from the direction of the territorial border. The midmorning sun beat down on the low tile roof and the hoof-beaten yard, driving off the chill of the darker hours. Most of the inn's guests had already continued on their way. Only a few locals loafed around the front entrance, quaffing beer and spitting tobacco juice in the dust. None was aware that the place was being watched—by us.

Crouched on the high slope overlooking the building, the Old Cougar peered intently at the premises below while I shivered and grimaced with pain from the previous night's adventure.

"What is it you're looking for?" I yawned.

"A sign . . . must be sure it's . . . ah, good! It's okay. Let's go at once."

"Wait," I hesitated. "You've helped me a lot so far. Maybe I should just be on my way." I was eager to separate myself from the nefarious business at hand, having gained what I wanted.

"Sure, if you wish. But you're still not out of trouble, and I might be able to help you yet. Tag along, if you care to."

We arose stiff-jointed from our lookout and ambled quickly toward the roadhouse. I was limping from the knee injury sustained in our night flight from the border patrols. In the backyard of the hostelry, a clothesline carried a green shirt, under which a washtub was turned upside down—apparently a signal. We entered by a rear door to avoid prying eyes. Inside the tavern, we sidled over to an obese man who sat listlessly behind the bar, chewing a strip of roast mutton. My companion plunked down a piece of silver as he inquired softly, "Anyone here yet?"

"Everyone, I guess," replied the innkeeper with studied indifference as he slipped the coin into his apron.

He gestured toward a side room. The low doorway was closed by a heavy mat of bullock hide, which we pushed aside in entering. There, ranged in a circle, sat seven men, six of whom I already knew. So all of the smugglers had eluded their pursuers, but not without mishap. The youngest one, barely a teenager, had a streak of dried blood running down his cheek and into his shirtfront from a bullet which grazed his forehead. It must have pained him, but he seemed proud of the wound. These people must have been intensely glad to be reunited safely, but there was little display of familial affection.

The seventh member of the group was a teamster who was their contact for disposing of the opium. With our arrival, there began a spirited haggling over price, which was only resolved after a lot of heated shimming and dickering. Finally, it appeared that the teamster was not to be driven up so much as another bullhead.

"Okay, enough money then," the Old Cougar conceded. "But you must throw in a ride."

The dealer looked at the mountaineer in bewilderment, as did the others.

"What's that? A ride, you say? What are you talking about?"

"A ride, that's all. You're going towards New Chalice. You have travel permits—bogus, no doubt, but they seem to work. This young fellow needs a lift. He'll pay his own expenses. A deal?"

Some of his kinsman were looking as though they'd throttle him, the others shifted uneasily. They had risked a lot on this venture and didn't want the deal soured on my account.

"Wait, what are you saying? Take him along? No, no, I can't do that. Just cash now, let's keep it simple."

"What could be simpler?" protested the elder, ignoring the baleful glares of all around him. "I can assure you from experience, he'll be no bother. Well then, there are six falcons in it for you extra."

"Uncle!" blurted several mouths at once, but they were stilled by a quiet, "Easy boys, I'm only spending the lad's own money for him."

The dealer was frustrated by this irregularity.

"Look, guys, I can't risk any complications. What if I'm stopped because of him?"

"You can say he's your nephew—no, he's too poorly dressed—one of your bucs, then. A deal?"

"I can't, that's all, you see. It's too big to risk."

"Then let's go home, boys. This fellow doesn't want our goods." I knew he was stretching the bonds of clan loyalty to the breaking point. I sensed a rebellion brewing, but it was the teamster who blinked.

"Now then, wait, wait! Not so hasty, good brothers. We've all come such a long way. Of course, I'd be glad to have the young gent's company. More work for the horses, of course, but for a mere eight falcons . . ."

"A deal, then! And well on with you, my young friend. You'll be in New Chalice within a week, though what good it will do you, I can't imagine."

*   *   *   *   *   *   *

I had hoped to get some sleep after the night's escapade, but my conductor was eager to be away from there, so we set off immediately.

The opium dealer had a "front" business as a peddler of products from the hill country: lambskins, fine woolen rugs, kid gloves, cowhide boots, saddles—that sort of thing. It was a bona fide business, all right, but it was the tiny sacks rolled up in the long carpets that made him a rich man. For he obviously was a rich man. Although he passed himself off as a trader of modest means, the pair of matched horses he drove was a bit too fine for a peddler's van.

The name he gave out was Fester Gilding, though he added that it was a name that served for business purposes. I concluded that an alias might serve my needs as well, so I contrived the identity of Dusty Wells, though I candidly remarked that it was a village I'd passed by last week. He agreed it was a nice touch.

Gildings was a corpulent man with sparse greasy hair and deepset eyes that shifted constantly. He seemed most ashamed of his legitimate occupation and made futile attempts to cover his sun-chapped neck and hands.

At first he seemed peeved at my company and showed little inclination to talk, which was fine with me. Feeling quite exhausted, I leaned back in my seat and tried to doze. We hadn't gone many miles, however, when a hissed curse from my driver brought me wide awake. Approaching us from the front were three mounted CADS officers. As my chest tightened in fright, Gilding reined in the team and greeted the group's leader like an old acquaintance:

"Good morning, Sergeant! How good to see you again. As I was just telling the boy here, this is bandit-ridden country around here. It's a relief to see patrols on the road."

"Yes, sir, we do our best. And the boy is . . . ?"

"Oh, Dusty Wells, one of my bucs' sons. It's getting harder for me to hoist the saddles and such, so I brought him along."

"I see," replied the officer with a tinge of suspicion in his voice. "Well then, he doesn't need papers while in your company, but I must ask to see your travel permit and manifest."

"Yes, of course." And he pulled a folded piece of pale green paper from his pocket. The officer scanned it quickly before handing it back.

"And the manifest."

"Indeed, here, Dusty, holds this a moment." While he groped through his baggage for the required document, I took a hasty look at the travel permit in my hand, committing as much to memory as I could before handing it back.

"And just by the way, Sergeant," Gilding was saying. "Those uniform boots may be quite all right for this rough riding, but a man in your position must cut a figure that will command the respect of your inferiors. Permit me to make a small gift of these boots I acquired recently—notice the fine tooling here—they'll do you credit."

"Why indeed, I'm most grateful . . . not necessary, of course, but many thanks." He swung the pair over his saddle horn. "Everything seems to be in order here. I see you've paid the proper fees at the border. You may pass. I would recommend that in future, your servant should carry his own permits in case you're separated. Could save some unpleasantness. Also, you should know that there are some bad washouts on the Huntstown Road. You'd be wise to take the Overland Bypass and camp at Carver's Spring.

"I thank you, sir. I shall follow your advice."

As our wagon rumbled on, I asked, "He was expecting those boots, wasn't he?"

"I travel this route often," he grunted.

*   *   *   *   *   *   *

After we had ridden for some time, Gilding asked, "Can you drive a team?"

I had been trying to doze off and was loath to do what his question implied, but I also was well aware that being useful to Gilding could only be useful to me.

"I used to handle a wagon for a man I worked for sometimes."

"Good, I want to catch some winks." He pulled up and handed me the reins.

I had driven a few miles when we came to a fork. I nudged my nodding companion. "Do we go through Tailorville or Fort St. Grace?"

"Tailorville," he murmured without opening his eyes. In a moment, he shook off his drowse and said. "I thought you weren't from around here."

"I'm not."

"How do you know the towns?"

"There was a signpost just back there."

"Oh, so you can read a little. Good for you."

"Actually, I can read quite well. In fact, I taught my foster sister to read."

"Can you really?" Gilding sat up now, looking at me as if I'd just now climbed onto the wagon seat.

"I learned to read as an adult," he boasted. "Paid dearly for the lessons. You don't look like a chap who's had much schooling. Your father taught you?"

"I never knew my birth father. I was raised in a Steward orphanage, they taught me. When I was eleven, I was adopted by a West Umberlands family, and I continued to practice with a few books they had in the house."

"Ah, so your adoptive father was a scholar?"

"Not hardly. I don't think he ever read any of them himself. He always said a few books gave a place a more genteel look, more progressive-like."

"Yes, indeed. I have quite an extensive library myself: more than fifty volumes, nicely bound things, mind you. But I read mine, classics mostly, works of theology. What sort have you read?"

"Just whatever we had. There was Reaping Justice, User-Built Windmills, and a large one called Crops Without Ploughs. I've read them all at least once. It's slow though, and I didn't understand everything."

"Oh, those things," sniffed Gilding. "Some rural types seem to go for those Esperian imports. Manuals really, nothing that could pass as literature. Not even leather-bound, what can one expect? I've met a few of those Steward folks. Pleasant enough, to be sure, but quite devoid of any spirituality. All they care to talk about is land reform and labour relations. Such drivel, really. Still, they are a kindly bunch of lumps . . . helped me out once when the horse broke my foot. And you say you taught your sister to read?"

"She's really quite good at it."

"That's a grave mistake. Scholarship is not a proper thing for women. No matter what some of these liberals say nowadays, a woman needs to know enough to make babies and get around the kitchen. More than that isn't good for them. Gives them ideas that only confuse them."

I didn't bother to add that Melody had taught several of her girlfriends to read as well, so that most of the literate peasants in Dryford were now female. I hadn't noticed any great increase in confusion there.

"You have a girlfriend back there in . . . the other side of Dusty Wells?"

"Yes, I . . . well, that is, I thought I did. Now I'm not so . . ."

"Ah, I know exactly what you mean! They're all a lot of sluts at heart. Can't turn your back on any of them."

He didn't at all know what I meant, and I was in no position to tell him, so I just let him run on. "But you see, that's why you mustn't teach them more than they can handle. They can't help themselves, they are born hornious. They need a man to keep them under control, preferably a philosophical man. Anyway, don't lose any tears over that one. Once you get to the city, you'll find plenty of places where you can dip your wick for a few coppers. Life's just too short to get yourself tied down, I say."

I was really keen to change the topic, so I asked, "What are these classics you refer to? I've heard the priest back in our village talk about the Holy Scriptures. Is that what you mean?"

"Well, among others, of course that's what it all derives from, yes. But it's all in the interpretation, you see. You have to read it right."

I was a bit bemused that this sleazebag fancied himself such an authority on the moral teachings of his culture, yet I also realized he knew more about it than I did, so I pursued.

"What then are the other books? The interpretations, I mean."

"Oh, there are many of them, and I have all the most important works. There is The Three Faces and Other Divine Mysteries Explained, *by Wrathson, and* Belief Triumphs Over Actions, *by Campford. Of course, the most important of all is Stone's* New Path of Manifest Destiny.*"*

"Why is it considered so important?"

"Well, you see, it gets us back on the right track, if we but follow it."

"What track?"

"Oh dear, I keep forgetting you are raised by . . . now surely, they taught you about the Calamities?"

"Of course, everyone knows about that."

"And I don't suppose they told you what caused them?"

"Well, I was pretty young when I left there, but I always understood that it had to do with misuse of the earth by the people that lived then. I'm not sure of the details."

"No, I dare say not. One detail in particular they never told you: it was they, *or rather their ancestors, who caused the Calamities."*

"Why did they want to do that?"

"Because they weren't content living in a Golden Age. They thought they knew better than everyone else, always dwelling on the negative. They ignored the great achievements of the era while obsessing over its flaws."

"Like what flaws?"

"Oh, minor things. A few species went extinct, none of which were of any use to anyone anyway. Scattered pockets of pollution and poverty. They refused to see the big picture."

"And that is . . . ?"

"Look, for once in its history, mankind was on the brink of curing disease, creating technologies that would enable individuals to live forever! And with limitless wealth. Why, just for example, you know aluminum, that precious metal they sometimes dig up in old ruins?"

"I've never seen any, but I've heard about it."

"Well, during the Golden Age, it was so plentiful that they made exquisite containers out of it and—get this—after one use, they'd throw it away! Too common to bother wash it! And they had infinite cheap energy, due to the sea of petroleum."

"Where was that sea?"

"Underground! It's everywhere down there, only it's too deep for us to reach today. They knew how to suck it up from great depths, so much of it that they burned it for fuel and made stuff like velcro and polyester."

"What are those?"

"Why, miracle drugs! Believe me, those people could cure cancer almost as fast as they caused it. They could fly to the moon, they could crossbreed fish with strawberries, they could do just about anything they wanted to. But those early Stewards, they said it wouldn't work, wasn't sustainable, even when it was working! A bit longer and all the kinks would've been ironed out. The Stewards complained that lots of people were being harmed by this progress, but that was mostly coloured people in other countries, stupid and lazy people who couldn't get ahead no matter how you helped them. It was the white nations that made all these miracles happen, so why shouldn't they benefit? And so what if part of the world became unlivable because of some pollution or other? The Stewards were so small-minded, they insisted that Earth is mankind's only home! As if there are not millions of other planets in the universe just as good as this one. Even their descendents today, your Esperian friends, always harping on pollution control and recycling. I tell you, man was placed by his Maker at the centre of creation for a reason. Is it proper for his children to be a miserable pack of ragpickers when they could be the rightful masters of it all? Oh, we'll regain that Golden Age sooner or later," he added darkly. "But probably not without first destroying those who opposed it all, then and now."

You may find Fester Gilding a disgusting hypocrite, a racist and a misogynist. He was all of those and worse, yet I feel a curious gratitude toward him. In my whole life, I had never heard the Anagaian worldview expressed so clearly, so candidly, as by this pompous and pretentious creep. Everything he said I had heard before, popping up here and there in bits and pieces, usually couched in more palatable terms. But he put his finger right on it, and to this day, I am grateful for that. It has proven more valuable to me than the ride.

*   *   *   *   *   *   *

The rolling foothills were lengthened as the setting sun sent their dark shadows sprawling off across the piedmont. At a small hillside spring, we two bone-weary travelers crouched beside a tiny heap of crackling twigs. Gilding was spit-roasting a piece of goat meat, while my supper required no preparation.

"Bread? That's all you have to eat?"

"Many's the day I don't even have that."

"Well, I'm not sharing my kid. That wasn't in the deal."

"Quite all right," I assured him with sincerity. "Actually, I have another whole loaf I bought today at that inn, but I have to make it last—it was quite expensive there."

"Well, you couldn't expect to talk the man down after he'd seen your silver. I won't ask where you got it, but others may. Anyway, bread will be cheaper at New Chalice."

"How so? Out here is where the grain comes from."

"Yes, but in the cities, there are price controls. The government knows expensive bread spells riots. Countryfolk are used to starving, and anyway, they have no political clout."

"If food is cheaper in the cities, won't all the poor peasants tend to move there and make matters even worse?"

"How should I know? I'm a merchant, not a farmer. All I know is that cities are where the money is, and that's where you have to go to trade."

The campfire sent up a few sparks to join the few stars that were already visible in the eastern sky. After eating, I borrowed some of Gilding's wool blankets to improvise a cozy nest under the wagon. I was about to doze off when I was bothered by the memory of a chore undone. My water bottle needed filling, but the little rill beside our camp was roiled by the horses. According to Fester, the spring itself was a couple hundred feet up the brushy slope. I didn't relish going back into the chilly air, but Fester planned to get rolling before dawn; so if I wanted to drink clean water tomorrow, there was no choice. I grabbed the clay jug and started up the path. It had no handle, so I snatched up my backpack and thrust the bottle back in. Finding the fern-rimmed spring, I squatted down to fill my jug. Setting it aside, I lay down flat to drink directly from the pool.

Somewhere in the quiet evening, I heard movement. Stray livestock perhaps, but I had grown extremely wary, and I rolled cautiously over into the ferns. Seconds later, the vague sounds became clear footsteps, moving furtively nearby. Frozen in fright beneath the ferns, I peered out into the deep twilight and saw a uniformed pant leg not four feet away. When I recognized the finely tooled riding boots, I knew Fester Gilding was a goner and probably myself as well. Just as I realized with horror that my knapsack still lay there beside the pool, the figure moved on, apparently too intent on the firelit camp below. When he was well past, I crawled out, snatched up my stuff, and slunk up the ridge as quickly as I dared. In a few moments, I heard a report from a nearby rifle followed by a muffled shriek. Two other guns barked from other points on the slope, and that seem to be the end of it. I didn't wait to investigate but ran for all I was worth. Then I heard a barrage of return fire from below, and I realized that Gilding, likely wounded, had leaped into the wagon bed, where he obviously had a cache of weapons. There was a furious exchange, but however many guns Gilding had, they held one shot each, and his situation was hopeless. As I scurried over the top of the ridge, a dusky silence testified that the teamster was finished, murdered for his little bags of poppy-gum.

And what about me? Those men knew about me and would surely assume I was nearby, a witness to the ambush. Running was painful with my backpack and injured knee, but run I did, my lungs screening for air. When I finally reached a road (different I believe from the one I had been on), I dared not walk along it but crawled into the first culvert I found, preferring the company of ticks and snakes to that of human vermin.

"The ball is up, finally," noted Wren, referring to the pressure indicator on the lock, and we poled slowly into the next section of open water.

Chapter 33

Marten was eager to hear more about my misadventures, but the next few days were preoccupied with business as we visited several steads on the upper reaches of Wapato and Stiles Brooks. They were unaccustomed to seeing tramp-boats, and we made plenty of good deals.

As dusk gathered over the brook on our last day there, a cold miserable rain set in, and we yanked the canopy over the cargo and crawled under to eat a cold supper. We were fed up with sleeping in that crowded space, but the nearest steadhouse was farther than we cared to run in the downpour. We saw a small saphouse near the landing, and we hustled into that. We knew that no one would object to our spending the night in its shelter. I was ready to go right to sleep, but Marten wanted to hear more of my story, and this time Wren seconded him. For want of more proper entertainment, I was elected. So we huddled in our dry blankets, and I took them back to Anagaia.

The rising sun struck patches of new frost in the rutted roadstead, kindling them into brief flashes of cold fire before they slowly dissolved into its waxy warmth. A passerby might have been taken aback to see a shivering figure emerge from a weed-choked culvert, much as a badger pushes out of its sod-rimmed burrow. I stood by the roadside a moment, stretching and taking my bearings. Then shouldering my small pack, I turned my face toward the pale warmth and started walking.

There was occasional traffic on the road: farm wagons and mule carts, pack trains and groups of travelers mounted or afoot. Most with convoy, because even though this area was more densely inhabited, there were still incidents of banditry.

That wasn't what I feared most though. It was terror in uniform that filled me with dread. People passing by were harmless enough, but how long before one of them would be questioned by the three officers and would remember the ragged youth they'd passed recently?

For one brief day, it had seemed there would be no more weary tramping, no more sleeping in ditches; yet here I was again, with more uncertainty than ever. But my encounter with Fester Gilding had provided me more than just a few hours of leisurely riding. I had also learned some important things. Here in Hither Anagaia, checkpoints and police inspections would be more common than in Umberlands. I must find a way to deal with them, and Fester Gilding had unwittingly shown me how.

I needed something that couldn't be found in the small villages I passed through. Only late the next afternoon did I come to a town large enough to supply my need. On a small side street, I found a bookstore which also dealt in writing supplies. Fortunately for me, there are few types of paper available in Anagaia, and the pale green stationery used by officialdom is also sold for private use, although it is pricey. I bought three sheets and a small bottle of ink with a quill. It cost more than three loaves of bread, but if my plan worked, it would be worth going hungry for. I found a secluded place to work, ruining the first two sheets in practice. In my all-too-hasty perusal of Gilding's travel permit, I had noticed that it wasn't a mass-printed form, but a handwritten letter from a provincial official whose name I had memorized. I also remembered the general contents of the letter with a few choice phrases of official-speak.

A major concern was the man's penmanship, which was unusually flowing and neat. I had trouble duplicating that, but by the third try, I had fabricated a reasonably convincing document. It wouldn't stand much careful scrutiny, but there was more to my plan.

I soon got my first chance to try it out. Just outside of that town was a bridge over a wide river, and on that bridge was a police checkpoint, which also collected tolls. I loitered around just out of sight of the guard post, watching for the perfect opportunity. Several wayfarers passed me on their way toward the checkpoint, but none quite suited my purpose. I especially noted their feet—I couldn't take any chances with clean-shod locals. Finally, a sedan-chair came past, carried by eight bucs. A glimpse inside told me the passenger was a priest of the MOTHS sect. Most importantly, the porters all had very dusty feet and appeared quite travel-weary. I noted their passing then waited several minutes until a large brewer's dray pulled onto the narrow bridge. I dashed in front of it and hastened boldly up to the guard.

"Did my master already pass by here?" I panted breathlessly. "Priest in a four-pair sedan, about fifty, blond, rather stout, gold chain around his neck?"

The driver of the van behind me was voicing his irritation at being cut out.

"Why yes, he went by not five minutes ago."

"Oh, thank goodness! I stopped to gamble with some lads in the town. He'll whip me good if I'm late. Here." I flashed the bogus permit at him as I raced on by.

"But wait! I need to . . . oh, never mind, go ahead." I disappeared down the road in hot pursuit of His Reverence. But you know, I never did catch up with the guy.

*   *   *   *   *   *   *

I was clearly at a turning point now. It was fully two weeks since I had crossed the border into Hither Anagaia. Some old difficulties vanished while new ones appeared. There were more police than ever here, but they weren't looking for me. There were more gardens here, but most were well guarded against the likes of me. This area had as yet seen no frosty nights, and I bought a few tomatoes as an extravagance; they were a delicious supplement to bread and raw sweetpotatoes. I had money to spend, but the silver coins caused suspicion whenever I used one to buy a loaf of bread; and shopkeepers always tried to shortchange me, assuming I wouldn't know better. I hoarded my falcons closely, not knowing how long they must last me.

I had seen so many hardships and narrow escapes, I can't even recall them all now. Six times I had come to police checkpoints, and six times I had resorted to my fake-passport ruse. Five times it had worked like a charm. I hit a snag once when a burly guard stepped in front of me before I could dash off. He snatched the paper and scanned it with an intensity that suggested the jig was up. To my amazement, he handed it back and told me to proceed. I suppose the fellow was barely literate and failed to recognize the forgery!

There were other dangers attendant upon the vagabond life. One cold night, I crawled under a bridge, nearly putting my hand on a startled copperhead. Every refuge I sought was infested with ticks and fleas, which found in my filthy and debilitated body a perfect host. Each morning and night, I search myself for parasites, but there was no keeping up.

One night, I huddled under the garden wall of a wealthy home. In the morning, I was awakened and driven off by the owner's children, chasing me with stones and dogs. I found that very heartening: they had no idea I was supposed to be a murderer, a cursed man. To those brats, I was just another homeless bum, to be taunted and beaten in fun. That was exactly how I wanted it.

Finally, I looked off from a low undulation of the coastal plain, and I could see my journey's end. I had already seen more marvelous sights than any country boy from the dusty river plains of West Umberlands could ever dream of, but I was awestruck at the vast flashing expanse of water before me. I had never imagined so much water existed in the whole world, yet this was only the Great Oyster Bay, a mere arm of the sea. One could barely see the far shore of the bay. In between, the water was dotted with vessels of every size and description. On the near shore lay my destination: the bustling seaport of New Chalice.

I've read that the ancient city, which once stood there had several times the present population of a hundred thousand and in much less space, but the metropolis I viewed certainly lived up to its reputation as the largest city in the modern world. I had never before seen a building more than two stories high; builders here were not bound by the constraints of mud brick and stone. The seaport gave access to imported timber, which allowed structures to climb four or even five stories high.

On the higher ground to the northwest stood the Onyx City, the walled Imperial enclave from which the Olotals ruled an entire civilization. For of course, the name "Anagaian League" was a charming leftover from the Tetrarchy Period when the four realms really were a voluntary alliance. While Umberlands was now in essence an occupied territory, Hither Anagaia had become the power centre of a far-reaching police state, with New Chalice as its hub. I didn't delude myself that I was "escaping" over the territorial border; I knew perfectly well I was jumping from the frying pan into the fire. Yet New Chalice offered one thing which Umberlands lacked: the hope of anonymity. Many an ambitious provincial came here, seeking to make a name for themselves, but my only hope was that everyone would forget my name. Let them all think I was dead; it was quite sufficient for now to be alive.

New Chalice was a great place to lose one's identity and don another. Surely I was not the only one trying to swap a past for a future. While New Chalice was truly the colourful showcase city of the Empire, it was also awash with all the riffraff and malcontents who drifted in from the hinterlands. Starving peasants left their drought-plagued farms for the tenuous security of the urban dole. Unwanted daughters were sent here to eke out a livelihood as servants or prostitutes. Political radicals sought to bide their time close to the centres of power. Crime was the greatest growth industry. The police were universally corrupt, and anyway, it was all too much for them to control. I was counting on that.

I had plenty of immediate concerns: how long would my silver last? I remembered how the opium smugglers had disdained to plunder me of it. How would I find a job with no skills that were relevant here? How could I protect myself from victimizers? If I so much as spoke to anyone, my accent marked me as a naïve bumpkin. Where could I sleep safely? Nights were growing chilly, and I had nothing to use for a blanket.

I began by exploring the city, no small undertaking. The areas around the bay were crammed with docks and warehouses. From these crammed precincts, several small streets fanned out, becoming major arteries as they cut through or bordered the major market districts. Farther out, away from the clamour, were the residential neighbourhoods of the urban elite, comprising rich merchants, professionals, and bureaucrats. Here too were many public buildings: government offices, museums, and theatres, and even a few small parks.

The four "quarters" were divided roughly according to the occupation groups of the residents. I had seen the small regional markets of Sycamore and Shoatmart, but they were nothing beside this teeming bazaar, athrob with the pulse of commerce which surged to and from its docks with every tide. In this cosmopolitan hive, preoccupied with bargains and profits, I felt a curious sense of security. If I felt out of place here, surely so did countless others.

The first quarter I entered was called Corntown. It originally centred around the grain export market in the days when there was surplus grain to export. It was now become an emporium for foodstuffs of all sorts: imported wheat, wine, and vegetables from the surrounding countryside; millet and sweetpotatoes from West Umberlands; meat and cheeses from the Foxfire Mountains; rice from the Palmetto Republic; fish and shellfish from the Bay; exotic spices from the Coquina Islands; and salt and maple sugar from Esperia.

The southeastern boundary of Corntown was a broad dusty avenue called Butcher Road. It was lined with pens where drovers brought their wares on the hoof. Goats, sheep, swine, and cattle milled around, awaiting their turn at the nearby slaughterhouses.

Beyond Butcher Road was the leather-workers quarter, or Tannertown. In addition to raw hides and finished goods like boots, gloves, and saddles, there were also stalls for bookbinders, lantern makers, and glue renderers. The entire length of Chandler Street was devoted to soap and candles.

From there, I wandered through Weaverstown, which extends down toward the docks. Of course, textile exports form a vital part of the Anagaian economy, and here workers could be found engaged in every conceivable aspect of the business. Much of the spinning was done in the provinces, but dyers', weavers', and fullers' shops abounded as well as tailors and drapers and lace makers. Nearer the docks were rope-yards and sail-makers' lofts.

In a very old section of the city, at the extreme east end of Weaverstown, I passed a large cemetery that attracted my attention. It abutted a depressed neighbourhood called Hell's Hollow, part of the shantytown which stretched along the sand dunes of the bayshore. I kept the place in mind as I went on to investigate Smithtown.

This quarter was the smallest but most diverse. Also the smokiest, filled with kilns and furnaces. It included many trades which have little connexion to metalworking. Skilled artisans hammered out fine works in gold and silver while gem cutters practiced their precise craft. Lovely blown glass was sold in the same alley as heavy crockery, a booth offering tinned hand mirrors was tucked in between a printshop and a coal dealer. It was like that everywhere; if you had the money, you could get anything.

As darkness approached, I made my way back to the cemetery. Perhaps due to my Steward upbringing, I had never really shared the superstitions of my countrymen, and now that was a positive advantage. No Anagaian in his right mind would enter that walled graveyard after dark, but to me, there was nothing there but buried bones. After all, it was the living I had to fear. Sleeping among the dead would help keep me from becoming one of them. In any case, in all that teeming city, I was never once molested during the many nights I slept among the tombs.

Chapter 34

Marten and Wren were both looking the worse for sleep, so I promised to continue later, and for once they agreed. Despite the frequent constant grumbling of the thunder, we had no difficulty dozing off. But Marten never seemed to tire of hearing my dismal adventures. The very next day, as we sat eating lunch at the mouth of Stiles Brook, he remarked, "Something I don't understand about that story. You went from being unwanted to being wanted dead or alive. But how did the police find out you were in New Chalice? From what I hear, it's a mighty big place."

"Yeah," added Wren. "I wondered about that too. When you walked right up to the ship that night, I thought you must be crazy as a rabid fox."

"I was, in a way. It was like this," I offered, as I set down my plate and leaned back against the wares locker.

Finding a safe place to sleep was only the beginning. I also needed some means of support. After paying Fester Gilding, I had only nine falcons left, which would not last forever, no matter how I skimped. I wasn't sure how to go about finding a job, but it happened almost accidentally. I was wandering around the side streets of Weavertown one early morning when the door to one of the shops opened and a stocky man poked his head out and peered up and down the street. Not seeing whatever he was looking for, his eyes rested instead on me. He paused a moment to look me over.

"Come here, boy," he demanded, and I hastened to comply. "Take this batch of roving down to Rowell's, on Dyers Street. Come right back, and I'll give you something."

I understood at once. I had seen clusters of urchins hanging around other shopfronts, hoping to run errands for a brass bullhead or two. In my ragged clothes, he had taken me for one of those, and indeed what else was I?

According to the sign, this man was Mr. Mullet, the owner, and he supplied raw materials to several of the sweatshops in the neighbourhood. Not wishing to show my ignorance by asking questions, I took the bundle and hurried off down the street. From passersby, I got directions to Rowell's, which was only a few blocks away. The business consisted of a small storefront with a large factory room behind it. There a dozen or so women toiled over looms amid a haze of lint-dust. The owner, a bald and hunched man, answered my bell and peered at me in surprise.

"Why, you're not Wily . . . ah, but you have my roving!" With no thanks or other acknowledgment, he took the parcel and disappeared back into the workroom. Assuming they already had some arrangement for paying, I went back to Mullet's for my reward. That consisted of a single slice of none-too-fresh bread. However, in the course of the day, I got other assignments and similar rewards, so that I went "home" to the cemetery with half a loaf of barley bread and two bullhead coins. Not so bad—at least I would not starve, and I might even accumulate a few coins to meet other needs, all without having to reduce my little hoard of falcons.

The next day, I returned to Mullet's to find another young fellow—obviously Wily—who clearly resented my presence. Whenever Mullet appeared, Wily showed his displeasure of me with his sharp elbows. He was bigger than I, and I might have been driven away from that patronage, but I persisted, and I discovered that Wily was not very reliable. He often disappeared for hours at a time, and in the morning, he often smelled of opium smoke. Mullet appeared not to fully trust him, and when Wily and I were both there, it was often I who was favoured.

This continued for a while, and I developed what seemed to be an almost sustainable lifestyle. Yet I knew I could not manage thus in the winter, and now and then, I even fantasized about going to someplace where I was not a fugitive. One afternoon shortly before closing time, I made a delivery, this time also at Rowell's.

"Wait just a minute," Rowell said as I started to leave. "What's your name anyway?"

"Dusty Wells, sir," I replied, a little ashamed of the lie.

"And where do you live?"

"On the street, sir. I've no home just now."

"Yes, yes, of course. Well, I can see you're a different cut from that Wily." He shook his head and sized me up a moment. "Can you do me an errand?"

"Yes, this is my last for Mr. Mullet today."

"Take this package and run it over to Swan's, on Pier Street. As fast as you can—it must be there before they close. I'll pay you in the morning. Now hurry!"

I ran as fast as I could with the awkward parcel. I understood why he was so carefully appraising me. A bundle of loose weft was nothing one would be tempted to steal, but a whole bolt of finished cloth—rather fine looking too—was another matter. Clearly he had decided I was trustworthy. I knew right where Swan's was, a big fabric export house facing the docks. I arrived there just as the manager was locking up. Having finished my business, my time was my own, and I idled along the quay, looking at the vessels moored there. I had been here before, and as usual, most of the craft were small fishing smacks, unloading their catches of shrimp or crab, or small cargo ships, which carried freight to ports all along the Anagaian coast. But this day, I saw a few larger ships in the harbour. One, a huge warship of the Imperial Navy, was moored a few *hundred yards out, and a lighter was ferrying out supplies to it. The second ship was a freighter, which flew the Imperial flag, though it had a Coquinese name. I assumed therefore it came from the occupied islands. Behind that, however, was a third ship I hadn't noticed at first.*

It was a smaller freighter—a two-master. Although I knew little of such things at the time, I now know it was a schooner. It came from the Palmetto Republic, and a team of ebony-skinned crewmen were rolling barrels marked Sugar onto the quay. There a white merchant was overseeing their loading onto a pair of large mule-drawn wagons. When they were finished, I discreetly approached one of the workers.

"Excuse me, but does your ship ever take passengers?"

He looked at me skeptically. "Like you? You'd be wanting to go to Palmetto?"

"Perhaps, or anywhere else. Would it be possible?"

"Well, let me just tell you, man, when we leave here, we're going straight back to Palmetto, not to Grand Coquina or anywhere else. Trust me, you don't want to go to Palmetto—they despise you there, just as much as they despise us here. And anyways, it costs more than I suspect you've got. Plus you'd have to have official papers, which I'm sure you haven't got."

I turned away, feeling discouraged, but not surprised. I sauntered up the streets of the warehouse district, consoling myself that I was doing all right for the time being, and that time was on my side.

Soon after—I think it was the very next evening—I was lounging about a small square when I happened to pass a small bulletin board. I paused to glance over the clutter of advertisements tacked up there, hoping I suppose to see some notice for employment or other opportunity. On the left edge was an official police bulletin, a wanted poster. I don't know why I even bothered to look at it, but my eyes were instantly drawn to a name halfway down the page: my own. Under that, I read a description of my appearance, followed by these words:

> *Wanted for two murders, in West Umberlands A. T.; believed to be headed toward New Chalice, considered dangerous and possibly armed. Anyone having info.on suspect's whereabouts should contact nearest authority.10 S reward.*

Whatever tenuous feelings of security and confidence I had gained in the past weeks were shattered in the instant I saw that poster. What was this all about? Before I was unwanted, but now I was wanted—no one had ever considered my life worth ten gold sceptres before! And now it was two *murders? Someone was very confused, and it wasn't only me! In the cities, it was a lot more common to find people who could read. In my mind, every head was turned my way, every eye was comparing me with that scanty description. What was I to do? Leave there and move to another town or city? Was there more danger in movement, or was it safer to stay put? Since every face that looked into mine seemed to pose a threat, I headed for the cemetery, which had so far been my refuge in this city. As I approached it, I took the usual precaution of looking around to make sure I didn't give away my hideaway. No one seemed to be following me, except a pedestrian far back on the opposite side, and he turned into a doorway just as I rounded the last corner. In the gathering dusk, I quickly slipped over the waist-high wall and found my usual sleeping place among some ornamental shrubs surrounding an old tomb. I slept uneasily, not only because of this new revelation of peril, but because the night air was unusually damp and chill.*

For many weeks, I'd worn the same thin cotton shirt, and it was about to rot off from me. I knew colder weather was approaching, and for lack of a better plan, I resolved to use one of my few falcons to buy a long cloak from the used-clothes dealers. It could double as a blanket in the months to follow, if there were any months to follow. I also figured I might draw less notice if I weren't always carrying my stuff around with me, like a newly arrived vagrant. People might be around the cemetery in the daytime, but I found a particularly dense clump of bushes and stashed my knapsack there. Minus, that is, the single falcon I rolled into the fold of my sash to buy a cloak. I glanced up and down the empty side street and scaled the low wall into the predawn city. I was hungry, as always, so I headed first for Mullet's to see if I might earn a crust for breakfast. Being so early, I was only a little surprised to find none of the usual street kids around. That was encouraging as it bode well for my eating before noon. I knew Mullet lived upstairs over the shop, and I loitered there awhile, waiting for him to open for business. When he finally stuck his head out the door, he looked startled, even frightened, to see me.

"You, you're here! Why . . . you're him, aren't you, that Seekings guy? No, never mind, just get out of here. They were here an hour ago, woke me up to see if I knew about you. I said no, but I know they didn't believe me. They'll be back anytime to put a watch on the street. You gotta get out of here fast!"

Then he pulled back in and slammed the door. I took to my heels even as he was speaking. I had to get back to my stuff fast. I scouted the cemetery quickly to make sure a guard hadn't been posted in the short time since I left. No one. I leaped over the wall—no time to be discreet—and ran to my hiding place. Even before I got there, I knew something was wrong. The knapsack lay there on the open grass, the jug beside it, and the limp coin bag. I didn't have to lift it to know it was empty. Stuffing it all together, I ran away from there, down toward the waterfront. Where to go? If they were closing in on me, was one place any better than another? The warehouse district seemed to have less traffic than other parts of the city, so I found a narrow alleyway and made myself a little nook among the rubbish and broken barrels there. A few rats skittered around in the debris, but they were the least of my worries—indeed I felt a kinship with them. We were all trying desperately to survive while the cats of the world were on the prowl for us. Occasionally, someone walked or drove past the end of the alley, but my hiding place seemed safe, at least for now.

When night fell again, my determination to not budge was somewhat weakened by discomfort, and I resolved to at least explore the immediate neighbourhood, in the faint hope of finding anything useful. Although there was a full moon, there were also broken clouds so that one moment it might be quite light, the next plunged into murky shadows. I certainly wouldn't venture into the street but climbed over a high board fence into an adjacent alley. From there I was able to slink across a darkful loading platform and down yet another alley. When I passed a wooden door in a warehouse wall, I must have stirred up a watchdog that was sleeping within, for there was an awful clamour of barking. I heard footsteps coming. This alley was blocked by a parked cart, half unloaded. However, the warehouse roof was pretty low on this side, so I frantically leaped onto the back of the cart and shinnied up onto the roof just as two men came out. I was surprised that two watchman would be guarding a single building, but apparently they had been in the process of unloading the cart when the dog sounded the alarm. They continued carrying the long heavy crates between them into the building while I flattened myself against the shingles above them. They worked very furtively, and I concluded they were moving contraband, possibly arms. The dog kept growling from inside, and I was extremely relieved when a rat darted down the passageway. One of the man muttered that the fool mutt wouldn't know the difference between a rat and a CADS spy. The second man rejoined that he wasn't so sure he could either. I waited breathlessly until they were both back inside; then I crawled silently across the roof to the other side. There I was able to lower myself onto a stable roof and thence to the ground. I found myself not in another alley but on the edge of Pier Street. I recognized the neighbourhood—in fact, the stable and adjoining warehouse belongs to the export company Swan's. For the moment, the moon was obscured, and I got on my hands and knees to search the ground in front of the stable door for any spilled grain the rats might have missed. Even raw chaffy oats would've been a welcome treat about then, but the pavement had been recently swept clean. Only then did I stand up and notice something new: across the street, a pier jutted out into the harbour, and beside it lay a new ship—at least I hadn't seen it on my last delivery there. A freighter it was, I could make out little else in the weak light. The figurehead was a carved whale, the name was stenciled in a foreign script I didn't recognize. But the flag, which hung limply above the naked rigging, was . . . yes, I could now make it out: a yellow flower on a green field. The flag of Esperia, whence came Faring and all the orphanage staff!

    To this day, I do not know why I was so foolhardy—I stepped out from the shadowy eaves of the stable and slinked across the street and right out onto the pier, totally exposed to view. Sidling up close to the hull, I peered at the marvelous vessel. It was going to a country about which we heard so many grand rumours and the so few reliable facts. The very name Esperia evoked so many emotions in me, I was momentarily mindless of the great risk I ran in just standing there. Nevertheless, my heart almost popped out of my chest in alarm when I heard a quiet voice from the shadows ask, "May I help you?"

During this narrative, my boatmates were all attention, but my voice was getting tired of always being the storyteller, so I suggested, "Wren, why don't you take it from here? You know this part of the story as well as I do."

"Okay, but I won't tell it as well. I was on watch that night—looters are a constant problem there. I saw this guy sneaking out of the shadows, only moments after the watchman had passed by. I assumed he was after pelf, but when he came right across and stood there in the open, gawking at the *Minkey*, I wondered if he was out of his head. I was about to blow the whistle for help, but I decided to watch him a bit longer—I didn't wish to get anyone in trouble for nothing. I was standing in the shadow of the deckhouse, and he didn't seem to have a clue that I was there. I finally figured that he meant no harm, and I hated to alarm him, so I just quietly asked, 'May I help you?' I thought he'd pass out, but he didn't try to run. All he said was 'You're from Esperia! You're Stewards!' I was going to say something cheeky, but this guy didn't look like he could handle much banter. I gotta tell you, Marten, he was a mess—filthy and tattered and malnourished, even worse than when you first met him at Stonesthrow. His eyes were sunken and glazed. He sounded like he had buzzard snot for brains, blubbering about how 'they' were after him. He admitted right away that he was accused of murder and that there was a price on his head. Imagine telling me, a stranger, that if I ratted on him, I could get ten fat sceptres for it! I knew there was something to it despite his ranting, the facts hung together pretty well, what facts there were anyway. Also, he wasn't even suggesting I should help him in any way. It just seemed like he was desperate to have someone to confide in, whatever the risks.

"He was either crazy or telling the truth, and I suspected the latter. And of course, I knew that if he was innocent, I and the whole crew were bound by our Refuge Laws to help him escape. Yet if he were guilty of murder, we were bound to turn him over to CADS, however distasteful that might be. It wasn't a decision I could make alone. We also couldn't converse out there in the open where a watchman might return at any time, so I pointed out a place under the pier where the stone pilings formed a sort of narrow ledge below the planking. I gave him a bit of my acorn cake and asked him to wait there for my return. I immediately awoke Arnica and the others and told them of this development. After hasty discussion, we all agreed that everyone couldn't go back up to interview the guy, yet we had to be more positive before risking the ship and all our lives by violating Anagaian law. It was decided that Arnica would join me in questioning the man, and the rest would abide by our judgment—a major show of trust, considering the stakes.

"Back under the dock, we crowded together to hear Yaro's story and to whisper questions we hoped would either trip him up or vindicate him. He showed us his single falcon and the note from his mother, and I asked about the knapsack and water bottle he'd mentioned. He didn't have them, which made us a little skeptical. He told us where he had left them, and I confronted him with an offer to fetch them for him. He was quick to agree, and sure enough, I found them in the alley exactly where he'd said. Later, before daybreak, I ducked back under the pier to return his stuff and offer him safe passage to Esperia. Then he got all emotional, and I had to calm him down, lest he give us away. Of course, we still had another two days of loading to finish—some of our cargo was still arriving from the countryside. We slipped him some food and told him to sit tight, which couldn't have been too comfy. We couldn't take them onboard with all the customs inspectors nosing about. The second day, I stopped by the CADS office where I found out about the second murder charge—his mother. I guess you already know about that. We realized that we couldn't possibly sneak him onboard before our departure. The government had leads of a major gunrunning plot—to the Coquinese rebels to fight their own troops—and of course, there were the usual drug smugglers and fugitives like Yaro. The harbour was under unusually tight scrutiny, which made his stroll on the pier all the more rash. Arnica hatched an alternative plan: he had some contact with this smuggler who was with the Brotherhood. He was really reluctant to use the guy for fear of exposing his own connexions, but he decided it was the only way we could rescue Yaro. You see, Yaro, if you'd been caught at that point, it would've been a lot more than your life: it could have destroyed a whole section of our intelligence-gathering network."

I didn't know quite what to say. All I could get out was "I'll never forget what I owe you guys."

Wren modestly added, "It was Arnica who really stuck his neck out."

"I know how that stuff works," I insisted. "The whole crew would've been blamed. You all probably would've rotted in jail, if not worse."

Wren shrugged, and I added, "As for your original question, Marten, I don't know how CADS knew I was in New Chalice as opposed to the other coastal cities. Probably an educated guess. But as for how they figured out I was working for Mullet, as I said before, a person was following me near the cemetery, but then he crossed the street and disappeared. I'll never know for sure, but in hindsight, I'm assuming it was Wily."

Chapter 35

By now, the Broadlea Valley had fully awakened from the clutches of winter. One might find occasional banks of rotting snow in the denser shade of hemlock thickets, but in general, the ground was clear as trout lilies and wake-robins announced the arrival of warmer weather. We often picked fiddleheads for supper, and each dusk, we were entertained by the clownish beeping of woodcocks as they spiraled upward from the flattened thatch of last year's hay stubble. Maple sugar making was done now, and many folks were busy with pruning orchards or cutting basket-willows. Even slower-flowing streams had a strong current at this season, and countless weirs and mill dams had to be passed, which slowed our progress. This problem was indirectly a boon for us, because any obstacle to larger boats created a special opportunity for *Come-What-May*. Indeed our business was going very well there, and we probably could have made a decent living in the Humps area alone, but Wren had decided it was time to head for the Upper Valley.

The distinction between the Upper and Lower Valley is no vague one, but rather as sharp a line as the mapmaker can draw. In the geological past, some writhing and twisting of the earth's crust caused the Upper Valley to be thrust upward (or perhaps the Lower Valley to settle downward—it all depends on your viewpoint). The resulting escarpment, which geographers call the Redwing Cleft, crosses the Broadlea Valley in a more or less straight line, visible in places as cliffs up to fifty feet high. It loses itself in the Humps, only to reemerge at such distant places as Juniper Wells and Cobbed Hill.

My first view of the escarpment was at Drumhead Falls, an impressive cataract where the Broadlea River thunders over a twenty-five-foot ledge amid great foam and mist. It is, of course, unnavigable, and the only means of passing it is by canal locks. To do so, one has to leave the Broadlea itself and go up a tributary stream called Solace Brook where four consecutive locks climb 30 feet in elevation. At that point, one can take a canal back over to the Upper Broadlea at a point well above the falls. That is called the Trillium Neck Canal, and it takes nearly an hour to negotiate the whole system. Nevertheless, it is the main avenue of transport in and out of the watery region called the Fenlands. The Upper Valley is a huge basin extending from the Sanctuary Mountains to the Talus Hills in the south. The same ice sheet which formed the Humps filled the basin with glacial sediments which remain trapped behind the escarpment rim. The result is a broad alluvial plain twelve to fifteen miles across, with poor drainage. The terms *Fenlands* and *Upper Valley* are sometimes used interchangeably, but correctly speaking, the *Fenlands* refers only to Pike Lake and the surrounding wetlands as far as the Margin Canal system, none of which varies from the rest by more than ten feet of elevation. For a further description of the region, I refer to my diary.

> 5/26/48: We entered Pike Lake this morning. What a curious place this is. At a glance, one might assume nature has played a cruel trick on this region, but as we entered the lake at Copseditch, it became obvious that the inhabitants have turned its shortcomings very much to their advantage. Unable to get rid of the water, the Fenlanders have learned to live with it—with it, around it, and on it. It permeates their very lives. On the marshy shore, people have built up artificial islands by dredging broad channels and filling in the shallows. Houses here have no dug cellars because of the water table. The main roads hereabouts are canals.
>
> The canals are all but choked with water lilies and river-oats, which people harvest right into their boats. There is also a tall reed whose seed is harvested for grain. Another plant called marsh-potato has an arrowhead-shaped leaf and thrives in the muddy shallows. We did not see any today as they are harvested in late fall by raking the mucky bottom and collecting the tubers which rise to the surface. To the Fenlanders, they are a staple; but elsewhere, a delicacy. None of these wetlands crops are wild, having been improved over the centuries by intensive breeding and cultivation.
>
> One of the most ubiquitous crops, here and in wetlands everywhere, is the cattail rush. It seems there is nothing folks here don't do with cattails. Wren says they eat the young shoots in salad, they steam the young green heads, they process food starch from the rootstocks, and they add the dried yellow pollen to pan-bread. They weave the stems and thatch with the leaves. My quilted winter coat was filled with cattail down, as were my boots, while the soles of my sandals are made of braided rushes. Back at Stonesthrow, the roof is insulated with cattails, and our chair seats are woven from the twisted leaves. The divider that forms my "bedroom" is a screen of woven rushes and, likewise, the beautiful mats which adorn and soften the walls. Martin says most of the communities in this region feature cattails on their banner emblems. It's really different here; even I can detect a subtle difference in people's accents.

It was no accident, this intensive development of wetlands for their own sake. It took centuries of effort to adapt these marshes for human habitation. I had to wonder what had induced people to settle them in the first place. Marten explained that during the Calamities, when most of the Stewards had fled into the Sanctuary Mountains, one group (the Southcamp band) managed to find refuge in the wild marshes around Pike Lake and Brass and Gander Lakes. Their enemies considered it a soggy wasteland, and indeed it was; but having little choice, the early Fenlanders learned to live with what the area produced. They even improved upon it to the point where today, wetlands are some of the nation's most productive lands. Not only are they rarely drained, but in some areas, they've been expanded to enhance their productivity.

As fascinating as this region was, Wren explained that we would not find good trading here. With so much water-transport infrastructure, the locals already had their own system of carrying goods that was too well-established for us to compete with.

We left the lake by going up Shadow Brook, but hardly had we started up it when we entered the Arum Canal and crossed over to Steppingstones Stream. The Arum Canal is a link in the ring of canals which surround the entire Fenlands. Wren had an old friend who lived in North Arum, and we stopped there for our day off.

Steppingstones Stream is essentially the upper continuation of the Broadlea. It winds and braids its way through an area littered with glacial debris. In some spots the soft bottom tried to grab our poles, and we had to yank them back from the sucking mud. Elsewhere the clean water rippled over hard gravel, and it was here that we saw the Steppingstones Placer Research Laboratory. I had no idea what that meant, and Wren said it was new in the last two years. We were all very curious to see it, so we tied up and went ashore to investigate.

A large shed held bins full of sand, which was variously cleaned and sifted. A technician explained that the sand was a by-product of numerous placer-mines in the neighbourhood. The local sand and gravel was run through sluices to capture any gold, tin, magnetite, or garnet in it. These all had various uses, and the remaining sand was useless to them, but not to the laboratory. The technician showed us a sophisticated apparatus: a round vibrating table which was slightly conical. By fine-sorting the sand according to density, they could remove most of the mica and feldspar, leaving nearly pure quartz or silica. Once separated, the actual sand particles were quite free of impurities. He said this quartz sand was potentially worth more than all the other products combined, if they could just find an economical method of large-scale cleaning.

Now I understood why this research was deemed so important that it was wholly funded by the VFC. It was about the impending glass boycott and the urgent need for Esperia to produce its own silica.

We hadn't expected to trade at the laboratory, but the head technician bought some miscellaneous hardware. He paid us in gold dust, which set me to thinking: I knew Esperians weren't big into self-adornment, and I wondered if there were even such a thing as an Esperian jeweler. Wren informed me that as far as he knew, there was not. However, there are Esperian dentists, and much of the nation's meagre gold production goes to that use. Some finds its way into international trade and may eventually return to us as Anagaian sceptres or Coquinese royalpalms.

*   *   *   *   *   *   *

"That's not it. It can't be it!"

"I'm telling you, that's it."

"There's got to be more to it. It's just too important."

"I suppose it is important, in a way. But nevertheless, that's all there is to it. What more were you expecting?"

"I mean, there should be some shrine built around it or something. There should be mobs of pilgrims. Look at that path—hardly anyone ever comes here. Have you ever seen many people here?"

"I've never been here myself. Too out of the way, and no reason to come."

"No reason? Why, to read it, of course."

"Yaro, it's in every history book. I believe they copied it right. Why do I have to see it for myself?"

I was shocked at the blase attitude of my two companions. We were in the banner of Markings, about a mile beyond the point where *Come-What-May* had hit bottom. In deference to my eagerness, Wren and Marten had agreed to take a short hike to this spot, which was such an historical landmark. Before us stood a large schist outcropping covered with the engraving from which the nearby bannerhouse took its name. Off to our right a few rods was beautiful Curtain Falls, and before us rose the steep flank of Stackpole Mountain, southernmost of the Sanctuary Range. Fine mist from the falls drifted our way as it must have done for centuries before. Lichens and mosses clung to the niches formed by the letters, nearly obscuring them. Surrounded by towering old-growth beaches and oaks, its presence here seemed almost enigmatic, although there was no puzzle at all about its meaning. Anyone in the nation could tell you exactly the day and month and year when the chisel had first gouged those words. One needn't be an historian; one simply had to know what today's date was, because the years of the Esperian calendar count from this one event. Actually, if one bothers to scrape away the rock tripe and read the words underneath, it is a rather prosaic document. It is a deed, or rather a treaty, and it commemorates an agreement between the early Stewards and their erstwhile enemies. Prior to the West Purchase, as it is now called, the Stewards were a miserable bunch of seminomadic bands, surviving in the upper reaches of the Sanctuary Mountains. However, as the civilization from which they had fled began to collapse upon itself, their persecutors withdrew to more favourable regions. The Stewards meanwhile had finally managed to gain a strong foothill in their highland home, building terraced gardens on steep rocky slopes and growing in numbers as only their vegan lifestyle could support. By then the fertile valleys below them were all but abandoned, except for a few squalid inhabitants who barely subsisted on desultory farming and hunting. In time the Stewards prospered to the point where they offered to buy out their neighbours, who eagerly agreed and moved away to join their racial brothers elsewhere. (Although the ethnic origins of the original Stewards are veiled in obscurity, it is likely that by this early date their appearance was much like the swarthy-skinned Esperians of today.)

The inscription describes the agreement in some detail: in exchange for three pounds of gold dust and five wagonloads of shelled corn, the Stewards and their heirs forever would own, possess, and occupy the lands and waters lying between the Sanctuaries and the Talus Hills to the south and west of Solace Brook and Stoutstaff Brook. To the lowlanders, who viewed the land as a wilderness waste, it was a bargain; but to anyone who looks at what it has become today, the "Old Ones" appear to have been shrewd businessmen indeed. This land, comprising what is now known as the Upper Valley, was but the first of several territorial acquisitions. All were the results of treaties, and all involved payment on mutually agreeable terms, the only form of "conquest" Stewards ever found acceptable.

*　*　*　*　*　*　*

In the course of the next few weeks, Wren discovered that some of his assumptions about this area were not wholly correct. For example, there is a network of tiny stead-built canals that connects Steppingstones Brook with Shadow Brook, but it is only meant for bantam-scows and is impassible by tramps. Or rather *was* impassible; we were actually able to get through with great effort (and a fair amount of help from neighbouring steadfolk who winched us out of a couple tight places). It took some unloading to get us over one shallow stretch, but it showed folks there how little was needed to make a usable link between the two brooks. As at Phoebe earlier, *Come-What-May,* by its very appearance, inspired a spate of local infrastructural improvements.

All this time, our trading had been wholly confined to the Broadlea fair. A couple times in our travels, we had been very close to the Laughingwater drainage; but there was no water passage over the Sanctuary Mountains nor, at that time, over the Humps. So according to my map, we could not enter the valley without going down to the Bluemeadow, up to Convene, and entering the Laughingwater at its mouth. I was looking forward to that move with eager anticipation for reasons I couldn't quite name. Perhaps it was because I had heard about Laughingwater since earliest childhood. Granted, I hadn't heard anything very specific about it, except that it was "home" to most of the orphanage workers. Since my arrival at Stonesthrow, I had been studying a lot about Esperian history, and I had learned that many of the seminal events which defined the modern nation had occurred in the Sanctuary Mountains, particularly in that part drained by the Laughingwater. Who doesn't know about the Juniper Legend, the Cairns Massacre, the Archives? Even before the West Purchase Treaty, which is a turning point in the modern era, the Laughingwater region was the cradle of Esperian culture, indeed of Steward culture. But was that the main reason I craved to see that upland valley? Or was it perhaps because of that certain reputation Laughingwater folk had even among fellow Stewards? Actually, each of the regions had its own stereotype, accurate or not: coastal folk were supposedly sharp-witted and cosmopolitan, Broadlea was viewed as easy-going, perhaps even complacent. But Laughingwater? Well, no one actually used the word *fanatic*, but the implication was that they took things very seriously, particularly things connected to the Vision. Set in the interior highlands with the lowest per capita consumption of all nine fairs, Laughingwater was nevertheless the largest supporter of the Vision Fulfillment Fund, far beyond their formal tax obligations, and they also operated the largest number of foreign missions. It sounded like a region where I might find people with shared interests, and I was excited at the prospects of trading there.

During the last two weeks of spring, we focused on Prism Brook and its tributaries: Kindred, Stoutstaff, and Rapshin Brooks. Gunkholing around those little brooks was slow and tedious, with frequent obstructions and endless lock waits, but it was usually well worth it. We picked up lots of the usual up-country merchandise: potash and maple sugar, odd lots of hemp and linen cloth, crockery, ash-splint baskets, tools, that sort of thing.

By now we were only nine weeks into the season, and we had already explored a large part of the Broadlea fair, including the upper extremities of most of its brooks, to Wren's satisfaction. That is to say, there was *lots* more trade potential on any of those brooks, but our job for now was to probe the area, test the infrastructure, and determine just where and how boats of our type could operate most profitably.

It was usually quite late in the day when we finished trading; often we would simply tie up somewhere, have a cold supper, and go right to sleep—two of us in the dingle and the other on the locker under the canopy. This was not particularly comfy, and of course, we were exposed to mosquitoes and blackflies. So occasionally, we would drop in at the nighmost stead and ask to sleep in their barn or shed. Most folks wouldn't hear of this; instead they'd invite all three of us into the steadhouse, usually in time for a hot supper. Of course, we were quite prepared with "host-gifts," as etiquette required; but whenever they spotted Wren's fine dulcitar sticking out of his pack, he'd be asked to give a tune. When they'd hear how good he was, it often evolved into an impromptu concert party, with neighbours invited in and special desserts served. In the morning, our host-gifts would be adamantly refused; instead we would be sent on our way with something home-cooked for lunch. Wren was really that good!

This stead-hopping had a great advantage for me: I got to visit a lot more households and make many more friends than if we'd stayed on the boat while Wren did the trading. For Wren, it was quite satisfactory too—he got lots of attention from admiring young people, especially females, his favourite kind!

That was just Wren's way: during the day, he was all hard-driving business, but when it was over, he was the fun-loving life of the party. He was good looking and popular; the girls all loved him, and he loved them all. He probably could have found a match among any of them, but he seemed to be looking for something in particular. Anyway, he always said he could never leave his life on the river, so I assumed his love life might always be a matter of flirting and flitting.

I probably would have taken less interest in his love life if I had any of my own. It was kind of funny in a way. I liked some of the girls, and some of them seemed to like me; but while Wren kept himself free of commitment, I already found myself deeply committed to futility. Although I had begun to question the wisdom of my relationship with Fawn, deep down I really loved her as a person, even if we were ill-suited for each other. Somehow I felt ashamed of my doubts—were they merely expedients? After all, she was still alive. I had heard stories about lovers being parted for years then one returning unexpectedly to find the other married to someone else. How horrible that must be! Unless time would somehow mend things, I could see no way of resolving this emotional quagmire.

* * * * * * *

One late evening after a hot and hectic day, we were poling down Prism Brook. It was long after our usual quitting time, but we were drifting leisurely in the gentle current to get an easy jump on the next day. Marten was sprawled in the dingle, savouring the cooler air of twilight, and I was in the stern, casually poling along. As we rounded a sharp bend, Wren called back from the bow. "Cease!" That was our signal to stop poling. Perhaps a rock or snag ahead? I peered ahead to see what was up, then I heard him call quietly, "Coming through!" There was a wide pool in the stream, and in the gloom, I could make out a dozen or more women skinny-dipping. It was, after all, not a time of day when boat traffic was much to be expected, and they were merely enjoying a respite from the day's heat. Now I could well imagine how such a scene might have played out back in my native Umberlands (assuming such a marvelous swimming hole could be found), so I was curious to watch this situation unfold. There was a calm hustle of brown bottoms and bouncing breasts as everyone reached for a towel or something. There were no prudish gasps or embarrassed squeals at the approach of strange men, just a reasonable effort to salvage a modicum of decency from the situation, on the assumption that we would do the same, thank you. And we did, although I confess it took a bit of self-control to keep my eyes on the water ahead. (What made me even more uncomfortable was that *they* were all staring at *me*, an obvious foreigner.) As soon as we had passed through them, Wren called, "Resume!" And we pushed forward again, the sooner to be out of their way. Once around the bend, we heard splashing and laughing as the bathing party continued behind us. I couldn't help teasing Wren.

"I never knew you to be in such a hurry to leave a party with pretty girls."

"We weren't invited to that party."

"Still, it was a public thoroughfare. No one could accuse us of peeping, yet I noticed you didn't"

"What's the pleasure of seeing what someone doesn't want to show you?"

That was the thing, I realized. Mind you, we were three virile males with quite normal instincts. Wren, of all people, was not puritanical. He was just raised in a crowded society where people learn from birth to value privacy by according it to others.

Chapter 36

Under the sun's steadier gaze, the whole valley was really heating up. All around were signs of the earth's great fecundity. Perennial crops were leafing out while tender shoots thrust themselves eagerly skyward. The green luxuriance all had an intensity about it that I had never seen on any Umberlands farm. Sometimes I seemed to actually feel with my senses the photosynthesis that Marten explained to me: the "sound" of sunshine striking chlorophyll, the smell of starch and sugar grains lining themselves up on tissue walls. With ample soil moisture, the corn and oats seemed to transpire like the damp exhalation of a living breathing earth.

The earth itself was not often visible, however—Esperians consider it no more proper to leave soil bare to the elements than to stare at the naked womb of a woman giving birth. Rows of tomato plants burst from a steamy straw mulch while chickpeas tucked their toes gratefully under a cool cloak of decayed black wood chips. Even the close rows of grain were not suffered to stand in unclad soil. Blades of spring wheat poked up through a light blanket of shredded leaves. They shared the same ground with field peas, whose broad leaves captured much of the otherwise-wasted sunlight. Together the two crops kept the ground beneath them moist and friable, allowing no weeds to take hold in their dense shade. At harvest time they would be threshed and winnowed together, then separated through screens.

I saw many other instances of two or more crops sharing the same ground. Indeed it is much rarer to see any crop growing all by itself. Currants throve in the half-shaded alleys between nut pines; runner beans scrambled up the sunflowers; snow peas clung to their trellises of woven alder brush, towering above crowded beds of parsnips or leeks. Some combinations of crops are more complicated, with one crop being planted while another is half grown, and still another is about to be harvested. It is not a casual business, Marten explained to me. For example, one must sow the right variety of field pea with the right variety of spring wheat, else the one might ripen and shatter onto the ground while the other is still green. Heights must be compatible, and fertility needs must mesh. Spacings of each must be precise. And overall hang the restraints of a short cool season. Yet the Esperians are not casual gardeners, as none can deny. They have spent centuries working out these details, and they attend to them diligently. As I observed how they managed to cram so many plants into so small an area, I began to comprehend why there are so many Esperians and none of them hungry.

*　　*　　*　　*　　*　　*　　*

The week before Banner Day, we all heard of the fall of Palm Bay, the capital of Grand Coquina. We were dismayed to hear that the Olotal's troops had triumphed at last, but there was some consolation: the Coquinese government was very corrupt and cruel to its own people, and Esperians had long been ambivalent about aiding the defending army. With the native government fled into exile, a true people's resistance emerged in the outlying provinces, with remnants of the defeated army joining the insurgents. Esperia immediately stepped up its shipments of "humanitarian assistance": food, medicine, tents, blankets. The Anagaians protested that we were violating our neutrality stance. They were bluntly reminded that neutrality had been a policy, but Esperia had never made a formal treaty to that effect. In fact, that neutrality had long been an agonizing source of contention within Esperia. Was not a native tyrant better than an imperialist occupier? Probably no controversy had ever divided the nation so painfully as the question of whether it was prudent, or even moral, to stand by while another nation was invaded.

Anyway, the Anagaian embassy was told flatly that our commercial relations with another sovereign state were our own business. To me at the time, this seemed audacious in the extreme. Had not Anagaia the mightiest military establishment on earth? What resources did tiny Esperia have to withstand an invasion? Yet most Esperians seemed fully confident that their position was not inferior. What did they know that I didn't? When I discussed this with the guys, Wren hinted that there was some special understanding with the Amanita; and that at some point, Esperians might be glad to see an Anagaian army on their own soil. I could hardly imagine what he meant.

Also in the news was labour unrest in Borealia. This also had to do with the Coquinese conflict. Although race mates of the Anagaians, Borealians generally consider Esperians to be preferable as allies. The two northern nations might not see eye to eye on many things, but Borealians knew they had nothing to fear from their darker-skinned neighbours. Still, Borealia knew where its economic interests lay, and they *did* have a strict neutrality pact with the Empire. Highly dependent on lumber exports, they had many contracts for the building of wooden warships. However, the Borealian government's actions were not based on consensus, and the shipyard workers themselves were unwilling to work on warships destined for the Imperial Navy. When the shipbuilders went on strike, their government repressed them, but there continued to be slowdowns and sabotage of their own facilities.

7/12/48: We hear a lot about the sheet glass shortage and the need to do something about it, but today we saw some real innovation, with an alternative material I never even heard of. Here in Shaley Woods, we visited a stead where they have a couple of large greenhouses with glass on the roofs only; the vertical walls are made of a new experimental material called cellopane. This slightly tinted glass substitute is made from "soluble cellulose," which in turn is made from wood, by some complicated process I still don't understand. The greenhouse manager explained that it may never be suitable for residential use, but it seems to work fine for greenhouses and cold frames. It is stiff like very heavy paper, yet more flexible than glass. Since much of the demand for glass is driven by construction of new greenhouses to extend the season for fresh salad greens, this cellopane must be a very exciting alternative, although it has some drawbacks. No wonder the VFC is heavily subsidizing the research.

Those particular greenhouses are wholly devoted to the commercial production of luffa sponges, which ordinarily will not mature here. We already have a few imported luffas in our cargo, but we bought several dozen of these despite the much higher price. Wren says people will snap them up, being domestic grown. We also traded for a keg of pine tar and five gallons of linseed oil, both of which are on Ermine's list. I assume they're for the rainwear shop.

We also passed a factory that makes saltpeter for the powder works down at Zenith, but according to the Pits-and-Parapets Laws, we aren't allowed to carry explosives in mixed cargoes.

It's dusk now, and just a few minutes ago, we had a really exciting experience, at least for me. We are on a part of Stoutstaff Brook, which is bordered by quite extensive forest. I saw several shadowy forms run across the brook and disappear into the trees. Wren says they are coyotes, probably from the nearby Sacred Groves, and that we shouldn't disturb them. Not disturb them! In Umberlands, there'd be a troop of bounty hunters out to exterminate them. But Wren says they are quite harmless to us since we keep no sheep or chickens, etc. What we do have in many places is deer, which destroy crops. Everybody hates the deer, but nobody likes to kill them since they're not valued as food; and so folks are grateful for the coyotes, which keep the deer thinned out. I'm nervous about sleeping on the bank, knowing the coyotes are close by; but Wren insists they never attack humans, least of all healthy adults. All the same, I'm sleeping on the boat.

In the morning, we're leaving early for Bluemeadow Fair since the day after tomorrow is Banner Day.

I got quite a surprise when I awoke the next morning. Another tramp was tied up on the other side of the pier—they must've arrived after dark when we were asleep. Wren was already up and fixing breakfast, but he had left it to go over and talk with them. What surprised me was that two of the three men were white and dressed like

Anagaians. Yet their boat, the *Amber Ambler*, was obviously of Esperian design, probably built at Longlogan. Despite my scary encounter with Lord Amberson, I overcame my hesitation and went over to join them. They were asking Wren detailed questions about goods and prices, routes and obstacles, and he was responding with as much candour as if they were fellow steadmates.

It turned out the white men were father and son; and the father had purchased the boat outright for his own trading, which apparently is perfectly legal here. In fact, he was in no way required to have the Steward as part of the crew, but had hired him to act as guide and interpreter. Not of the language—both father and son spoke quite acceptable Mok, but rather to interpret the customs and regulations, which they needed to understand to do business here effectively. I asked the son why more Anagaians didn't trade here, since it was obviously permitted. He gave me this explanation: "There's a lot to learn, that's why we have Linden with us. The others, they always try to cheat, so they ruin it for the rest of us, the bastards. They short-count, they lie about boycott exemption, they adulterate their goods whenever possible. But you can only do that once, even to these Esperians. Once they get the idea that you dwell in a Small House, as they call it, you're all finished. No fines, no jail, word just gets around, and nobody will deal with you. We've been trading here for years, my dad and I. It was hard at first, no one trusted us, but by now, lots of people have figured out who we are and that we're trying to do things their way. It's worth it, believe me. My uncles own a trading company back home, and when we show up each fall with our Esperian merchandise, it sells right off the wharf for top-falcon. Everyone knows you can't beat the quality."

"So you go back and forth each year, but most of your lives you spend in Esperia. Wouldn't it make more sense to become citizens here?"

"We have to keep going back. We have family there, if you know what I mean. And anyway, Esperia wouldn't let us immigrate—we're white, after all."

"It's not because of that," I explained, a bit defensively. "I'm white too, and I'm an immigrant."

"Must be a special case, then. They don't usually let outsiders in, not as permanent settlers anyway."

"I got in under the Refuge Laws," I admitted. "But the main reason they're closed is because they feel the country is about as crowded as it should be, and they don't want to overstrain their resources. After all, they limit their own numbers even more strictly, through birth control."

"I suppose that's so. Anyway, it's nice to be living here, even as outsiders. They use us better here than our own people do at home."

Later, when we were by ourselves, I asked Wren why the Anagaian government would let them come here in the first place. After all, most people had to have special permits to travel around, even within the country. His reply:

"I'm sure there's a lot in what he said about his family back home. With their extensive business interests and all, they probably make very good hostages. Unlike you, these two don't have a stead sponsoring them as sojourners, so they have little choice but to go back from time to time, if only to refinance. But I doubt that's the only reason the Olotal lets them hang out here."

"What you mean?"

"It's generally known that those guys are acting as spies for their government."

"Really?" I gasped. "That fellow seemed really sincere when he said how much he likes it here."

"Oh, I'm sure he was. Still, he probably feels he's got to do what he's got to do, for his family's sake, you know."

"If they're known to be spying, why doesn't someone throw them out?"

"I guess everyone likes them too much. They seem like nice guys, don't they?"

"Nice guys?! But think of the harm they could do!"

"What harm? What information can they collect that we wouldn't gladly share? If they give the Olotal and his advisers a better understanding of us, what more could we want?"

"How about military secrets? Defense plans?"

"Our defense plans are well-known. We've certainly told everyone. There may be some classified details, but those two are unlikely to stumble onto them. Besides, there's little mischief they can do with that fellow Linden tagging along. I wouldn't be surprised if he picks up more useful information from them than vice versa. Don't worry, people will keep an eye on them."

I understood what he meant. Most folks were very friendly to me here, but I knew I could do nothing suspicious without it being noticed.

Chapter 37

Banner Day is the closest thing there is to a national, or patriotic holiday. Like every other Esperian holiday, it has several names: Gathering of the Banners, Mid-Year, Unity Day, and of course, Summer Solstice.

We hurried through breakfast and pushed off for Bluemeadow. It was easy going this time, with the current always with us. In the evening, we encountered swarms of people heading the opposite direction, toward Broadlea Fair; but once through the Trice Canal, traffic was moving with us. Though it was all downstream, it was midmorning of Banner Day when we finally tied up a half mile above the fairgrounds—there was no way to get near the piers with that crowd. Marten and I knew we'd be meeting our steadmates there, so we took as much of the stuff on Ermine's list as we could carry.

Surrounding the fairgrounds was a forest of flagpoles, one for each of the banners comprising the fair. We arranged to meet back on *Come-What-May* that night, knowing that in that milling throng, we might well not see each other for the rest of the day. Near the Alga banner pole, we found lots of familiar faces, including several of our steadmates. We received an especially warm embrace from Ermine.

"Just look at you two—a rougher pair I never saw! Why, Marten, if you get any darker, we'll mistake you for a Palmettoan. Here, Myrica, what do you think of your cousin?"

"More like a couple of Coquinese pirates, the two of them," sniffed her granddaughter teasingly. "Marten looks like he never slept under a roof in his life. And Yaro—he's so fit, it's disgusting! Where's that sickly white fellow who stepped off the *Minkey*? And they both smell as if they didn't have a bottle of soap in their whole cargo."

"Unfair!" Marten protested. "We bathe daily, sometimes hourly, and we both put on fresh togs this morning."

They continued with their jibes, but I turned to Ermine.

"And you made it here," I remarked, knowing she rarely left the island.

"Couldn't keep me away with chains. Hewn and I came up yesterday on the *River Harp*—so crowded I thought we'd swamp it! We stayed with old friends at The Hedges, not far from here. We'll do the same tonight, so we can miss the mob going back."

We continued to visit with all our friends and neighbours from the island, except those who were themselves visiting elsewhere. Ermine was delighted with the wares we'd brought from the boat, and we showed her the cargo inventory so she could check off anything else she felt we or our neighbours might need. Marten and I would take those items toward our share of the profits, leaving them at Bluemeadow for our steadmates to haul home on the ferry. Everyone was excited to see how many brooms and brushes and raincoats we had sold. Combined with sales elsewhere, profits for the year were already looking very good indeed; Stonesthrow was clearly going to get its new bicycle.

At midday, food hampers were unloaded onto makeshift tables and blankets spread on the ground for a communal picnic of epic proportions. The whole idea of Banner Day is a great reunion, an affirmation of the connexion between all the people who share this vague thing called the Vision. Probably not one in a hundred could explain just what that Vision is, yet everyone understands it because it is manifested in the rivers and forests and canals and steadhouses and bannerhouses that make up the land. Esperia is first and foremost the land. Secondly, it is the people who live on the land. This day was a celebration of both and of the powerful bonds between them.

In addition to eating and visiting, group activities were going on all around the fairgrounds. Young and not-so-young enjoyed tug-of-war, sack races, and that sort of thing. Knots of men and women arguing politics, lovers announcing their intentions, new babies being presented to the assemblage for their blessing. I noticed several times that Ermine was positively aglow with the pleasure of renewed acquaintances. Despite her complaints about the crowd, I could see that this event meant an awful lot to her. I said as much to her, and she pressed my hand with youthful verve.

"You can't imagine," she explained, almost tearfully. "For so many years, we were away from this. In Anagaia, there was no feeling of 'tribe,' no powerful sense of support, or belonging . . . you know what I mean, of course. When we finally came back here, I just . . . well, I just had to take stock of it all, to rethink my role in this great storytelling."

"That storytelling being the Vision?"

"That's how I like to view it," she nodded. "I myself will not go on forever, Yaro, but the story will. That's what feels so good. I'm not sure if you can understand that."

I couldn't answer her—it wasn't a question, after all—but I thought a lot about it.

I thought even more about it as the holiday neared its culmination. Every day—even this longest day of the year—must come to an end, and as the shadows began to lengthen across the intervale, there began a keening wail of many bagpipes and the sonorous cadence of great wooden slit drums, announcing the beginning of a ceremony called the Sunflower Dance.

Actually, *march* is perhaps a more apt word for it. The Esperians have intimate dances for lovers, but this is not one of those. They have artistic dances which showcase the talent of the individual, but this is not one of those either. One doesn't *perform* the Sunflower Dance; one *enters* into it. It all began in a small cleared area around the pole bearing the national flag, a yellow blossom on a green field. As picnickers moved away toward the edges of the grounds, a few people began moving around a pole, crossing each other's paths and weaving toward, then away from, the centre. Others quickly joined, and in moments, the swirling figure had coalesced into a galaxy of bodies, numbering in the hundreds, then in the thousands. The formation grew or shrank as spectators joined the dance and later left to become spectators again. Dozens or thousands might dance—it was all the same, so long as all could hear the rhythm-keeping pulse of the drums and pipes. It didn't seem to require much skill; the steps were simplicity itself. People of even less ability than I were participating and having a grand time. I felt a surging eagerness to join in—I thought I had it figured out—but an innate voice held me back. "Be certain," it said. "Make sure you know the rules, even the rules behind the rules." Almost angrily, I answered the voice, "But there's nothing to it! I want to be one of them, why not now?" But the voice would not be ignored, and in the end I waited, impatient with that part of me which had always before seemed wise.

I was able to do one thing though: there were several lamp towers which gave some illumination to the grounds. These were not yet on, but each one had a small service platform near the top, from which an intrepid climber could get a better view of the goings-on below. A few young people were already up there, and with some effort, I joined them. As I looked down on the human kaleidoscope, the reason for the dance's name became obvious: the undulating gyre looked ever so much like an enormous sunflower head, with each dancer a seed, moving in tight spirals within the slowly rotating disk. It occurred to me that if one dilettantish individual were to decide to do their own thing, it could create a chaotic snarl. Or perhaps not; I saw one person stumble and fall down, and somehow everyone managed to make way just a bit until he was helped to his feet again.

I was quick to see the symbolism in all this. It's not about making some classy moves, it's about belonging. It's not about the individual, it's about the people. It's not enough to remember all the steps; you have to feel the rhythm.

Of course, Anagaians have a dance too—everyone does. The difference is that in their dance, you can make all the right steps and still mess up. And if you fall, no one will make way to help you up; they will trample you.

After a while, I climbed back down and prepared to head for the boat—I knew there'd be no finding Wren in this throng; but I chanced to bump into Marten, and we two went back to the Alga banner pole to take leave of our friends, some of whom had already left. Ermine was still there, and she grabbed me by the sleeve.

"Oh, Yaro, I almost forgot! How could I? I've a letter that came for you a couple weeks ago. I knew you'd probably get it sooner if I kept it until I saw you here."

It was the eagerly awaited reply from Mallard of Greengate, Otterbank, and I read it on the spot.

Dear friend,

Re your letter of 4/26, requesting information about a volunteer at the Mid-Umberlands Orphanage at Cleftridge, U.T., A.L.: we do not ordinarily release such information to Anagaian nationals without the explicit consent of the individual involved. However, given the unique nature of your situation, I have sought and rec'd permission from the Oversight Committee to make an exception to that policy.

    The individual you describe is Faring of Two Chimneys, Otterbank. In fact, his family are neighbours of mine, and I knew Faring as a young child. I asked his parents for news about his well-being, but they have not rec'd any personal communication for the past three months. The embassy at New Chalice tried to send an agent to investigate, but he was denied permission to travel to the area due to political unrest there. One should perhaps not take too great alarm at this as it is hardly the first time the authorities have blocked contact. I'm extremely sorry not to be able to give you more certain or encouraging news. I can personally appreciate your concern as my own niece is also a worker at one of the hospitals there.

    Meanwhile, I have been asked by Faring's parents to urge you to visit them here. There are old and rather poorly, but extend their warmest greetings.

    If I may be of further assistance, do not hesitate to ask.

Mallard Greengate, Otterbank.
Exec. Steward; L.F.O.F. Mission Projects
cc. Oversight Committee

I was upset and I crumpled the letter in my fist. Not that it was so surprising; throughout my childhood at the orphanage, there was a near-constant sense that the outside world might come crashing down on us at any moment. Apparently, that was exactly what had happened. Hard to be certain—news from Anagaia was so unreliable. This was not a day for brooding, however, and I tried to uncrumple my emotions and fold them neatly into my pocket.

*   *   *   *   *   *   *

The day after Banner Day was unlikely to be good for trading, with so many people still traveling home. We took advantage of the hiatus to move our operation over to the Welcome Fair. Not that we weren't doing just fine in the Broadlea, but we had a mandate after all to try out *Come-What-May* in different environments. Getting to Welcome was no easy chore, though, as the central Bluemeadow has several major falls which must be passed. At Gentian Falls, a single high lock with a long canal carries one past the rapids and another at Wright's Woe. A complicated set of self-opening and self-closing locks must be negotiated at Cataracts. In between these lie several miles of deep swift channel, which most boats can only manage by using the river-trams. Bluemeadow locks are exceptionally long and wide to accommodate the huge lumber barges, which come down from time to time from the upland fairs. Because it requires so much time and water to fill those locks, the toll is rather expensive for small boats, so we often waited for other boats to show up so we could share the toll.

At Gentian Locks, we were waiting below the nether-gate for one of those barges to pass through so we could enter and rise on the refill. Wren was explaining to me how those awkward giants could only go downriver, not up. However, they didn't need to as they were only built for one-way, one-time use. There wasn't much to operating them: a pair of sweeps to keep them in the channel and a winch to tow themselves through still water. When they reach their destination, usually Harking Bay, the lumber was loaded onto ships for export to Anagaia or the Coquinas. The barge itself was dismantled and sold for lumber too. Then the crew would walk or bicycle back home.

One of those very barges showed up while we were awaiting some upbound traffic. This particular barge had a crew of four women, all very pretty and all of them built like prizefighters. While we were waiting, a heavy shower came up and soon blew into a squall. We took shelter under our dingle, and we saw the women climb under a hastily erected canopy. However, theirs was flimsy and soon collapsed. They were getting drenched, so we yelled over to them to join us while we extended our boat tarp out over the cargo lockers to protect them and make room for our guests.

The squall did not pass over quickly, and we got well acquainted with the barge women, who it turned out were from way up in Shingletree, near the Tarnish Hills. Apparently, it was inevitable that we would soon turn to telling stories, or rather lie-swapping. Wren told a ridiculous tale about how in Ancient Times a cosmonaut got into his skyship and sailed off to some far corner of the universe to collect some magic crystals. His return was later than expected, and he admitted that he'd got lost among all the stars. His base commander asked, "So how did you finally get back?" "Oh, that part was easy. I finally ran into some tramp-traders, and they gave me directions."

Not to be outdone, the steward of the barge crew came back with a whopper of her own. Let's see if I can get it right: "Now the greatest barge that ever floated down to the sea was also the only one to have a name instead of a serial number. It was called the *Portage Pioneer*, and that monster was as wide abeam as today's barges are long. Its first and only run was with a load of oak ship-planking—enough for the entire Coquinese Navy. That vessel was as heavy as duty and harder to control than a sailor's girlfriend. Now in those days, the Bluemeadow was such a terribly winding river that it took months instead of days to run a load of cargo to the sea. In fact, it twisted about so that some vessels would round a bend and crash into their own stern; others found themselves back home and had to start out all over again. Well, mate, the *Portage Pioneer* took all summer to get as far as Jug Slough, what with getting stuck in every bend and having to be winched out. Once they reached the Estuary, the tide grabbed them and drove them along like an avalanche. The crew feared they'd miss Harking altogether and be carried out to sea—not a good idea for a lumber barge. The steward's daughter was a lusty nimble-witted girl, and she snatched up one of the huge sweeps. Standing at the bow, she thrust that oar down into the gravelly riverbed and held it with all her might. When her father and brothers saw what she was about, they did the same with the other sweeps. Except they couldn't hold on to theirs; they tried their very hardest, but they might as well have been pissing into the wind, so the daughter reached over to help them with her free hand. Well, they stopped that barge all right, but soon they heard a terrible rumbling and saw the banks and the trees go rushing past. When it was over, they saw that they were right at the Harking pier, and they had pulled the Bluemeadow into as straight a river as it is today."

Before we had finished chuckling and groaning over that one, one of her bargemates jumped in with a sequel.

"In fact, on her way back upriver, the daughter felt it was *too* straight and so she stopped to consider what to do about it. She broke loose one of the Calendar Hills and rolled it over beside the river to sit down on while she thought. Well, that river had to curve out around that hill to go on its way, and that's how Mallow's Bight came to be there. The rock she sat on is now Cobbed Hill."

This went on, back and forth, and after a while, I began to get the idea. "We had a tramp-boat come to our village once," I offered casually. It was a bald lie, of course, but what else was this about? Everyone, even my own crew mates, turned to me skeptically and asked. "Really?"

"C'mon," said Wren suspiciously. "You told me the Possum River is dry much of the time."

"Oh, it is," I agreed mischievously. "I didn't say they followed the Possum."

"How then?"

"They poled overland, but of course they could only travel at night, when there was enough dew to float them."

This one-upmanship continued with Wren and the barge steward doing most of the yarning. Some of their stories began with things like "Why does it take four people to handle a barge?" or "How does a tramp-trader teach his kids to swim?" Not all the stories were kind, or even tasteful, and I hoped Wren wasn't giving offense; but the burly barge steward was a match for him—in more ways than one as I would learn later.

On the fourth evening of summer, we were camped at the junction of the Welcome and Bluemeadow Rivers. There was a small stone fireplace there, specially built for the use of water travelers. The worst of the blackfly season was past, but mosquitoes continued to annoy in the cool of dusk, especially if you weren't daubed with pennyroyal. We had finished a generous and leisurely supper, and it was right about the time you could count on Marten to say, "Well, Yaro, so what happened after such and such?" But this time, Wren beat him to it.

"Say, Yaro, we've been hearing a lot of your adventures, and that's great, but I for one would be curious to learn more about some of the people you've mentioned."

"Fine with me. Like who?"

"Like your adopted parents, for beginners. You never talk much about them, and what little you have said isn't very flattering. I've never even heard you refer to your adopted mother as anything but Mrs. Seekings."

"Then perhaps I do them wrong. I mean, they were well-meaning folks, I can't deny, it's just that Archer failed me at the very time he should've supported me. I don't doubt they thought they did me a favour by taking me out of the orphanage. Apparently, they started out life with some real promise—their own land and all—but things just turned sour for them. Archer always seemed bitter about his lot, and I suppose that quashed whatever gentlekindness he might have had in him before. His best efforts in life never seemed quite good enough. I only saw him drunk once—he was usually very sober. I don't know how it came about. He was a pathetic blubbering fool, crying about all the right choices he might have made. He never got like that again.

"He never asked me to call him 'Dad,' which was just as well—Faring was the nearest thing to a father I ever had. Archer was just a guy I worked for. As for Mrs. Seekings, I really don't know why she ever wanted kids anyway. You see, in Umberlands, girls aren't valued very highly, but sons are all-important. Seekings already had a daughter, but I'm sure Mrs. Seekings had been raised to feel unfulfilled until she had a son. Leastwise, when I first got there, she fell all over me, showed me off to everyone in town. You'd think I was the answer to all her prayers, yet within a few weeks, her motherly affection tapered off real quick to the point where she practically ignored me, just like she ignored her own daughter Melody. Frankly, it didn't hurt my feelings in the least. I never had anything against her, but it was hard to express affection that I didn't really feel. Actually, I'd have to say we never had a relationship—we never quarreled, we never hugged, we never talked about anything important. Except religion—she was extremely devout and tried for a while to influence me but soon found me a lost cause. She consulted the priest almost daily, usually about her physical ailments, which were supposed to be many. I shouldn't say 'supposed to be.' I believe she was in genuine pain from something, but she sure made the most of it. She took to her bed more and more often and dosed herself with laudanum. Now it was the priest who came to see her almost daily, and he often urged Melody and me to copy her example of piety. The fact is, even if we'd been so inclined, we were both too preoccupied with holding the place together to pay much attention to him. By the age of fourteen, Melody was in fact the woman of the house. Most of the cooking, and all the laundry and mending fell to her. I could see her torn between loving her mother and despising her for putting a daughter in such a position. I like to think I was a comfort to Melody, but I don't think she could have held up without friends like Fawn and Crag. We all watched helplessly as Mrs. Seekings's condition worsened, and she became a hollow shell of her former robust self. Even Archer seemed to grow distant and blamed himself for not being able to afford her better care. Dr. Borestone did look in on her a few times, and said that what was ailing her was beyond medication. When she finally wasted away and died—I know you'll think this is terrible, and you're right—we hardly noticed it. She had been fading away for so long that the last final step seemed like just that.

"I'm most of all worried about Melody, how they'll keep the place now with me gone. Unless she and Crag get married soon, so she can inherit it. And even that may not help much. Crag's a real nice guy, and we are good friends, but he's not a farmer at heart. He'd rather hunt and trap or race horses. He has a weakness for gambling."

Wren poked a glowing coal back into the fire pit as he asked, "Did you have many other friends in the village, besides Melody and Fawn and Crag?"

"Well, of course Archer kept me pretty busy on the farm, so I didn't have any too much time left for socializing. Also, my upbringing was somewhat different from theirs, and I didn't really fit in. I guess I had quite a few casual friends—most people seemed to like me okay—but I didn't really have any close buddies."

"Tell me if it's none of my business," he murmured discreetly, "but did you have any connexion with the Brotherhood?"

"Well, I never belonged to the Amanita myself, but I know plenty of local guys who did. I'm sure Crag belonged—he hardly made a secret of it. Of course, technically I was a landowner's son myself, though in our condition, I don't expect that would've kept me from joining. Archer always spoke ill of them, but then he was too cowardly to participate in anything political. I think the main reason I was never invited was that everyone saw me as kind of an outsider. No one knew quite where I stood, and neither did I, I guess."

The conversation turned to other topics. I remember we discussed the fighting in Grand Coquina and whether Esperia should provide more direct support of the island, which was desperately resisting the Olotal's attacks. We talked about a new "multilogue" the VFC was promoting to arrive at a more detailed consensus on national defense strategies. We critiqued a play we had all attended at the Hoots bannerhouse the night before. But as we arranged our ground mats, my mind kept looking back to other concerns of my own; and as I pulled the quilt over my shoulders, I found myself commenting to no one in particular: "It wasn't that she was rich."

"No, but what was it then?"

Leave it to Wren—it was as if he'd heard me unfolding my whole sequence of thoughts instead of dropping haphazardly into the midst of them. Marten just stared blankly.

"I've been wondering that. I mean, she's awfully pretty too, but it's not really that, either. She's got more freckles than a killdeer's egg—more than me—and the big sorrel braid with a cute chin and all. And that voice, like a glass wind chime! What I should be wondering is what she saw in me. Now Ash Shackleford—there is a bold and handsome fellow, aside from his family's wealth, reeks of confidence. Compared to Mr. Less-Than-Average Me, he's the obvious choice."

"Well, I don't have any trouble seeing that side of it. After all, we know you, and from some other stuff you said about this Shackleford guy, he's a moose's prick. Are you surprised she's not a fool?"

"No, but thanks. Anyway, it's something else about her. I guess it's her spark, her spirit. Her mother is that way—full of opinions and speaks them freely. Umberlands women aren't supposed to be like that, you know. Husband always knows best, even when he doesn't. But Fawn couldn't stand to be dominated. I think she gets that from both parents."

"Isn't that it, then? Do you suppose this Shackleford fellow would tolerate any of that? Or most other Umberlands men? That's what she saw in you, Yaro, but it also sounds to me like that's what you saw in her."

"Maybe so," I conceded, staring into the dying fire.

I continued the discussion in my own mind now because there were thoughts I wasn't comfortable sharing just yet. Thoughts that had given me twinges of anxiety even before the banishment. You see, I had tried before to imagine myself in Jasper Gates's place, or rather, as his heir, a prospect which would have delighted any other young peasant. I could, with some effort, picture myself as the master of Hunter Hall; but no way could I bring myself to run it the way Jasper did. During my first eleven years of life, I had seen an example that was too compelling to ignore. I had little idea of specifics, but I could imagine myself doing things like getting rid of all the livestock or planting fruit trees instead. Like diversifying crops and allotting land for the bucs to grow their own food, at less cost to me, rather than sell them inferior goods from the provisioners. In short, I'd want to invest a lot in improving the land and the lives of the people who worked it. Now in the long run, this all should bring a more stable prosperity to the estate, but in the short run, it would cut into income sharply. In raising the workers' standard of living, it would inevitably reduce mine. I was quite comfortable with that idea—would it be any less than I enjoyed already? But that's just it, you see. Fawn was accustomed to a more genteel lifestyle than could ever be sustained under such a management régime. Could she adjust to such a comedown for the sake of our love? Could I ask her to? Mind you, Fawn was not snobbish or insensitive; she was a very caring person. She had a kindly heart, but this would be different. It's one thing to wish all the best for others, to bestow charitable favours as long as you've got yours; but what if that makes you *worse* off, perhaps even like one of them? As our liberalism became less fun, would she begin to despise me? Or if she withstood me, as she most likely would, what would happen to my feelings for her? Of one thing I felt certain: I loved Fawn with all my heart, and I always would. Knowing about our kinship would not have changed that.

So here I was, locked in a sort of limbo, emotionally bound by promises I could never fulfill, plagued by doubts I could not resolve, and surrounded by people who could not quite see what any of that had to do with my present situation.

Chapter 38

The great Bluemeadow Basin is asymmetrical in that most of the drainage is from the west. Most of its eastern tributaries are minor streams of less than twenty miles in length. A major exception is the Welcome River valley, which was our second major arena for exploration.

We spent two whole weeks there before Wren was satisfied of its potential. At first glance, it seemed an ideal region for tramp-boats with its well-developed system of waterways and great diversity of small industries. But the same features that made Welcome an ideal place for tramp-boats made it less suitable for *Come-What-May* in particular. There was already so much infrastructure that the territory in which *Come-What-May* could compete effectively with larger boats was relatively small. Wren concluded that one or two boats of our class were probably all the fair could support, and he made due note of that in his log.

Here we found basically all the same products that were made in Broadlea: cast-iron and glassware, paper and soap, baskets and bricks, and so forth. That was just as was envisioned by the Vine Laws—that each region should be self-reliant for the majority of its industrial needs. That did not stop us from dealing in those same goods from other fairs. For example, at Cloudbridge they weave an elegant style of bread basket out of reed cane. They are unlike anything made in the Broadlea, and indeed later that summer, we sold a couple at Recompense, a banner renowned for its reed craft. We also bought several of those woven-rush rugs that everyone hangs on their walls for warmth and beauty. Many places weave them, but these were Lustre-Oldbrooks, much sought-after for their warm colours and intricate patterns. And of course, the banner of Cassiopeia is synonymous with exquisite wooden musical instruments, which are famous even in my native Umberlands. I recall our old neighbour, Mr. Canes, played a fine dulcitar, which his father had once imported from Esperia. In two generations, they had taken great care not to remove or mar the glued-paper label with the constellation logo. That status symbol was worth near as much as the instrument itself!

We invested in several fiddles, dulcitars, guitars, and balalaikas. They were expensive, but lightweight and compact. Seeing the dulcitars made me feel glum about the cheap one I'd traded for at Stubs Pond; but Wren assured me it was worth all I paid for it and more, and that it might rather be he who had traded unwisely, shelling out so much for those top-of-the-line Cassiopeias, which many would consider an unaffordable luxury. That cheered me up a bit, but I soon had much greater cause for dismay.

I had been assuming that our next "sphere of operations" would be the Laughingwater Fair. This upland region of lofty peaks and tumbling streams had long held a special fascination for me, and I was excited at the prospect of seeing it, but Wren threw cold water on that idea.

"We won't be trading there on this trip," Wren informed us. "We are only going up as far as Hazard to drop off that crate of window glass for Meridian. A local tramp will take it from there."

I mentally pictured the map of the district. I thought I knew it pretty well, and what he was saying didn't quite make sense.

"If I remember right, Meridian is only a couple miles beyond the Hazard Canal. How come we don't deliver it ourselves and make more of the profit?"

"What your map doesn't show is that the Hazard Locks are shut down."

"Whatever for?"

"Last year, we had some freak flooding, especially in the Laughingwater. It took out a major bridge, and the debris from it clogged up the Hazard Canal, so the river gouged out a whole new channel around the locks. It'll take at least two years to repair it all.

"So how are people moving goods in and out of the valley?"

"With difficulty and at great expense. There is a temporary railroad spur around Hazard, but it wouldn't carry the boat loaded. We'd have to unload and transfer everything, and that's more expense than I want to incur right now."

"So we won't be able to trade there until two years from now?"

"It isn't quite that bad. There is another canal, the Sundew, that was under construction before all this happened. It comes over the Humps from the Broadlea, connecting Furnace Brook with Kettlehole Stream. We were quite near it when we were at Maxim's. It was scheduled to open sometime this fall, but reports I've heard aren't encouraging. Don't worry, we'll trade in there next spring, but for now, we won't be poling on the Laughingwater."

"But if their infrastructure is so messed up, wouldn't that make it perfect for *Come-What-May* now? We could get where others can't and get top-falcon for our goods."

"I thought of all that, Yaro, and I don't think it's worth it, at least not right now. Besides, we've got other work upriver."

"But that's exactly what *Come-What-May* is . . ."

"Listen, Yaro, would you get off my back! I've got to make decisions based on what seems wisest to me, whether they make sense to you or not. Face it, your own eagerness to be there is based on considerations that are no more rational than mine. I may be wrong, but so far this season, my instincts have worked out pretty well, including bringing you guys along."

I backed off quickly because I knew he was right about that. Wren was always firm but never arbitrary in his use of authority, and his instincts were indeed excellent, which is why he had been chosen as boat steward. I just thought he realized how eager I was to go there, yet he had never mentioned this before.

Marten had been silent through all this discussion, but now he injected quietly, "You may as well know, Yaro, it has also become a military priority. Every time the Olotal does a bit of sabre-rattling, we look at our possible responses to an invasion. Having this thing out of commission right now is considered a real vulnerability."

In fact, I did get to see only one mile of the storied river, from its mouth to the Hazard landing, which sits at the foot of the locks. Looking up the gorge and seeing the torrent of water booming over the mist-veiled ledges, one needn't have asked why that way was closed. Nor when one saw the gateless locks, now drained and choked with rubble from the flood.

While Wren was arranging to leave the glass for pickup, Marten and I went over to examine the little railroad, which began at the landing and ended above the gorge. It was pretty much like the quarry railroad on Alga, but I had never really examined the roller mechanisms on the flatcars. Instead of wheels, a sort of steel box was fastened on the bottom of each corner of the car, facing downward onto the tracks. In this channel were a dozen or so large steel balls, which rolled on the rail. Considering how heavy these cars are when loaded, they can be pushed with amazing ease on the level. On grades, such as around the gorge, they are hooked to a steel cable and pulley which, in this case, was driven by a capstan.

I couldn't hide my disappointment as we pulled away from the pier and drifted back down to the Bluemeadow. After all, the main point of my coming on this venture was to scope out possible places to settle. I'm afraid I grumbled a good bit, which is not usually like me. Wren and Marten tried to ignore me graciously. The strong current carried us along in ease, with nothing to do but steer, but once back on the main river, it was a different story. Now we all grumbled—at the channel, at our poles, at each other. The current was very exhausting here, yet apparently not enough to justify installing a tram-cable.

Although we were still on the Bluemeadow River, we were now in the Portage Fair. Once above its confluence with the Welcome and Laughingwater rivers, the Bluemeadow is quite reduced in volume. It remains wide, but there are many rocky shallows, and the actual channel is narrow and elusive. We had to be alert for down-coming boats, which might have trouble squeezing by us. Once, just below Mallow's Bight, we nearly had a catastrophe. One of those great lumber barges came hurtling down around the point. They were on the outside of the curve where the channel was deepest and swiftest. They had plenty of momentum and didn't seem to be in full control. We had just rehooked past a pulley onto the upbound cable and couldn't easily maneuver out of their way. Only Wren's quick action saved us from being run down. He yanked the cable-release line, which instantly set us lose, so that we were being swept back downstream too. That gave us a few precious moments to push ourselves out of harm's way although one of their long sweeps caught under us for an instant and almost turned us over. As they rushed by us, we hurled some angry words, but they were struggling to control their own craft and never stopped although we heard some faint shouts that sounded like apologies.

"Those booger-pickers!" fumed Wren. "A flagrant violation of the Pits-and-Parapets—they should've been using the cable for restraint, instead of rolling along full tilt. If I knew who they were, they'd sure hear from me!"

"I noticed their number stenciled on the side," offerred Marten. "It's 52512CF."

We both spun around to stare at him in astonishment.

"How could you possibly remember a number like that? It all happened so fast!"

"Easy: the first three digits are the year of my birth, and the last two are the sum of the first three."

Who else, I thought? Who but a Keeper of Numbers could peer into the looming face of disaster while memorizing of five-digit number?

CF, we knew, meant Crescent Falls, and we also knew Wren's letter of complaint would receive a swift and humble apology. The Pits-and-Parapets Laws deal with liability for safety violations, and they're taken extremely seriously. The steward of that crew would be roundly rebuked for his negligence, which in Esperian culture is a harsher penalty than any fine.

We were hardly out of Portage Locks when we turned up Sharpshin Brook. According to Wren, it would pose a new challenge to *Come-What-May*'s special capabilities. The Sharpshin Basin is very high and steep-sided, with numerous falls and rapids.

The area produced a fair diversity of trade goods, including tarred-hemp cable, linen, blown glass, potash, gold and tin, abrasives, maple sugar, and biolumes. Most of these goods were quite portable by handcart and required only decent roads. But like Laughingwater to the south, they also produced lots of furniture and latheware as well as cooperage and other bulkier merchandise, which were expensive to haul overland. The problem was that most of the steads in the basin were inaccessible by common tramp-boats. And what about *Come-What-May*? That's what we were to find out. It was not only our Longlogan sponsors who wished us to check out Sharpshin Brook; we had also received a special request from the Highlands Development Commission (a VFC agency) to report on access issues for the area. If a dearth of infrastructure were the only obstacle to greater prosperity in those banners and if that obstacle could be removed by a reasonable infusion of well-targeted investments, then they wanted to know at what specific points they should direct their efforts for maximum return. To that end, we spent several days exploring the watershed, certainly more than what was warranted by our profit. We traded for all the items mentioned and more, but considering how much time and effort we expended just getting around, the return was rather disappointing. Probably the most valuable result of our time there was Wren's numerous recommendations to the HDC for navigational improvements.

Chapter 39

As I squinted despairingly at the long steep grade ahead of me, I wondered if this were such a good idea after all. This just had to be the last big hill. It surely looked like it, but so had all the others. I mean, I had never assumed that I could pedal 380 pounds of merchandise over the Calendar Hills without working up a sweat, but at times, it seemed like it would get the best of me.

It had all started early that morning, after a mosquito-plagued night on the south shore of Rebus Lake. I guess we were all a bit worse for sleep as we sat eating our breakfast on the gravelly beach. We had accomplished what we came for, and we were preparing to head back down to the Broadlea where we would spend the rest of the season. Or so I thought. Coming back from relieving myself, I heard Wren and Marten chatting about something to do with bicycle parts and dried fruit, but I didn't hear just what it was about. When I came back to the shore, Wren was passing down boxes to Marten, who stood knee-deep in the Lake.

"C'mon, Yaro, give us a hand lugging these ashore."

"Sure, but what for? Why's that stuff going here?"

Instead of answering, Wren started unstrapping Bumblebee from its rack on the lockers.

"Here, get this side, would you? There, all set. Well, I guess you're ready to go."

"Me? Go? Where am I supposed to go?"

"Where you've been aching to go. See that road up there on the shore? It follows Cinnabar Brook and goes right over the Calendar Hills to Laughingwater. Today's their fair, and if you hustle, you can be there in a few hours."

"What? Why do you want me to go there?"

"Because you want to so badly."

"But I haven't complained, have I? I didn't mean to."

"You didn't need to. We can smell it on your breath, like raw garlic. You can't wait until next season, and we can't put up with you until then. If you keep thinking about it, you'll imagine it to be more than it is. So get this stuff loaded on and grab a map. We'll meet you at the Lower Dapplefawn landing tomorrow evening."

I hadn't argued at all then, but if he had given me the choice now, I might have been less eager. I slipped the lever into the lowest gear and crept up the long hill slower than I could have walked. I had to stop often to catch my wind and mop the sweat off my face and neck. I was not the only one on the road, but I was the only one making such heavy weather of it. I was wondering whether my knees would hold out when a rather elderly looking man pedalled up from behind me, calling out a breezy good-morning as he churned on past. I returned the greeting with a polite grunt, but inwardly snarling. I consoled myself that he had probably had a good night's sleep, and anyway, he was mounted on a sleek Purple Martin, not a heavy-laden Bumblebee.

However, this was indeed "the last big hill." Once I topped the crest, I had a relatively flat stretch for a mile or so, then lots of downhill. I still had to pedal, but it was no great effort; and I could make reasonable speed, at least ten miles per hour.

After leaving Lynx Pond, I knew I was in Laughingwater fair, although the fairbanner itself was still a good twelve miles away. Now I could make up for lost time. Mindful of what Wren had said about hitting the rear brakes first on steep downhills, I coasted cautiously at first. As I gained confidence, however, I really poured on the speed. I swooped along the reedy margin of Horizon Pond and roared through East Fetchworth. Things were going very well indeed. I should be at the fairgrounds by midmorning. I had been hearing a little rattle behind me, but it had gone away, so I assumed whatever it was had corrected itself—why do we often assume that about machines? Just beyond Weeping Springs, the road plunged down a long steep grade followed by a couple of moderate rises. Soon after that would be the flatter valley floor. I decided to really put on the power, to build momentum for the rise beyond. I was really barrelling along—it seemed like everything was passing in a blur. A woman was jogging along the road and I rang my bell, as is the rule, to warn her of my approach. She moved over to the side, and I whizzed past. It wasn't long after that I realized something wasn't right. I felt a jerk and a wobble at one of the rear wheels. I hit the rear brakes hard, and suddenly, things got much worse. There was a jolting thud, and I knew that my right rear hub was scraping on the ground. I completely lost control of the cycle, and had I not been slowing down, I might have been more seriously hurt. As it was, the thing spun around hard and flipped me and half the cargo into the ditch. The rear wheel was still to be seen, bouncing off across a field of young buckwheat.

Before I could collect my wits, someone was at my side, gently helping me to my feet. "Are you hurt badly? Careful now, don't move too fast. Make sure nothing is broken. Sorry I'm not too good at your language."

Indeed she wasn't speaking my language that well, though close enough to be understandable. It was the woman I'd passed several hundred yards ago—how had she gotten there so fast?

"No, no, I'm all right, thank you . . . just a few scrapes, I think. I speak Mok some."

I looked around at all my trading goods. Some were still strapped on, but most were strewn all over the road and ditch. As the woman helped me gather them all up, we found that nothing much was damaged, beyond a few scratches in one of the dulcitars (*not* one of the Cassiopeias!). I thanked the woman profusely for her help, but she insisted on examining my scraped knee. The scrape was right below the healed-but-scarred injury from my fugitive days, so it looked worse than it was. She produced a wet cloth from somewhere and tenderly sponged off the grit and blood from the area. Then to my surprise, she pulled out a vial of some tincture and daubed it on the knee, wrapping it in several layers of gauze bandage.

"Well, you certainly come prepared," I commented admiringly.

"You never know. There, that should do it nicely, if you keep it clean."

"Yes, thank you very much. Now if only my cycle were as easy to fix."

She turned her attention to the crippled machine—I hadn't meant that she should bother herself about that too!—while I limped over to retrieve the errant wheel. When I got back, she had flipped the thing over—it had landed on its side, but the wrong side—and was examining the bent axle.

"We can straighten this easy enough, but . . ."

"Look, this is awfully nice of you, but—"

"The wheel won't go back on unless we—"

"I mean, this never would have happened if I—"

"The brake assembly has turned inward, where . . . oh, dear, I'm doing it again, aren't I?"

"Doing what?"

"Oh, I'm terribly sorry! They say I'm always trying to run everything, whether I'm wanted or not. I just . . ."

"But I'm quite happy to have your help. I know so little about cycle repairs . . . we don't have these where I come from, you know. I just didn't want to bother anyone else with my problems."

"Oh, but it's no bother, really. You see . . . since you don't mind . . . we've got to get the brake-assembly out of there, and to do that, we must undo the shoes. Now one of them fell off back up the road when you passed me—here, I picked it up—but the other is bolted tight. Where's your wrench?"

"Ah . . . I'm afraid I didn't bring tools along," I said.

"No matter, I have a little adjustable which should work." She rummaged through a large shoulder bag. "Let's see . . . salt tablets, waterproof matches . . . ah! Here it is."

I could only stare at her in bemused wonder.

"Do you have everything under the sun in there?"

Almost," she laughed. "I try to be prepared. People say I go out of my way to look for trouble, so I can use all this stuff. Okay, that's off. Now before we put the wheel back on, let's straighten out this axle."

The axle was a rather light piece of steel rod, threaded at both ends in opposite directions. One end was slightly bent from the mishap, not much but enough to make the wheel wobble hopelessly. I wouldn't have had any idea how to straighten it, out there in the roadstead with no vise or other tools. But this woman took that rod and walked up the road to a little outcrop of slate ledge. Finding a suitable crack, she wedged the rod in to the point of the bend and pried it carefully until it suited her. I guess she must've gotten it right—it looked fine to me and never gave any trouble afterward. The hub-nut had come off way back up the road where there was no chance of finding it, but she—why was I not surprised?—she had one right in her universal-disaster kit. It was a wing-nut rather than a hex-nut, but sufficed wonderfully; and I never bothered to change it. Having made me roadworthy again, we chatted for a few minutes.

"So they don't have pedicycles in Borealia?"

"Actually, I'm from Anagaia—West Umberlands, that is."

As I said that, her eyes grew even wider than they normally were.

"In Anagaia then, but however do people get around in a hurry?"

"On horseback, usually."

"Oh, of course, how silly of me. I've never seen a horse, except in pictures. Kind of like a moose without antlers, aren't they?"

"Yes, I suppose so. Actually, I only saw a moose for the first time a few days ago, up at Window Lake."

"So you look like you're going to the fair," she observed.

"Yes, at least for a while. I have other stops after that."

"Well then, I mustn't keep you."

"Oh, I didn't mean that. I just meant that I won't be able to see as much of the fair as I'd like. Are you going there too?"

"No, I'm heading back to Ravenswing. I've been visiting a great-aunt who wasn't able to come to Banner Day."

"Well, I sure appreciate your help . . ." And I tried awkwardly to straddle the seat of Bumblebee.

"Listen, I realize you haven't time to waste, but I really think you'd be wise to rest that knee a few minutes, if only to make sure it's really okay. Look, I haven't had my breakfast yet, have you?"

"No, I was waiting until I got over that last grade. And you're quite right. I know very well what happens to neglected knee wounds. So sure, let's eat together."

We both sat down on the sunny road-bank, and I opened my lunch basket as she reached into her bag. But then she leaned back very quietly and said, "Actually, I'm really not all that hungry yet. I'll just sit with you for a few minutes."

I was suddenly filled with acute suspicion. I couldn't help teasing.

"Ah! So you're not prepared in every single way?"

Her dusky cheeks became quite red, and she stammered in embarrassment, "I really did pack a breakfast, but . . ."

"But it's sitting on the kitchen counter back at your grandma's stead."

"My great-aunt, actually," she corrected meekly.

"You know, if you're going to run around solving everyone else's troubles, you need to take better care of yourself too. The next person you rescue may not have more food that he can possibly eat."

"Oh, that's very kind of you, but you don't need, mmph—"

She couldn't finish the thought, because I'd shoved a dried apricot into her lips and a bagel into her hands. Once she'd resolved to share my meal, she interspersed her chewing with lots of nosy questions, like "How did you get all the way up here?"

"I pedaled over the Calendar Hills from Rebus Pond."

"No, no, I mean all the way from Anagaia. Surely you didn't ride that thing here."

"Oh, of course not. I'm a refugee. I came here on an Esperian freighter, and now I'm working on a tramp-boat."

"How adventuresome. Then how come you're not with your boat?"

"I've been really wanting to see the Laughingwater Valley, but because of the Hazard Locks construction, we won't be trading here this year, by boat that is. So I'm cycling to the fair today and meeting my boatmates at Dapplefawn tomorrow. It's silly, I realize—I'll not see much of the valley, but I'm terribly excited to be here anyway."

"Terribly excited? And what's so special about the Laughingwater, I mean compared to the other fairs?"

"Oh, I guess it's partly the historical traditions. After all, the whole thing started here, didn't it?"

"What thing?" she asked a bit tentatively, as if she knew the answer perfectly well but wondered if I did.

"Why, you know, the Vision—the Larger House, and all that."

"Sure, but since you're not a Steward, what would you care about all that?"

"How do you know I'm not a Steward? Because I'm white? Because I was born outside the Covenant? Because I didn't know about the Vine Laws until a few months ago? Don't you think that someone who wasn't raised with the Vision can acquire it somehow?"

She smiled weakly, no more sure of herself than I was of myself.

"But the Vision isn't like a religious sect," she suggested. "Something you can convert to by accepting a few doctrines. I mean, it's deeper than that. I just don't see how someone raised with one mythic vision can easily swap it for another."

"Not easily, but possibly, I'm sure. As I understand it, you internalize it by living it, which is what I'm trying to do. And besides, I was raised half of my life by your people, and I was always a misfit among my own, so I'm not really sure I have much of a mythic vision to swap."

"Oh, I'm so sorry. I was just assuming . . ."

"But you can't assume all that!" I snapped, feeling that a raw nerve had been pricked. "Because if an individual can't acquire a new vision, how can a whole civilization? Like Anagaia. Don't you see? Unless Anagaia can change its mythic vision, then they're doomed to fail and maybe take others down with them. Like Esperia."

She just looked at me hard as if I'd suddenly sprouted a third eye or something.

"I . . . I didn't realize anyone in Anagaia even thought about things in that way."

"They don't, so far as I know. I've learned a lot here that I never would've learned back there."

"But then, what can anyone *do* about it?"

"About what?"

"All that stuff you were just saying: learning a new vision. That's what my dad is always saying: you'll never get a better world until you get a better vision of that world. But I mean, how can Anagaians, or anyone else, learn a different vision, especially when they think they know everything already?"

"Someone must teach them?"

"But who and how?"

"I'm sure I don't know. I'm in no position to teach anyone anything or to suggest what anyone should do. I'm just trying to figure some things out for myself. Maybe someday I'll know what action to take."

"Well, I can't wait for someday. I'm trying to take action now, but I do want to act in the right direction. I need more than a concept, I need a day-to-day plan."

I shrugged. "Don't look to me. I'm not even close to that."

As we munched our breakfast, I tried to size up my newfound companion. Her name was Cherish, after the heroine of the third-century epic, and she was every bit the heroic type herself. A sometimes-awkward heroine, it seemed. Forgetful and clumsy on occasion, but intensely focused and competent when it mattered. That she was a woman of action was reflected in her physique, as well as her speech. At twenty-two, she was lithe and muscular, dark-skinned even for an Esperian. Although highly intelligent, she seemed more comfortable with direct concrete action than with introspective thoughts. Her core nature was motivation, especially motivation on behalf of her people's Vision.

In Anagaia, what would be the chances of bumping into someone who was even aware of their people's mythic vision or even that there was such a thing? Not one in a thousand, perhaps not one in a million. Yet was I to assume that this woman was unique among her compatriots in having the concerns she expressed? Not likely, especially here in the Laughingwater, whose people were known for their visionary zeal. After all, wasn't that what had drawn me to this valley more than seeing the lay of the land? And here, the very first person I'd met was practically a caricature of the Laughingwater "type." Then something occurred to me.

"When I first passed you, you were running along at a pretty good clip. I hope I'm not keeping you from something urgent."

"Not really. I run most everywhere. You see, I'm in training to be a Swallow," she offered as if it explained everything.

"Oh, I see," I nodded, trying to hide the fact that I didn't see at all. I had heard something somewhere but didn't care to show my ignorance just now, so I merely suggested, "It must be a pretty rigorous business."

"It's quite demanding," she agreed, "but terribly fulfilling. Doesn't leave much time for anything else."

I tried to think of a discrete way of asking the next question without giving the wrong impression.

"Do all your family live at Ravenswing?"

"My immediate family. There's my parents and the twins and so forth . . . I'm not married, if that's what you mean."

"I was just curious," I responded gauchely. "It's just that where I come from, a woman in her twenties is usually married and with children, if she's going to be. My own fiancée is only eighteen. But of course, things are very different here. I just wondered, that's all."

"Well, I'm not married—nor engaged," she shrugged with no apparent regret. "I just can't get interested in all that just now."

"Ah yes, I know what you mean there. At least, I know what I want to do with myself, and anything else would seem like a great distraction."

"Exactly. And what would *you* like to do? Get back to your fiancée, I suppose."

"That's quite out of the question. I have a price on my head there, and she couldn't leave to come here, even if she wanted to."

I explained about the curse. Then I confided something I hadn't seen fit to share with anyone else—in fact, I'd only recently begun to realize it myself.

"Quite frankly, I sometimes wonder if it was such a good idea to begin with—our engagement, that is. I mean, I still love her very much, so much in fact that it doesn't feel like there's enough love left in me to start again."

I wasn't wholly comfortable with all this soul-baring, so I shifted abruptly to a topic I was more comfortable with.

"Anyway, I believe I've found my real place here. You see, I've long wondered what makes our countries so different and why Anagaia can't be a little more like this. It's just not enough to point to the mythic vision. I need to understand how the vision affects society, and how someone might alter either one. Isn't that what you're getting at?"

"Please continue," she said without answering. There was a quiet intensity in her stare, almost a ferocity that I found disconcerting.

"I really don't know . . . I just mean that when I lived there, it didn't matter whether I understood why things were as they were—there was nothing I or anybody else could do about it. But here, you see, there are such possibilities, it seems. Like you, I want to be actively engaged, doing something, but I know that any amount of effort will be futile unless we understand better what's behind it all. According to my friend Orris, our vision—anyone's vision—is a result of how we live our lives, which in turn is a result of our vision. He says whether the oak begets the acorn or vice versa is probably irrelevant, but in the case of this vision thing, it may make more sense to impact the way of life, and the vision will eventually morph to reflect the new reality. I kind of get all that, but as you were asking, how do you impact the way someone *else* lives, especially when that someone is Anagaian? That's what I want to know."

She was peering at me as though I were a bug under a microscope. She pointed an insistent finger at me.

"You must come visit us some time. You would like to talk with my father, and he would like to talk with you. He says that Anagaia and countries like it will always be a threat to us unless they can somehow learn to tell a sustainable story—that's how he puts it. Not *our* story—just a story of their own that lets them live within their own resources."

"Sounds like your dad thinks a lot about this stuff. And has he any ideas about how to teach a different story?"

"Ideas, yes. But he says they're irrelevant now. It's impossible to teach a different story than what they already know, especially when their own story still seems to make sense to them. Even here, most people are just beginning to discuss the issue in terms of changing visions as opposed to specific programmes. After all, visions are an abstraction, something folks like me have trouble latching onto. I mean, what can you *do* with it? That's what they keep telling Dad, but he insists they're trying to deal with weeds by snipping at the shoots when they should be attacking the roots."

"They? Who are they?"

"The Foreign Missions Committee. Dad's on the board of directors, and he's always looking for new insights."

"Well, I know that I don't have any new insights, but I surely would like to meet them someday, if only to express my gratitude."

"For what?"

"For my life." I went on to explain how I was raised in an orphanage sponsored by the Laughingwater FMC, which until ten months ago had been my sole connexion with Esperia.

Although we both shared an obvious passion for the things we were discussing, we soon found we had pretty much exhausted what we thought we had to say about them, so our conversation turned more to our own personal lives: gardens and tramp-boats and buckwheat and the view.

There was much to like about this woman; indeed, she was quite lovable—in a sisterly way, of course. What really appealed to me about her was the fact that she wasn't "looking for someone"—she had clearly said that, hadn't she?—and she understood that I wasn't either. What freedom that gave us to be "just friends," something I was quite eager for! Yes, surely I would visit her someday, since my intentions would not be misconstrued.

After a while, a couple of bikes speeding by reminded me that I had an itinerary to keep to. I had everything packed together again, and there seemed no further excuse to linger, so we each turned our separate ways. I offered my heartfelt thanks and remounted Bumblebee for the remaining few miles. Her repairs were well done, and there was no more shaking or rattling. My stinging knee reminded me to restrain myself on the downhills; indeed there were few downhills left, for I soon reached the intervale where it was fairly level all the way to the fair.

Chapter 40

At the fair, all the sellers' stalls had been taken, but I didn't want one anyway. My merchandise didn't justify renting a covered space for only part of the day. I simply found a place at the end of a row and spread out a brown-and-blue Lustre-Oldbrook mat on the ground and arranged my wares to advantage on that.

I immediately realized that there was no way I was going to take in much of this fair myself, not if I meant to do any trading. How could I get free to walk around when people kept stopping to look at my stuff? I saw why Wren had said it takes at least two to run a booth well: one to shop and one to keep shop. But even from my spot, I could see quite a lot. Laughingwater Fair seemed to have pretty much the same products as other fairs, with a few exceptions. In particular, there was an enormous volume and variety of quality hardwood products: large bowls, fine furniture, wheelbarrows, tool handles, wooden machine parts, etc. Some of these were for local or regional sale, but since the other fairs produced many of the same items for their own use, the preponderance of merchandise on display here was destined for export to Anagaia and other lands, which lacked the rich forests and abundant waterpower of the Esperian hill-country. In fact, I was surprised to see several foreigners there, buying whole consignments of woodenware and arranging for them to be delivered to Fairhaven, Harking, or Goosegrass for shipping to southern ports.

My own trading was a bit sluggish at first since my wares had to compete with local made, plus the added cost of my bringing them there. To have a competitive edge here, one must be able to get to the remoter steads with greater carrying capacity than the Bumblebee. In short, I needed *Come-What-May*.

I did have some luck selling clocks and musical instruments, due to their special quality. I unloaded two of the three Cassiopeia dulcitars for a handsome profit. Imported figs and apricots sold briskly because there was no competing source within the valley. Of course, no one really needed to buy them—they produce lots of other dried fruits here—but their leaders were encouraging them to support the conversion of Anagaian and Palmettoan cotton lands to tree crops.

A special complication was that I could only accept payment in goods that were easy to carry on Bumblebee. Several times, I was only able to do business by resorting to very complicated exchanges with third-or fourth-party dealers. One woman wanted to buy my last dulcitar, but only if I would barter for cordage. We couldn't find anyone handy who was willing to take four reels of tarred hemp-rope, so the deal fell through. I invented one strategy I hoped would meet with Wren's approval: I would accept promissory notes for a rather standardized commodity, usually maple sugar or lye, which we would collect whenever *Come-What-May* finally entered the valley. This was almost like having cash, and it made room on the load to accept other less-compact items.

Through all this, I was generally pleased with myself for managing the language so well. Although I had studied feverishly during the winter and had mastered a reasonable level of conversational Mok, that is not at all the same as listening to three fast-talking customers at the same time, all quoting a jumble of prices, measures, and quality-grades, sometimes about articles I'd never heard of before. How was I to know what molybdenum was, let alone how much it was worth? It was never a question of anyone trying to cheat you, but in this floating-value market, you had to know enough not to cheat yourself.

In all the flurry of trading, I was wondering when I was going to get a chance to eat. At midday, the crowds thinned out as others began to think of their own stomachs. I had brought along cold food, but as the tempting aromas wafted over from the caterers' tables, I yearned for a hot meal. While we were all queued up at the concessions, the fellow in front of me struck up a conversation as if we were old acquaintances. He shared an anecdote about someone he knew who lived very near to the fairgrounds. One day during fair-market, they were cooking up a stew that was so tasty that its savoury fragrance attracted the notice of some fairgoers. A couple of them showed up at the door, asking for lunch. Of course, they could not be turned away—it was the custom, after all—so the cook, who was the only one home at the moment, invited them in to dine. They enjoyed the meal so much they told their friends, who also invited themselves. Although they could not be charged for the meal, the guests all observed proper etiquette and left gifts to compensate. In fact they were very generous, and the stead realized a handsome profit on their "hospitality," but when the rest of the household showed up, they found the house full of strangers and the kettle nearly empty, so they were all sent over to eat at the caterers.

He chuckled at his own story, and I joined him, pleased that he assumed I would "get it."

I made my selections and headed back to my spot where a lone shopper was looking over my things. I recognized the athletic figure from behind, so as I came up behind her, I quipped jovially, "I doubt that you'll find anything here that you don't already have in your bag."

She burst into laughter as she turned around to face me.

"I figured you must be around here somewhere. I recognized your bike—the only one with buckwheat straw tangled in the spokes."

"I thought you weren't coming to the fair."

"So did I, but I remembered a couple of things we need. I thought as long as I'm in the area, it would save someone a trip later."

"Ah, so what do you need?"

"Well, ah . . . paprika, for one thing, and . . . uh . . . garden seeds too. Probably other things too, but I'm not the supply steward, so I'm not sure what."

It struck me as a happy coincidence that I just happened to have both items on display.

"You're in luck, I have just the thing."

"So I see. I think we can use about eight ounces of paprika. And a packet of that kohlrabi seed: Courier's Giant Winter Keeper. Oh, and that Purple Bead fava. I'll just take a packet and propagate it myself. I am garden steward at our stead, and I'm always eager to try new varieties. What can you tell me about that Torchfield Extra-Early Bell Pepper—is it earlier than Mountaineer?"

"I can't tell you any more than what it says on the packet. It was developed by the Cinderfield Breeding Station for cool short seasons. I've never grown it myself."

"Oh, that's right. I guess you don't do much gardening when you're traveling all the time."

"And I sure miss it. It's the first summer in my life that I haven't been growing things. The main reason for my taking this job was to see the country and find a suitable place to settle down."

"And you haven't found it yet? Just what are you looking to find?"

"I'm not exactly sure, but I'll recognize it when I see it."

She looked at me thoughtfully for a second, and said, "Well, I'll try some of that pepper seed, then maybe we won't always be buying so much paprika. We have awful luck ripening peppers where I live."

"At Ravenswing, right?"

"Why, yes. So you remembered that."

"In this business, you learn to remember place-names."

As I weighed out the paprika, I remarked, "It's too bad we didn't think of this back at Weeping Springs. I could have saved you going out of your way."

"Oh, it's just as well. I wanted to see if you got here all right. My goodness, I just realized I don't have any trade-goods or coins to cover these purchases."

I assured her that it was I who was in her debt, but she would not hear of it, and by now, I knew better than to withstand her. She went looking for someone she knew—quite unlikely, I thought, among all these thousands of people from all over. Yet she soon ran into a trader she knew who was happy to take her note for some goods—a small sweetgrass sewing basket and some maple sugar—with which she paid me. She could settle with him later, whereas I couldn't say when I might see her again.

She stayed and chatted awhile between the customers. In fact, she was very helpful to me once, when a woman wanted to buy a few pounds of figs. I was preoccupied with other customers, so Cherish quietly weighed them out for her. After the buyers

246

had moved on, she commented, "What a lovely dulcitar you have there! I adore dulcitar music—I wish I could play. Do you play it?"

"Er, well, actually, I've just started learning. My boat steward is teaching me." Why on earth did I ever say such an outrageous thing? It was just that she was so all-capable that if she had any deficit whatever, it was my duty to make it up, although I had never done anything more musical than whistling. And all those strings!

Shortly thereafter, she took her leave. "I meant it about you coming to visit," she reminded me. "A lot of our neighbours have similar concerns to yours. With enough folks asking the same questions, maybe somehow we'll start figuring out some answers."

"I just might do that," I called after her as she strode off in her deliberate fashion.

I ceased to think about her as I continued trading through the afternoon. I sold lots of pump-washers and jar rings, several recorders and many fine combs and brushes. I probably could have sold out everything if I'd stayed until the end, but I had one more important stop before night.

So I left the fair a little early and pedaled over to Otterbank, a few miles east and right on my way. I looked up the home of Mallard of Greengate, and he very graciously offered to guide me to the home of Faring's parents, less than a mile away. Actually it wasn't all that simple; as soon as word spread—and it spread instantly—that an Anagaian whom Faring had raised was come to visit, half of Mallard's household insisted on accompanying us. We passed a couple other steads, were still others joined the parade—for such it had become. I was mortified with embarrassment to show up at Faring's old home with a score or more of noisy gawkers. Everyone trooped right into the steadhouse, whose occupants seemed surprised but unoffended at our arrival. Now ordinarily, Esperians appreciate privacy since they have so little of it, but all these neighbours assumed they had every right to be part of this reunion, and I suppose they did. Apparently, every letter sent home from the missions is shared with the entire neighbourhood; interesting passages may be read from the pulpit or published in the newssheets, so these complete strangers had heard my name and had heard reports about me and my orphanage-mates since I was an infant. These people supported the foreign missions with a fervour, and if an actual beneficiary of their kindness had miraculously appeared in their very midst, they were entitled to see him.

I was immediately introduced to Faring's aged parents, who greeted me with great warmth. That is, his mother did. His father, who had obviously suffered a stroke, greeted me as profusely as he was able, with a loppish grin and a palsied grip on my hand. His words were incoherent, but the sentiment was crystal clear.

Indeed, the only person there whose welcome was less than warm was a woman in her midforties who entered the room after I'd been there a while. Upon being introduced as Faring's older sister, she gave the obligatory handshake and left again rather brusquely soon after. The mother (whose name was Rejoice, but she insisted I call her Grandma) apologized for her daughter's rudeness.

"You must forgive Celandine. He is her baby brother. They played together, she taught him to swim and to whistle. She implored him not to go, and when he persisted, she hid his favourite tunic, in the vain hope it would stop him. And now this . . . she can't help herself. When we told her that you were coming here, she said she had no use for any of those folk who cherish their misery so. She's become quite racist, you see. She just can't seem to understand that you are a victim as well. But at least you were rescued. Please, I can't excuse her, but I hope you can forgive her."

My new "grandpa" continued to grasp my hand, and I saw in his eyes a look that was at the same time stupid and all-knowing. Somehow, his piercing stare expressed things that his faint babbling could not. It said that although he didn't even know me, I was his last hope, his final stab at immortality. Whatever had become of Faring, this daughter would never fulfill the hopes of a Steward father—she was far too blinded by bitterness to even see the Larger House, much less dwell in it.

I finally felt I had something useful to say. "You said that at least I was saved, but you must know that there were others too. Even while I was there, several older ones came and went. We were all changed from having lived there, in different ways and to different degrees, but changed, all of us. Even though the rest struggle just to survive, they all dwell in Larger Houses than before. Most of us would not even be alive. At best we'd be beggars and thieves and prostitutes. And it's more than us children. A few local peasants can read now, an injured workmen didn't lose his arm, a widow was given home employment to support her children. I just want you to understand that whatever has happened to Faring and the others, he did not go there for nothing. He once told me something: 'When you plant a seed, you never know what the harvest will be or who will eat it, but it's worth planting nevertheless.' We were in the garden at the time, and I thought he was talking about muskmelons."

We continued to visit at length. It was eerie to hear these strangers in a strange land tell me stories about myself which I thought I alone knew. About the freezing day soon after his arrival when Faring had thought he heard crying in the woodshed, and Veerio had assured him it was the incessant banging of a loose shutter. And how he had investigated and found a baby wrapped up in newly washed rags and tucked into a laundry basket with a note, the same note I still carried in my pocket. And how I was so malnourished that he struggled for days to keep me alive, carrying me around in his warm shirtfront like a pet puppy, concocting various milky broths from peanuts and barley and stuff, trying to come up with something I could keep down.

These were all things Faring had never told me, and it made me feel all the more that he was my "real" father, far more than the birth father I had never known or the adopted father who had failed me. My dark-faced grandma told me another story that helped explain a seemingly impossible mental picture I had always carried in my mind: one spring (it must've been during the carnival at Sycamore), I was playing with the others in the alleyway that served as our playground. At one point, I suddenly left my playmates and, before anyone could stop me, ran up the alley and across the street, somehow dodging through the hooves and the wheels of all the merchants and pilgrims bound for the shrine at Sycamore. Faring ran after me as quickly as possible, having more trouble than I getting across the traffic. When he caught up to me, I was looking up at this young woman who stood in front of a wall right across from the alley, and I was saying to her, "Were you looking for me?" Faring said the woman looked stunned and embarrassed, like she wanted to run away. He apologized to her and picked me up to go back. Apparently, he wrote home to his folks about the incident.

Years later, Faring had told me that he had noticed a woman watching us children from afar and he had drawn his own conclusions, but he never told us all those details. However, I always had this image in my head: of a woman's pale face backed by a stuccoed stone wall. The stucco was peeled and flaked off in places, making the wall look pocked and blistered. Was it the wall that made her seem so sickly looking, and whose was that voice asking, "Were you looking for me?"

It wasn't just me they knew about: they remembered as well as I did the rainy night the Blotch children were brought to us, following the murder of their derelict father by a landowner's agents. The next year, they heard the sad news of Opal's death from tuberculosis. They even knew about the terrible fight between Boon and me, when he had snatched my mother's note, and how later we became the closest of friends. They knew something, but much less than I, about the night old Mr. Canes, our neighbour, had arranged for all three of the draught-age boys to be at his house, under the pretext of entertaining them while a press-gang was raiding the orphanage for fresh recruits. Of course, Faring had been very discreet about what he put in writing, so I filled them in on such specific details as I remembered. After all, even though old Victor Canes was safely in his grave by the time of my visit, it was young Canes, an army corporal, who had tipped off his father.

Such stories continued until dusk. Everyone was assuming I would stay the night, but I explained that I had to hurry off to a previous appointment. I did promise to keep in touch and to visit again when I could, and with that, I took my leave.

The plan had been that I would spend the following day trading my way toward our rendezvous at Dapplefawn. I wanted to visit as many steads as possible on the way, and that meant getting a head start on the morning, so I made use of the remaining twilight to pedal as far as Boneset. There I simply parked Bumblebee in someone's woodlot and pulled a tarp over the load while I myself slept on the ground under it.

Waking before dawn, I breakfasted on a roadside raspberry patch (it's quite acceptable; many steads plant such things beside the road purposely for travelers). I then spent the whole day bartering around those parts of Netherstone, Sundry, and Chimes, which are least accessible by water. The idea was to probe the potential of our Bumblebee strategy, and I wanted to make a good showing to justify this side trip in Wren's eyes. Skipping lunch, I covered a lot more miles than necessary as I scoured the crossroads for good deals. Indeed I found so many, I was loath to quit; but as the day waxed late, I headed across the Hazard Bridge and rolled into Lower Dapplefawn with barely enough light to see the road.

Since I was a little behind schedule, I fully expected to find *Come-What-May* waiting for me at the landing. Instead, I found it was they who were delayed. At least I assumed that was the case; I checked the message board in case they had come and gone, leaving me directions to an alternate meeting place. But among the collage of messages, ads, and announcements could be found nothing from my crewmates. Two other Longlogan boats were tied up there: the tramp *Mudskipper* and the liner *Big Dipper*. They had both come down from Salmon Falls that afternoon, but neither had seen any sign of *Come-What-May*. As the darkness deepened, so did my concern. Their itinerary was simpler and shorter than mine; it didn't seem quite right that I should be there first. But that was the nature of tramp-traders. Hopefully, they had run into some opportunity that was too good to pass up. In any event, there was nothing to do but make the best of it. They had obviously tied up for the night somewhere above here, so I might as well settle in myself. The crews of the other boats knew of a nearby outbuilding that was reasonably mosquito-tight, so we all filed in there to sleep. It was an apple-drying shed, so there were lots of screened windows, a welcome feature in the sticky night air. I was bushed from my very full day, but sleep did not come quickly. Flitting figures of new acquaintances danced around in my restless mind: the palsied old man—my "grandfather"—his wife, as full of love and hope as the daughter was lacking, and their son. Yes, he was but a faint shadow to me now. Were he suddenly to appear before me, alive and well after all these years, would I know him? Surely he would not recognize me. Silhouetted against all those pathetic figures, I saw the colourful character of my newfound friend Cherish, sort of like a harlequined clown, stumbling through the curtains to find herself standing center stage in someone else's tragedy. I couldn't help chuckling at the thought—would she think me unkind? I couldn't bear that; she was such a dear, with her insuppressible enthusiasm and her infirmary in a bag. Yet there was something so appealing, so admirable, about her quest for clear-cut goals, unambiguous channels into which she might pour her boundless energy. It would not be unpleasant to meet her again—had she not invited me?—to continue the conversation we both found so satisfying. Hardly likely, though.

As I finally dropped off into oblivion, I was vaguely aware of distant lightning.

* * * * * * *

I was roughly awakened by the commotion of people stumbling over me. Loud yells were lost in the din of thunder as the downpour broke all around. Everyone was fumbling in the dark to close the shutters over the screened panels where the wind-driven rain was already gusting in on us. Shaking myself into wakefulness, I rushed outside to cover my cycle and its load. Someone had already been thoughtful to do so, but they hadn't done it well enough, so I hurriedly retied the corners. Back inside, we scurried around, pulling our stuff away from the sides and hanging our damp clothes on the empty apple racks. The wind died down in a while, but the rain continued. With seven sweaty people crammed into the tight-shut shed, the air was pretty oppressive; and every so often, the drying clothes would drip on our heads, reminding us that the morning would be no less damp.

Thanks to a lot of popular songs that romanticize the life of a vagabond trader, there are many Esperian adolescents (and some adults) who would give anything to go on a tramp-boat. But that night in a rain-besieged shack near Dapplefawn landing, we all longed to be farmers.

Chapter 41

Morning dawned clear. Everything that had been drenched during the night gave off a warm fog, which would burn off by midmorning to leave a refreshed landscape, something which people in this country take for granted. The other crews were on their boats and gone before the sun had cleared the horizon, but I, having no need for haste, walked to a likely looking stead and invited myself to breakfast. The residents were all very hospitable, considering that they lived near a major landing and probably had many such self-appointed guests. I placed on the table a bowl of dried figs, which were much appreciated. The fact that I was a foreigner made me the centre of attention, but I must have been a disappointment since I brought no fresh news from abroad. One woman asked if I believed Blaze II was really serious about his threatened retaliation for the boycotts and whether he was contemplating military action. I assured her that I knew as much about the Olotal's intentions as she knew about the weather on Jupiter.

Back at the landing, there was still no sign of the *Come-What-May*. I thought of heading upriver to meet them, but the road wasn't always in sight of the river, and we might miss each other. There was no point in my trying to trade in that neighbourhood where access to big well-stocked boats kept prices low. If I ventured farther afield, they might show up and be waiting for hours—there would be no profit in that. It occurred to me that I had had three nights of very poor sleep and that catching up on some rest might be a reasonable idea, especially if they arrived to find me a refreshed and energized boat hand. So I stretched out on the sun-warmed wharf and napped for an hour or two. I was roused by a hard thump against the pilings. It was not *Come-What-May*, but a strange tramp out of Cornshocks called the *Sallyforth*. They had just come from up-valley and brought me a note from Wren.

> Yaro,
>
> We've had a mishap near the mouth of Sharpshin Brook. A stub caught us in some quick water, punched a hole in the sheathing. Nothing ruined, but we had to get everything undercover before that heavy rain. It will take awhile

to make a patch, and then we have to reload everything. Meanwhile, M's not feeling so great—some stomach thing. If you took any of that tempeh with you, throw it out. He thinks he'll be fine tomorrow. No point in coming up. Do whatever you can there, will join you ASAP, hopefully well before dark.

W. P.

So that was it! I immediately felt guilty for not staying with them. Still, we did that regularly as a trading strategy; and anyway, it wasn't my idea. So how to use my time well other than trading? Not far from the pier stood a grist-mill. Leaving Bumblebee and its cargo parked on the pier, I walked in and asked the mill steward if they had any stones that needed retouching. She showed me a couple of worn burrstones behind the door. They had their own grooving tools, but with the winter wheat crop coming in, they had been too busy to catch up on maintenance. When I explained that I was trained at cutting them from scratch, and could even correct any errors or uneven wear, I was given the job on the spot.

I had left a note on Bumblebee, telling Wren where I was; and sure enough, early in the afternoon, just as I was finishing the second stone, he showed up to meet me. I took my pay in cornmeal for our own use, and we went back to the landing where Marten was over his intestinal complaint, but still not feeling full-strength. *Come-What-May* looked almost as good as new, although the unpainted patchboards didn't match. And Wren was clearly feeling a bit overwhelmed by having to deal with everything all alone. He seemed genuinely pleased with all the trades I had made. I frankly think the two of them considered my junket more vacation than business trip, so I was proud to impress them with my entrepreneurial skills.

We all got something of a respite for the rest of the day since our traveling was all downstream. Most of the time, there was no point in poling at all, the current being adequate to carry us along at a leisurely speed. That evening, we were camped by Gentian Falls on our way back to the Broadlea. Wren seemed more subdued than usual, or maybe he was just tired from the strain of coping with the accident. Anyway, we quit a bit early and made ourselves a nice hot supper. Afterward, we ate on a ledge overlooking the cascades, and Wren pulled out his dulcitar. That gave me an inspiration.

"Hey, Wren, why don't you teach me how to play one of those things?"

He stopped playing and cast a suspicious glance at me. He didn't need to say what he was thinking: he had offered to teach me before, and I had declined on the grounds that it looked too complicated. I didn't wait for his comment before adding, "Well, it can't be all that hard to play. After all, you do it . . . I mean, you make it look so easy. Maybe I should give it a try, seeing as how we have all these instruments. And look at all the host-gifts you've saved us."

"Sure, but we've got a couple of fiddles too, and you said you preferred—"

"Oh, forget that. When you've got a good teacher available, it's foolish not to take advantage of the instrument he plays."

The upshot was that he agreed, and we immediately added dulcitar lessons to my math and science studies. I used the cheap scratched instrument I had bought at Stubs Pond (I hadn't sold it yet, probably because I insisted on putting such a high price on it). Whenever we had a few moments to spare, Wren would coach me on proper fingering technique.

I had told them all about my visit to Faring's home, and of course, there was no hiding the fact that Bumblebee and I had been in an accident. I told them about the woman who had helped me out and later dropped by my booth at the fair. I mentioned it as casually as I could for fear they'd assume some connexion with my sudden interest in the dulcitar. It was hard to talk to the guys about certain things without them jumping to wrong conclusions. Anyway, one day I noticed a pair of women jogging along the towpath, and it reminded me of something.

"You guys know about some people who call themselves Swallows?"

Wren swung around to stare at me and said, "Wow! You don't mean she's one of those, do you?"

"What do you mean 'she'? Who said . . . ?"

"Oh yeah, sure. It makes sense, the way you described her."

"Described whom? I never—"

"That woman you met back at Laughingwater. The big handbag, running everywhere . . ."

"Well, I was just generally curious. What are they anyway?"

"Service group, you might say. Really elite. You've got to be pretty dedicated to get in, and really tough to stay in. You have to go through all kinds of rigorous training: running, swimming, rope-climbing, self-defense. You have to practice search-and-rescue. You have to learn to be a paramedic, and—oh yes, and you have to be a woman."

"They are a sisterhood," Marten added. "Sometimes called Candle's Daughters."

You mean, Candle as in that woman back at Alga?"

"The original Candle, a folk hero from the second century. As a youth, she was kidnapped by the Tannerites and raised by them."

"Who are they?"

"*Were* they, you mean. There's a part of Goosegrass fair that was once controlled by a warlord named Cleave Tanner. He and his followers were enemies of our ancestors until an epidemic wiped out so many of his people that they were too weak to defend themselves from another warlord to the south. By that time the Esperian nation had grown strong enough to defend its own borders, and Cleave Tanner tried to form a defense alliance with us, but our ancestors weren't willing to get into such a tangle. Finally, facing annihilation from the south, he became so desperate that he proposed to *bequeath* his territory to Esperia with the understanding that his remaining followers might live among us as sojourners for all their days. According to legend, it was Candle who, as an adult, persuaded the Stewards to accept them by appealing to the Refuge Laws. A lot of heroic exploits are attributed to her, including founding the Swallows."

"And are these Tannerites still there?"

"Very much so, but no longer as sojourners. They grew up among us, and one by one were assimilated into the Covenant. The only reminder of that territory today is a banner named Cleave Tanner's Will."

"So back to the Swallows. Why did you react that way, Wren? Is something wrong with them?"

"Not at all. They're really role model types, every one. No emergency should be without one. It's just that . . . ," he added significantly. "Well, not just everybody would want to be married to one."

"Not that I was planning to," I assured him quickly. "But why not?"

"Wren is exaggerating," Marten objected. "I know a guy who's married to a Swallow, and they're extremely happy together."

"That's true," conceded Wren. "I guess some guys just have trouble living with that much attitude. But Marten's right—they're nothing but admirable. Practically every little girl wants to grow up to be one, though very few do. Anyway, don't let that turn you off to her."

"Assuming I was turned *on* to her," I frowned.

*　　*　　*　　*　　*　　*　　*

Back in the Broadlea, we continued more or less as before, trading in areas where tramps weren't usually seen. As summer progressed, the territory accessible to *Come-What-May* was reduced somewhat by lower water levels. It was hot and humid now, and people around me complained of the "drought." I had to laugh in their faces. What did they know about that? Every stream still ran clear and cool, and the deep-mulched crops continued to make explosive growth. These people rarely knew the need to irrigate. It was true that *Come-What-May* wouldn't find the same channel depths we had during those early months, but we could still get to places the other tramps could not.

One result of the shallower waters was that we spent less time actually *on* the boat itself. That is to say, it was often easier to pull *Come-What-May* from towpaths on either bank or, when lacking those, to simply wade up the shallow streambed itself. A great advantage of this was that the removal of our own weight floated the hull a little higher, an important consideration when rocks and sandbars lurked just beneath the surface. It also allowed more efficient use of muscle power than poling. The wading was okay, but the cold current really got to your shins after awhile, and the water-worn rocks were often coated with greasy algae. We traded for some tough hemp-soled sandals, but I remember always having pebbles in irritating places.

Because of the importance Esperians give to food self-reliance, many enterprises were shut down or on skeleton crews at this season as nearly every able-bodied person spent some time helping with crops. Librarians were swinging scythes, engineers were pulling weeds, and Vision-Councilors were turning compost piles. If you required a doctor, you might have to fetch him or her from the orchard; teachers and scholars alike might be found threshing field peas. Clearly, others were not obsessed with buying and selling, least of all now. It seemed we tramp-traders were the only ones having nothing to do with food production. And quite frankly, if there was anything I missed during our vagabond life, it was the diversity of work that one found in Esperian agriculture. There were in fact a few occasions when the commodity most valued by our trade-partner stead was our own labour, and we would be draughted to help in the fields for a few hours. I loved it, but Wren usually refused such offers, considering that our time on *Come-What-May* was worth more than they would care to pay us.

$$* \quad * \quad * \quad * \quad * \quad * \quad *$$

The next several weeks passed in a kind of a blur. By then, I was used to the routine. We explored some of the smaller brooks we'd missed before, but mostly we revisited our old territory. There was less exploring, less innovation now as Wren sought more consistent returns from proven strategies.

One "experiment" we did continue was my use of Bumblebee. In fact, my overland excursions became more important as I could help compensate for *Come-What-May*'s shrinking range. With lower water levels and slower currents, it was easier for the two of them to manage without me.

Wren was great at adapting to new challenges. We had noticed that goods mentioned in the production inventory tended to have their channels of distribution already worked out. Households, on the other hand, were far less predictable. It was impossible to anticipate what they might want (if they even knew themselves) until we showed up. Likewise, there was no foreseeing what a hodgepodge of valuables might lie in their wares rooms, waiting to be exchanged. This unknowing was either an obstacle or an opportunity, depending on how you chose to face it, and Wren chose the latter.

I kept wishing we were over in Laughingwater, even more so now that I had seen it and met some of its people. Yes, especially one person in particular, and why not? As I reminded myself, she really was just an intriguing friend with whom I'd like to get better acquainted. I don't mean that I dwelt on it much—I certainly didn't talk about it. For now, I had my work to do, and in my spare time, there were my studies, my drawing, and oh yeah, a lot of dulcitar strings to figure out.

About this time, I began to notice a subtle change in Wren. He seemed less impulsive, more subdued. When the workweek ended, he sometimes borrowed a bike and sped off for somewhere, even though there might be a dance or other event right in the neighbourhood with lovely girls inquiring after him. Or sometimes, he just stayed aboard *Come-What-May* (quite unlike him), writing letters or resting quietly. Even during the workweek, his mind seemed less focused on business. He forgot where things were and didn't always seem to care that much.

$$* \quad * \quad * \quad * \quad * \quad * \quad *$$

The days continued warm and dry, but there was a distinct chill in the night air. This was especially apparent for those of us who lived on the water and slept on the wharves. In the world around us, harvest was beginning in earnest. Spring grains were being cut and stooked, flax was being pulled, and field pea vines were being heaped on poles to cure. Again there was demand for salt as mustard, rape, and other greens were packed into large crocks.

Finally, just after the equinox, we awoke one morning to see the fields all rimed with frost. We knew there was no point in trading for the next couple days—everyone's attention was devoted to getting in those tender crops which had been frost-hit. We three hired ourselves out to a couple of nearby steads where we picked squash, peppers, and tomatoes and helped haul them under cover.

When we did return to the water, we set our bow toward the Humps where we had not been for several weeks. We had a specific errand to do there: the delivery of some supplies to the Sundew Project. The banner of Tenacre had some foodstuffs which were part of their cost share for the canal, and we were to deliver them to the work camp. Of course, we did other trading on our way there; but once we arrived at Sundew, we discovered that our free-roaming days were over, at least for a while.

This great construction project was in a flurry of eleventh-hour activity. By that I mean that it was scheduled to open late that fall, but there remained a long stretch of blasting and dredging before the Broadlea watershed would at last be directly linked to the Laughingwater. In a couple more months, most work would grind to a halt for the season, so everyone was in a dither to finish up. One thing that was hampering their progress was the inability of supply boats to reach the work camp due to the lack of water in the last section of the canal. Water from the Heathlands was being diverted into Towsack Brook in order that the worksite might not be flooded, but that left too little depth in Furnace Brook to float larger boats. Handcarts were being used to carry supplies, but they were woefully inadequate for the volume needed. We had no sooner arrived at the project than we were recruited to haul supplies the last two miles. We were very well paid, and the work was predictable—too predictable for a crew used to hopping from place to place with the spontaneity of a damselfly. The project loaned us a couple of workers to help unload all our cargo into a store shed near the Sundew pier, and for the next couple weeks we were tethered to this new job.

This is how it worked: larger boats would come up Furnace Brook as far as Sundew landing. There they would transfer their cargoes to us or pile it on the wharf, whence we would ferry it the remaining distance. It was a short-enough haul, but the volume of supplies required many trips back and forth. Often the load consisted of food for the mess tents, which served hundreds of workers; at other times we carried tools—picks and shovels and drills—to replace worn and broken ones. A few times we hauled explosives for blasting the slaty outcrop which blocked the last section.

I was amazed at the tremendous quantity of supplies needed to keep so many workers fed and supplied. The huge temporary camp was more like a city than anything else in the nation. Just the logistics of financing such an endeavour were mind-boggling.

Many banners paid their share in provisions or labour; others provided coins or cashlike goods with which to pay the expenses of others. No small amount of planning was needed to guarantee a steady rotation of workers and to keep them well furnished. We were duly proud of our role in that, and others were proud of us; *Come-What-May* became sort of a camp mascot. Every morning, when we finished our first run, which included fresh provisions and mail, our arrival would be greeted by loud cheers from the work gangs.

Chapter 42

One evening after work, we were tied up at Sundew landing, the end of the line for other boats. We had just transferred sixty-eight kegs of black powder onto *Come-What-May*, to be hauled into camp at first light. It had been an exquisite day; bright-coloured maple leaves were beginning to fall, and the air was as sweet and tangy as new cider. Though bone-tired from the day's work, we weren't in a sleeping mood quite yet. There was a small stone fireplace on the shore, and we warmed our fingers over it while Wren and I played our dulcitars. I should say Wren played while I plunked along on the simpler parts. He was playing some of my favourites: "The Tramp Traders Lament" and "The Party at Cloudbridge." Marten nodded away at the flickering embers, determined to keep awake.

The Party at Cloudbridge

(Some versions of this very old song contain many more verses; these are
all I remember)

The Cloudbridge folks are a fun-loving crowd,
They smile real easy and they laugh real loud.
They work all day and they dance all night,
And they love each other in the pale moonlight.

(refrain)
Now I've got a fiddle and I've got a bow,
And I've got a girl that I love so,
I'll fiddle in the rain, I'll fiddle in the snow;
if there's a dance, that's where I'll go.

Now one bright night, so goes my yarn,
Folks were gathered in a neighbour's barn

To kick up their heels and have some fun,
But it seems they weren't the only ones.

A pair of skunks came in at the door,
Everyone rushed to clear the floor;
Now there was no one left in sight,
But I decided to sit real tight.

Stuck in the corner, where could I go?
So I just rosined up my bow.
I scratched away like a fiddlin' fool
To see what them two skunks would do.

With paw to paw they both began
To promenade and allemande,
Now to the left and now to the right,
They danced away that summer night.

As if that weren't enough surprise,
There now appeared before my eyes
Two red squirrels and a couple of hares.
They walked right in and stood in pairs.

While they began to do-si-do,
Others crept in to watch the show:
A bold raccoon with his banded tail,
A flock of geese and a covey of quail.

The white-tailed deer did snort and prance,
A fat muskrat joined in the dance.
A painted turtle and a pair of loons,
And I was there to call the tunes.

Now as the dawn commenced to break,
The critters all their leave did take,
While I was left with an empty barn
And no one there to believe my yarn.

There were two other boats moored alongside *Come-What-May*: the liner *Zenith Stalwart*, which we had just emptied and whose crew had gone to stay at a nearby stead, and a local tramp, the *Harbinger*, which was laden with new-made cedar barrels. The *Harbinger* was down-bound in the morning, and like us, they were camped at the landing.

We had barely met the crew and assumed they had gone to bed; but as soon as we started singing, they showed up on the pier, eager to join the impromptu party. So the six of us huddled around the little fire-pit, enjoying the cheer and the music. We broke out some apples and roasted them on sharp sticks. At some point, one of us commented, "Ah, what a luscious night! The smell of sizzling apples and cedar smoke."

"Not cedar," Wren corrected. "I'm just burning up some oak scraps." Still there was the undeniable bitter pungence of cedar in the air. Suddenly, Wren's eyes met mine as the same thought occurred to both of us at once.

"Say, you guys don't have some kind of fire going on . . . ?" Before finishing, he had leaped to his feet and was running toward the *Harbinger* with the rest of us close behind. Sure enough, a column of smoke was billowing out of its stern, which at that very moment burst into a flash of flame.

If there is anything that kindles and ignites faster than a dry cedar barrel, I'm sure I don't know what it is. Unless of course, blasting powder, which was parked less than thirty feet away. Within seconds, a bunch of the thin-walled barrels were flaring like torches, spitting sparks into the surrounding water. Wren acted as if by instinct. Grabbing a boat pole and leaping onboard the *Harbinger*, he began pushing the burning barrels overboard. It was an excellent idea, and others searched for poles or fallen limbs to do the same. But it was too late—the reed-mat roof of the dingle had caught on, and no one could get near it. Again, Wren was the quick one, snatching an unburned barrel and using it like a bucket to dip river water and fling it at the flames. I didn't participate in any of the effort as I saw a much graver threat. Despite shouts to stay away, I leaped into the water beside *Come-What-May* and, yanking loose the painter, tried to push it out into the stream. I was fully aware of the great risk, but in the commotion, it occurred to me that if sixty-eight kegs of blasting powder were to go off, it really wouldn't make much difference whether I were on top of it or thirty feet away. The water was hardly knee-deep, but it wasn't easy getting the boat in motion all alone. Two tons of inertia isn't overcome in a moment, and from the heat on my back and the scorched smell of cinders landing in my hair, I knew there weren't any moments to spare. Finally, I got *Come-What-May* drifting down the brook, and I waded ahead of it, pulling for all I was worth until it was safely out of reach of any stray sparks. I retied the painter rope carefully to an overhanging limb and hurried back to help the others.

By this time, the fire was quite out of control, and all one could do was watch as showers of glowing embers shot up and drifted all around, many landing where *Come-What-May* had been. In the end, it was a sorry sight indeed. The *Harbinger* was burnt to the waterline. All of their personal possessions in the dingle were destroyed, and of course, the cargo was now ashes. I received a lot of praise for my quick action; and indeed, if anyone had doubts about the danger, they needed only look at the scorch holes in the dingle of the *Zenith Stalwart*, which was moored beyond where *Come-What-May* had been.

There was no one more dejected than the *Harbinger*'s crew. It was not only that their vessel was gone, along with its cargo. They also were keenly aware of their liability:

apparently in their eagerness to party, they had left a smoldering brazier in the stern, too close to the highly flammable cedar. As serious as was their loss, the magnitude of what might have been was sobering. I wasn't disposed to point fingers, but a more flagrant violation of the Pits-and-Parapets Laws would be hard to imagine, and I didn't envy them going back to their employers and steadmates. It would be in the newssheets, and their humiliation would be hard to bear. If anyone thinks a society without fines and police is necessarily a permissive one, they have never been to Esperia.

* * * * * * *

As autumn progressed, we began to hear rumours out of Anagaia that there had been an assassination attempt on the Olotal. At first, a government spokesperson for the Onyx Palace denied it ever happened, but as days passed, further news releases confirmed much of what we had already learned through underground sources: Blaze II had survived a poisoning attempt, not by the radical opposition, but by someone within the Imperial court itself. Still later, it was officially announced that the Duke of Seabridge, the Olotal's first cousin, had been executed for treason against the state.

Every day, I made a point of checking out any bulletin board we passed for the latest newssheet. It was generally assumed that there would be a retaliatory bloodletting, but happily, it never came to that. If the duke was acting in league with any faction, they were never identified, beyond a couple of palace kitchen staff who were hanged along with him. Quite predictably, the Onyx Court became more secretive and reactionary than ever.

In Esperia, the incident was greeted by a spate of editorials espousing different opinions. As far as I could make out, they all boiled down to two views: one was that the late duke was a reform-minded liberal who would have made great improvements, and therefore it was a great shame the coup had failed. The second view held that an aristocrat, however liberal, could be counted on to make only the most superficial changes, which could only dampen the zeal of dissidents and delay any real change in the system—a good thing he was dead!

Relations between the Empire and its neighbours were at a low point. New Kalmia was increasingly resentful of its status as a client-state, and it was claimed by the Onyx Court that separatist groups in Tramont received support from clandestine groups in Lacustria.

Of particular interest to Esperians was the fighting in the Coquinas. Although that conflict appeared to be at an all-time low from the islanders' perspective, many Esperians felt that with the Olotal's forces spread so far and thin, it was an opportune moment. But for what? Esperia's entire military posture was defensive, and some wondered if it were adequate for that. Surely the tiny country was in no position to confront the Empire on the battlefield. Our leaders insisted, and most of the people agreed, that Anagaia's greatest weakness was within, which is to say the Amanita, and that foreign intervention would be futile until the Brotherhood got itself in readiness. In the meantime, the best

Esperia could do was keep supplying the Coquinese Free Army with the means to continue resisting. Of course, Esperia's neutral policy was not binding on individuals acting on their own behalf with no support from their government; and indeed hundreds of Stewards, from Esperia as well as pacifist Concordia, had formed the Tropic Brigade in support of the rebels. Many in both countries were alarmed that those "free agents" might precipitate an invasion of their homelands while many others were frustrated, even angry, with their nation's reluctance to get directly involved in the struggle. The Council continued to urge restraint, while Blaze II, despite his frequent sabre-rattling, still refrained from sending his troops northward.

About the same time as the assassination attempt, another incident had ratcheted up tension levels in both nations. *The Cormorant*, a freighter flying the Esperian flag and carrying food, blankets, and medicine—but no weapons—was stopped on the high seas by an Imperial warship. The Anagaian captain assumed, reasonably enough, that the cargo was destined for the rebel-held parts of Grand Coquina. The ship and cargo were impounded and the crew taken forcibly to New Chalice and jailed. The Esperian ambassador protested strenuously, threatening to sever relations. After a week of negotiation, the crew were freed and returned to their ship. Indemnity was paid, but the cargo itself was never released.

After 11/11, the newssheets carried reports of a new crisis. Following the *Cormorant* incident, the Council had authorized merchant ships to defend themselves "by appropriate means." Of course, the Council never had the power to forbid anyone from defending themselves; the authorization simply meant there was a formal consensus behind them that the nation would approve and support their actions. At the time, I wasn't clear on just what that meant, but everyone else seemed to get it.

Anyway, on the afternoon of the eleventh, another Esperian freighter, the *Dauntless* was challenged by an Anagaian gunboat while approaching the Coquinese coast and ordered to heave to. When they refused, their deck was raked by gunfire with one sailor wounded. It's not clear exactly what happened next; an Imperial government investigation was "inconclusive," because the gunboat went down with all hands. No wreckage was ever found. This seems the more incredible since the *Dauntless* was known to be unarmed—that is, there were no cannon onboard. To this day, the returning crew have told no one, at least publicly, about what happened.

Chapter 43

A week after the tramp-boat fire, the last series of charges were set; and with that blast, the channel through the Humps was opened. The various locks en route had already been completed by other work teams, and with the removal of debris from this last section, small boats could pass directly between the two valleys. On the official opening day, *Come-What-May* was invited to inaugurate the new canal. We repainted the patched part of the hull and replaced the cinder-holed canopy with one bearing a new public service slogan. I thought it highly fitting that the new message, a promotion for the Non-Combustion policy, said simply "Learn Not to Burn."

Many hundreds of onlookers lined the banks, and loud cheers and whistles greeted us the whole four miles from Sundew to Dikemoor. But for me, the most exciting part was when we *left* the canal, and *Come-What-May* began trading in the Laughingwater fair for the first time. There would not be many weeks left in the season, but by now, both Wren and Marten were as eager as I was to explore the region sometimes referred to as the Heartland of the Vision.

By this time, I had seen at least parts of Bluemeadow, Goosegrass, Welcome, Portage, and Broadlea fairs. The valley in which we now proposed to trade was distinctive from those in its physical character. Like the Broadlea River to the south, the Laughingwater rises in the Sanctuary Mountains, several of which reach above four thousand feet and wends its way eastward to join the Bluemeadow. Like the Broadlea, it debouches through a narrow gorge, which requires several locks to bypass. And like the Broadlea, it is rife with historic landmarks, evoking the memories of the Covenant's long past.

But unlike the other fairs, the Laughingwater is higher in elevation; and except for Portage, it lies farther north. Its lakes are fewer and smaller. Its streams spend more time tumbling through shaded ravines than meandering across warm silty floodplains. Its three constricted intervales are prone to spring flooding, and its slopes tend to be steep and rocky. Many of its ridges are naked spines of schist or granite, and several of its tributary brooks are unnavigable. Summers are short and cool, winter snows lie very deep. The rugged nature of the land is reflected in the hardy character of the people. However, the region is not poor. Its inhabitants are frugal with themselves, yet generous to others. They are hardworking and enterprising, making maximum use of their two great resources.

First, fully two-thirds of its area is covered by mighty forests rich in valuable hardwoods of many species. The lower elevations abound in oak, ash, elm, chestnuts and bastwood; the rocky but well-drained slopes are clad in beeches, sugar maples, yellow birches, hornbeams, and hemlocks. The higher ridges are dominated by paper birches and spruces while the acidic wetlands are carpeted in cedar, larch, red maple, alder, and willow. These forests aren't merely allowed to grow; they are pruned, thinned, replanted, and managed with the assiduous care of a garden.

Secondly, the clear and full-rushing streams provide power for countless small industries, many of which convert those woods into quality manufactured goods. The river of lumber, furniture, and other wood products that pours out of Laughingwater and flows to foreign shores would have allowed the valley's residents to live high and handsome had they so chosen, but that is not the Laughingwater character.

In proportion to its population and wealth, the Laughingwater supports more foreign missions than any other part of the country. It also sends more missionaries. And although its interior location causes it to see fewer foreigners than other fairs, I read somewhere that Laughingwater has the highest percentage of people knowing a foreign language, perhaps due in part to the mission effort.

Since the land of Laughingwater is not overly productive by nature, the people have toiled relentlessly through many generations to make it productive. Sandy soils have been amended with clay while clay soils have been loosened with sand, and all have been shaped into sod-banked terraces so that no hard-won topsoil should erode into the waterways. Such unstinting effort has enabled the region to feed itself amply on less than a third of its area, leaving the rest free for forests.

Of course, much of the forest also produces food, either directly as chestnuts, acorns, and maple sugar or indirectly as leaves and ramial chips, which nurture the croplands. But the production of the forest goes far beyond food, fuel, lumber, or even fertilizer. The ingenuity of the people has enabled them to turn trees into a vast array of useful materials, such as paper, cellophane and cellopane, synthetic fibres, and chemicals for many uses. Much of their technology has been rediscovered from the pre-Calamitous world, but they have learned to adapt it sustainably.

Our travels in the Laughingwater Valley were constantly hampered by the topography. The rapid drop of most streams makes them wonderful sources of power but real obstacles to navigation. Every single dam or weir requires a lock to pass it as well as a fish-ladder, making progress very slow. Where waterfalls are not equipped with locks, there is often a short steep railroad around the ledge. One simply moves the boat over a half-submerged car, then a capstan is used to winch the whole thing up the tracks and back into the water on the other side. The car, boat, and cargo together may weigh over three tons, so working the capstan can be hard work, but the main problem is the time involved. Trading requires making lots of contacts, and every hour spent getting to those contacts is costly overhead. It was in this region that we found the Bumblebee strategy to be a real winner. As in Broadlea, there were already trike-traders in the area, but we were unable to coordinate with them much since they had no way of knowing our movements—we barely knew ourselves. Whenever I crossed paths with them, however, I was quick to unload on them anything they wanted since cooperation seemed more profitable than competition, especially on their own territory.

In the course of my overland rambles with Bumblebee, I saw or heard about a number of enterprises which intrigued me immensely, in part because of their fascinating work, but also because they were not set up to make profit. These were the various research and development institutes which operate under the aegis of the Vision Fulfillment Commission, and their purpose is to work on certain technologies, which are very much in the national interest yet which require more long-term capital investment than any one stead or banner could muster. These are spread around the country, but Laughingwater seems to have an unwonted share of them, especially those related to forest products. I've already mentioned the glass research facility back in the Steppingstones area and the experimental cellopane greenhouses. Here in the Laughingwater, I heard about a pilot plant which was actually producing cellopane; they were also developing a silklike textile fibre, also made from soluble cellulose. I didn't get to visit the place at the time, but I did visit another materials-development centre called the Synthetic Polymer Research Institute. I didn't even understand what the words meant, but in essence, they were trying to re-create some of the amazing materials from the Ancient World by using stuff like corn and wood pulp instead of petroleum. I looked in on still another facility, which was exploring new adhesives and protective coatings, some derived from soybeans and tree resins. Of course, many of these are already in common use, but they were working to create greater bonding strengths and durability by manipulating the molecular bonds—it was all way over my head. One place I stopped to trade turned out to be part of the Alternative Fibres Project, which Hewn had defended so stoutly. They were working mostly with conventional cellulose fibres already in use, like nettles, hemp, flax, bast, and sunflower, but using improved postextraction technology to get a "clingier" fibre that would spin more like protein-based wool.

I saw one research laboratory, essentially a great barn, where technicians were learning to artificially grow large crystals of silica (basically glass); but this was only the beginning. They were also trying to re-create an invention built by the Ancients: a device which could create a beam of perfectly aligned light, which in turn could be used to slice off those silica crystals into extremely thin wafers. Wired together in a laminated panel, those wafers had the incredible talent of converting sunlight into the form of energy so widely used by the Ancients: electricity. Did I mention the Ancients? Oh yes, guess what is the main objection to all this newfangled technology? That the Ancients used it! And after all, who wants to be like them? How unlike the Anagaians who slavishly emulate anything they perceive as coming from the "Golden Age." However, I was told that the reactionary position here has weakened in recent years, as it has been strongly argued that such technologies are perhaps not inherently flawed. Perhaps in a sustainably construed society, these clever wonders might indeed fulfill the promise that was originally seen in them (if only they could have figured that out *before* the Calamities destroyed so much of that knowledge!). Perhaps polymer plastics can indeed be made from crop residues without ultimately releasing fossil carbon; perhaps axle grease and paraffin wax can be derived from growing wood, just as tar and charcoal are produced today. Perhaps we can have all these things without adding an unsustainable burden to our forests and to the earth. Perhaps.

Whatever hopes and doubts others might have about these technologies, two aspects of it all impressed me greatly. One was the fact that the society could marshal such enormous resources for such research, some of which might never justify the expense. After all, the Ancients had a vast reserve of discretionary energy-wealth; not only the sea of petroleum, but a whole global empire of deprived classes and exploited colonies, which allowed certain elites the freedom to develop sophisticated arts and sciences, even to walking on the moon. Of course, the Esperians have none of this "slave labour," not even of draught animals, although they certainly try to make it up by harnessing the winds and currents. Lacking any great "windfall" resources, they rather avoid the squandering of what they do have. They live modestly, and the surplus fruits of their labours are freed for reinvestment in such research. Their grandchildren will reap the benefits, just as they are enjoying the results of their forebears' efforts. As Ermine put it so well, "When you dwell in the Larger House, you can afford such things."

A second aspect of all this that struck me was the manner in which such changes are made. These new technologies have great consequences for all of society, and so all of society is involved in an ongoing dialogue about them. Technological innovations seem invariably to raise political, economic, and ethical questions: where will these changes take us, and do we wish to go there? A logical-enough question, but one which is rarely asked in Anagaia or, I suppose, in other societies. Some elite group of researchers and investors pool their talents and resources, with profit the main driving force and with little or no input from the wider stakeholders. By the time problems arise, it is too late for questions, too late for anything but the most meagre safeguards.

Of course, Esperians are rather unique, so far as I know, in this self-conscious internal dialogue over their common destiny. All of which made me wonder: how did this situation come about? Is it transferable to other societies? How?

*   *   *   *   *   *   *

One day, we poled around a river bend and saw a dramatic landform far ahead of us. It was a very sharp ridge, sticking out at us like a bony finger from the main block of the Sanctuary Mountains. When I was told that this was Covenant Ridge, my interest quickened immediately. It was the one place in Esperia I had heard about since I was sixteen. Standing in my little garden in Dryford, two Esperian surveyors had told me about a marvelous place called the Archives where carefully guarded caves held the published wisdom of the ages, rescued from the ruins of a fallen civilization.

Now I studied the landmass carefully. The valley forked around the ridge, the Laughingwater on the left, or south side, while a major tributary called Wisewoman Brook carved into its north flank. The upper slopes were clad in white birch, mountain ash, and moosewood with stunted spruces clinging to the cliffs. The crest of the ridge was all above timberline, naked ledges etched and scoured by the primeval glaciers.

Wren pointed out that the Archives themselves were not visible from where we were. Perched atop the schistose spine, it was, after all, originally intended as a fortress against their enemies. Even now, five centuries later, access to the place was restricted by a community of monastic types called Keepers of the Lore, who made it their life's work to preserve and protect the knowledge of the ancient world from oblivion. One didn't just drop in there, especially known enemies of the Vision who preferred to view history from their own perspective, unencumbered by awkward facts. Visits to this great library were by invitation only.

Later in the day, we passed the mouth of Wisewoman Brook above Evenswap, but we did not enter it. According to Wren, it was only navigable for the first mile, even by *Come-What-May*. Above Stoutbridge, the first of a long series of dams and rapids made passage quite impractical. It is the only major stream in the country which is devoid of locks and canals. The same might have been true of the Upper Laughingwater; however it led to White Mica Notch, which was a major pass over the Sanctuaries to the Five Fairs district and points west. Wisewoman Brook, on the other hand, only led to a few banners which were backed up by Sacred Groves—a dead end for travellers.

For the moment, Wren was only interested in the Upper Laughingwater because he'd heard that the White Mica Notch cable railroad might be able to carry a boat of *Come-What-May*'s size, fully loaded, without having to transfer the cargo. This was of dubious usefulness to us since we didn't wish to go over the Notch, but it was of great interest to the cable operators since it would remove the main disadvantage of that route for tramp-traders wishing to pass directly into the western fairs. Of course, the toll rate would include the weight of the boat itself, but in our case, the toll was waived since the experiment was in their own interest.

After a lot of lock portages and tram-links, we finally made it to a point above Colliers' Rill where the railroad begins. Since the track was beside the stream and not down into it, as in other places, we had to waste a lot of time while the operators improvised a temporary section of track to get us up out of the water. Then *Come-What-May* had to be maneuvered onto two eight-foot cars, and because these were common flatbeds, some bunking had to be arranged so the boat would not rock. Then we eased onto the main track and hooked onto the cable. There was a suspenseful moment as the hemp lead line stretched a bit to avoid a stressful shock to the system; then a gentle jerk and we were on our way, the cable towing the cars, boat, cargo, and us all together. In the beginning, the tramline was powered by waterwheels in the stream below; the same rapids and cascades which blocked navigation now provided the muscle to tow us along the stream bank above. At that late season, the flow was barely adequate for power. Once we were stalled for nearly half an hour while small dams upstream released enough water to get us moving again. Still, it was little worse than waiting for canal locks to fill. A couple miles below the summit of the Notch, the stream becomes too meagre for a power source, and a new cable was driven by a pair of huge windmills right up in the Notch itself.

Long before reaching the windmills, one could see and hear them, and I noticed their design was somewhat different from others I'd seen. The turbines were essentially the same shape, except there was only one per tower. Height was of little consequence in the exposed notch, but these turbines were very much wider—over forty feet—and the vertical oak shafts were at least eight inches in diameter.

Ordinarily, each windmill powered a tramline of its own, each serving either approach to the notch. In times of inadequate wind, the two could be engaged so as to give double power to one line or the other. That was rare enough, since a nearly constant wind funneled through the narrow pass, producing ample force. Each car had a hinged brake-stick dragging beneath it so that if anything let go, it would not go careening off down the track. I found that especially reassuring on the last section, which was extremely steep.

I have to say the view was breathtaking, as we sat lazily on the bow of our boat, with the breeze in our faces doing all the work. It was the season of maximum fall foliage, and across the mountain saddle stretched a Coquinese carpet of brilliant hues: dark mahogany-purple, fiery scarlet, bright gold, and muted ochre accented by the scattered dark greens of spruces and hemlocks. Nestled into the Notch, the rock-cradled Tarn glistened like a polished sapphire under the brilliant autumn sky.

For Marten and me, it was worth it all for that alone, but Wren was too absorbed with the ascent to fully appreciate the scenery. If something had lurched the wrong way, it might have smashed or damaged the cargo. As it was, all went very smoothly, if agonizingly slow. At the summit, a carload of cargo had been waiting its turn, and it would have to wait still longer while we hooked onto the other side of the same cable loop and started back down. It occurred to me that if there were a second track, a car could be going down while another came up; and its descending weight would help pull the other up, cable power making up the difference only. However, I don't know where they'd have put a second track—in some places the close sides of the road-cut barely left room for one.

When we reached the bottom of the line, the other car was close behind us as it didn't take much power to ease us both down. We found out that they were loaded with soapstone griddles from Concordia, and we traded for some. That was the only deal we made in that whole day, due to the cable experiment, but Wren didn't seem to begrudge the lost time as much as I would've expected. I guess he knew our sponsors would value the information gleaned from our experiment more than whatever trading opportunities we missed.

Collier Rill and Auger Rill were not passible at all, but we decided that I should take Bumblebee through the area and rendezvous on Spodumene Brook. The whole area has numerous pegmatite formations, which are mined for a variety of useful minerals. The chief product is quartz (the nation's main source of clear glass), but they also mine sheet-mica for stove and furnace windows. Kyanite and feldspar are also mined for specialty ceramics; garnet is mined for abrasives although gem quality stuff is exported to countries which value that more. The same is true of the area's beryl and tourmaline although the latter is also made into polarizing lenses for navigational instruments and astronomy research.

Being on my own, I hardly knew which of these specialty products I should take in trade or how I should value them, but I did buy a lot of isinglass panes and some optical lenses.

*　*　*　*　*　*　*

The Spodumene bannerhouse was near the landing where I was to rendezvous with *Come-What-May*. Arriving there early, I saw a lot of activity in the field behind the building. It looked like an archery contest, so I perched on Bumblebee's saddle and watched awhile. I had often seen two or three people practicing target-shooting in backyards, so I assumed that must be very popular sport here, but I'd never seen anything like this: dozens of men and women with bows nearly seven feet long and quivers full of yard-long arrows all aiming at a row of targets fully a hundred yards away. It appeared to be some sort of regional tournament. After several rounds of shooting and noting scores, the distance was changed, and everyone began shooting again. A woman would call out some number, and everyone would raise or lower their aim accordingly.

I was only mildly curious, but with time on my hands, I continued to watch from a distance. After a while, a man in his thirties appeared next to me—I didn't see where he came from—and struck up a friendly chat. He asked me what I thought of the proceedings, and I merely commented that it looked like fun. He gave me a curious look and asked where I was from.

"Stonesthrow, on Alga Island."

"Oh, but I thought you looked Anagaian, or Borealian, maybe."

"Well, I mean I am from Anagaia originally. But now I'm a refugee, and I sojourn at Alga."

Another curious look, carefully taking in my short beard and longish hair.

"Oh well, you're probably not a spy then?" He looked a bit disappointed.

Now I suppose I gave *him* a curious look.

"Why? Do you assume every foreigner is a spy?"

"No, of course not, I mean you're dressed like one of us, and you appear to be a trader, but you seemed pretty interested in the exercise. I mean, don't get me wrong—if you were a spy, we'd be very happy to have you watch."

"Forgive my obtuseness, but why would a spy want to watch folks playing with bows and arrows?"

"Playing with . . . ? Oh, dear me, no no no! You see, this is part of their military training. These people are preparing for war, and we want the Olotal to know we are prepared."

"Prepared to confront guns with bows and arrows? Are you serious?"

"Quite. That's how we fought the last war."

"Over a century ago. Don't you suppose guns have been improved since then?"

"Yes, I do. And so have our bows and other weapons. Don't assume because they're basic that they're primitive."

"But what's the point? Why not guns?"

"Several advantages. One is that they're cheap enough to manufacture so that every citizen who wants one can have one. Even if the Olotal dared to supply his entire citizenry with guns, it would be prohibitive. With those longbows, it's quite possible."

"Frankly, I hadn't even realized that Esperia had a standing army."

"A much larger army than the Olotal's. Every citizen is in effect a soldier, and they're far more loyal to their nation than the Olotal's troops are to him."

I certainly couldn't dispute that. Indeed, as I looked at the large gathering of self-styled militia, I noticed that they ranged widely in age—some were probably in their sixties—and included plenty of women.

Watching their next round of shots, a realization came to me: from where I was sitting, I could clearly see the archers and I could clearly see the targets, but the way the land was curved, the archers probably couldn't see their targets at all! That's why they were so dependent on the leaders' calls. My acquaintance pointed out that each of the bows had a tiny spirit level and compass attached, and he explained that the leader called out the angle of inclination, the direction of fire, and how far to draw the string. Therefore their aim did not depend so much on expert marksmanship as on their leaders' calculations and their own ability to follow instructions. Large groups fired simultaneously. They pointed in the direction indicated and let fly. Of course, this was not a very accurate way to hit a specific point, but when the target was an approaching mass of enemy troops, the rain of deadly shafts from on high would be devastating. Many shots would miss, but plenty would find their mark, and the effect would be all the more demoralizing since the enemy couldn't return fire! Rifle bullets travel farther than arrows, but they also travel in straight lines, and require visual contact to be effective.

Yes, I could see some advantage to this mode of warfare, but I feared this fellow was mad if he thought the Olotal would be intimidated by his spies' reports of teenagers and grandmothers awaiting his troops with bows and arrows.

That evening, reunited with Wren and Marten, I told them about the things I'd seen.

"Does Esperia really think it can repel the armies of the Empire with only weapons like those?"

"No, it doesn't. We have a whole array of strategies at our disposal. Firearms just don't seem compatible with those strategies. In guerrilla warfare, it's best to use a weapon that doesn't give away your position the very first time you use it. And anyway, some of our most effective weapons are not projectiles of all, but rather strategies which exploit our own strengths and Anagaia's weakness."

"But what is the Olotal's weakness? He has tens of thousands of troops, warships with cannon, all the latest developments in weaponry."

"And does he have the support of his own people? Is the average peasant, in his heart of hearts, willing to give his life to fatten the aristocracy?"

"We both know that answer."

"Then he is militarily weak. And moreover, he knows it. That hasn't stopped him from attacking others when he can attack their weaknesses. See here: Grand Coquina had a nasty dictator—many people weren't sure whether the Olotal would be any worse. And the Amanita is divided against itself, torn by infighting. That fellow on the throne is not our main worry. There are others in the Onyx Court who believe we are pacifist, like Concordia. Because we have no fortresses or great warships, they assume we are vulnerable, unable and unwilling to defend ourselves. Fortunately, Blaze knows better. The last invasion of Esperia, in 425, ended in the toppling of the Zirconid dynasty and brought his ancestors to power. He and his family have never forgotten that lesson: whatever despots they may be, they've always left little Esperia at peace. I don't believe he will attack, but if he does, we are ready."

"So what is the draught age here?"

"There is no compulsory service. People are simply urged to get as much training as possible—I'll be continuing mine this winter. If and when we're attacked, plenty of volunteers will come forward, you can count on that."

Chapter 44

One evening over our supper fire, I asked Wren, "Have you ever by any chance ever heard of a banner named Ravenswing?"

"Nope, there isn't any. Are you sure you don't mean Crowfoot?"

"Nope, I know where that is. Besides, that's in Broadlea, Ravenswing is in Laughingwater.

I had already pored over the map, vainly trying to find it, but I figured Wren knew every place in the country.

"It's not a banner. Might it be a stead name?"

Now that set me back a moment. Of course, I had assumed Cherish was telling me her banner, but to one whose activities were more centred on the local community, it might doubtless seem more natural to give her stead name. That was a discouraging thought. With scores of banners in the fair, each comprised of dozens of steads, it would be a long shot to come up with this Ravenswing.

"Why? What's there?" It was Marten who asked. I had tried to make my query casual enough so as not to arouse the obvious question.

"Oh, just that friend I met at Laughingwater Fair back in Eighth-Month. I didn't know but that we might be near there sometime."

"Quite likely," agreed Wren. "But we may never know it. A Swallow, you said . . . what's her name?"

"Oh, I don't remember . . . Charity or Cherish, I think, or something like that. Never mind. I just enjoyed talking with her at the fair."

"Sure," agreed Wren without further comment.

Oh, that Wren! I just knew he was assuming some kind of romantic interest. He never put it like that, of course, but everyone imagines more than he says.

As I mentioned before, my loneliness was only intensified by gnawing doubts about Fawn. Not doubts about *whether* I still loved her, but about *how* I loved her. (Keep in mind that I still knew nothing about our biological connexion). I now wondered if Jasper had perhaps spoken truly when he said we were ill-matched for each other. After all, that light gaiety of hers, that sweet frivolity, had seemed all the more charming until I tried to imagine myself arranging my life around it. Yet if Fawn were so certain about *me*, who was I to cavil about her? Had she not spurned Ash Shackleford, scion of a wealthy landowner dynasty, in favour of the adopted son of a down-at-the-heels peasant? I felt ashamed that *I* should be the one having second thoughts.

As if I weren't already torn by these conflicting sentiments, Wren had a habit of aggravating my discomfort by occasional remarks. He certainly intended no harm—he only meant to help—but his situation was so different from mine that he simply couldn't understand my turmoil.

That same evening, as we stood together in the stern, steadying the boat while Marten tied the painter to a dockpost, he reminded me. "You know, Yaro, as far as she knows, you're probably dead."

He could do that: follow my thoughts for several minutes, sometimes hours, without our speaking, then pick the thread right up as if everything in between had been said out loud.

"Yes, I know, but she doesn't know for sure."

"Really? Don't you think CADS has announced to the village of Dryford that Yaro Seekings was picked up and executed?"

"Yeah, probably. But she might know better than to believe it."

"Maybe. But even so, she knows you can't ever come back. Are you sure she's letting her life be held hostage to what might have been? For all you know, she may have found some—"

Quicker than I could think better of, I lunged at him. And quicker still, he grabbed my thrusting arm in a deft defensive maneuver, pulling me off balance. Although he surely didn't intend it, I tripped over the gunnel and toppled into the cold knee-deep water. In an instant, he was in with me, helping me to my feet.

"Shit, Yaro, I'm so sorry . . . an insensitive jerk . . . I just wanted you to . . ."

We were both blubbering: he from the water he'd just swallowed, and me from the emotions I'd swallowed for too long. There were a few passersby on the bank, attracted by the two splashes. They were glad to see that we didn't need any help, and we were glad to be dripping wet, so no one could notice that we were both crying.

*   *   *   *   *   *   *

One rainy morning, the weather was just too nasty for trading. Wren said the weather prophecy was for clearing later in the day, so we decided to hole up in the Troutbridge bannerhouse library until things improved. Wren had some bookkeeping to keep him busy, and of course, Marten had a backlog of trade data to compile from his countless notebooks. I hadn't had a chance to keep up with the news of the past fortnight, so I grabbed a handful of old newssheets from the recycling pile and scanned them hastily. One article of great interest to me concerned a recent discovery in the storage tunnels of the Archives, up on Covenant Ridge. According to the article, workers were moving some chests of old books around when someone noticed a place in the wall where a fissure had been sealed over by a mixture of small stones and ash slurry. For some reason, no one had ever noticed the difference in the texture of the material, although it may have been centuries old. It was in the original tunnel, only yards from the now-blocked-up portal. When they chipped away the grouting, they found a little cache of books—eight, I believe the article said—written in Old Mok. Actually, the "books" were more like loose bundles of handwritten pages tied together with some kind of material no one knows about today. Amazingly, the papers were not wholly disintegrated due perhaps to the airtight cavity, the alkalinity of the mortar, or whatever. Restorers had already begun the painstaking work of peeling away the brittle sheets and transferring them onto a more stable backing.

I was so intrigued by all this that I rummaged through the stack of newssheets until I found a later follow-up article. It reported that linguists and scriptologists had been examining each page as it was restored and deciphering the often-blurry handwriting, which only vaguely resembled modern standardized Mok script. They had only begun the work, but they had already determined that they were dealing with diaries, all written by one individual. The name and gender of the diarist were unknown, except for the initials J. L. What made these diaries so extremely rare and important was that they were clearly the firsthand eyewitness accounts of someone who actually lived during a pivotal phase of the Calamities. I watched future editions for further developments, but if there were more, I missed them.

Whenever I was alone on Bumblebee, I asked nearly everyone I met whether there was a stead called Ravenswing in the neighbourhood. On *Come-What-May*, it was a bit awkward since I didn't like to inquire when the guys were within hearing, knowing how much they liked to read into everything. But no one seemed to know the place, and I really began to wonder if I had misunderstood something.

Chapter 45

There were increasing signs of winter's approach. We saw many wedges of geese fly overhead, even the habitually late snow geese. Our hot breath hung in the frosty air, and it became ever harder to sleep aboard *Come-What-May* despite several warm quilts. Every night, a thin skin of needle ice formed around the dock-pilings; and every morning, it took longer for the rising sun to melt it away. But we stuck to it as long as we could, for the same reason that we had started so early in the spring. Not only was it a matter of pride to be first on the water and last off, but those opening and closing weeks were prime trading periods. With months of virtually trade-free winter ahead, supply stewards everywhere would be thinking about last-minute stocking up; and as the fairs were now closing for the season, prices would rise for those who remained.

Nevertheless, we awoke one morning to find flurries swirling around us, and we decided over breakfast to call it quits and head for Longlogan. Our least perishable cargo was stowed in various depots where it could be retrieved next spring by us or our sister boats. *Come-What-May* was winched up the ways into its Pierstead boat shed where it would be refurbished for the next season. Marten and I took what we could carry of our pay goods and headed home to Alga.

Arriving back at Stonesthrow, we were welcomed like returning heroes. Marten in particular was a changed person, swollen with new muscles and newfound confidence. As for me, I felt like a contributing member of the household, not merely a dependent sojourner. In addition to the wealth that Marten and I brought back to Stonesthrow in the form of goods, coins, IOUs, and other credits, we also had some useful ideas for the stead's enterprises. For example, we brought back a scrub brush to show Alaria how the holes were drilled and the back plate mounted in such a way that the bristles were slower to wear off. And we showed Corolla a style of raincoat made in Morningside, which had fringe sewn into the chest and shoulder seams. This caused much of the rain to drip off before reaching the hem and soaking one's pants' knees. Canny buyers would prefer those over ours. When the Sundew Canal was completed, we were right there to get some terrific deals in slightly used hand drills, which Stonesthrow resold to the Alga granite quarries.

The island's shallow soils were not conducive to raising sugar beets, so the ten gallons of beet molasses we brought back were a welcome alternative to honey. Several new cedar buckets, a bolt of stout hemp cloth, some oil paints and charcoal pencils for Teal, a fine maple rocking chair for Discern, spare tire rinds for the Purple Martin, several demijohns of sunflower soap, a wooden clock for the laundry. And so on and so forth.

It took us a whole day (two trips on the ferry) just to get all our pay hauled back and stowed in the waresroom at Stonesthrow. And much more stuff we didn't expect to ever use ourselves—we carted it down to the bannerhouse waresrooms to pay our taxes. It was quite unlikely that either of us could have contributed so much prosperity by working at home. Moreover, Marten profited from his data-collection work, and we both had enjoyed a summer like none before or since.

* * * * * * *

Soon after returning to Alga, I enjoyed my first Esperian harvest feast. Several steadmates were invited to share the holiday at various friends' homes, but their places were much more than filled by our own guests. That was largely due to Hewn and Ermine's enormous prestige, but of course it reflected well on the whole household, and we were honoured to have our tables so crowded.

I could hardly imagine anyone having more cause for thanksgiving than I, yet I still had some major unfulfilled needs. I hadn't yet found a permanent homestead, although I seemed to have narrowed the search considerably. I felt pretty certain that the place I wanted to put down roots was somewhere in the Laughingwater Valley. Also I still had a compelling need for a purpose: some clearer idea of what part I might play in all this Larger House thing. I wasn't very far along with that, but on the other hand, I had met a very special friend who shared that compulsion and with whom I could exchange ideas—that is, if I ever met her again. And of course, there was the loneliness thing—ah well, that might just never be resolved.

For all that, I was delighted to be back with my friends on Alga and to throw myself into my studies with renewed zeal. My Mok was now good enough that I attended school each morning at the bannerhouse. Although I had made fair progress in math and science during the summer under Marten's tutelage, I still found myself with students who were two or three years my junior.

That fall, some important changes were made at Stonesthrow. Fulmar had just been married to Maize, a much younger woman from Chagrin Lake. They were to move into Discern's room, which was a couple's room. Discern had been alone in it these many years since his wife had died, as no one had the heart to suggest he move out, but it was he who now insisted on turning it over to the newlyweds as his "wedding gift" to them. That meant moving him into the men's dormitory with Marten, Burnet, and myself. Actually, it was a wise move for everyone as Discern's health was declining noticeably, and he often needed attention in the middle of the night. Although it was usually I who had to tend to Discern's needs, I didn't mind it in the least. He was such a likeable old guy, and we hit it off so well, I could hardly resent sharing the reduced space (and I trust *he* didn't resent it; after all, it was his home since long before I was born!). Anyway, we didn't expect the arrangement to last that long, either for me or for him.

Although the nation's "capital" was soon to move to Welcome Fair for the year (which is to say, the Council of Vision Keepers and the VFC would be meeting there), the consulates continued in their permanent location at Goosegrass; and so Hewn had now to travel to Welcome for most of his business, whereas the ambassadors at Goosegrass had to make special trips to Alga to consult with *him*. This they willingly did, and he bore with them patiently; well, patiently for him, anyway.

Alaria had to delegate more of the work in the brush factory to us youngers, not only because her arthritis was bothering her more, but because she wanted to use what dexterity she did have for sewing baby clothes (Fulmar and Maize's wedding was not a wholly spontaneous idea).

I continued to work at the stone yard or wherever else I could be useful. And on my own, I spent lots of time reading history. My steadmates all seemed to find this arrangement totally acceptable, although I couldn't quite explain to anyone, not even Hewn, why this research was more important to me than eating or sleeping.

Without thinking much about why at first, my studies of the past focused on two historic eras. One was the time, thousands of years ago, when humans first developed agriculture and settled in towns and cities and invented writing and metalworking and all that goes with those. The other period of critical interest to me was the Calamities and the century or two leading up to them when an entire global civilization slipped into a dark age, in effect annihilating its own culture and much of the memory of what led up to it.

An obstacle to studying either period was the dearth of surviving records. The first period was many thousands of years ago, and there are few, if any, surviving written records. After all, the invention of writing is one of the hallmarks of that era. Modern knowledge of that time and those people is largely derived from indirect evidence: pot-shards, stone tools, burial sites, and such. As for the Calamitous Times, that was mere centuries ago, and those were a highly literate and record-leaving people. That is, they left us detailed knowledge of the centuries leading up to their own. But during that dark tumultuous time when everyone was struggling for bare survival, there was little opportunity for observing, reflecting, and recording the events of daily life. Much of what was written did not survive the turmoil and destruction of the age. Were it not for the Archives and the Keepers of the Lore, how much more would have been lost forever? Occasionally the literature would contain some obscure reference to this or that book which was in the Archives, but which had never been published and was thus inaccessible to the general public. Although there was a serious effort to get such single-copy works into circulation, there was just too much of it, and more works were always coming to light. A board of scholars worked to prioritize new discoveries, and Orris, our vision-keeper, happened to be on that board, which is how I knew about it. He often directed me to new releases at the library which he knew I might find interesting.

I thought it strange indeed that I could find more information about the builders of ancient pyramids than about the comparatively recent founding period of our own culture. I also thought it strange that the people we commonly referred to as the Ancients (with a capital *A*) often described their own era as the information age, yet they left such a scanty and superficial account of themselves. (Of course, it doesn't help that so many of their records are in a form that we cannot access today.)

As I studied about these two periods, I began to understand their common appeal to me. Both periods were times of profound upheaval. In both cases, the technologies that were gained or lost were no less significant than the groups of ideas which accompanied them. From what Orris and others had taught me, the first revolution (sometimes called Neolithic) was accompanied by a change in the primordial mythic vision of those cultures. That vision-shift had led them to live unsustainable lives, or was it the other way around? Was their mythic vision merely the result of an unsustainable lifeway?

In the more recent case—the Calamities—we know that a small radical minority among the Ancients had perceived that their life was unsustainable, that is to say—doomed. They had embarked upon a new life, a life containing the seeds of hope; and in the process they had seen a new mythic vision, or as some put it, they began to tell a different story.

Or was it, again, the other way around? This much we think we know: this latter revolution, this return to a sustainable vision, was a deliberate and self-conscious act. Many, at least, of the people involved knew exactly what they were doing, at the active level, and apparently, even at the abstract level. Which is to say that unlike most of the people around them, they were explicitly aware of the mythic vision they were rejecting and where they wanted their own mythic vision to take them. In that, they were probably unlike the cultures of the past vision-shift, the Neolithic, who may have been simply following the path offered by their new circumstances, not realizing whither it was taking them nor whither they wanted to go. I wasn't sure how important that last aspect might be. However I was becoming more mindful of something Orris had said—the oak and the acorn thing: whether the vision begets the reality, or vice versa, might be irrelevant except when you wish to have some impact on them both. I couldn't say what that might mean, but I sensed that it mattered.

I also realized that the two revolutions, or vision-shifts, were different in another crucial way: the first revolution was accompanied by, if not caused by, technological innovations and population changes which enabled the new vision-holders to dominate or annihilate the more sustainable peoples around them. Enabled? No, it *forced* them to, because that's what unsustainability is all about. By contrast, the sustainable, or Steward, societies which developed after the Calamitous Times evolved into viable, even powerful, cultures which had the technology, the political cohesion, the wealth, and the population density to defend their cultures and their territories. In fact, it now occurred to me that any society, no matter how benignly it occupies its territory, is not truly sustainable unless it can hold its own against all comers.

There was an obvious problem with using historical models for such an objective: previous shifts in mythic vision appeared to have always risen from within, in response to a crisis. I could find no example in history of one culture converting another culture to its own mythic vision, except by overwhelming and absorbing them. I most certainly couldn't imagine an arrogant hubristic civilization like Anagaia recognizing that its own worldview was not serving it well. But while I did not, for a moment, imagine that I or any other individual had any power to bring about such a profound change, there could be no harm in at least trying to understand that better.

With this general picture in mind, I now focused on the details of the Calamities themselves. As I read about them, I took voluminous notes, then periodically I'd try to organize those notes into an overview. That was about as close as I could get to the definable cause I was seeking. It wasn't enough, but I hoped it was a first step. I frequently summed up the results of several days' research in my diary. I guess it's easier if I just give some excerpts from those diaries, which best demonstrate where my understanding was at the time. The entry dates don't matter, and I've skipped from one section to another for the sake of clarity and conciseness.

> Busy week, rolling snow and helping Corolla. No time for drawing. I spent most of my little spare time reading a new anthology of histories recommended by Orris. It consists of works by several prominent historians, describing what happened just prior to and during the Calamities. One problem for me, the reader, is that all of those writers are relying on older sources, at least twice removed from the events themselves. The original sources are by no means in agreement with each other, and in turn, the contributing authors have widely differing interpretations of the recorded facts . . . . The first thing I've discovered was that the specific cause or causes of the Calamities are in dispute . . . . One theory (Burl of Linstead) is that foreign terrorists or desperate fanatics from oppressed colonies made security such an unsupportable burden that the whole global economy collapsed, or that the reaction to terrorist threats, real or perceived, created a police state where vast segments of the population became enemies of the establishment. Calyx of Madderfield refutes that whole idea, questioning whether any amount of lawless activity could topple an otherwise-stable society. She rather points to the appearance of bizarre plagues which decimated the population, not only new plagues, but old ones which were considered vanquished. Those plagues, according to Madderfield, were serious enough in the beginning, but when a disproportionate number of the victims were healthcare specialists, emergency and security personnel, the whole fabric of civilization was rent by panic. A climate of despair and cynicism fomented an ever wider crisis as masses of refugees were turned away or massacred, disease-ridden corpses lay unburied,

unchecked vermin carried deadly pathogens from community to community, and food and water supplies became tainted. Decades of misguided medical and nutritional policy had produced a population with little immunity to disease, while creating pathogens with ever-greater resistance to medicines. Most of the world's peoples couldn't afford those medicines anyway, and so disease ran rampant, overwhelming the medical establishment's capacity to protect anyone.

Another writer (Reed of Oakknoll), who largely agrees with Madderfield, points out that aside from human maladies, both crops and livestock were inundated with one plague after another. Field after field of genetically uniform crop plants, propped up by humusless and chemical-laden soil, offered little resistance to diseases or pests, especially once their protective chemicals were withdrawn or became obsolete. With little capacity to outevolve their enemies, whole crops succumbed, along with the human communities they nourished.

Closely paralleling Linstead's theory about international terrorists is Anagaian historian Brant Wilderson, who focuses on a particular cluster of events which are popularly cited, at least in Anagaia, as causing the collapse of the Ancient World. According to this hypothesis, dissidents within the society itself perpetuated a building wave of sabotage. These appear to have been a combination of organized groups and disgruntled individuals mostly acting on their own. It may be inaccurate to brand them all as "terrorists," since many of the perpetrators were apparently not intending to attack society itself, but rather specific sources of environmental damage or social injustice. However, Wilderson insists that all of these saboteurs were integrated into a larger conspiracy, an assertion which most Esperian authors question. Wilderson bases his reasoning on at least one wave of nearly simultaneous attacks, which included targets as diverse as aluminum smelters, government offices, coal-fired electric generators, livestock facilities, and sports arenas. While Wilderson claims that the timing is too close to be coincidental, others suggest that the varied nature of the targets indicates different groups with different agendas. Whatever the case may be, these had a profound impact, especially sabotage of the power and transport infrastructure—electric lines and railroads. (It is hard for us living today to even conceive how much of people's food and energy came from hundreds, or even thousands of miles away). These latter were most vulnerable because they traversed vast areas, thinly populated and impossible to guard. By themselves, most of those attacks would have been no more than a major nuisance but orchestrated (as some claim) to occur simultaneously, the effect snowballed, bringing the entire system to its knees.

It looks to me like none of the Esperian authors refute any of Wilderson's facts, but all of them seem to challenge his insistence that these events were the root cause of the Calamities. The last author in the series, Mortise Fenman (a Borealian and thus not a Steward) claims that all the other crises, serious enough by themselves, were aggravated and in some cases instigated by changes in the global climate itself. This is a pretty bold stand for a Borealian to take, since many non-Stewards still refuse to admit that the very skies could be threatened by human activity. Nevertheless, Fenman acknowledges that elevated levels of CO_2 released from fossil fuel, combined with deforestation, set the stage for a chain of epic disasters: ozone depletion, shifting ocean currents, rising sea levels, droughts, floods, storms, fires, and freakish weather of all kinds. While most non-Steward historians are quick to blame the early Stewards for causing the chaos which drew the curtain on what they wistfully referred to as the Golden Age, Fenman rather describes the Ancient World as a sickly old man, tottering on the edge of a cliff, and those wild-eyed saboteurs, whatever their intent, did little more than shove him over, sooner rather than later.

Well, this is all terribly interesting to me, but frankly it's still not addressing some of my underlying questions. I'll keep reading tomorrow, but for now, I'm going to bed.

Chapter 46

On a blustery late afternoon in the early new year, Hewn came home from a trip to Welcome (that being the government seat that year) where he had been called in for urgent consultation with the Foreign Affairs Committee. He was visibly perturbed about something, and without bothering to sup, he invited me to take a walk with him. I myself had just returned from a stint on the snow roller, and frankly, I was tired and hungry; but Hewn seemed set on it, and besides, I knew Ermine didn't like for him to be walking alone in such cold weather. It was less than an hour after sunset, but the gibbous moon was bright and the footing firm on the new-packed roads. We didn't walk all that far anyway; when we reached the landing, he plunked himself down on the bench by the wharf and motioned me to do likewise. I sensed it was not merely exercise he sought but conversation, and with me in particular.

"It's been a trying day at the Committee meetings. I need to hear some of your stories, Yaro, they often give me ideas."

I couldn't imagine what ideas he'd gotten from my stories so far, so I asked, "Something in particular you wish to hear about?"

"Yes, indeed. Back at that orphanage—before you were adopted—a little village in the Flint Hills, if I remember."

"Yes. Cleftridge."

"What sort of a place, that Cleftridge?"

"Well, a rather nice place, at least by Anagaian standards. Relatively cool, lightly wooded, overlooks the Upper Possum Valley to the west, the Umberlands Valley to the northeast. Nearest town of size is Sycamore, three miles away at the foot of the hills on the river plain. Its economy is based on textiles and pilgrims."

"Pilgrims?"

"Just outside of town, there's a spring—it's supposed to be the source of the Possum River. They say it's artesian: the rain water seeps down through the chert and flint formations and wells up at the spring. They also say the flint is crypto-crystalline. That means it's made up of zillions of quartz crystals so tiny no one can see them. Well, the water percolating through all those crystals is supposed to pick up some kind of magical properties. There are a lot of stories about miracles and such coming from the spring. There's a shrine built around it, and folks come from all over to get healed or improve their sex life or whatever. It's a big money-catcher for the town, even more than the cotton spinneries. Actually, I only went there a couple times even though it's not far from Cleftridge."

"And the people?"

"At Sycamore, mostly factory workers or shopkeepers."

"And at Cleftridge?"

"Some of the same, but a lot of gentry and retired military, planters, and merchants. They tend to settle there because of the more congenial climate."

"And what about relations? How did you, the orphanage folks, get along with these villagers?"

I just knew Hewn was going somewhere in particular with this; his questions were never as casual or as random as they seemed. I couldn't imagine where he was headed this time, but I knew he'd tell me when he thought right. Meanwhile, I'd just give him anything I thought might interest him.

"Mostly we got along fine. Stewards in that area had a special reputation. You see, when I was real little, a fire broke out in one of the spinneries over at Sycamore. When the subscription firefighters arrived, the mill owners told them to turn their water on the ground floor where the valuable machinery was. But several workers, mostly women, were trapped on the second floor where bales of stored cotton were smoldering and filling the place with dense smoke. A few Stewards showed up from somewhere and bursting through the ring of onlookers, they entered the burning building. For several minutes, they lowered the helpless women out the windows until everyone was rescued. One of the Stewards later died from smoking inhalation. You can be sure folks didn't forget about that soon."

"And so no one gave you any difficulties at the orphanage?"

"Ah well, I wouldn't go so far as to say that. There were some racists and ne'er-do-wells who would harass the staff from time to time, or pick on us kids because we were illegitimate. On the other hand, there were some locals who actually helped support the orphanage. I mean, we didn't get much help from the community—let's face it, people couldn't give what they didn't have. Still, there were some folks, like old Mr. Canes, who gave us the property. It had been his cloth warehouse, but he was retired, so he and his wife lived in a tiny house at the back of the lot. Then there was this guy, a local fuel dealer, who used to send his driver around every New Year's Day with a cord of pine limbs for the stove. They say the deliveries began sometime before I was born, the year a new girl was left on the back porch. I remember when she was seventeen, she ran off and married a young farmer from Priesthill. There was no firewood delivery that year or ever after. Some folks were just like that, for better or worse.

"But then there was another fellow, Lord Pitcannon, an estate owner from somewhere the other side of Sycamore. He was a really decent sort, a bachelor. I think his older brother had died, leaving him the estate and the care of his nephew Jade, who was about my age. Lord Pitcannon was a very progressive type, eager not only to improve the yields of his lands, but also the well-being of his workers—not very typical, as you know. Anyway, he was also a major supporter of the orphanage. But he was not content to merely give and forget. He dropped by occasionally to see what we needed and to bring special treats for us kids—one time he brought a whole bushel of ripe persimmons! He used to talk a lot with Veerio, the elderly woman who ran the orphanage at that time. She used to give him lots of ideas for improving his estate. Once, on her recommendation, he planted several acres of ridgeslope to pecans with scuppernongs in the undershade! Jade became a good friend of ours. Needless to say, we kids were always delighted when Lord Pitcannon visited."

I paused in my narrative to consider whether I was answering Hewn's original question.

"Look here," I suggested. "I've got a story in mind that will give you some idea of how different people related to us. That is, if you care to hear it."

"I care very much, if you'll indulge an old man's curiosity. Let's just set this bench around the corner here, into the moonlight and out of the wind. Get comfortable and don't leave out any details."

And so we did, and so I began.

The orphanage family was gathered for supper one early spring evening when Veerio announced, "Tomorrow, we're going for a picnic hike in the chalk bluffs behind town. It's a good time of year for studying the ferns."

There was an immediate chorus of delighted cheers. Although it was all in all a rather tame expedition, it was rare that the staff ventured to take the entire group anywhere—our reception by some in the community was unpredictable. One of the children asked, "Will we all get to go?"

"Actually," Bracken clarified, "Yaro and Boon and Kit will be unable to go."

I felt a keen pang of disappointment, and Boon's face began to tense in resentment while his deaf brother merely reacted to our own expressions.

"Is it because we haven't finished hoeing the favas?" I asked.

"The favas will have to be hoed and mulched before it turns hot. But everyone will turn to and help you finish it after supper because you boys are going on an outing of your own."

"But we can't go anywhere by ourselves," I objected.

Veerio answered by taking a letter from her apron.

"Lord Pitcannon's servant dropped this off today." And she read, "'Dear Y, B, and K, Uncle is taking me to the carnival at Sycamore tomorrow. He says I may take a few friends. Can Faring bring you? Meet us at the statues on the mall around eight.'

The botanical expedition into the hills was a clever ploy to keep the others from resenting our good fortune. The garden work was quickly accomplished by many hands, and we were all early to bed in eager anticipation. Morning brought us a hasty breakfast as we all set off on our separate adventures.

It was a rare spring day, the sort of day which is even rarer out on the torrid river plain. The roadside was bedecked with spring wildflowers, and the air full of song made by the many birds which are unique to the Flint Hills. The three-mile walk was a bit much for Kit, and Faring carried him part way on his shoulders.

We arrived to find our hosts waiting on the crowded mall. Jade and his uncle were fine-clad for the festivities, and we were dressed as well as we might be. Although I sensed that Faring was inwardly repulsed by the religious excesses of the festival, I think he was also curious to understand it all better. The orphanage-keepers never talked much about their religion or ours; I think they assumed we would grow up to share in the beliefs of our own people, and they didn't wish to put difficulties in our way. While the shrine was thronged with pilgrims and cure-seekers, the streets around the central mall were filled with stalls and booths which catered to them. At this table, one could buy prisms to keep your energies aligned. At the next were holy statues and god-eyes and vials of holy water from the spring, fresh-blessed by the resident hermit. Read your signs, check your lines, get on the inside track to glory—all right there for anyone who had the wherewithal. Scattered through the multitude were jugglers, mimes, stilt-walkers, and strolling musicians. Vendors of food and drink vied loudly for the attention of passersby. And ever on the fringes of the crowd hovered the pickpockets and prostitutes. For the townsfolk of Sycamore, this was payday.

On a side street, we passed a goatherd who led a string of full-bagged nannies, which he milked into an enamel cup on demand, for a copper. On a busy corner, a bear-leader was putting his beast through its paces to the delight of a knot of children. Lord Pitcannon couldn't help but notice that Faring was disgusted at the sight, and he asked him about it.

"I'm puzzled at your reaction, my friend. I realize you don't approve of killing animals, but . . ."

"In fact, I don't object to killing animals when it's necessary. It's just that this is so wanton, so cruel."

"Cruel, you say. Why, most people here will kill a bear when they get a chance. I'd say this fellow was lucky—he has an enviable life."

"If it's lucky to be castrated and have your teeth and claws pulled out. I shouldn't envy that."

"Well, I suppose, but consider, Faring. These brutes are the scourge of the land."

"Yes, of course," replied Faring with sudden and uncharacteristic docility.

"Oh-ho, no, you don't! What's with this 'yes, of course' nonsense? I can see you have more on your mind than that."

Faring chuckled in embarrassment. "Well, it's just that we are your guests after all, and . . . I don't mean to always be so disagreeable."

"Now see here, Veerio is always disagreeing with me, and there's no one else on earth with whom I'd rather talk. If I want to hear my own opinions, I'll talk to myself. Now spill it. Can you deny that these brutes kill sheep and goats, which are the wealth of our nation? "

"All right, if you insist. No, it is the sheep and goats which are the scourge of the land. The predators are important to keep the herbivores in balance. Your real wealth is the crops and fuel which that land would produce if the livestock weren't there."

"But those are marginal lands, unsuited for cultivation."

"Not all food crops require cultivation or rich soil. Look at your own plantings of pecans. Aren't they more profitable than the wool or milk from that area would be? No society will ever reach its full potential while its adults suckle at the teats of dumb beasts."

They both seemed to be enjoying their controversy, but we kids had other muffins to bake, so to speak, so we pulled them apart and continued our tour of the festivities. There were games to try and shows to watch—Pitcannon insisted on paying for everything. As morning wore into midday, we became increasingly interested in the food concessions. There were smoked sausages and cheeses, sandwiches with ham or beef—all special delicacies for the poorer classes who could rarely afford them. But Lord Pitcannon knew our habits, and he looked about until he found a booth with sweetpotatoes sizzling in fat on a hot iron plate. The woman had already served the other boys, and I was greedily reaching for one when I heard Faring say, "Actually, I'm not hungry quite yet." I withdrew my hand as if the proffered sweetpotato were a scorpion. Faring tried to encourage me. "Now, Yaro, you know you're famished."

"Uh-huh, not hungry yet."

I had no idea why Faring wouldn't eat them, but I didn't need to know. It was enough that he considered them unfit. This created a dilemma for our host. He was astute enough to see that he wasn't going to get me fed unless he found something that satisfied Faring. He looked around for a few moments and found a nearby stall selling boiled salted peanuts in their shells. He offered some of these to Faring, who eagerly accepted them, and I quickly followed suit. I think Lord Pitcannon was amused to see that the best customers at that booth were the two who were "not hungry."

We spent the long afternoon hours taking in more of the carnival's attractions. On one street, our passage was blocked by a crowd watching a puppet show. The skit included a subtle satire about a recent scandal among the leadership of the MOTHS sect. Of course, it had to be very subtle, since MOTHS is the state religion, and to criticize it publicly is to attack the state. Nevertheless, everyone got the point, and many snickered at the ribald lampoon. We watched it for a while, and as we jockeyed for a better view, we got separated a bit in the mob. I was standing near Faring when a stranger approached him and murmured something in his ear. I was a couple paces away, but I was sure he said something like, "Excuse me, my man, but have you seen my brother's jacket around here?"

Faring just stared at him in utter bewilderment and finally said, "Why now, I haven't . . . I mean, I don't believe I even know your brother . . ."

"Quite so, pardon me, would you." And the man moved quickly away. Faring just shook his head as if saying to himself, "Is he quite all right?" I was wondering the same thing a few moments later when another man, a tall brawny fellow wearing a butcher's apron, *furtively nudged Faring and asked him the* exact same words. *I've never seen Faring look so confused.*

"Er . . . perhaps if I only knew what you mean by . . ."

"Oh, I'm sorry, my mistake, excuse me . . ." And he would've vanished into the crowd as quickly as the other man were he not so tall. We caught a glimpse of him looking back our way, as if to be sure he weren't followed, before turning down a narrow side street.

Faring and I just looked at each other, wondering what to make of it all. The two men were very different in every way, except for the curious words. Well, not quite. I had noticed that each of them had a bit of scarlet thread tied about his left wrist as if to hold some trinket that wasn't there.

Some minutes later, we had almost forgotten the strangers when Lord Pitcannon and Jade moved back around to our side of the crowd. I alone was aware of a slight young man—a clerical student, perhaps—standing close by Faring's elbow. He seemed about to speak when Lord Pitcannon joined us and began chatting. The nervous-looking stranger withdrew quickly into the audience, but not before I noticed a scarlet string on his left arm. I didn't know whether Faring noticed that, but as soon as he could discreetly do so, he whispered into my ear, "Let's keep this curious business to ourselves, don't you think?"

"So you had no idea what it was all about?" Hewn asked me through his tight-wrapped scarf.

"At the time, I was baffled. I've since figured out, as I'm sure Faring did, that those guys were connected with the Amanita, and the 'brother's jacket' thing was some sort of password. But what I never understood was why they tried to contact Faring when he was obviously an outsider, a foreigner."

Hewn made no comment, though I sensed that he might have enlightened me a bit had he cared to.

"But yes, I can see what you mean about the relations with locals: it's more nuanced than I had imagined."

"But there's more. I can tell you the rest, if you're not getting too cold."

"I'll manage. Please continue."

"Well, as the afternoon wore late, we followed the general flow of traffic back toward the central mall where the pageant was to take place. I suppose you've seen that before."

"Most surely, several times. In New Chalice, it's quite a grand spectacle."

"Then I'll skip the details about that part, although I think Faring was rather fascinated by it. Anyway, as you know, there's this great climax where good triumphs over evil. At that point, things started breaking up as people headed home or for the nearest tavern. We took leave of our hosts and started for Cleftridge."

Chapter 47

We figured we'd had enough excitement for the day, but then, well, Faring was sure he knew a shortcut out of town that would avoid the big crowds, so we went down a side street and then up another. Then he said it didn't look quite right, so we backtracked, but apparently missed the turn. Well, the upshot of it is that we were soon quite lost in a city none of us knew, and with dark approaching.

At one corner, Faring told us to wait while he stepped into a shop to ask directions. While he was gone, a pair of drunks came staggering out of a tavern across the way and plunked down on a bench near us. They ignored us, but it was hard for us to ignore their brewful dithering.

"Yessir, I tell you, it's no fault of our'n," one was saying. "He says we're unreliable, but he just don't want to admit it. The mortuary business is flat, and that's why he's let us go."

"God's truth, that's so," the second man hastened to concur. "He don't need me to dig the hole, nor you to make the coffin, if there ain't any bodies to be buried. Folks just ain't dying like they'd ought."

"Worse than that," grumbled the first. "Even when there's corpses enough to go around, there ain't enough lumber."

"Oh? Say, why is that, Newt?"

"It's because it's all imported. You need fine wood, like rum cherry and butternut to make a proper box as is going to hold your bones 'til judgment. They only have that quality of wood up in Esperia."

"So what's the problem with that?"

"Well, they won't sell us enough of it, the bastards. They say they're sending all they can, that they're not going to cut all their forests like we did."

"They say that? Why, the nervy snots! They care more about their damned trees than about people's jobs."

They were both oblivious to us, but I didn't care much for the trend of their conversation, especially when I saw Faring coming out of the shop beyond them.

"Yep, it gripes me fierce, Honer. And then they send them missionaries—godless perverts, every one of them—coming down here to mock us. Why, if I got my hands on one of them, what I wouldn't do."

"What would you do, Newt?" badgered the one called Honer. He wore a cynical grin, and I could see he had spotted Faring coming toward us.

"Why, I'd make him swallow a few teeth, and then—"

"Hey, Newt, lookee here what's coming!"

"Huh? Oh him, well, I just—"

"What do you mean, Newt. This is your chance."

I tried frantically to make some kind of signs to Faring, but he was jotting down the directions he'd just got. As he came in line with the bench, the one called Honer shot out a foot and sent him sprawling. As Faring got up, flustered, the man called Newt said, "Hey, what's the idea of kicking my friend like that? You half-niggers got less breeding than a full darkie."

"I'm quite sorry . . . I meant no harm, but your foot—"

"You saying his foot meant to get hisself kicked. Don't contradict me, you squint-eyed bastard. I've had enough of your kind!"

By now, both drunks were on their feet, and Newt took a wild swing at Faring's face. Of course, Faring was trained in defensive arts, like all missionaries, but before he could fend off a second blow, Honer had sneaked around behind and pinned his arms. We kids were terrified at all this, and Boon and Kit rushed off to find help. I couldn't bring myself to leave Faring, although I was of no use to him. By now, Newt had worked up enough anger to pummel the restrained Faring with his fists. Faring later insisted that Newt wasn't doing much damage; his drunken punches were often wild, and his heart wasn't really in it. Although it appeared to me that Faring was quite helpless, he was merely exercising great self-restraint, choosing to sustain a few cuts and bruises in hopes the bullies would be satisfied with humiliating him. No doubt that's what would have happened if I had not interfered. I ran up to Newt and grabbed his leg to pull him back. Angrily, he cuffed me away with his left hand, which apparently had a ring on it. It left a scratch across my cheek, which was really superficial; but when Faring saw the streak of blood, I could see his self-control snap like a linen thread in a candle flame. A pair of bony elbows thrust like pistons into Honer's kidneys, and as the latter momentarily loosed his hold, Faring reached back and yanked him across his hip and into some shrubbery. Then as Newt tried to grab him from behind, Faring managed to flip his assailant over his right shoulder and slam him down on the cobblestone pavement. I hadn't noticed a crowd beginning to collect in the dim street. The stunned coffin-maker tried to stagger to his feet, but with a shriek of pain, he collapsed again. Instantly, Faring's anger turned to concern.

"Oh, what have I done now? A real street ruffian I've become! Hey, are you okay?"

As he reached to feel the man's back, a new groan escaped the former tormentor's lips.

"Oh dear, it seems I've cracked his shoulder blade. I need to get this man home."

Then, appealing to the bystanders, he asked, *"Does anyone know where he lives?"*

"Lives?" scoffed one of them. *"Why, he doesn't live anywhere. That's Newt Hobbling, the good-for-nothing. He just sleeps on the street. He'll be fine right where he is."*

"But he can't stay here, he's injured. He could be crippled without proper care. Where's his friend?"

"Honer Smart? That coward is no man's friend. He lit out as soon as things looked to be going the wrong way."

"Don't trouble yourself, Steward," another advised. *"Newt Hobbling's a bigot—hates your people. He got what's coming to him."*

"But I can't leave him here. The man's hurt. It's my responsibility."

"Uh-oh, he may have even bigger problems now," someone remarked. Farther down the street, we could see Boon and Kit returning with a CADS officer. *"Old Newt has had law troubles before that don't bear looking into. You might want to make yourself scarce too, Steward. Disturbing the peace and all . . ."*

But it was too late, the officer was pushing his way through the gathering gawkers.

"Just what's going on here? Fighting, eh?"

Faring tried to explain. *"I'm afraid this fellow is injured. He needs medical care."*

"And who did it? You, from the looks of those shiners."

"Yes," admitted Faring. *"I was defending myself, and I guess I got carried away."*

"Well, I'll have to take you in too. We don't care much for foreigners stirring up trouble—"

"He's lying!" interrupted one of the onlookers, the one who had urged him to get away. *"It was me that beat this guy up."*

"Oh, really," said the officer suspiciously. *"Then I suppose I'll just have to arrest the three of you, won't I?"*

"It was me!" insisted yet another voice from the edge of the crowd. *"These guys don't know nothing about it."*

The officer was nobody's fool, but I could see he didn't like being toyed with. The tension was thick enough to slice when another voice piped shrilly from the back, and an elderly woman with a cane hacked her way to the front.

"I did it and I'll do it again! How dare he make indecent suggestions to me, the bum!"

The crowd broke into guffaws, and the officer couldn't suppress a grin.

"All right, I can see what's going on here. You all can go about your business, and I'll take this character down to sleep it off behind bars."

"No!" objected Faring as Newt blinked in confusion. *"I mean, it's nothing really. I get nosebleeds easily. I'll take care of him."*

"You'll take care of him?" chuckled the officer skeptically. "Yeah, I'll bet you'll take care of him real good. Well, what do I care? I'm about to go off duty. One less bother for me."

As soon as he was gone, Faring looked around at the crowd. "Thank you very much for that. But now I've got to get this man back to the orphanage. Will someone help me out here?"

Reluctantly, one of the crowd stepped forward. "What have you got in mind, Steward?"

"Well, we could improvise a litter. Boon and Yaro together could take one corner, and I another. That leaves two corners. I really do need some help."

"Hey, you, Garish, give us a hand here. We're going to the orphanage."

"The orphanage at Cleftridge? That's three goddam miles!"

"Just do what he asks, will you?"

"The hell I will. You think I've got nothing better to do than lug Newt Hobbling around the countryside? It's no business of mine."

"Oh no? And whose business was it when one of them pulled your sister-in-law out of that mill fire? I don't care two farts about Hobbling either, but I say, if this Steward wants a hand, you'll give it to him if I have to break it off first."

"Shit!" snarled the man, pulling off his cloak as his companion, and Faring did likewise. From somewhere, someone produced a couple of poles, not really long enough, but adequate. They managed to fabricate a crude stretcher, and Newt Hobbling was rolled onto it, whining piteously with every move. The rest of the crowd dispersed as we five lugged the unappreciative builder of caskets up the long lurching road to Cleftridge.

"I assume he was grateful in the end, though," asked Hewn.

"If so, he never showed it. We didn't have any too much room or food to spare, but we set up a cot in the corner of the main room. For a week, he just lay there, glaring at us. He tried to get us kids to sneak him some booze. When we wouldn't, he cursed us a lot. After a while, he didn't say much, good or bad—I think he just didn't know what to make of his situation. Then one morning, we came down to find him gone. Faring was worried because he was far from healed. We asked around town, but no one seemed to know what became of him. We never did find out."

Hewn leaned back and took a deep breath of the icy air.

"Well, you've certainly broadened my understanding of how the missions are viewed there. And now, I have some information to share with you. Do you remember reading about that fracas last month, when the Imperial Navy began seizing our ships on the high seas?"

"The *Dauntless* incident? Yes, of course."

"As you know, the Cleftridge orphanage hasn't been heard of in the past year. Well, the embassy in New Chalice has recently received confirmation that that facility was destroyed. It's believed that the staff are dead, but the government won't confirm that yet."

I was stunned at this news, although it was hardly unexpected.

"And what has that to do with the *Dauntless* incident?"

"I'm not sure, maybe nothing. The Onyx Court denies any complicity in the orphanage attack. Anyway, the very latest news—announced just yesterday in the Council—is that *all* Steward missions in Umberlands and Tramont have been shut down and their staffs deported. It is generally assumed to be in retaliation for the sinking of their gunboat. I've got a list here—hold it under my biolume—I want you to tell me if you recognize any of these names."

I scanned the list in frantic hope, but to no avail.

"None of these are familiar . . . So that means . . . ?"

"I'm afraid we must brace for the worst. In fact, we may never learn the truth about what happened at Cleftridge. Their government insists the attack was perpetrated by a local mob. That is why I was curious to hear your comments, in case there is a shred of truth in their claim."

"We had enemies, it's sure, but I only know of one man who hated the orphanage enough to destroy it."

"And who is he?"

"You know him better than I do," I said bitterly. "He lives in the Onyx Palace."

"Well, as I said," Hewn continued, "this was just announced in Council today. Tomorrow it will be in all the newssheets. I wanted to tell you first."

As the cold began to penetrate our quilted coats, we headed back to the steadhouse. After several moments of walking, during which we were each lost in our own thoughts, I stopped and turned toward Hewn.

"There is something that puzzles me about you."

"Yes?"

"Since I've been here, at least a dozen people have asked me if I was connected to the Amanita. But you never asked, you who of all people should want to know."

He smiled enigmatically. "I didn't need to ask. The first moment I saw you, I knew you were not one of them."

"But how could you know? Couldn't I hide it, if I didn't trust you?"

"You would have told me in a way that didn't betray yourself."

"But how?"

"Yaro, a lifelong ambassador acquires a lot of secrets. When he retires, he doesn't retire from those secrets. He either takes them to his grave, or he sends others to their graves. My friend, be grateful for what you don't know."

Chapter 48

1/11/49: overcast, no wind, flurries.

Sci. and geom. this a.m. Started a new grindstone after lunch, till midafternoon then read anthropology books 'til I'm bleary-eyed and achy-headed. Ermine showed me how to massage my temples, but it's little help.

I keep running into confusing ideas. I'm not really sure what I've learned, but I'm writing out some of it for my own benefit—doubt it would make sense to anyone else. Okay, here's what I think I've figured out from today's reading: up until maybe 10,000 years ago, all humans lived in countless societies which differed in practically every possible way. The only trait they all seem to have shared was that they all worked out some way of living on their own bit of real estate without trashing it. That is to say, they were sustainable over time. That is *not* to say they were all nice folks; some of the sustainable societies practiced cannibalism, infanticide, human sacrifice. And they all seemed to be constantly at war with their neighbours—rarely an all-out war, but just a chronic feuding, fending off encroachment on their own territory while occasionally trying to bite off a chunk of their neighbours' territory. They kill one of ours, we kill one of theirs. Life is tenuous and brief. Tons of room for improvement, but their sustainability meant that time was on their side, and given that time, who knows what improvement they might have made?

Somewhere along the way, relatively unsustainable lifeways caught on and even seemed to triumph. That's one point I can't figure out yet: what made them start down an unsustainable path in the first place? And if that path was indeed so patently unsustainable, how were they able to continue on that path for so long? I mean, empires came and went, but overall it took mankind many millennia to reach a crisis as profound as the Calamities. It makes me wonder if there were degrees of unsustainability and if those accumulated and multiplied toward the end. I think this just may be important: if this sustainability thing, and the mythic visions that accompany it, is not a discrete black-and-white phenomenon but rather part of a continuum, might that explain how one group of lifeways, or mythic vision, evolved *incrementally* into another? And if so, might that have implications for how Anagaia could become a gradually more sustainable civilization? I'm not sure I'm suggesting that evolution can proceed without revolution; even in what Hewn has told me about biological evolution, there's this idea that change doesn't always happen at a constant rate, but rather by jerks and jolts.

This idea of incremental change toward greater sustainability has really got ahold of me lately, if only because it may offer hope. It may even offer ideas as to how this change might be encouraged from outside. I've got to ask Orris about this.

I feel like I've been spending a lot of time reading and thinking lately and maybe not enough time helping out. No one complains, but I fear they may get to thinking I'm a Smaller House dweller. To bed now.

I did have several discussions with Orris about this and other things. He didn't really agree or disagree with most things; instead he usually suggested I read this or that and encouraged me to keep thinking about stuff. I sometimes worried lest he think me presumptuous for sticking my nose into things that were so far beyond me. Later, I learned that he told others I had some "important ideas." What ideas? Anyway, sometime later that month, an opportunity arose which changed my life in more ways than I could have imagined. Perhaps I can explain it best by sharing more diary entries.

1/11/49: The first big snowstorm of the season yesterday. It was all they could do to get the roads cleared by sundown. Not that many people made it out to meeting this morning, what with the roads drifting back in. Pity because Orris preached a really interesting sermon.

As we were leaving afterward, he called me aside and asked me if I could do him a favour. There's a conference over at Telling tomorrow, and he needs someone to row him across the channel. It's not far, but he is in no shape to do it alone, and I guess everyone else is tied up. I'm really glad to be doing something for him for a change. Also, I can drop in to see Myrica. In Anagaia, people are celebrating the New Year today.

1/12/49: Blustery but clearer. What an unforeseen day! Here's how it went: I helped M fill all the wood boxes, then we both helped shovel the snow off the little pond we share with Scallion Rill. This makes the ice freeze clearer and sooner so later we can saw it into blocks for storage. At midmorning, I got Orris into the skiff and rowed him across the Thoroughfare. He mentioned that the conference was one where Keepers of the Lore meet with publishers and others to decide which of the hundred-thousands of books in the Archives get first priority for issuing, that is, before their paper disintegrates. Of those, some 200 selected titles are then translated into modern Mok and sent to the publishers, some of whom are right there on Telling Island. Myrica's parents both work there, and her mother's press specializes in ancient documents, so she was there. I had no business of my own at the conference, but I had a couple hours before taking O back, so once I got him comfortably situated at the bannerhouse, I went over to Myrica's factory to check it out. Her mother doubted she'd be there, but she was. She gave me a tour of the place (it isn't all that big) and showed me a specimen of latex rubber from the tropics, which is superior but too rare for general use. But she says there is some kind of dandelion that's almost as good, and they're also experimenting with a synthetic process that starts with milkweed juice. Myrica is really a remarkable person (not to mention very pretty). The guy she picks will be a very lucky one.

At the appointed time, I went back to pick up O. He was sitting on a bench near the door, chatting with a few other conference attenders. He called me over to meet a man whom he introduced as Curlew, one of the Keepers of the Lore. Then O introduced me—I can't believe this!—as a "serious scholar of Calamity studies"! I looked at him to see if he was teasing me; he looked completely serious!

O explained that Curlew is leader of a research team at the Archives, which is working to restore the J. L. papers. Of course I remember all I read about those newly discovered diaries in the news last fall, and I asked enthusiastically how the translating was going. Curlew, who seems to be a pretty aloof and self-possessed type, seemed to warm up slightly at my interest, and I feared he would ask me something about my own "serious studies."

Instead he went on to explain that they were halfway through the first book and finding many unexpected revelations. They still don't know the author's name (it would probably mean nothing if they did), but they now assume it is a female. Various features of the writing style may indicate a feminine hand, but in particular they've noticed a curious mark (sort of an asterisk) which occurs in the lower left corner of about every 28th day. This leads them to suspect a female of childbearing age. This gave me an idea, and I pointed out that according to my reading (I was about to say "research," but I figured O had gotten me in enough trouble already), we have no idea what became of the legendary Juniper after her namesake feast. Curlew, who seemed delighted to have a "colleague" with whom to disagree, said that others have suggested the same; but he dismisses that because by the time Juniper would have reached adulthood, the situation was probably much less precarious than those diaries seem to indicate. I countered that "childbearing age" doesn't necessarily imply "adulthood" as he assumed (if he lived in Anagaia, he might be more aware of that). If the legend is to be taken at face value, Juniper might well have been within a year or two of the onset of menses, if indeed that's what the marks were indicating. Curlew conceded the point rather grudgingly, but he now seems to take me seriously, certainly more so than I deserve. We went on to discuss the known details of that period and how this new discovery might bear on them. Orris pointed out to him—I wish he hadn't—that I am particularly keen on understanding the bigger picture of just *how* and *when* the Calamities were coupled with a shift in the mythic vision. Big mistake: this Curlew chap now has the impression that I'm not only an historian, but a vision scholar as well! Luckily for me, I'll probably never see the guy again.

I'm not sure just how much later it was—maybe a couple weeks—that I got a letter via Orris from Curlew. It had a sort of stuffy formality about it, not at all like scholars I'd met at the Archaeological Society. In fact, he addressed me as "My esteemed colleague"—Orris said he was trying to ingratiate himself, apparently convinced that I was someone he should impress.

My esteemed colleague,

Per our conversation of last 1/12 re. the J. L. diaries, I am pleased to inform you that there will be a gap in the access schedule at 6 a.m. on 1/27. A previously scheduled examiner has been forced to cancel, which would allow you a two-hour slot. Please realize that this is an unusually generous time stretch, given the intense demand for viewing opportunities, and it will be essential that you arrive promptly. Considering the earliness of the hour, you will of course want to arrive the day before, and we shall be honoured to accommodate you in the guest quarters. Please confirm by signal ASAP.

Looking forward,
Curlew of Archives, via Fortyfold.

cc. Orris Gables, KoV, Alga.

I shared the letter with Orris as we sat in his office.

"Why did you set me up like this?" I complained. "I'd just make a fool of myself if I went up there!"

"Come now, Yaro, you underestimate yourself."

"No, I don't, he overestimates me. He has got me pegged for a 'serious scholar'—those were *your* words. What makes it so embarrassing is that you used a lot of influence to get me invited up there—I just know you did—and for what? It would be wasted on me."

"I will admit, Curlew does feel a strong need to accommodate my wishes—we won't discuss why—but I can't agree that it will be wasted. Yaro, can't you see that you are on a vision quest, a pilgrimage of sorts, to find that clearer understanding that will bring fuller meaning to your life and to your actions? You've told me as much several times, in different words. Trust that good power that is in you—you don't have to clothe it in 'spiritual' trappings. It's as real as your right hand. And don't be in such awe of Curlew. He is a fine scholar, but I know him well, and he dwells in a Smaller House than you, believe me.

"Furthermore, I think you're more prepared than you realize. You've been studying and searching for the right questions. The Archives may hold some of your answers, or maybe just clearer questions. Either way, I'm confident you will make the most of it. Go, Yaro, look around up there and be awake to whatever you may find."

Chapter 49

The wind whipped across the ice on Piper Lake as I skirted its shore. A few people were skating on the large windswept areas, but I had no time for such recreation myself. It was still over forty miles to Covenant Ridge, and I was determined to cover that before nightfall. The message from Curlew had arrived late on the morning before, and although I had taken the next ferry, I had only gotten as far as Stubs Pond by dark. I spent the night there with friends whom I'd gotten to know on one of my bicycle trips from the *Come-What-May* last summer. They seemed pleased to see me and were a bit surprised that I not only still had the cheap dulcitar I had bought there, but had acquired a modicum of skill on it. However, I declined their invitation to visit longer and, early morning found me skimming along the road past Piper Lake. This long-distance skiing did not come as easily to me as to the "natives." Where I come from, a man rarely went more than fifteen or twenty miles from home in a lifetime, and if so, it would surely be on horseback. Esperians of all ages are great walkers, and in the winter months, they think little of skiing twenty or thirty miles to make a social call. The roads were rolled hard now, and I was surprised that even I, with clumsy technique and occasional spills, could cover distances at a fraction of the time it would take to walk.

My route took me through the Humps, so I stopped in at Maxim's stead in Sundew for a light lunch and the briefest of visits. As I was strapping on my skis to depart, Oriole, the pencil-maker, cautioned, "There is a storm in the offing. The barometer has been dropping fast for hours. You know, if you bided here the night and went on after it was over, you'd probably get there just as quick in the end."

I had enjoyed their hospitality a couple times before, and the suggestion was tempting, but my appointment was for six on the following morning; and anyway, I was certain that I could reach the Archives before either dark or snow set in. Based on the distance, I'd already covered, I figured I was more than halfway there, so I ignored the warning and struck off. Crossing the Heathlands, I was aided somewhat by a stiff southeast wind at my back; and as I glided on down the valley of Sweetwater Brook, my daring plan seemed vindicated, for there were lots of long gentle downhill grades where I made marvelous time. The first few flakes began to fall somewhere beyond Foresight

Corners, but they swirled and eddied with such a leisurely grace that I saw no threat in them. By the time I crossed the Laughingwater at Upper Intervale, I had to make a decision: to stop for supper or continue. I hadn't allowed for the effect of strenuous cold-weather exercise on appetite, especially after having eaten lightly all day. Now I berated myself for not grabbing a sandwich to munch while on the move. Snow was falling faster, and daylight would soon fail if I stopped to dine now. According to the map, it was only four or five miles to the Archives, so at my present rate of travel, I should be there in less than a half hour. The choice seemed obvious: make a dash for it.

The problem with my reasoning was that I had made a foolish assumption, foolish because I knew better. Back in the summer, I had viewed Covenant Ridge from a distance below. I had seen its steep cliff-girt heights, and there was no excuse for my thinking I could scale them on skis in thirty minutes. Still, the beginning of the road up Sugar Rill was reassuring enough, well rolled and of moderate grade. Climbing up out of the intervale, I began to have real doubts as I realized what a wild place this was. In most of Esperia, one rarely goes a half mile without passing a steadhouse; here, there was none in sight. The narrow road was close-flanked by rock maples and then just by rocks. There must have been a grand vista out over the high valley, but I was wholly socked in by now. I had never seen a snowstorm set in so fast, and it clearly had no intention of quitting soon. The road, or perhaps I should call it a track at this point, was only four feet wide where it snaked up the ridge's steep flank. It made frequent switchbacks in climbing around the impassable ledges, and visibility was so bad that I had to beware lest I miss a turn and ski over the edge. At one point the road appeared to fork—it was hard to be sure in the driving snow—and I chose what seemed to be the main branch. Before long, that petered out, and I headed back toward the fork. Or where I thought the fork was; the snow was coming so fast now and the late light so dim that it was hard to make out my own tracks. On what I thought was the right track, I began to catch my skis on low juniper bushes. Clearly this was not well-used road; it wasn't any kind of road. I was in the middle of the woods without the faintest idea where I was. Fighting down a sense of panic, I deliberated on the only two choices: if I headed down, straight down through the woods, I would eventually come to the Laughingwater River and a stead where I could wait out the night. If I went upward, I would have to come out somewhere on the crest of the ridge where I knew was the Archives community. I felt sure I was much closer to the top than the bottom, so I opted for that. Progress was very slow now. I stumbled often in the dark, and the brush grabbed at my skis and lashed at my face. As I climbed higher, the rock maples and beeches gave way to stunted white birches. There was a time when I was convinced I had blundered back onto the road, but if so, I soon lost it again; the going was that blind. It occurred to me that my skis were more of an encumbrance than they were worth, but when I unstrapped them, I sank in up to my crotch. My cold fingers had difficulty redoing the straps in the dark, and when I succeeded after several minutes of fumbling, they were colder still. I was cold all over, I was wet with sweat and melted snow, I was hungry and tired, I wondered if I could reach the top.

When I finally broke out from the timberline and found myself atop the craggy spur, I fancied that my woes were at end. The Archives must be close by, but which way? The fluffy bits of snow, which had wafted so gracefully below, were turned by the gale winds into stinging missiles, driving horizontally against my parka hood. I shouted for help, knowing that no one could hear me unless they stood within two rods downwind. I spent many valuable minutes slogging over the ledges, looking in vain for any sign of habitation. There were several acres of relatively level ridgetop, but there simply was nothing there. I was in the wrong place. The ridge crest had its ups and downs; surely if I persisted in going one direction or another, I would blunder onto the settlement. But I no longer had the energy to gamble. I couldn't remember why it had seemed so important to get to this forsaken place, but now I was desperate to get away from there alive. I had chosen to go up, and I had been wrong. There seemed to be no help within miles, and the only hope left was down, down in the snug steads of the valley. Although I had no idea where I was, down seemed pretty clear, after all.

The descent was quicker than the climb, though far more dangerous. I could not doff my skis, though they were a nuisance. In the blackness, I dared not actually ski on them; but I hurried down as fast as I dared, feeling myself in a race to get somewhere safe and warm before my strength gave out. My blood sugar was low, and I began to think about things I'd heard: how people died from the cold, painlessly perhaps, but nonetheless dead.

I kept dropping, down into the taller timber, down past the cliffs, down into the maples and beeches. Once, I slipped over a ledge and found myself pinned in some snow-covered rocks at its base. The deep snow had saved me from getting badly hurt, and I was able to extricate myself with only a collarful of melting snow. I thought one of my skis had cracked, but I had only torn part of the binding. I needed that piece to hold my toe in place, so I managed to improvise something out of a snapped-off hazel twig. It worked but was a poor makeshift, and it slowed my progress even further.

In my obsession with getting off the ridge, I lost track of time, but I'm sure it was over an hour before I found myself on the intervale once more. I reached the riverbank, but in the storm, one couldn't make out any light from steadhouses, if there were any near about. I could see the river well enough to discover a shocking fact: it was flowing the wrong way.

Sure enough, the direction or flow was toward my right, which was all wrong. The Laughingwater flowed south-eastward, toward my left. Clearly I was disoriented, but at least I could make out a roadway on the opposite bank—that much was as it should be. There was no crossing here though; the water was mostly open and fast. I schussed along the near bank for a hundred yards or so until I came to where a stone dam formed a small millpond. There I knew the still water would be more thickly frozen. I had to take the chance. My skis were now extremely helpful as they spread my weight out over the gelid surface. Almost to the other side, I passed the mouth of the mill race and felt a *whumpf* under me as a section of thinner crust collapsed. I felt myself slide, skis and all, into the water which was only knee-deep. Drowning was not my worry; simply being wet was danger enough. Already damp from floundering in the deep snow, my legs and feet were now drenched. Using my ski poles, I quickly worked my way up the bank and onto the roadway. At the end of the dam, a large frame building loomed through the snow-streaked darkness. I couldn't tell which way was the nearest stead, nor how far; so the vacant mill looked like my only salvation, at least for the moment. The door was hooked shut on the outside, and I ploughed my way in, skis and all, with difficulty, closing it against the snowdrift again. There was a narrow wooden shelf just by the door, and I groped there almost instinctively for what I needed most. It was there: a lamp and matches. I ruined two matches trying to strike them with my numbed fingers, but the third one lit, and I managed to get it to the wick. In the glow I could see that I was in some sort of woodworking factory. At one end I saw a large pile of chips piled under a lathe, and they gave me an idea. Pulling off my boots and liners, I thrust my feet into the pile of chips, hoping the insulation would let them warm themselves up. I sat on the work stool and held the lantern in my lap with my hands around the globe. This had the desired effect; I could feel a small measure of warmth seep back into them. Not so with my feet. The idea was good one, but it presupposed that I had some body heat to be held in. My system was too exhausted to generate any heat, and the cold chips only stung my bitten feet as if I were standing on crushed glass. I just had to get out of there, venture back out into the jaws of the blizzard, and wander about until I found some dwelling. My body parts were not in agreement with each other; fingers said, "Tarry just a bit longer, the lamp feels too good," while toes screamed, "Go on! Go on! Before it's too late!" While I was trying to muster the courage to referee in favour of the lower extremities, there was a renewed shriek of wind outside, and I heard the door burst open. Looking around for a stick to prop it shut, I heard a new sound at the door, bellowing over the storm, "Anybody in here?"

I nearly fell over myself in eagerness to respond, but I had to speak twice before a sound came croaking out. "Yes, over here, I am here, oh help!"

The man at the door held up a lantern and, seeing me at the far end, called out the door: "Somebody in trouble here, come quickly!" Immediately, there were four men and women around me, helping me to stand. I was all broken up now, sputtering and trying to stand up on my numbed feet. All my fatigue and fear and frost pain welled over in sobs and shudders.

"Why, the poor man, he's an Anagaian peddler, lost in the blizzard! Say, fellow, can you understand us . . . ? I don't know much of your language."

"My language is your language," I stammered as they held me up. "I'm from Alga. I've been lost . . . I am lost . . . trying to get down off the ridge."

"Which ridge?"

"Why Covenant Ridge, of course." I was puzzled at such an obvious question.

"It's a good thing you spotted that lamp glow in the window, Kindle. He's got trouble, maybe frostbite," said the man with a lantern. "Monarda, yours is the closest place. We'd better get him there quick."

It turned out they were a snow-rolling crew, and they lifted me gingerly into the weight-rack of their roller and pulled me to the nearest steadhouse, only a quarter-mile away. I'm not sure I could have made it on my own, even had I known where to go. The searing pain raged in my feet so I couldn't stand by myself.

Many thoughtful arms carried me into the house where gentle hands peeled off my cold stiff clothes and replace them with flannelled quilts. Kind voices murmured around me, offering suggestions. Through my convulsive shivering, I could catch snatches of their talk: "Up on Covenant, he says . . . then how on earth . . . ? Lucky to be any pieces left . . . may lose them unless . . . Kindle, your sister will know how . . . bring her back quickly . . ."

Pumped full of warm broth and wrapped up close to the restoked stove, I felt myself slowly reviving, except for my feet. The soles were shot with pain, and those toes that were not numb seemed to be afire. I asked if I could have some hot water to soak them.

"No, my dear, we dare not. If there's frostbite, that might be just the worst thing. Someone's coming who knows how to treat this right. Just hold on."

"Holding on" was not easy; it was quite a few minutes before I heard a door opening and voices in the front room.

"So sorry to rouse you at such a night, niece, but he seems to be in sad shape. I have no idea, some white fellow, not from around here certainly, yet not quite a foreigner either. You'll see what I mean."

I was huddled deep into my quilts, facing the stove, so I heard her before I saw her. There was a little gasp, followed by "Why, it's Yaro!"

Startled by the familiar voice, I was stunned to see Cherish, my savior of the bicycle-wreck incident. You might suppose I would feel sheepish at meeting her again under such beholden circumstances, but I was nothing but grateful. I knew what everyone else was thinking: that my toes might be injured beyond recovery and require amputation. If anyone could offer hope, they were welcome on any terms. Yet surprised we surely were. I had no idea where she lived, nor for that matter did I know where I was. She, of course, had no reason to expect me to show up in her neighbourhood, least of all under such circumstances.

Nevertheless, she set right to work, bathing my feet in tepid water and gradually warming them. She also served me some overly sweetened mint tea and insisted that I drink every drop. She sat up by me all through the night, constantly adjusting the water and checking my own temperature. In my exhaustion, I eventually fell asleep despite the stinging, but I don't think Cherish did.

The next morning, after the storm had blown over, a middle-aged man showed up, introducing himself as Cherish's father, Herald.

"My daughter says there's a reasonable hope of saving all your toes."

"Yes, so she tells me. In fact, they feel somewhat better already, as long as I don't touch them with anything rough."

"Well, what we'd like to do is move you up to our place, Ravenswing, so she can look after you. She says the toes on your left foot will bear close watching, lest they go to gangrene."

"That's fine with me, only I'm not sure I can walk up there."

"Oh, most assuredly not. You'll be off those feet for days. Cherish has gone down to the bannerhouse to fetch a drawchair from the waresroom. She will be along pretty soon."

"Oh yes, speaking of bannerhouses, I was in such discomfort last night, I didn't think to ask, where am I anyway—I mean, what banner?"

"Why, it's Navestock you're in."

"Navestock! But that's not on the Laughingwater."

"Indeed not, we're on Wisewoman."

"But Wisewoman Brook is on the north side of Covenant Ridge!"

"I'm sure that's a surprise to no one here."

"But I went up Sugar Rill and meant to come down the same. How could I have gotten over here?"

"I suppose you got confounded up on the ridge—I needn't tell you it was a thick one last night. What we're all trying to figure out is how you managed to pick your way down over the cliffs in one piece. There's scarcely a break on this side."

"Dumb luck, I guess. So I must have passed right near the Archive settlement without even knowing it."

"It's likely. That's not so hard to do, even on a fair day. The Archives was never meant to stand out. You may have marched right over someone's roof without ever being the wiser. So you have business there that couldn't wait out a blizzard. You're a scholar, then?"

"No, not really, just a busybody with questions about the past. I had hoped to get them answered there, but I guess I've ruined it now. I must get a message back to Alga so they won't worry about me."

"We already sent one—found an address stamped on your skis—but the signal won't get through for a while. Seems the storm hasn't cleared the coast yet, so the towers there are shut down. Not much you can do except work at getting well."

In fact, my recuperation went a lot faster than even Cherish had expected. Either the damage to my feet was much less than it appeared, or Cherish was remarkably skilled at her art. From the way my toes looked and what I already knew about Cherish, I was quick to assume the latter. Within a few days, I was able to walk with relatively little discomfort; indeed I would've been fit to travel within the week had I not also contracted a serious cold which turned to pleurisy and lingered for the better part of another week. Cherish was not yet a fully trained healer like Ermine, since the Swallows put more emphasis on emergency procedures, but she consulted with the local healer and tended to me assiduously herself.

It was not as though she had nothing else to do; I saw that she had a number of important stewardships and was somehow active in many aspects of her stead's life.

Though only two years older than I, she was looked up to by the entire household. Despite all her other duties, she found some time each day to administer the vapours, hot and cold baths, and poultices which are a mainstay of Esperian healing.

During the days of my convalescence, I had several opportunities to speak with her father. The more I gained his acquaintance, the more interesting I found him to be. He was rather stocky and vigourous beyond his fifty years. He impressed me at once as a man of keen perception; while more brilliant lights were still probing at the fringes, he lost no time in getting right to the heart of the matter. When he spoke his mind, one could be sure he had reasoned carefully and had formed a strong opinion—otherwise, he was wont to remain silent.

Like nearly every Esperian I ever met, he was versatile in his pursuits. The orchard was his special responsibility, but he also operated a lathe down at the same turning-mill where I had taken shelter. He had only one good eye, having lost the use of one in a woods accident. However, his inner vision was keener than most. No scholar himself, he greatly admired those whose learning gave them insight into matters that he himself wished to understand. Both his wife and his daughter overstood him by a couple inches, yet there was one trait he had undeniably passed on to Cherish: they both had a zeal, even a lust, for the fulfillment of the Steward Vision.

I had assumed that I had missed my opportunity to visit the Archives, but I had a surprise in store. Herald sent them word of the mishap which had thwarted my appointment, and Curlew himself promptly flashed back a conciliatory message, wishing me a full and speedy recovery. He said I had indeed missed an important window, but that he could arrange a very short viewing most days at noon and to let him know before I came. I thought this far beyond anything he owed me (or rather Orris), but he obviously felt otherwise.

As soon as I began to feel stronger, I mentioned my intention of trying again to reach the Archive. Cherish seemed a bit concerned, but Herald didn't try to discourage me. "You'll have little trouble now, with the roads all opened. There is a narrow track which goes up this side; it starts from the Fortyfold bridge about two miles above the mill. It's well marked, and it skirts around the higher cliffs. When you walk it, you'll see how lucky you were to blunder down from there alive. I do hope you'll drop in and see us on your way back down. I know Cherish is still concerned about your lungs."

Chapter 50

I left early on a totally clear morning—I was taking no chances now. A bitter blast bore down from the peaks of the Sanctuaries, sculpting the stiff-drifted snow into grotesque alabaster heaps. The trail (for it was little more than that) had been rolled recently, but here and there tongues of snow had drifted into it, nearly blocking passage. I had left my skis at Ravenswing, knowing that they would be of little use on the ascent; whereas the return trip would be too steep, at least for a novice like me. I remembered that Herald had described the Archivists as being almost hermitlike; they hauled in most of their supplies in late fall and were quite content to hibernate for five months in their bookish seclusion. Were it not for the Cutoff Laws, they might even have felt disinclined to bother rolling their two access roads.

It was a dramatic climb, the "East Road," with frequent vistas of the entire Wisewoman Valley. The high buttressing cliffs of Covenant Ridge were rimed in the thick black ice which welled out of fissures in the towering palisades. From my history reading, I knew the word *palisades* was not a mere figure of speech; the sheer walls of schist had been the main defense whereby the early Stewards had withstood their attackers.

As I neared the crest, I hailed the gatehouse before it was in sight, as Herald had advised me that these folks didn't always take too kindly to unexpected visitors. I was expected, however, as I assume Curlew had notified the guards of my impending arrival. There was a dry-laid stone wall perched on the rim of the crest. In places it was at least eight feet tall, and that puzzled me greatly, because I realized there was no way I could have blundered over that wall in a blizzard without realizing it. Even though the snow was deep-drifted into the lee of the wall's one side, the wind had swept it bare on the outer side. With the encircling wall on both sides of the crest, how could I have missed the Archives even in the blizzard?

I believe I now know the answer; the actual Archives compound area is only a couple acres, including the entrance to the tunnels. Outside the wall to the west lies only the windswept crest. There are several outbuildings there, seasonally occupied by visiting scholars and support workers, and those are so incorporated into the ridgetop that one might easily passed right by them, or even *over* them, in a storm.

At the gatehouse, I found a man and a woman on sentry-duty. That duty was understandably light, since visitors of any ilk were rare enough at this season, and the chances of an enemy attack seemed ludicrous. Nevertheless, the collection of crossbows and other weapons hanging on a wall proved that they took nothing for granted.

The woman was engrossed in reading while the man (her husband apparently) was occupying himself over a small backstrap loom, somewhat like the one I had used back in Dryford, only his was much better. He paused to make a show of checking his logbook as if to certify my appointment. Looking over his shoulder, I could see my name surrounded by a lot of white paper. Clearly I could have come the day before or the day after and still have been the only visitor. Was all this stuff about busy schedules just a put-off? The guard's next comment cleared that up for me.

"Curlew says to hold you here until . . ."—he turned to look at yet another log, this one penciled in on every single line, including the night hours—"until noon sharp. There's a thirty-minute gap here, between sessions. That's the best he can give you today. The pressure's really building on him."

Within an hour, Curlew showed up with greetings and concerns for my improved health. He apologized for making me wait until the precise appointment time, and I assured him of my appreciation for the priviledge of viewing the manuscript at all. I was astute enough to mention that I would certainly let Orris know all about my gracious reception there, and I could see Curlew was greatly pleased at that.

"This must seem like a foolish question, but why has access to these documents been so restricted in the first place? After all, we're talking about a copy, not the original. Couldn't at least a few handwritten copies be released before general publication? Or couldn't the translation go to press in installments, as it is completed?"

"It's not a foolish question, and many prominent people are asking it. To answer you, I must first explain a bit about the process: once the restorers have pieced it together so it can be safely handled, the text is copied as exactly as possible. Next, classical scholars translate it into modern Mok. Many feel that at this point, it should be published for the general public, but the Archives Board insists that the translation must be further peer-reviewed. This is partly because translation is not always the same as interpretation, and contextual considerations may put a quite different slant on certain passages. Foreign scholars in particular are unhappy with this policy, even though in the end, they will get to look at everything and judge for themselves. They want at least for the already-completed translation to be released, but the board feels that until the document is viewable in its entirety, any releases would merely invite unfounded conclusions. It is creating a controversy, both here and abroad, but I must tell you that I am in sympathy with the present policy. In fact, I was one of those who recommended it."

Knowing what very little I did about this fellow, I could well imagine he might cherish his role in all this. Having such control over a chunk of knowledge at which the scholastic world was salivating seemed quite in character for him. On the other hand, the policy might be altogether reasonable; who was I to refute his arguments? It only deepened my appreciation for the absurdity of my position. What influence could Orris have over this intellectual hoarder that he should make an exception for me, of all people? To this day, I have no idea, but I determined to make the best of my thirty minutes of privilege.

We entered a fairly large building, whose entrance was framed by two solid-looking guards—the first armed men I had seen since coming here. I have no doubt that were I not escorted by Curlew, I could never have entered that building alive. Inside the door, we found ourselves in a small chamber where we removed our coats and boots and donned paper caps and white smocks and soft slippers. As we washed our hands thoroughly in a basin, a group of similarly clad workers came up a stairway and went out the door, giving me a courteous but thorough look-over as they passed. These were the translating team who were just breaking for lunch, and I knew that when they returned in a half hour, I must be gone. We went down the narrow stairway and immediately climbed up another narrow flight. Curlew explained that all the workrooms had elaborate provisions for controlling temperature, humidity, light, dust, and airflow.

Passing through another sealed door, we entered a larger chamber, which like the tunnels was lit only on demand by piped-in reflected light. A whiff of acrid and not wholly pleasant scents permeated the air. At a long table in the far corner, an elderly man was labouring over some very exacting restoration work. Although the room was generally rather dim-lit, his area was illuminated brightly by the reflector tubes. He looked up at our arrival and padded over to speak privately with Curlew. Drawing him aside, the restorer spoke in annoyed whispers, glancing occasionally at me. Curlew spoke reassuringly to him (I thought I heard Orris's name mentioned), and the man returned to his work, rather peevishly it seemed to me. Culew led me over to another table on the rear wall and opened one of the reflector tubes on the area. It was then I noticed that two other men, also armed, were standing beside the door we had just entered. I gulped, feeling very glad I hadn't come here to do mischief. I realized more than ever what enormous value these people place on the contents of this snow-swept ridge.

On the back of the table were several steel shelves, holding assorted bundles of paper, some looking very old indeed, and tied in some kind of shiny material I didn't recognize. Curlew made it quite clear that I should under no circumstances touch those papers nor even reach toward them, implying that the guards might take great umbrage at such a gesture. Then he offered me a comfortable chair and presented me a file folder containing the copies of which he had spoken back at Telling. Placing them on the table before me, I saw at once it was far more than I could read in the remaining twenty-seven minutes, so I asked Curlew if I he could recommend any selections for me to focus on. He seemed pleased to be consulted, and drew out one sheaf from the others.

"In my opinion, this is the most packed entry, the most central. But see what you think. The bracketed sections are either difficult to make out in the original or there is disagreement on the exact translation."

And so I read.

Now that the snow is almost gone, we dare move around a lot more, with less fear of leaving tracks. Emery returned this morning from visiting the Northcamp band. He said they had some wheat flour they found in the abandoned store down at the forks. Wheat flour! I declare I've had nothing but acorns and maple seeds for so long, I'm not sure my guts could tolerate bread (try me!). They've had lots of trouble though: they lost their vision-keeper during the starving time, and Emery says they're all adrift. But Aster says we mustn't worry about her; she says we'll go all right, even if she doesn't make it through. I wonder though. I wonder if any of us knows what it all means. I mean, even if any of us survives all this, what's to stop us from going back to [the same ways that got us here]?

Emery is certain he spotted a couple of [down-countrymen] yesterday. They weren't soldiers, he insists, but hunters after venison. Not much difference if they spot us; they just as leave shoot us instead. I sure hope no one from the other band tries to put sand in their oil or anything else that delays their getting out of here.

Tomorrow, Zeal and Robin are going back down to the old camp. We left a big patch of [??] there, and if it's thawed out enough to dig, we'll have enough to fill our bellies for the first time in months! They won't take us all along, lest we walk into a trap, like happened to part of the Highcamp band last year.

[Obliterated gaps, about six lines]

It's funny; they say black folks can't stand the cold as well as whites, but [Red or Roan?] and his [adopted?] kids came through the winter OK; most of the other families got at least one dead; little Fluoresce lost every one of [next three lines obliterated]

Summer solstice next week and it will have been a full year since any flyovers; no [missiles?], no soldiers. Emery came back from another explore. Aster thinks we should stay together and everyone does, but Emery says we can't afford not to know what's going on outside. He was gone over a week, went as far as Oakland. He found it completely abandoned, except for some stray cats. He thinks those who survived the epidemic have all moved toward the coast. On foot, mostly, vehicles left behind. Hardly any gas around. It's like every oil well's gone dry. Of course they haven't, but with everything disrupted, it's not getting distributed, and those who haven't any are killing those who have some. I wish he'd quit leaving the forest like that. Sometimes he's weird, but we can't afford to lose him.

[Gap of several lines here, perhaps intentional or perhaps obliterated]

We all crossed the ridge yesterday to join the Southcamp band for solstice. What they see in those swamps! Safety, I guess. We haven't dared to before. After Avalanche Brook, it has been too dangerous to gather all in one place. Much safer to be scattered, but lonelier. They had a new fellow with them, a stranger from beyond the White Mountains. I thought it a terrible risk, but he claims he comes from a community that thinks a lot like us. Like us indeed! He is a meat-eater and a believer. Says he's not religious, but 'spiritual.' Aster says that doesn't mean we can't work with his people, if their vision is sustainable. He did seem like a gentle type, but kind of trippy.

He was real full of news, though. One of his community is a [pig-meat?], and can talk to people everywhere, if someone's listening. He said the trick is to not say too much, not to give yourself away. He heard that there is lots of fighting everywhere. The epidemic has wiped out lots of the [channels/ networks?], everything is all broken up into little pieces. Some groups have formed alliances to protect themselves and to get what they want. Everyone needs food and not many know how to get it, short of stealing or killing for it. That probably explains why we haven't been attacked for so long: everybody wants pizza and we've just got acorns!

It seems we may be safe here anyway, at least for now. We've decided to try again to build. Lots of logs cut. This time we're building one big house for everyone, then we'll add more as we can. Hopefully we won't get burned out this time. Chandler has a crew clearing more land on the south slope, but it's so steep we must terrace every square rod. At least our gardens won't have to be so hidden now, so we can grow grain instead of just . . . . and apios.

Rusty is such a pest. He still [rest of that page obliterated]

Myrtle says I should keep writing all this stuff down, but when I use up this batch of paper, I'm not sure what I'll find to write on. Or what to do with it when I'm done.

There was more, lots more, but I closed the translated copy carefully and laid it on the table before me. I looked up at Curlew, who seemed barely able to contain his excitement.

"Isn't it fantastic?" he gushed. I nodded silently. "I mean, isn't it exactly what you're looking for?"

"Well, I can see its importance, of course. Second only to the Juniper legend, I'd say."

"Not second, Yaro. That is legend, after all, oral history handed down for nearly a century before it was written down. This is firsthand stuff, recorded as it happened. It's big."

"Yes, I completely agree." But my enthusiasm was a bit too lukewarm for Curlew.

"You're disappointed then."

"No, not disappointed, certainly. Who could be, after all? As you say, it's big. But . . . well, yes I'm disappointed, not at the significance of all this . . . it's just that . . . I mean, it's mostly details, isn't it? What else would one expect of a diary, after all? But I'm trying to get behind it, to see something that's probably too abstract for me to recognize. I think I just need to ponder it awhile. Listen, Curlew, I want you to understand how much I appreciate this. It's immensely thoughtful of you. You see, Orris told you I was a serious scholar of this stuff. Well, I don't consider myself a scholar of anything, but serious, yes. I'm trying to understand not only what this diary-keeper is saying but what she *isn't* saying—isn't saying because she doesn't need to. It's part of her vision, and she's assuming that it's part of ours, the readers'. You were raised with that vision, but was she? At what point did it become hers, and how? That may all lie in these pages, but it's not obvious, at least not to me. Perhaps as the rest becomes available, over the next year or two. As I say, I need to ponder it awhile."

Curlew seemed a bit peeved, and I felt guilty. In a way, I blamed Orris for my situation. Had he not urged me to come to this place where I had no business being? He had pulled strings, called in debts, to give me an opportunity I was not prepared to use. He should have known better.

During this time, the head of the restoration team had been working intently over a brittle scrap of brown paper, trying to coax the faded lines into contrast with some kind of chemical bath and special lights. Occasionally he had glared across at us to express his annoyance at having his concentration disturbed. I wasn't sure the security guards were overjoyed with my presence either. As they prepared to escort me out, a loud throat-clearing issued from the far corner of the room followed by a gruff voice. "Please come here a moment." The "please" sounded like a mere formality, and I wondered how the security men would react if I did not "please." But I stepped over to where the restorer was now looking up from his work.

"Kindly sit down carefully so as not to stir up the air here. Thank you. Now tell me, have you ever worked on a jigsaw puzzle?"

"Yes, well . . . I helped a steadmate to assemble one. But I see the parallel: one sneeze, one drag of the shirt sleeve, and you can mess up a lot of your work."

"Actually I was speaking of *your* work."

"My work?" I stammered as he peered from behind a gauze mask.

"You are not an historian."

"Er, well, I myself never claimed—"

"You are a philosopher."

"Oh my goodness! I'm a grindstone-cutter and a tramp-trader and this and that, but I'm surely—"

"You must see that you are a philosopher, or you'll never be any good at it. Everyone here does many jobs. Why wouldn't a philosopher also cut grindstones? But in this case, you are seeing only the puzzle pieces, and you're trying to grasp the whole picture. Or as you yourself put it, to get behind the details. Maybe you're looking in the wrong place. I don't think you're interested in how yesterday shaped today so much as how today might shape tomorrow. And correct me if I'm wrong, but I think you're not concerned about Esperia so much as Anagaia."

I was amazed that this stranger had sized me up so accurately, so quickly.

"In fact, I believe I'm interested in history and archaeology for its own sake, but you're absolutely right, of course. I do have a very applicable interest as well."

"Well, I have no great answers for you there, but I have a suggestion. If you think you may have enough details, then look next at their connexion. Find a pattern, if there is any. That's what I'm trying to do here. Now on your way out, take care to close the door slowly. You can't imagine what currents it can set in motion."

*   *   *   *   *   *   *

As I came back down off Covenant Ridge, I looked out over the snow-choked valley with a new appreciation. The diary account I'd just read was no legend—the events it chronicled had happened right here within my field of vision. Off to my left lay the cirque where the Cairns massacre had happened. Above that loomed the peaks named after the fabled Wisewoman. This very ridge had supposedly hosted the first Feast of Juniper. My own footsteps had crossed the paths of Kindlefire and Rainwalker.

Curlew was right; even more than the Juniper legend, this new discovery opened up a whole new insight into Esperian, indeed Steward origins. It seemed the writer could hardly have crammed in more pregnant references to things which have become key features of Esperian culture: the dependence on forests for food and security, the focus on self-reliance and barter, the vegan diet, the communal mentality centred on the stead, the "devout" atheism, the moral leadership of the vision-keepers, and of course, the knee-jerk rejection of nearly everything they had left behind. Were not all of these alluded to in that diary? Not to mention many details: the terraces, Banner Day, the racial makeup of modern Esperian, even the actual mention of the historic leader Wisewoman (whose given name is believed to have been Aster)! Also, one thing I had been looking for but never yet found: use of the words *vision* and *sustainable* in the same context! So much detail and so little explanation. It was like a portrait, which may depict all the details of that captured moment, but cannot show the sequence of steps which led up to that moment. Perhaps the fault would be remedied as the restorators and translators unveiled the rest of those diaries, but somehow I doubted that. I was beginning to think I already had enough data, but I had to fit it together. As the restorator had said, I must now make the connexions.

As I picked my way down the newly rolled switchbacks, I found myself thinking about something Hewn had explained one night when he came home from an Evolutionary Biology lecture. He explained that the inception of an evolutionary change requires *first* that there must be some negative stress, some crisis, to induce a predilection to change. If everything seems to be working okay, there will be very little pressure to adapt. Secondly, there must be some alternative, some benefit which will be reaped by making the change. Thirdly, the organism (in this case a society) must be mutable; that is to say, the potential for the change must already lie within (for example, scales must be capable of morphing into feathers). I tried to connect these to the reality that was Anagaia.

To me, there wasn't the slightest question that Anagaia is in crisis, that it just isn't working. But obviously, many people there, perhaps most people, don't see it that way. Or at least they don't understand how deep the roots of the crisis go. I suppose they see it as a "sustainable disaster," which isn't quite the same as a crisis. A sustainable disaster is when things are miserable, but you can keep muddling through, especially when you see yourself as a little less miserable than others. Misery may be sustainable; doom isn't.

Secondly, here was *an* alternative, Esperia, a working model of what might be. For even though it might be no utopia, it had so much to teach about sustainable living. But how many Anagaians ever got to see, or even hear about, that alternative? And those few who did were usually two blinded by hubris and their own propaganda to realize what they were seeing.

And thirdly, what about this "mutability" thing? Where, in all of Anagaian culture, was some feature, some institution which was so particularly adaptive that it could morph into a sustainable analogue of itself and eventually pull the rest of the culture along with it? I kept reminding myself that it didn't need to look like Esperia, but could—indeed must—find its own evolutionary path toward a sustainable future. I kept telling myself that Esperia was merely *my* ideal of a homeland. I kept telling myself that Ravenswing was but one of the many places I could be happy living. I kept telling myself that Cherish was just a dear friend whose sisterly company it would be fine to enjoy. I kept climbing down off the ridge.

Chapter 51

Back at Ravenswing, I sat at the long dining table across from Herald and Cherish. The rest had already supped, but Haven, Cherish's mom, had ladled me out some hot leftover soup made from chestnuts, dried green beans, and leeks. I had promised to come back before heading home to the island, and anyway it was the end of the week, so they prevailed on me to bide another day.

I told them about my visit to the Archive, about the exciting things I'd seen and read, and about my disappointment at realizing that what I'd been seeking was not to be found up there. I also tried to explain about my thoughts on the way down, but that was difficult, for me and for them. I kept going off into abstractions where I was even confusing myself. I especially sensed Cherish's frustration at all these ideas, which were so tentative and roundabout. Her eyes seemed riveted on my mouth, which kept spooning down chestnuts without ever once burping up some kernel of wisdom. I just knew that if I could have given her one concrete tip, if I could have said, "Just swim from here to Grand Coquina and all will be well with the world," she would have dived into Harking Bay without a second thought. But of course, I had no answers; I was only beginning to ask better questions.

I did have one insight, something that had occurred to me as I was crossing the bridge at Fortyfold. It was such a jumbled idea that I would have been hesitant to present it were I not among people who were so eager to share any fresh outlook on the world's affairs.

"This will seem bizarre," I began falteringly. "But why do things happen here? I mean, what factor most strongly guides people's actions? What induces change?"

"The Vision, you mean?"

"But as you yourself reminded me the other day, the Vision manifests itself in many aspects, many facets of life. It's everywhere, but there are places where it bubbles up closest to the surface, and those places are different for different societies."

"I'm afraid I don't see what you're getting at," Herald admitted.

"I'm discovering that in Esperia, it is religion more than anything else. This may be an atheist society, but I've noticed that decisions, even including market decisions, are always based on religious considerations: what do the vision-keepers say about it? How shall we interpret the Scriptures to deal with this economic question? Admit it, you can't imagine doing it any other way."

"Hmm. Well, then suppose you tell me how else it would be done."

"Look at Anagaia. Ostensibly a very religious society, yet when push comes to shove, what decides how things go?"

"Why, I always assumed the priests had control over that."

"No way! It is the marketplace which ultimately drives everything, including religion. Like you, Herald, I always assumed that was the only way it could be, until I came here and saw how things run here. They're exactly reversed! So paradoxically reversed that I couldn't see it."

"So what?" interrupted Cherish impatiently. "What does it mean? What can we do with it?"

"I have absolutely no idea," I confessed in some embarrassment, knowing how imperative it was to her. "I'm not even sure I'm right about it all, but it seems that way. It just seems that if you wish to induce any change in a society, especially one not your own, then you need to figure out what drives change in their world. People have told me that there's no point in converting Anagaians to a different religion—that makes more sense than ever to me now. But maybe if we could somehow make changes in their market system, that would have a more profound impact on the rest."

"Even if that's all true," mused Herald, "I can't imagine the Empire willingly accepting any changes induced from outside. Nowadays, they hardly tolerate our presence there, let alone our influence."

I continued to sip my soup quietly. He was right, and I knew it.

*   *   *   *   *   *   *

The first morning of the new week, I joined the steadmates of Ravenswing for breakfast before leaving for home. The night before, I had wearied myself to sleep, thinking about how much I would miss these good people, especially Cherish and her father. But, I assured myself, next spring this region would see a lot of me and my boatmates as we continued trading in the Upper Laughingwater. I would visit here often, especially when the weekend found us near Wisewoman Brook, and Herald and I might continue our conversations about saving the world, or at least our part of it. And of course, it would be wonderful to see more of my dear new friend Cherish.

I remember that breakfast more clearly than most: they stewed dried apple wedges and other fruits and hazelnut meal, and onto that they dropped yeasted wheat dumplings spiced with coriander, one of my favourites. However, it's not just the delicious fare that keeps that repast in my memory. As we were finishing up, Herald, who sat down-table from me, said, "Yaro, I don't know if you're inclined to consider this, but seeing as how we appear to be so like-minded, you and all of us, I wonder if you wouldn't do well to bide here with us awhile, as a sojourner, at least."

I tried desperately to conceal my own feelings, which were as mixed as the stewed fruit in my bowl. One part of me wanted to say, "Yes, of course, I'll just go home and move my things here right away." But something else in me raised warning flags.

"I quite know what you mean, sir . . ." I felt everyone at the table stiffen a bit "I mean, Herald. I guess I'd have to give it some thought. I mean, I'm flattered you feel that way, but of course there are other people to be considered."

"Actually, I've spoken to everyone else here, and there seems to be a consensus about it. It's only been a fortnight since you stumbled into our valley, so of course you don't know us that well, nor we you, but then a sojourn doesn't require a long-term commitment either way."

I glanced quickly over at Cherish, and saw what I took for a nervous, self-conscious look.

"Yes, well, I thank you all for the kind invitation. As I say, I will have to consider it."

We dropped the subject then, but as Cherish had some business down at Evenswap, she skied along with me that far. Finally I turned to her with what I hoped was an unassuming smile.

"Cherish, I have to admit your father's idea appeals to me enormously, but—"

"Yes, I understand."

"Do you, then? It's just that you're such a wonderful friend, and I can't help worrying that if I lived there, people might misunderstand our relationship, and I might become an impediment, a nuisance even. I shouldn't like that."

"Oh well, I don't think you should let that stop you. After all, I have plenty of other male friends, and anyway, everyone knows I'm busy with other interests just now. We're not a nuclear family, Yaro, we're a household of thirty-one members, and no one is likely to read too much into a newcomer's intentions . . . and if they did, we could just straighten them out, couldn't we?"

"I suppose so . . . yes . . . of course. And yourself . . . it wouldn't feel awkward having me around?"

"Of course not. I understand your position clearly. I just know Dad would love sharing ideas with you, and . . . well, I'd like it too . . . sharing ideas, that is. And as he said, you don't have to stay forever."

By now, we had come to the bridge where I had to turn off while Cherish's way lay straight ahead.

"Then this is what I'd like you to do: when you get back, tell them all that I need a week or two to get things settled at Stonesthrow. Then I'll come back. We'll just see how it works out, okay?"

"Okay," she said simply. "See you then." And she stuck her ski poles into the hard road snow and pushed off.

*　　*　　*　　*　　*　　*　　*

It took me a day and a half to get back to the island. Much of that time, I mused deeply over this new turn of events. My excitement was tempered by uncertainty concerning Cherish. Or rather uncertainty concerning myself. They say that absence makes the heart grow fonder, but in the case of Fawn, it only made my heart grow confused. And instead of absence, what might presence do to my feelings for Cherish? In frequent company with her, might I find myself developing the very sort of attraction I've been trying to avoid? I wasn't quite sure how much I trusted myself, for the simple reason that I was less and less certain of what I expected of myself. And if such an attraction did develop on my part, it would be doubly complicated by the fact that Cherish clearly had no such feelings for me. That at least was the safety lock: however confused I might get, she knew her own heart, and it was securely kept.

Back at the island, I had intended to complete a project I was working on at the stone yards, but Burnet insisted that he'd be glad to finish it for me. I had been in the middle of reading several textbooks and histories from the library, but at Ermine's suggestion, I made a list of their titles so I could simply find them at the Navestock library. I sent a note off to Wren, informing him I probably would not be available for the *Come-What-May* in spring. In only three days, I was ready to return, but I waited a couple more so as not to appear overeager. It was a pretty emotional leave-taking—I hadn't realized just how attached I'd grown to all these people and to this windswept island. I promised to keep in touch and return to visit now and again, and I kept that promise. Those folks were my first refuge when I arrived on a strange shore, and I can never repay all they gave me.

Chapter 52

I arrived at Ravenswing to stay on a very cold day in mid-Second month with a knapsack full of sturdy but comfortable clothes and a gift-quilt from my former steadmates and wrapped in that a third-rate dulcitar, which was more than my talent merited. In my pocket were the three souvenirs I had on my arrival a year and a half earlier. One was the note written by my mother when she left me on the orphanage steps. The second was a friendship token given me by a chum when I'd left the orphanage: a rough shard of pottery with Boon incised in one surface and my own name in the other side. The third was a solitary silver coin from the little hoard my mother had surreptitiously left for me shortly before falling to her death. Those three items were the only tangible mementos I had of another life in another world. However, I still carried many memories of people and commitments, memories which would continue to complicate life for me in my new home.

*   *   *   *   *   *   *

Ravenswing was, in every respect, larger than Stonesthrow. Thirty-two steadmates (counting myself) lived in a huge three-wing wooden house situated on 133 acres of mountain slope which, though rocky, was nevertheless well drained and fertile. Its walls were of square-hewn logs, a foot thick and blackened with age. The building was much older than Stonesthrow, one part dating back at least three centuries. The actual site had been occupied since around 180 ACT, but the original stead had been leveled by fire in 255. Even with thirty-two residents, both the house and the land could support more. Indeed Ravenswing had a real need for more labour, to develop and exploit its considerable resources. They occasionally hired extra hands from neighbouring steads, but that worked both ways, so able newcomers like myself were generally welcome. Like every stead in the country, Ravenswing had its own mix of subsistence activities and commercial enterprises, many of them connected with forest products. Although most of my skills were not applicable here, everyone was happy to teach me, and I was eager to learn.

This was the makeup of the household at the time of my arrival, in case anyone is interested. (If not, feel free to skip over it—you'll meet them sooner or later, if it matters.) Cherish's parents, Herald and Haven, had three children, which would've been scandalous in this population-conscious society; but they were not at fault. After Cherish, Haven had borne twin boys. Kindle was a regular sort of fellow, always cheerful, whistled a lot. Hale was strange in a hard-to-define way. He could be quite eccentric, yet when it came to certain things, like devising useful gadgets, he was really quite remarkable. I've already described Herald. As for his wife, Haven, she was very soft-spoken in manner; yet like her husband, she exuded a quiet exuberance that only bubbled to the surface in their daughter. I mostly picture Haven cooking, for which she has a great passion and talent.

Herald had an older sister, Ivy, who was unmarried. Like him, she originally came from Welcome Fair. It didn't take me long to realize that she and Herald generally didn't get on well . . . I could see why. She always expressed Steward ideals in a vociferous and self-conscious manner, but it was all a façade. She showed in many little ways that she was insecure and only concerned about herself. She fooled no one but annoyed everyone—how could one live in intimate daily contact with someone and not see through them?

Fairfield and Holly were Cherish's maternal grandparents. In their early seventies, both were very active members of the household. In addition to Haven, they had a second daughter Candle (a very popular name in Esperia). She lived at a stead down on the Valley Road, the one where I was taken on the night of my mishap on Covenant Ridge. (Her husband, whom I never met, was also a healer in the tradition of his in-laws' family. He was serving a five-year missionary stint in Anagaia at the time of the persecution; he was one of those who never returned.) Fairfield had a half brother Rufous. Rufous had been born with a birth defect that caused him to limp badly. The deceased father of these brothers had been a physician of some renoun. In his time, Prosper of Ravenswing was said to have healing skills equal to the great Shiningsea (whom most people remember only for her epic poetry). Cherish had childhood memories of her great-grandfather, and I'm sure she had been inspired by his example. According to the family story, Prosper had taken his family to live in Tramont where he had gone to train local doctors. While there, his wife was stricken with cholera and died. Two years later, Prosper remarried a Tramontese woman, and the family had moved back to Ravenswing. That second wife, Beryl, was still alive when I moved there, a remarkably spirited woman of 102 years. It was not so much her age that was remarkable (centenarians are quite common in Esperia), but also her race. It was no small coincidence that I had chosen the one stead in the valley where another white person was already living. Her one son, Rufous, had reddish hair that justified his name; yet he had the broader nose and full lips which characterize the hybrid Esperians. He was a chemical engineer at the local soluble cellulose plant, doing research for the Alternative Fibres Project. Rufous' wife, Lily, had been only nineteen when their first child was born—that's considered very young here. That child, Slate, was now married to Autumn, a woman from Stubs Pond in the

Broadlea. Her birth stead was neighbour to one where I stayed a couple times; in fact, my dulcitar was made by a distant kinsman of hers. Slate and Autumn were childless, not by choice.

Slate had a younger sister, Rowan, who was very artistic; in fact she helped me continue with the drawing lessons I had begun with Teal at Stonesthrow. A curious thing about Rowan and her husband, Rampion, was that they were both born and raised at Ravenswing, though in no way related. They had a four-year-old son, Scoter. Rampion also had a younger cousin, Ember, who had come to live there as a teenager because her parents were divorced and she was unhappy at that stead.

Now Rampion's mother, Clarity, was also born and raised at Ravenswing—in fact her lineage goes back to the very founding of the stead in the second century. As I understand it, Clarity's parents moved away long ago after a falling-out with the household. Their daughter either chose to stay, or perhaps moved back—I never asked which. Anyway, she and her husband Reed had another son, Ilex. He in turn had two daughters, but his wife had died of childbirth complications with the second. The daughters, Linnet and Willow, were eight and twelve respectively. Willow idolized Cherish and tagged around after her whenever possible.

There is still another partial lineage to be mentioned: old Bower was cousin several times removed to Clarity and, like her, had very deep roots at Ravenswing. This ninety-year-old widower was slow-moving but still pretty capable. In fact, he was steward of the flowers. In his many years he had acquired quite a colour assortment of iris and had developed several new varieties of his own. He had one daughter, Grace, who was married to Bidewell; I usually chose to avoid them. They had a daughter, Quail, in her early thirties. She was in charge of the stead's soy-paste enterprise. She had a thirteen-year-old son named Larch. At first I was under the impression Quail was a widow, but I later found out that she was divorced. I was interested to learn that her ex-husband's parents, Greybirch and Ravine, continued to live there, although their son had remarried and moved to another fair while Quail remained very close to her in-laws.

The only other steadmate to mention is Jay. He was not in any way related to anyone else at Ravenswing. He came fom Cleave Tanner's Will and was at Ravenswing for essentially the same reason I was: he liked it there. He was twenty-eight. It was rumoured that he was sweet on Cherish's cousin Monarda, who lived at a neighbouring stead. But if so, nothing ever came of it; at this writing, he is still single.

The reason I remember all those people's ages and relationships is that soon after joining the household, I made myself a list and lineage tree so I could keep them all straight. But it was of limited use; it wasn't long before new babies were born and old folks died, new members married in or just moved in while others left for the same reasons. A stead is like that; the place is never sold. People come, and people go, but the flow of stead life continues as it has for centuries. Many of the steadmates I loved dearly, some were less than lovable, but steadmates all the same. It's just the way it is here.

*   *   *   *   *   *   *

For a couple weeks after my arrival, one snowstorm after another continued to dump snow into the narrow basin of Wisewoman Brook. It seemed like I spent half of my working hours pulling the snow roller, though in fact I spent plenty of time studying and doing other work. The entire household was of the opinion that I should continue my education. No one seemed to have a lot of spare time to tutor me, nor was it necessary. By now, I spoke rather fluent Mok, so I was sent down to the regular bannerschool even though I was older than most of the other students.

Whenever I wasn't in class, I had various opportunities to work. There was almost always a crew working in the woodlot, and occasionally I could work with Herald down at the tool-handle factory. And of course, there was always plenty of household work to be done—just cooking meals for such a crowd required at least three people in the kitchen.

Working in the woods was a new experience for me. Where I come from, wood is only used for fuel—there's rarely anything big enough to be used for lumber. Esperian forestry, like everything else here, is very complicated, as I learned one day when I joined Rampion's crew. This part of the woodlot was a more or less natural forest; that is to say, trees came up wherever they seeded themselves, a mix of species and ages. Some of the trees were either overmature or injured or too crowded. Rampion put Cherish and me on opposite ends of a crosscut saw and showed us where to cut each of the trees which the others had felled.

"The ash will all go to the handle-mill, if it's over five inches and straight. I've marked the lengths with chalk. Smaller than that goes for firewood or charcoal. Pile that over there. That big beech will go to the bowl-turners, but for now, cut it five feet long, and they can size it at the mill when it's cured. Same with the yellow birch, but pile the brush separately so the chips can be distilled for oil."

He gave us a lot more specifications: crotch-sections were to be left intact and hand-cut later in a pit saw. They were very valuable for laying the keels of ships. Fir logs would be milled into boards, and shorter pieces would be ground for paper. Even the small tops would be limbed and used in the garden for bean poles and trellises.

It was too much for me to keep straight, so I just got on the end of a saw and let my partner (Cherish) make the decisions.

*   *   *   *   *   *   *

For several years before my arrival in the Wisewoman Valley, a major construction project had been progressing, albeit at snail's pace. This was the railroad that was eventually to reach from Evenswap to Hanging Bridge. In almost a decade it had been completed only as far as Navestock bannerhouse. Ironically, it was a lack of resources that hampered the work. Although all three of the valley's banners were quite prosperous, they had persisted in sending a disproportionate amount of their wealth off to support foreign missions and the various projects of the Vision Fulfillment Commission. There was a vocal faction which contended that this investment in infrastructure would only increase their productivity, and thus enable them to support such projects even more. It had been a hard sell, but now the plan was finding vociferous advocates *outside* the valley. The VFC itself had made a strong argument that such a railroad would be a vital strategic asset in the event of an invasion. The nation was eager to throw lots of resources our way if we would just step up the pace of construction.

Even though Ravenswing's own heavy transport needs were largely filled—or perhaps because of that—we were eager to help in extending the main line upstream. Two or three of our household were regularly part of the rail crew, and we had contributed quite a lot of oak for the rails.

There was, however, a shortage of chestnut for crossties. This tough, rot-resistant wood was always in demand, and with similar projects elsewhere boosting the demand, the price for large logs was through the roof. Now Ravenswing had several rows of chestnuts, and one of those rows was of the old kind, which have to be inoculated occasionally with a subvirulent fungus to keep the trees from succumbing to the blight. These trees, eighteen in all, were old and enormous, far too big to reach around. In fact, they were ailing, and their nut production was declining so that another row of resistant young trees had already been planted to replace them. We would have kept those old ones a few more years, but in view of the pressing need, it was decided that they should be cut.

The felling had already been done when I moved there, but I helped a bit with sawing the trunks and limbs to length. It was like sawing bone—we had to keep the blade very keen. When cut to five-foot lengths, we rived the logs with mauls and gluts (also made of chestnut) into the approximate size. Then we used the windmill cable to drag them through the snow to our spur line. Loaded onto a flatcar, they'd be eased down the track alongside Thunder Rill to the main line where others would hew them into final shape. The trees were so huge that even some of the limb pieces could also be cleft and made into sleepers.

In all, Ravenswing's single contribution enabled the line to be extended almost three-quarters of a mile farther. It garnered enormous prestige for Ravenswing and just incidentally, nearly doubled our household income for that year.

Chapter 53

The possibility of invasion was on everyone's mind in those days, and Esperia was busy cultivating its ties with the other Steward states and with Borealia, our neighbour to the northeast. Ever since the *Dauntless* incident and our continued supplying of the Coquinese rebels, many assumed that the Olotal would feel there was nothing to be gained by continued peace with tiny Esperia. But it appeared that Hewn had spoken truly when he said Blaze II would not dare to attack, at least not yet.

Be that as it may, citizens of all ages, male and female, continued to flock to training sessions of every kind. There was archery and crossbow practice, martial arts, winter-survival skills. Mass meetings discussed mobilization/evacuation strategies, supply logistics, contingency plans. I started going to training sessions myself. Although no one ever said so, I supposed there must be some who questioned my loyalty. Anyway, I just wanted to.

I came home from one of these training sessions to find we had company. He was a couple years older then me and came from somewhere in the Calendar Hills. A very likable fellow I thought, and obviously Cherish thought so too. His name was Wells, and she greeted him warmly. It became clear she was the main cause of his visit, although he was on intimate terms with the whole family. I put two and two together and thought it made four, yet whenever he got a bit demonstrative with his affection, she would push him away. That part shouldn't surprise me too much since she had, after all, expressed a disinterest in pairing. Whenever Wells was around, she usually took care to involve me in their conversations or activities. That made me nervous; as much as I enjoyed being with her, I didn't want her to see me as an obligation, someone who had to be included in everything. Or at least I didn't think I wanted that. Sometimes she would act kind of shiny with him, and then I would seek some excuse to leave. Inexplicably, that seemed to irritate Cherish, though I was merely trying to give her some privacy!

All this vacillation must have been really frustrating to Wells, but he seemed to take it in stride. I feared he might see me as a rival, but once when I was chatting with him in Cherish's absence, he told me that they had some kind of "understanding." I really liked the guy; it was easy to see what Cherish saw in him. I was happy for her. The only thing that bothered me was that I was *jealous*. There it was; I had tried to ignore it, but Wells made me acknowledge it, if only to myself. I was sorely vexed with myself for such feelings. Was I not still in love with Fawn? What if the impossible were to happen and we got back together? A good thing, I told myself, if Cherish had a beau—at least one of us knew what they wanted!

The last night of Wells's stay, the thermometer dropped low, yet the first day of the week warmed very quickly—coatless weather—followed by another freezing night, and another day so bright and warm the paths were speckled with bluish snow-fleas. This was the long-expected signal that the sweet sap was rising in the maples. A large crew—fully a dozen—donned snowshoes and slogged up to the sap-berth with drills and elder spiles and wooden buckets. I helped out awhile until Herald summoned me down to the sugarhouse to assist him. A large part of the boiling is done by huge solar reflectors, and he feared the frame had shifted a bit over the winter and might not be properly focused. One by one, I would unmask the six-inch-by-six-inch mirrors and adjust their angle with a setscrew until each one shone on the proper point on a coil of pipe, as Herald directed me. When we were done, the bright sunlight blazed off from a hundred square feet of reflecting surface onto four square feet of water-filled tubing. When we opened the faucet, a burst of live steam testified to the power of the concentrated beam. It was good that the reflector array and its target were several feet above the ground; if you passed in front of it, even ten feet away from the focal point, you could be badly burned. Now we were ready; as soon as the sap began to pour in, we would drain off the water and begin to boil sap instead. It is convenient that the sap flow is greatest on bright sunny days. The fluid was already at a rolling boil when it hit the pan, and except for cloudy days, the wood fire was mainly needed to finish it off. We busied ourselves collecting the buckets that were nearby the sugarhouse, but by midafternoon, the gathering crew was bringing in the new sap in a sled-mounted tank. Predictably, Cherish had appointed herself to the team. This first day of the season, the hauling trail was not well broken, and the breeze was too light for cable power. They were all making heavy weather of it, none more than Cherish, yet she complained least. I knew better than to discuss it with her, but when they had gone back for more, I asked Herald, "What is it with Cherish? As fit as she is, she seems to get winded easily, and it takes her longer to regain her breath."

Herald was up on "the brow," a platform from which one could dump the sap directly into the raised holding tank.

"Oh that," he said with what seemed like a forced casualness. "Well, I guess she's her father's daughter."

"What's that supposed to mean?"

He set his bucket down and looked at me square. "You don't see me flailing around up there in the deep snow, do you?"

"So?"

"Heart murmur."

"And what's that?"

"A valve that doesn't close just right. When your heart doesn't pump efficiently, you don't get enough oxygen. Makes you tired, breathless. Cherish seems to have the same problem, but not so bad . . . yet."

"But couldn't it . . . harm her to work it so hard?"

"I'm not sure. In my case, it just slows me down, tells me when to ease up. But you know Cherish, no one tells her when to ease up. Maybe she can work around it. Hard to say."

I wanted to know more, but Herald wasn't very forthcoming, perhaps because he had already said more than his daughter would have wished.

*   *   *   *   *   *   *

On windy days, when conditions weren't right for a full flow of sap, some of us would go up into the woods with the chipper-shredder and shred up the piles of brush which were emerging from the fast-melting snow. The cable from the upper windmill snaked around the woodlot on a trunk-road, and at any fixed pulley, one could loop a side-cable off from that pulley to another, thus delivering power to almost anywhere you needed it. The same cable that shredded the brush would later tow a sled, hauling those chips to the cropland. But it was noisy—oh, what a racket it made! Those of us working close to it had to wear ear- and eye-protectors at all times.

One morning toward the end of sapping, we were finishing off brush-piles in anticipation of the crop season. The snow had all gone slushy, and not too much of it at that. As I gathered armloads of branches and dragged them to the chipper, I found my thoughts turning toward Wren and the *Come-What-May*. Surely they would be taking to the water about now, but who was aboard? A letter from Myrica had informed me that Marten was staying ashore. Wren's cousin? We had discussed whether a third crewmember was really essential for the smaller boat, and the consensus had been that the added flexibility was worth it. Oh well, it wasn't any of my business anymore.

Just then I happen to look up from my reverie and was startled at what I saw. I was just below the border of the Sacred Groves where a high laid stone wall marked the boundary between manicured woodlot and untended wilderness. Standing atop the wall was an old man I had never seen before. Not that he looked feeble—far from it. He was moderate in height and looked as strong and supple as a hazel whip. But he had a forked white beard that lay broad and long on his quilted overcoat. His face was so creased and weathered that one could imagine he had never slept within walls.

He had emerged from one of those clumps of fir that spring up around the corpse of a fallen hardwood. Evidently he was drawn by the clatter of our machine, for he stood there awhile, looking down at it. He did not notice me far off to his right, and I wondered at first if he were lost or something. Where had he come from? Where could he live? I had met most of our neighbours. Behind him lay hundreds of square miles of mountain wilderness devoid of roads, houses, or even trails. I called out to him, but my voice was smothered in the din of the chipper. That racket seemed to annoy the old man, for he scowled at it. Then looking down at the wall beneath him, he shrugged and disappeared back into the thicket. I started to follow him then bethought myself to ask my workmates first. The last time I had pursued a helpless-looking person through the wilds, it had resulted in the death of my mother. Running down to Rampion, I tapped him on the shoulder. After he pulled aside his ear guards, I told him what I had seen.

"Ah, that would be Candid. He was probably checking up on us. No need to worry—he's far safer up there than you or I would be."

I could see he was eager to resume his work, and since I was assured that all was well, I did the same. But as we walked back to the house that evening, I brought it up again.

"You see, he's the Keeper of the Sacred Groves for this area. A loner, for the most part, as many of them are. I mean, he's friendly enough—he drops by to visit once in a great while and can be quite jolly when he does. He's full of endless stories about wild animals. He likes people—he just seems to prefer his lonely mountaintops even better. I believe he had some bad times in his younger years and he finds solace there. He's really a remarkable follow, lives for weeks on end just eating what he finds in there or nothing at all."

"But what exactly does he do?"

"Good question. I'm not exactly sure. His only real job is to 'keep' the wilderness: to patrol it and make sure no one violates it. Not so difficult, I suppose, since no one would dream of violating them—it's a really big taboo. But I know he's always busy with something in there. He calls it 'just looking around,' whatever that means. He sure does get around though. You saw him here today, but tomorrow he is just as likely to show up on the Weasel River somewheres. As big as that area is, he knows it better than you or I know the stead yard. If an old tree blows over or a coyote kills a deer, he'll know about it within the week."

I was deeply fascinated with this steward of the wilderness, not only with the person himself, but with the idea. I was to discover later that Rampion had a slightly skewed idea of the man and his activities, but he got it about right. I hoped to catch sight of this Candid again, perhaps even make his acquaintance, but to my knowledge, he did not appear again that spring.

*　*　*　*　*　*　*

According to Esperian law (which is to say, tradition), a sojourner may not become a full stead member for at least a year, for a foreigner usually much longer. But that in no way made me feel that I didn't belong at Ravenswing. Although I had no formal vote in household affairs, no communal decision was ever made without consulting my views. Here it was not assumed that I would be moving on soon. As far as I was concerned, I had definitely found my home, a place I could strike root. I could only look forward to the day I could cease to be known as Yaro Seekings and become Yaro of Ravenswing.

Resolving this issue in my life had only complicated another one: my relationship with Cherish. I had begun to realize that my feelings for her went beyond friendship while I still had not come to terms with my separation from Fawn. And even if Fawn were not part of the picture, as anyone else might reasonably assume, Cherish also seemed to have some commitments of her own although I wasn't quite clear what those were. The fact was that she viewed me as a friend, no more. If I now took the role of a suitor, would she not feel shocked, betrayed even? Perhaps wish I hadn't come there? The best I could do was hide my feelings, rejoice in her happiness, and give her whatever space she needed.

Herald and I had grown very close as we found other shared interests. We continued our incessant brainstorming over "the Anagaian problem." We hatched countless schemes for business ventures, which might somehow inoculate the Anagaian mindset with sustainable, if not Esperian, values. We realized, of course, that such ideas were pure fantasy. Imperial law, to say nothing of popular prejudice, made Steward commercial enterprises virtually impossible, except on terms which nullified their social impact. But Herald insisted that such conditions might not always prevail. Great changes were part of history, he said, and doubtless part of the future. Nevertheless, one could envision, one could ask "what if?" and we most certainly did.

On the day-to-day level, I had come to appreciate the emphasis on permacrops, which were Herald's principal stewardship. The idea of producing staple human foods without ploughing the soil appealed to me enormously. This included several specialties, most of which were delegated to others. The hazelnuts had been Rufous's responsibility, but he also had the currants and gooseberries. With his age and infirmity, these were becoming a burden, so I was asked to take over the hazels. I took great pride in the assignment, which might seem like a minor one, but considering that hazels are such an important item in the Esperian diet, I felt a great deal of trust was being put in me.

That crop alone occupied the equivalent of one and a half acres. I say *alone*, though in fact, hazels are rarely planted alone but in combination with other crops, and I say *equivalent* because this intensive intercropping makes it difficult or impossible to calculate what portion of the space is occupied by any one component. What is clearly calculable is that the total food production per acre from these overlapping crops is much greater than it would be from those same crops planted separately.

The cultivation, or should I say noncultivation, of hazels requires mainly the pruning and thinning of suckers, mulching with leaves or chips, and the harvest and processing of the nuts. At critical periods, I could call on steadmates to help out. At other times, when the hazels were taking care of themselves, I might be recruited to help with someone else's stewardship. My responsibility was to see that the necessary work got done in a timely fashion.

I regularly attended the Hazel Breeders Club. Although they focused on improvement of that crop through selective crossing of promising types, there was also a lot of discussion of other aspects: control of circulio worm, new pruning techniques, cracking-machine design, etc. Our regional chapter met at Fortyfold, and I attended every meeting I could.

I also continued my membership in the Archaeological Society, but with the nearest chapter meeting down at Stoutbridge, it was much more ado to get there, so I attended only occasionally. Two big topics seemed to dominate the discussion at those meetings. One was the continuing hunt for new insights into the Founding Era, given a new impetus by the discoveries of what were then being referred to as the J. L. diaries. The fact that I had actually seen them firsthand myself and read the initial draught translations made me a minor celebrity at the meetings. Embarrassing, really, since the group included several bona fide scholars who had been unable to gain access to the originals. It made me realize what powerful strings Orris must have pulled to get me up there, and how wasted it all was on me.

The other hot topic at our meetings was the recent discovery of the so-called Harrowyards Midden, a wooded knoll which was nothing more than ancient garbage, a vast dump from the pre-Calamity period. The incredible thing about the landfill site was the degree of preservation in that artificial anaerobic environment: readable papers, uncorroded metal, and synthetic materials which have been virtually unknown for centuries. In fact, the excavation leading to its discovery was prompted not by archaeological interest, but by concerns that wells in the area continued to contain bizarre toxins, centuries after such substances had ceased to be produced. Aside from its scientific interest, there was also great hope that the site might be "mined," particularly for glass and semiprecious metals like aluminum.

I also made a friend at a nearby stead who was willing to give me dulcitar lessons. I already had a tiny modicum of ability, but I was eager to develop it. After all, I'd once lied to Cherish that I was already learning to play, and I didn't want to look too foolish.

I got to be around her a lot now. When I wasn't on her garden crew, I was usually pruning the hazels and berry bushes that bordered her vegetable terraces. We saw a lot of each other, but I was careful not to get into her space too much. She, in turn, acted a bit more aloof than before, almost cool at times. Yet when I tried to avoid her out of respect, she seemed hurt—I didn't know what to make of it.

Cherish had a little shadow, Willow that is, who absolutely adored her. Perhaps because Willow had few memories of her own late mother or perhaps because she was herself an elder sister, she viewed Cherish as a role model; and in fact, she could hardly have chosen better. She dogged her every step and hung on her every word.

One afternoon as I was spreading chips on the hazel rows, Willow was hanging around me, only because Cherish had been called away suddenly to help with a birthing. We chatted a bit about the neighbour who was in labour, and I discovered that Willow was quite a little gossip.

"She's such a bubblehead, you know. I don't know why she ever got knocked up by him."

"Well, I don't think that has too much to do with how bright you are. And anyway, they're married, aren't they?"

"They say they are. But he's such a worm—would you believe, he still flirts with other girls. Cherish says people should grow up more before they do that boy-girl stuff.

She says if you give your heart away too soon, you can mess up the whole rest of your life. Like Liatris."

"I don't know that story, Willow, and Liatris might not like you to tell it."

"Well, anyway, I know Cherish would never make that mistake. She's keeping her heart to herself until the perfect person comes along. That's what I'm going to do."

"An excellent idea. But what about Wells? You don't think he's the perfect person?"

"Oh, I like Wells a lot. He's real nice. But I don't know . . . I mean, Cherish never tells me stuff like that. But she did tell me something once . . ."

"Are you sure you ought to be telling me all this?"

"Well, it's nobody we know. But if you don't want to hear . . ."

"So what did she tell you?"

"Well, she came back from one of her visits to her great-aunt's back in the Calendar Hills. And she said she'd just met the most interesting person, someone who made other guys seem boring. She was kind of excited, like she doesn't usually get about boys."

"Ah well, that would be Wells, don't you see? He's from back there, and he fits that."

"Yeah. I suppose so."

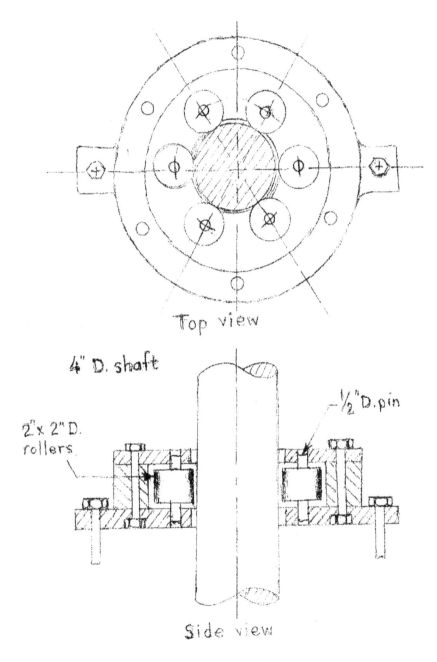

Top view

4" D. shaft

2"x 2"D. rollers

½"D. pin

Side view

Windmill shaft bearing

Chapter 54

To grasp the scale and complexity of Ravenswing's agricultural enterprise, one must consider that this household of thirty-two mouths required each year at least two and a half tons of grain alone. And that was only because it was supplemented with dried chestnuts and sweet acorns along with many bushels of dried peas, beans, soy, favas, and other pulses. Nor does it include the mountains of vegetables and fruits that filled the cellar. All this production required the most attentive management of resources: labour, seed, water, and fertility—all must be applied at the right time. Although everyone in the household had some part in food production, none were full-time farmers. We all had some other specialty (or many) which competed for our attention. The solution was intelligent planning. For as all the world knows, Esperians are skilled cultivators of the highest degree. For centuries, they have been reinvesting themselves in their land: building terraces, removing stones (and often returning them to the soil as rock-dust), breeding superior crop varieties for specific conditions, controlling the flow of water, and managing the forests for production of soil-building material. All this has created an agricultural system which is stable, efficient, and enormously productive.

For several weeks after the snow left, nearly everyone in the valley was occupied with planting. Luckily, the permacrops required little attention at this time, but grain-sowing was a major operation. Some steads use a small version of a mouldboard plough drawn by teams of several people, but most prefer to use a type of heavy broadhoe, or mattock. This requires more people, but it does a better job of making a friable, weed-free seedbed. I knew that soil would not be left bare for long. As soon as the soil was warm and the plants were above ground, a new mulch would be applied. Even close-spaced barley and durum would get a light covering of shredded maple leaves to retain moisture and repress weeds. For many vegetable crops, they don't turn the soil at all but simply part the existing mulch to plant the seeds. More mulch is added during the season so that when the piece is rotated into grain the following year, the rotting debris has left the soil incredibly rich and mellow. I could see why foxes and skunks were so appreciated here: without them, the thick mulch would be overrun with mice and moles.

Cherish's stewardship was particularly complicated. Such a diverse array of vegetable crops I had never seen. Moreover, those crops overlapped into Herald's permacrops and Lily's field crops. For example, squash and pepita vines were allowed to run into my hazels since they would be frost-killed by nutting-time, and some of Cherish's early vegetables would be out in time for Lily to sow winter wheat there. As in the woodlot, nothing was simple, and everyone seemed to like it that way.

I was pleased to see among Cherish's seed inventory a number of varieties which she had bought from me only the year before, improved strains from the Cinderfield Research Station. For the most part, our seed was propagated right on the stead with careful attention to maintaining true type. This is pretty much the case at every stead in the country with a result that there is a dazzling amount of regional variability, each neighbourhood having its own strains which are uniquely adapted to that niche. For example, we grew at least a dozen different kinds of potatoes at Ravenswing, including rough-skin bakers, yellow-fleshed fingerlings, red potatoes, blue potatoes, lumpy potatoes so nearly black it is hard to see them in the moist humusy soil. There was a kind of soup-pea we planted in the spring wheat, another taller kind we planted in the oats, and still another—a huge fat, speckled brown pea—that we grew by itself on alder brush trellis. To use any of these pea types in the other context just wouldn't work; it was that carefully managed.

Springtime is also the season of full mill wheels, and those few who could be spared worked at the sawmill or the turnery. Shaping and finishing could be done at a more convenient season, but rough-milling needed the power of the spring freshet. On rainy days, I sometimes worked at my own new specialty: assembling windmill bearings. It was a careful bit of work, laminating three layers of seasoned hardwood into a finished bearing that could hold a windmill shaft in place as it turned. Rather than describe it in detail, I enclose a cutaway drawing for clarification (not that anyone cares, but because I'm proud of them). I made very many of them, and to my knowledge none of my bearings ever came back damaged by normal use.

*　　*　　*　　*　　*　　*　　*

There is a special garden at Ravenswing, as at every stead, and it is called a memorial garden. It serves as a cemetery for the stead's deceased members. That is, for their ashes, I should say, since cremation is universal here. There are no graves as such, only inscribed marker stones scattered among the perennial flowers and ornamental bushes. Although Ravenswing's memorial garden is less than a quarter acre, the remains of twelve generations are interred or spread there. The garden abuts and nearly surrounds the steadhouse itself, yet no one seems to have any qualms about living so close to their departed loved ones. Indeed, several stone benches and picnic tables are set up there, and in warm weather, the household often chooses to take the midday meal in the open air amid fragrant beauty and reminders of those whose memory they treasure.

In the last week of spring, we were all deeply saddened when Beryl died rather suddenly following a bout of pneumonia. I had only known her a few months, but in that time, I had grown to love her as much as the rest did. She was a lovely person, cheerful and brave-spirited even in her last hours. It had been fifty years since she had come to the Wisewoman Valley as the white wife of a returning missionary doctor. Her five descendents all still live at Ravenswing, and all of them seem as dedicated to the Vision as any native-born Steward.

*　*　*　*　*　*　*

In the course of my first season as an Esperian farmer, I learned things I never dreamed existed: about mycorhizae and actinomycetes, cation exchange, and beneficial insects. I came to recognize specific diseases and pest damage. I acquired specific skills like bud-grafting and was exposed to big concepts like "bioefficiency."

That last one came up one late spring day when a small crew of us was working in the upper orchard. The grass had recently been mown and hauled off to make compost. At the sides of the piece lay great piles of woody chips (they call them ramial chips) which had been made from last year's apple prunings, plus brush-piles in the nearby forest. Having sat there a whole year, the chips were blackened with decay and festooned with a downy white mold. We were there with wheelbarrows and dung forks, spreading the chips on the hay stubble. Actually, *spreading* isn't quite the right word because we were very careful to *not* strew the chips evenly. Rather we would drop a forkful of the mouldy matted stuff in one spot then another forkful a couple feet away. Wherever we had been, the sod looked like the pockmarked face of a measly kid. I couldn't imagine why we were doing this.

Cherish was with us today, not as steward, but a mere worker like me with the understanding that on the morrow, we'd be working for her in the vegetable garden. Whenever I had questions, I usually asked her, not only because of her incredible knowledge of all this stuff, but also because she was patient with my ignorance. I understood clearly that the chips a fertilizer, but this part didn't make sense.

"If we're trying to fertilize the hayfield," I asked, "then why did we just remove all the grass, which also adds fertility?"

"Oh, I see what you mean," she answered after a moment's thoughts. "Well, you see, the chips are much more bioefficient."

"What does that mean?"

"Well now, let me think. Back in your garden in Umberlands, you used animal manure, right?"

"When I could get it, certainly, but that was rare. Mostly I made do with weeds and tree leaves that no one else wanted. I only knew to do that from being at the orphanage."

"Exactly, because animal manure, including human manure, is very rich. But as you apparently discovered, weeds and grass and leaves also contain plenty of fertility, but in a less concentrated form. So do these chips. The thing is, did you ever consider how much fertility went into *producing* that fertility?"

"No, I just used what I had on hand."

"Understandably. But when you're dealing with a whole system instead of just a garden, you want to look at all the parts in perspective, and see who's really pulling their weight. Now the richness in animal manure came from the food the animal ate, minus a great deal that was destroyed in the animal's life processes. In terms of soil fertility, it's a net loss."

"Ah, so when we use the grass more directly to fertilize our gardens, it's less wasteful or more—what's that word?—*bioefficient*."

"Exactly, but it doesn't stop there. Grass is more bioefficient than any animal manure, but many plants are way ahead of grass. Maple trees, for instance."

"Really? How can you know that?"

"Well, look at any place on the planet where grassland is the climax ecosystem: the Prairie Federation, for example. The ecosystem stops evolving at grass for one reason only: lack of water. Add water to any true prairie, and it will soon evolve to forest."

"But why?"

"Why not? Just think of it: given enough water, forest trees can reach out to the sky with millions of horizontal green surfaces to catch every bit of sunlight. And tree roots are more aggressive collectors of deep-lying minerals. Nothing else would be able to mine those soluble nutrients and pump them up to the biosphere—the land of the living. By comparison, grass is downright wimpy. The reason that mixed hardwood forests are the climax cover for so much of the world is because they're the most evolved—nothing can compete with them."

"Then how come grasses and weeds grow where a tree blows over or where there has been a fire?"

"Because it's a wound site. When you cut yourself, do you start worrying about your long-term nutrition? Of course not, you say, 'Give me a bandage quick!' Stop the bleeding, worry about efficiency later. In the long run, weeds and grasses are merely bandage species. So are most of our garden crops, which were bred from those weeds and grasses."

"So we humans aren't very bioefficient?"

"None of us. But some less than others. When we eat from animals, we are most inefficient of all. If we could eat just tree crops, we'd be doing real well but our stomachs are too used to eating those domesticated succulent weeds and grass seeds that we've had for so long. Maybe the best we can do is to use forest stuff as the fertility base for all the other food."

"I'm starting to get it. But then, why not use only forest stuff for fertilizer, instead of composting all that grass and weeds, which is less bioefficient?"

"Well, we have the grass and weeds anyway, since we can't garden right up to the edge of the forest. And besides, those bandage species are quicker to decay and release their fertility. In fact, they help the chips decompose faster. Our garden crops have generally evolved in grassland soils, not forest soils which are cooler, more acidic, and fungal. They seem to do best in the mixed habitat we've created, but at least we can maximize the forest's role in maintaining the fertility of that system."

"Wow, that's quite a lot to get my head around. But it still doesn't answer this: why are we making these little chip-humps instead of spreading them evenly?"

"Because here we're using it less as a fertilizer than as a mulch. It's just one of the many ways we use chips. What will happen here is that the sod beneath the chips will be partly killed out. As it decays, the sod around it will reinvade the decaying chips, making rings of richer and lusher grass. That's the effect of any mulch, regardless of its inherent fertility. Those rings will expand inward and outward, coalescing until the whole piece is much lusher. The important thing is that the result—increased grass—will be significantly greater than the fertility value of the chips which created it. In effect, we are parlaying something we have in abundance for something that has relatively more direct value. We're spinning gold thread out of straw."

I was incredulous. "So that means we're eating directly from the forest with the chestnuts and other tree foods, then we' re eating the trees indirectly when we compost leaves and chips for the crops, and now we're using the forest again to feed the grass that feeds the crops that feed us."

"Isn't it lovely?" She smiled as she turned to toss another forkful of chips.

*   *   *   *   *   *   *

As spring progressed, I couldn't help notice that Wells didn't come to visit. I remarked on it once to Cherish, and her only comment was "He probably won't be coming to visit again."

I suddenly felt terrible, realizing how insensitive I'd been. "Why, I'm so sorry, Cherish! I hadn't realized . . . I hope I didn't . . ."

"You didn't do anything." She almost snapped at me, then more quietly, "You didn't do . . . anything."

Thank goodness, I though to myself; at least *I* wasn't part of her problem. At the same time, I was aware of a selfish part of me that was glad to have nothing interfere with our friendship. But it seemed that might be at the expense of her own happinesss, and I wasn't proud of that.

It didn't escape my attention that she continued to get mail from Wells. Not that I pried into her business, but there was no mistaking his sloppy writing on the addresses. I assumed she answered his letters, and one weekend, she even went back to the Calendar Hills.

*   *   *   *   *   *   *

One day when I was helping prepare the ground for sowing wheat, I was surprised and delighted to hear a familiar yell from across the field. It was Wren and Marten, and

I ran over to embrace them. They told me they were on *Come-What-May*, with Wren's cousin as a third hand. They had tied up down at Evenswap and walked all the way to Ravenswing to see me.

"But I thought you were staying ashore this year," I said to Marten.

"A last-minute change, just like last year," he grinned. "But only for a few weeks. I'm just filling in until the wedding."

"The wedding? I hadn't heard you were getting married!"

Marten rolled his eyes upward and shook his head while pointing at Wren's sheepish smirk.

"I brought your invitation," he confirmed. "Hope you can make it."

"But who?" I demanded as I catalogued the myriad possibilities.

"You remember that time in the Gentian Locks, we invited those girls in out of the rain?"

"Yes, and you were swapping tall tales with that . . . Wren, are you serious?"

"Yep. Two people can insult each other just so much without getting intimate. Pachysandra's moving down to Pierstead tomorrow. In a couple weeks, she'll join us on *Come-What-May*. I'll bring her around so you can meet her again before the wedding."

"And so you won't leave the river after all?"

"Never. She'll just have to swap a barge for a tramp, which is hardly a comedown, the way I figure it."

"And your cousin, won't he feel strange, living in such close quarters with you two?"

"Won't 'she,' you mean. She says she'll manage fine. If you recall, one of us often slept ashore anyway."

Cherish was working nearby, so I introduced them to her and others of the workgang. It was a totally ordinary meeting, yet I felt nervous about all the things no one was saying. I walked them down as far as the house where they also met Haven, who forced a loaf of fresh-baked bread on them. When they were gone, I went back up to the wheatfield, feeling a trifle nonplussed.

Married? Just like that? I thought about Wren and that barge girl . . . Pachysandra? Yes, I could just imagine them being a perfect couple, though I never would have guessed so before the fact. Back in line next to Cherish, I continued chopping.

"What are you chuckling about?" she pried.

"Oh, just Wren and that girl. I mean, who would have thought?"

"Not you, obviously, but they seem to have thought."

"Yes, of course, it's just . . . I don't know. It's great that it works out that way for some people."

Cherish said nothing, just chopped a little faster as we buried the old residue to make way for new growth.

* * * * * * *

The banner of Navestock numbered 1,310 occupants, living on a little more than eight square miles. That's almost exactly one person for every four acres, which is very much less than the average population density of the whole country. In the early days, this was the most populous section of the country—after all, it's where it all began. But as other regions developed, the Upper Laughingwater lagged behind, perhaps due to the paucity of transport infrastructure. Not to say that it was ever depopulated, but the rest of the nation outgrew it. By the time I arrived in Esperia this trend had begun to reverse and many people, especially on the crowded coast, began to view the Sanctuaries as the ideal place to settle.

Unlike Alga Island, Ravenswing had plenty of potential for expansion without depleting its precious forests. The house itself could hold another six or eight people without feeling crowded (at least to a people who were used to "scrunching up"), and of course, no additional fuel was needed. It wasn't even necessary to expand the gardens; Ravenswing was still at a point where new mouths did not require more cropland, just more work. Cherish insisted that our existing gardens were capable of even greater productivity, given more compost. That meant more leaves, more chips, more rock dust. Our woodlots could supply much more of those then we were using as yet. What was needed was labour—labour to rake and shred leaves, labour to chip brush, labour to turn and spread more compost—and presumably newcomers could provide more than enough labour to carry themselves.

Obviously, Ravenswing could have generated its own "newcomers" by having more babies. But to ignore the "two is enough" policy, when places like Alga were already overcrowded would've been seen as "dwelling in a Small House," and certainly no one wanted that.

Every single one of Navestock's fifty-three steads was a dealer in forest products of one form or other. Like everywhere else, the various enterprises were a maze of partnerships, co-ops, consortiums, stock companies, and every sort of ownership scheme imaginable. Perhaps the best way to portray this byzantine interlocking of enterprise is to describe those in which Ravenswing shared. A few small endeavors were completely in-house: we sold tempeh, soy paste, vinegar, and dried apples. Bower grew iris bulbs for sale. There was a tiny shop attached to the barn where someone, usually Herald, made rake teeth. With several other steads we co-owned the sawmill up at Rainbow Falls while we were partners with Withegate, Limbertwig, and Bastrill in running the turnery down at the millpond. There we made ladder rungs, handles, axles, and machine shafts; we provided much of the labour and material, and we owned the actual mill wheel, but the building and water rights belonged to Bastrill. We were also part of a cooperative furniture factory on the lower millpond, which made chairs and hardwood bowls mostly. We mostly supplied the beech and maple blanks for them and occasionally some labour.

Beside such "direct" business activity, we also owned stock shares in several toll canals, including both the Laughingwater and the Sundew, and a share in the lamp fluid plant and tar-works—that's where we sent our crude resin. Some years, we even bought shares in ships, or rather ship voyages. This usually was because we had supplied a significant part of the cargo and wished to invest rather than sell outright.

This diversity led to stable, yet flexible employment. If the turning-mill had produced more wheel spokes than were likely to be called for, they either shifted production to some other products or simply closed up shop for a while and went to work for someone else. No one had a monopoly on any facet of production, and there were no booms or busts.

Chapter 55

There was other news from Anagaia that summer of 549, which impacted me less directly, at least for the time being. The Olotal's armies were having some reverses in the Coquinas, after rolling up one victory after another. The islands had finally managed to ignore their differences and begun to mount a united defense. Most of the Coral Cays had been liberated, and temporarily the siege of Mace Harbour (the only remaining rebel port on Grand Coquina) had been lifted. This turnabout was indirectly the result of turmoil in the Palmetto Republic. That nation had been agitating for the removal of Anagaian troops from the enclave of Upper Tupelo, which had been occupied for the past eight years. At that time, most of the black population of that largely white enclave had fled to other parts of Palmetto. Having insured the "cultural integrity" of the enclave (each generation invents its own euphemisms for race policies), the Olotal now tried to annex it to the Empire much like his predecessors had done to Umberlands. What he had not counted on was the fierce resistance of the *white* inhabitants, most of whom preferred to work out their problems with a black majority government than to submit to the control of the Anagaian police state. Nevertheless, there was a small pro-Empire faction, and on their behalf more troops were sent in to quell the unrest and established a "protectorate," which would eventually become an "autonomous district" of the Empire, after the pattern of Umberlands and Tramont.

The upshot of it all was that military resources had to be withdrawn from the Coquinese theatre, just when those islands were beginning to get organized. There was rejoicing in Esperia, even though we knew the Coquinese gains were temporary. As soon as the Olotal's press gangs had swept through the slums of Anagaia, conscripting homeless teenagers, there would be new waves of recruits to throw at the palm-fringed beaches.

*   *   *   *   *   *   **

Back home at Ravenswing, we had accumulated enough extra oak and chestnut limbs to fill the charcoal pit. I helped with the initial firing, covering the huge mound with several inches of leaves and mud. Then while others tended the smouldering heap, I went back to mowing grass for the compost piles. We usually did this in teams, scything a series of swathes across the broad terraces while others raked the grass and carted it to the compost bins. There it was mixed with shredded leaves, chips, weeds, and threshing waste, and covered with a layer of pond muck or stone meal.

Meanwhile, after several days of seething in its oxygen-starved hole, the charcoal was finished and the heap opened. We scooped up the sooty chunks into hempen sacks and carted them down to the smithy, one of several in the fair which recycle scrap iron.

There was a brief lull before the winter wheat was ripe, and I requested permission to leave for a few days on an adventure of my own. Ever since seeing the old man on the snowy ridge, I had nurtured a fantasy of meeting him and seeing something of his domain.

Although they told me how to find his cabin, I realized the chances of finding him there would be slim at that season. If he were off "on patrol," it would be impossible to locate him in that huge area of unbroken wilderness, but I went up anyway, up the steep track that leads over Antler Ridge to Calliope Falls in the next valley. His tiny cabin was set back from the narrow road, just under the brow of the ridge. There was hardly any clearing; an aged yellow birch towered over the woodshed, and in the yard a gnarled apple tree stood in need of pruning. Like the Archivists, he was subsidized by the society at large, but one could see at a glance that his upkeep was not setting anyone back very much. As I neared the cabin, a ring of splitting wood told me I had lucked out: someone was home.

He looked quite surprised to see me, or rather to see anybody at all. I had so expected to find him not at home that I was rather at a loss to explain myself. I introduced myself clumsily, mentioning that I had seen him in the woods one day last spring. He shrugged noncommittally as if to acknowledge that such an event was hardly remarkable—he was after all the Keeper of the Sacred Groves.

"Since I came to this country a year ago, I've been trying very hard to understand this place, in order better to belong to it. Not just the people, you understand, but the land itself. I've traveled a good deal and seen much of what is to be seen, I think. Of the settled land, that is. But this, the Sacred Groves, that's quite something else, isn't it? I have seen that bit of it that borders our land at Ravenswing, but I'd like to explore farther into it, and I would like to do it with you. Not only because you know how to live in it, but because you can interpret it for me in ways no one else could. Would you be willing to take me?"

The old man sat down on his chopping block and ran his fingers through his tousled white hair.

"I have, from time to time, let friends accompany me on my walks," he replied tentatively. "The trouble is, all but a few of them don't last. Your average Esperian is used to his hot meals and snug house. That's not what the Sacred Groves are all about."

"I realize that," I persisted.

He sized me up for a moment. "You see, if you get worn out or lose interest, it's not as simple as just turning around and heading back home. You'd be hopelessly lost by yourself, so I'd have to break my rounds and escort you back, and that's no good. This is a busy time for me."

"I believe I could keep up, and I can guarantee I would not lose interest."

He shook his head brusquely at my tenacity.

"It's not for everyone, I tell you. No one may kindle fire in the Sacred Groves, so there is no hot food and sometimes no food at all. If it turns cold, so do you."

"I was a fugitive for many weeks. I slept outdoors with less than I'm wearing now and ate only an occasional raw sweetpotato. Even before that, I was used to being hungry. To be lost in this wilderness is better than to be poor in Anagaia."

He chuckled softly at this last.

Then he stood up and, without further reply, went on splitting his wood. I stood awkwardly by, wondering what kind of answer this was. After several minutes, he stopped and leaned his maul against the cabin wall. "Well, grab some of this and help me stow it inside. If I need to pack for two, you'd better give me a hand. I plan to leave right away."

In less than a half hour, we were packed and on our way. Everything I carried was borrowed from Candid: a linen canvas knapsack containing a spare shirt, a bowl, waxed paper packages of rye crispbread, and assorted dried fruits and vegetables. Between us, we also carried a hatchet, a knife, binoculars, a latex-impregnated tarp, and several notebooks. We carried no matches, even for emergencies.

I saw at once why he preferred to travel alone: despite his very advanced age, he moved through the woods like a deer, and sometimes it was all I could do to keep him in sight. He even made Hewn seem like a laggard. I had been used to the managed woodlots of Ravenswing where the ground was generally free of brush and blowdowns. In the Sacred Groves, there was no such neatness. Sometimes we passed through stands of towering maples and beaches whose arching crowns nearly blotted out the sunlight. Wherever the canopy admitted light to the forest floor, young saplings presented a nearly impenetrable thicket. At Candid's mile-eating pace, we proceeded up Antler Ridge. We were only a mile above the Fortyfold steads, and occasionally the ring of a woodcutters axe drifted up to us.

When Candid moved, he really moved, and when he stopped, he really stopped. Often after loping for a mile through dense old growth, he would halt by a tiny spring-fed pool and remain there for an hour, staring into its waters to find who-knows-what. He might scoop out a palmful of the seemingly clear liquid and examine it with a hand lens he carried in his pocket. Then he would jot a few words into one of his notebooks, and we'd be off again. At the head of Avalanche Brook, we came to a huge heap of stones. I didn't have to be told what it was; I knew we were in the vicinity of the Cairns massacre site, where one of the early Steward bands had been nearly annihilated in an ambush. Under this crude monument lay the bones of those victims. We each added a stone to the heap and continued on our way. Later we climbed into a pass called Steward's Notch where we settled in to spy over a series of beaver ponds that were the source of Wisewoman Brook. We spent the remaining hours of the long summer day crouched in a clump of bog laurel, and as the sun dropped behind Sentinel Mountain, I began to wonder when we were going to make camp. What I didn't realize was that we already had. Candid had laid out the rubberized tarp under us, to protect us from the damp spongy peat. Supper was as unceremonious as one can imagine; Candid allowed us each a single crispbread. For the rest of the meal, we foraged without even leaving the tarp. We simply reached over to the water's edge and pulled a few cattail shoots from the mud. At the base of each plant was a tender young pithy heart, not unpleasant to taste, yet hardly filling. Candid also pulled up the starchy rootstocks and rinsed them off. Chopping them into his bowl with some clean water, he mashed the whole thing then poured off the milky extract and drank it raw. I tried the same thing, and although it had a decidedly muddy flavour, it was more satisfying than the shoots. I was by no means sated, but food was clearly not a priority on Candid's list. As dusk deepened and the evening quiet grew, we could hear many smaller noises around us. A pair of shy muskrats fed almost at our feet, making a supper of the same cattails we had used. Candid had been taking notes furiously all day, not only of the beavers and muskrats, but of every living creature which frequented the Notch. Whether a majestic deer or tiny water strider, all were duly recorded in his notebooks. Not only their presence, but their number, size, apparent health, what they were eating, how they acted—it all mattered to Candid. Sometimes I helped by timing how many minutes a great blue heron spent feeding at one spot, or measuring the leaves of watershield.

When darkness came, we simply bent over some nearby willows and pulled half of the ground cloth up over them, making the very crudest of shelters. Of course the air was not very cold, but it served to keep the dew off us while we slept. I suppose I should say "while *I* slept"; as I dropped into a deep slumber, I was aware of Candid still sitting there, his eyes and ears straining to penetrate the secrets of the boggy darkness. When I awoke in the morning, just before sunrise, he was already at it, scribbling notes with his night-chilled fingers.

When he saw that I was awake, he immediately rose and prepared to move on. That too was as simple as could be; after all, there was no tent to strike, no fire to build, we didn't even breakfast until later. Sometimes it seemed as though the old mountain man lived without sleeping or eating, but from somewhere he drew sustenance that kept him running like a windmill. We climbed up the broad west flank of Wisewoman Mountain. I was amazed to see the remnants of terraces right in the middle of the ancient forest. Candid explained that they were over five centuries old, built during the first century ACT when these steep slopes constituted the Esperian heartland.

We spent several minutes on West Peak, surveying the country in every direction. Although I did not realize it at the time, we were standing on the boundary line between the so-called Nine Fairs or Bluemeadow Region and the Five Fairs or Turtleshell Region. To our north lay the Misery Basin, and beyond that a vast expanse of unbroken wilderness extending all the way to the Borealian border. We spent the next five days tramping over that forest vastness. I could see no particular system in Candid's movements, yet system there was nevertheless. We left whole valleys unvisited while passing hours in some undistinguished spot, watching for something unseeable.

On one day, we would gorge ourselves on wild cress and bunchberries; on the next day we might eat nothing but a single crispbread with a few dried apples or elderberries. Candid always seemed to know where to find clean fresh water. Even far above the clear brooks, he knew where every tiny spring seeped out of the ancient rock.

When you spend five days in the wilderness with only one other person to talk to, you cannot help but come to know that person very well. Nearly every minute of our days was taken up in counting deer and birds and salamanders or inspecting skunk droppings and leaf galls. However, one afternoon blew in rainy, and for a few hours, even Candid was content to lie about in our cramped tarp shelter until the showers were passed. We fell to talking about all kinds of things, including our own pasts.

"You sure know a lot about this wilderness," I observed. "You must've been doing this all your life."

"Only the last half of it. Before that I was a ship steward."

"Really!" I remarked, remembering that Esperians used the term *steward* where Anagaians would say *boss* or *chief*, or in this case, *captain*. "However did you happen to make such a drastic career change?"

"It all came about quite unexpectedly," he replied, and with a sad shaking of his head, he began his story.

"I served on a small coastal freighter, sailing out of Mercy Bay. On one trip, I had my whole family along, wife and two children. They were to disembark at Galeslee where my wife had relations. My wife never could abide a rough sea, and she was sick below deck the whole while. My fourteen-year-old son was tending out on her, and I assumed my three-year-old daughter was down there too. Somewhere off Point Turnagain, we got caught by a northeaster that threatened to drive us ashore. In order to save the ship, we made for open sea, hoping to ride it out. But as darkness fell, we had trouble keeping our bearings—we thought we were far offshore, but suddenly we heard surf breaking right ahead of us. The wind was hard abaft, and we were driven on to a ledge before we could steer away. We struck hard, and it was clear we were going to break up. While the three crewmen tried to lower a dinghy, I made my way toward the hatch to get the family. It was a struggle just to move on the slippery lurching deck. Waves were crashing over the side. I heard a shout and saw the dinghy break loose from its davits. One of the men tried to leap into it from the deck. Just as he disappeared from view, I looked toward the hatch and saw the cook emerging with my daughter is his arms. Putting his mouth close to my ear, he shouted over the wind, 'The other two are working their way up. The boy's helping her. I thought this one needed—'

"Before he could finish, a huge wave smashed over us, nearly tearing my daughter out of my grip. Before I could grab onto the rail, we were swept over the side. I'm a good swimmer, but clutching the terrified child to me with one arm, I could barely tread water. I never saw the cook again, and I was sure we were lost too. Then I realized from the crash of the sea that we were near some rocks, part of the ledge that had wrecked us. With my free arm I tried to swim toward them, but although they were not thirty yards away, it took me an eternity to reach them. I pulled us up onto the jagged reef, though I feared the churning surf would either suck us back in or pound us to a bloody pulp. There was no part of the tiny ledge that was well above water, so I never dared let go of my hold. In the dim light, I could barely make out the form of the nearby wreck, heaving and grinding against the hidden portion of the reef. In a few minutes, I stared in helpless horror as the hull split open, and with a final shudder the ship sank beneath the surging waves. I could not repress a shriek of dismay, realizing there was no way my wife and son could have escaped the wreck. For hours I clung to the ledge, trying to shield the shivering child under my body."

At this point, the old man gave a shiver as he recalled the tragic incident of long ago.

"When the storm abated, we saw that there was one other castaway on the ledge with us: the crewman who had leaped into the lifeboat but then been unable to control it. It carried him near to the ledge before capsizing and throwing him into the surf. The boat itself was now grounded with us but smashed beyond use. We were able to tip it up to serve as a crude shelter, giving us some protection from the wind and rain. If the storm had not been followed almost immediately by bright sunny weather, I'm sure that all of us, especially the child, would've perished. For a day and a second night we waited without food or water. My daughter suffered badly from exposure. The other man and I tried between us to keep her warm, but we had little body heat of our own. On the second morning, we were picked up by a sloop that had been searching for us in the Random Islands, twenty miles away. My daughter was very sick for a while, but she lived. I regained my health but remained sick at heart. I could not cope with the sudden loss. Friends tried to help me, but I was inconsolable. I kept telling myself I still had obligations. I still had one child who needed me. But it was no good. Others at our stead took care of her while I wandered around aimlessly for weeks on end, trying to find myself. I happened once to find myself on the Calliope Hill Road, right near where my cabin now stands. The wilderness seemed as good a place as any to run away from myself. I think I expected, even hoped, to get lost and perish there. Of course I didn't. I was already as lost as one can be, so any direction I turned had to be the right way.

"It had never occurred to me that a place could heal, but slowly I felt that happening. I could not forget the past, but I could conceive of a future. I wasn't sure exactly what I should do, but I knew I must remain in or near the Sacred Groves. It was about that time that I learned that the keeper of that division had died the year before, and no one had replaced him yet. I decided at once to become the new keeper and set out to get my daughter. My steadmates were strongly opposed—no single Keeper of the Sacred Groves had ever taken his daughter there to live; how would she go to school? How would she grow up normal without other children to play with? I finally managed to allay their concerns by agreeing to join a stead bordering the forest and leaving the girl there while I was on my rounds—in those days, I rarely patrolled for more than three days at a time, so I was with her regularly. As she grew older, she would accompany me on my hikes. Of course, she had to make up the lost schooltime, but she learned many things that others never know. It may surprise you to know that I belong to Withegate, the stead across the road from yours. Yes, that's right. In forty-four years, I've never stayed there more than a couple days, preferring the woods and my little cabin. I hardly even know my steadmates or neighbours—you, for example."

"And your daughter?" I asked. "What has become of her?"

"She has become a keeper herself. She's thirty-seven years old and married to a naturalist from Quaggy Lake. They're not as hermitish as me, I'm glad to say. They participate more in the life of their stead, but nevertheless, they spend much of their time in the Sacred Groves, doing the same things we're doing. And much more: my daughter is an accomplished mycologist, among other things."

"A what?"

"Come here, let me show you."

I was glad for Candid's sake to have the conversation flow into happier channels. Our tarp was tied to the trunk of a great beech for support. Without even leaving its shelter, Candid was able to kneel down and scrape away some of the forest duff beneath us. He pointed out a mat of fine whitish hairs which interlaced with the fine roots of the beech tree.

"See now, these are mycelia of a symbiotic fungus."

"You're losing me again. A fungus—that's like a mushroom, right? But a sym . . . symbi . . ."

"Symbiotic. Actually many fungi are not mushrooms. This kind sends its tiny tentacles into the rootlets of the beech, where it feeds on the tree's nutrients."

"Oh, so it's a parasite."

"But not really—this fungus pays well for its keep. It enables the tree to take up phosphorus and other nutrients. If it were not 'infected' by this fungus, the beech would be much less healthy. That's what symbiosis is all about. Other species of trees have their own fungal associations, and my daughter is quite an expert on them."

"Oh, I'm beginning to see; this has some very practical applications."

"It well might. That's none of my business."

"But why not?"

"You're missing the whole point of the Sacred Groves. Don't you understand that this wilderness is not intended to be useful to humans?"

"Yes, yes, lumber and all that. But surely knowledge . . ."

"And why not knowledge as well? In fact, we received great benefits from the Sacred Groves. They keep our wells and canals full, they lock up the CO_2 from our fires, they regulate the climate. Likewise, the knowledge we get there may be useful to us, but that's not their purpose. Man is not the centre of creation, after all. All these things: muskrat and herons and beech trees and fungi have their own reasons for existing. In the same sense, knowledge is worth having for its own sake, regardless of whether we can do anything with it."

Ironically, even this "pure knowledge," which Candid sought, was extremely valuable in many "practical" senses. For example, I later learned that one of those many fungi which Candid's daughter studied was a subvirulent strain of chestnut blight. It did not harm the tree, but repressed the virulent strain, enabling the host tree to survive. By grafting patches of the subvirulent tissue into the bark of cultivated trees, the inoculated groves became immune to, or at least tolerant of, the otherwise-lethal blight fungus. It was the chance observation of this phenomenon that made it possible for the noble chestnut to become a major food source for Esperian civilization. Similar research is also underway for diseases of elms and other trees. However, it is this self-justifying view of knowledge which has supported such centuries-long studies which a results-oriented approach would have spurned.

Every morning without fail, Candid took a bath in whatever brook we were near. I followed his example without enthusiasm, since even at this season, the water was always frigid. His fastidiousness was not motivated by any social custom—after all, he usually went for weeks without meeting anyone, and he certainly was not fussy about his own comfort. His greater concern was to be unnoticeable; he might stalk a black bear for hours to measure its territorial range or lie in wait to observe the mating rituals of a fisher, and one couldn't expect wild animals to behave normally if they were surrounded by human body odour.

Eventually, we reached the shores of Misery Lake, where Candid had arranged to rendezvous with his daughter and son-in-law. I left them there and made my own way down Misery Brook to where it leaves the Sacred Groves above Axle Falls. From there I took a road back over the High Meadows to Antler Brook and finally to Ravenswing. I arrived tired and eager for things like hot baths and cooked meals, but feeling that I had experienced an important dimension of the Steward Vision.

Chapter 56

The steadhouse at Ravenswing consisted of three adjoining wings, partly surrounding a sheltered courtyard which opened to the southeast. Along the west side of the building, a screened-in veranda overlooked terraced gardens which marched downhill in the direction of Wisewoman Brook. In warm weather, much of the household was wont to sit out there for meals or just visiting. There was a lovely view up the valley, and off to our left were the cliffs on Covenant Ridge. We could see the signal tower on Chairback Mountain, and some of the kids liked to watch it through Hale's telescope when it was transmitting. They all knew the codes by heart, and they got a kick out of announcing all the latest news to the grownups a half day before it appeared in the newssheets.

One day in late spring, most of us were lounging around the veranda, enjoying a cold picnic lunch. Bright golden-crowned thunderheads reared overhead, which were as dazzling as they were welcome. Everything was planted and mulched, so whatever water fell could sink right in and do its work. It was sticky hot, and no one was in a rush to get back to work. Everyone chatted about crops and new strawberries and the upcoming Banner Day festivities. Larch was narrating the news from the tower.

"Hey, that's strange!" he reported. "They just stopped in the middle of a sentence. 'Continued progress reported in talks with . . .' That doesn't make any sense."

All eyes turned toward the tower. It was eleven miles away, so the actual tower structure was barely visible.

"There are some awfully dark clouds closing in on them," observed Quail. "They're probably scared of lightning."

Down by us in the valley, hardly a breath was stirring, but I felt a familiar sensation that made me nervous.

"Back where I come from," I began, "when it gets quieter than quiet like this . . ." But even as I spoke the words, we began to hear a roar in the back of the house, like a hundred mighty rivers rushing through. "Get into the cellar!" I hollered with more authority than I was used to exerting. In fact, everyone was already heading there, but we had barely gotten everyone down there when the roar began to die down. Less than sixty seconds from when it began, it was all over.

We all went around to see what damage had been done. The actual tornado, if in fact there had really been one, had missed us. Up in the Sacred Groves, a few overgrown old trees had been hurled to the ground and some limbs had been whipped and twisted off. Around the house, there was regular wind damage, but nothing devastating. Everyone looked at the garden in horror, everyone except me.

"This is nothing," I reassured them. "A little mulched tossed around, some poles blown over . . . you don't know how lucky you are."

In fact, not everyone in the area was quite so lucky. Our neighbours over at Withegate lost one whole side of their saphouse roof, and up at Fortyfold, a windmill had all of its three turbines trashed. Yet even they were lucky; they had neglected to secure the idle turbines, which were up to twelve feet in diameter and eight feet tall. With that much sail area and made of light cedar, they must have been spinning at a fantastic rate. If anyone had been close by when they broke up, they could've been killed by flying fragments. Fortunately, our turbines were all harnessed tightly in their frames, and the guy wires tight on the tower, so no damage was done. Cherish was crestfallen to look at the gardens, but again, I tried to console her. The winter wheat and rye were flattened, but that would straighten itself up in a few days. All of the supports: trellis, bean poles, pea fence, had all been hurled about and tangled up, but the plants themselves were still too short to be much injured, except where buried under wads of flying mulch. In the orchards, a dogwood cherry was uprooted, and several pears had broken limbs but no worse. It was all pretty trivial, as disasters go, but try telling that to people who strive to work with nature and expect a little cooperation in return. Later, they said it hadn't been a tornado at all, but something called a wind shear.

We soon learned that we were not the only ones to suffer damage from the freak storm. It had cut a diagonal swath across Antler Ridge, leaving several acres of down and tangled trees in the Sacred Groves. From there it blasted through Chill Springs and Longfield where a few barns lost their roofs and several windmills were severely damaged. The very next day, we were not surprised when the turnery received urgent orders for new windmill parts. One stead over in Lone Spruce was in particularly bad shape since their main windmill was out of commission, and they needed it to pump water. They had managed to locate new tower beams and shafting, but they also needed to replace two of the four thrust bearings.

We happened to have a couple of the kind of bearings they needed, but they couldn't wait for us to ship them over. They were willing to pay extra for special delivery, so I was asked to carry the parts over on a bicycle. It was only ten miles over to Lone Spruce, and even though I left after lunch, I expected to be back well before dark. It took longer than expected because the road still had numerous trees and limbs across it, forcing me to dismount and lift the bike over them. Little wonder, I told myself; after all, I had picked the road which nearly paralleled the path of the wind shear. I delivered my burden all right, hoping to take my pay home in falcons or conches. However, the stead was short of both coins and ingots. I could simply wait to settle later or accept a promissory note, but they offered me a good deal on some glassware they had themselves received in trade. From my days on *Come-What-May*, I knew it was a bargain I couldn't refuse, but the problem was getting it safely home. I decided not to return by the same limb-littered route I had come, instead taking the Wisewoman Brook Road, which was longer but smoother. I wasn't sure how to connect with the road over to Stoutbridge, so when I got back to the bridge over Longfield Dam, I looked for someone to ask directions.

As I crossed the long trestle bridge, there was a person standing in the middle with another person sitting in a drawchair. Apparently, the seated man was an invalid whom the other was moving, and they had parked there on the bridge to admire the sunlight dancing over the tumbling current. They appeared to live in the neighbourhood, so I asked them to point me toward Stoutbridge. As always happens in this tight-knit country, we fell to talking about other things: of wind shears and lodged hay, of turbines and shingles. The invalid seemed to pay little attention to me; I assumed he was senile or perhaps a stroke patient. But at one point, I noticed he had jerked up his head and was staring at me very intently. For the first time I took closer note of his contorted face as he seemed to be studying mine. He looked strangely familiar, and I realized he was much younger in years then he seemed. His awkward features: widespread ears and prominent Adam's apple, carried my mind back to another time and place. At the same moment that he blurted out "Yaro?", recognition hit me too, and I practically screamed, "Faring!!"

"It is you, then!" he gasped, struggling to his feet; but apparently he was too weak to stand, and only the quick action of his companion saved him from falling onto the bridge planking. She eased him back into his seat while he and I showered each other with embraces and choking sobs. It was no wonder I had been slow to recognize him: he was a mere shadow of the man I had last seen over eight years ago. He couldn't be over forty-three years old now, but he could've passed for seventy. As for me, I had been a mere child when Archer Seekings had taken me from the orphanage, and here I was now, bearded and wearing Esperian clothes

"So you did escape," he rasped joyfully. "I knew something was up when they let me go all of a sudden."

A horrible thought crossed my mind. "They did this to you because of me?" Neither of us had the slightest doubt about what the other meant by *they*.

"No, no, not that time anyway. Nothing to do with you."

Gradually, as we both regained some composure, we began organizing our stories for each other. The woman stood discreetly by, and it never occurred to Faring to introduce us, so immersed were we in our mutual debriefing. At his insistence, I first recounted in some detail how I had managed to elude the CADS surveillance network and slip over the border into Hither Anagaia after finding my birth mother.

"Yes, yes, we heard something about that poor woman, and I have no doubt that she must be the woman who used to spy on the orphanage when you are very little. A pity, but you mustn't blame yourself for the tragedy. She had already put her head in the noose by merely leaving something for you. The CADS would have done her in as soon as she came back to town."

"And what about you? You obviously knew something about what happened. Did they make trouble for you too?"

"Not worth mentioning. They picked me up for questioning, slapped me around a little, and held me in detention for a few days. They kept telling me that they had you in custody, so I might as well talk. I knew they were bluffing until they finally let me go. When I overheard a guard mention that it didn't matter anymore, I figured you were either dead or had escaped. I never knew which until now."

So I continued to relate my adventures with the opium smugglers and all the rest: the ambush of Fester Gilding, my life as a fugitive in New Chalice, and my eventual escape on the *Minkey*.

"But that's nothing now," I said. "I am here, safe and well and happier than I ever would have been there. But you, what happened? What have they done to you?"

"Ah, badly enough, it's true," he sighed with a stifled sob. "Yet not as badly as they intended. After all, I too am here, what's left of me."

Then he proceeded to recount, in a sometimes muffled voice, the sad events that had befallen him in the past year.

"After I was released, I set out for Dryford to learn whatever I could there. No one there knew any more about your whereabouts than I did. When I returned to Cleftridge, the local CADS agent was furious to learn that I'd been traveling without proper papers. They locked me up again for a few days as punishment, but that was the worst of it—I think the fact that I went to Dryford instead of after you convinced them that I really didn't know anything. Anyway, except for the usual harassment, they left us pretty much alone until last winter, when Boon came around . . ."

"Boon Blotch? Is he still alive?" I fairly shouted. Boon was my bosom buddy who had mysteriously disappeared from the orphanage while I was at Dryford.

"Yes, at least he was at the time. I was never able to tell you in letters that he was picked up one night by a press-gang and forced into the army. His little brother Kit became a camp follower. When Boon learned that his unit was about to be sent over to Grand Coquina, he deserted. We heard that he and Kit had joined the Amanita and had gone underground somewhere in the surrounding hills. One night, there was a raid on their hideout, and everyone ran for their lives. Young Kit didn't make it however. Being deaf and dumb, you know, I suppose he didn't react soon enough. Anyway, he was killed. That was the last straw for Boon, as you can imagine. He always was bitter toward the world, and with Kit's death, they say he has gone berserk. Now he has become a leader in a revolutionary cell and wants any excuse for vengeance. One thing is clear to everyone, including CADS: they'll never take him alive."

"So how did all this affect you?"

"About four months ago, he showed up again at Cleftridge. We keepers never saw him, but he invited some of the draught-age boys to join him, and two of them went. Some time later, they raided an estate near Ramparts, in an attempt to replenish their supplies. They were surprised by an overseer, and there was a shoot-out and one of the boys was killed. On his body, CADS found some papers or something that connected him to the orphanage. CADS ransacked us and found nothing, but we knew that was not the end of it. A few nights later, we heard shouting outside and shots. When Bracken opened the door to see what was wrong, they cut him down in cold blood. We immediately barred the doors and shutters as a storm of gunfire rained on the building. Before long we realized that the roof had been set afire. If you remember, there was a well in the shed behind the building, which we dug after that time when someone tried to poison the well in the courtyard. They had me take as many children as I could into that shed and crowd them all into the shaft. I climbed in above them to pull the heavy slab over the top, leaving just a crack to breathe. We couldn't hear much down there, but the air got so bad I feared we would all suffocate. The best I could do was keep the children from screaming and giving us away. Hours later, everything seemed quiet out there, so I crawled out and lifted the children after me. The mud brick walls were mostly still standing, but the roof had fallen in and was still aflame. We crept out of the shed and over the back wall. I succeeded in guiding them down a couple of back alleys and on to another part of town. There we all split up, the older ones carrying the younger ones, since to stay together was to guarantee our capture. I'll never know what became of all those children—I shudder to think of it—but at least they were all safe when I left them. Toward dawn, I doubled back to see if I could do anything for the others, though I feared the worst. When I finally reached the building, there was no more shooting, no more screaming . . ."

Here, Faring paused and sobbed convulsively for a moment before collecting himself.

The building was nothing but smouldering embers. The yard was filled with bullet-ridden bodies, fallen in groups where they had tried to help one another. Some had obviously been badly burned as they tried to stick it out inside. I was poking around in the ashes, trying to account for everyone, in case anyone else had escaped. What I found was the most grisly evidence that I was the only survivor. I was so overcome by shock that I couldn't give any thought to my own safety. Just before daylight, a neighbour showed up—no one else dared to be seen there, although I learned later that the police blamed the massacre on them. It was Ernest Canes, one of old Victor's sons who had inherited the adjacent place. He grabbed my arm and pulled me hastily into his own house. For two days, he hid me in his loft. He couldn't tell anyone, not even his family, since one of his brothers was in the army. Several times, CADS agents had been seen inspecting the orphanage site; since there were few children's bodies, they could surmise that someone had led them off. It was clear that the massacre was intended to be complete, leaving no survivors, even children, to carry away the truth of what happened. That put my protector in grave danger. I convinced him that I must leave, so early one morning, I sneaked out of his house and right into the arms of a pair of CADS officers who had staked out the place next door. The man who had hid me was executed on the spot, before his wife and children, who knew nothing of my being there. I would've been shot too, of course, but when they learned my name, they took me into custody. Again I was interrogated, this time about Boon Blotch and his band. They were totally convinced that I knew much more than I admitted and were determined to wring it out of me. Under torture, I told him everything I knew, which was nothing at all. So they continued. After weeks of deprivation and abuse such as you can't imagine, I was more dead than alive. I knew it was just a matter of time before they would give up on me and finished me off. I began to yearn for that time since I had no hope of escaping, and life seemed worse than death.

"Then one night—I suppose it was night, it was always night in there—they threw me back in my cell where I lay barely conscious. I dimly remember hearing a new voice say, 'Wait a minute before you lock it. I'm s'posed to check him.' Then a dim light came back into the cell, and I felt a light touch of my hand. I made an effort to open my eyes and saw a face just inches from mine. It took a moment to recognize him, but it was . . . say, Yaro, do you remember a couple of drunks that roughed me up one time when we were at the carnival at Sycamore?"

"Why yes! You pushed one of them back and he fell and broke his shoulder blade. We doctored him for a while, then he disappeared without a word."

"Well, my dear friend, that was him. The face before me was none other than Newt Hobbling, the coffin maker. He slips something in between my fingers and whispers, 'Here, man, at least I can do you one right, for old times, y'know. As you value your life, do as I say. As soon as you hear the fourth bell, you take what's in this paper and you eat it all, hear? Not sooner not later, and don't spill a bit of it. If they give you water, don't touch it. This will make you feel terrible, but you'll be worse if you don't. It's tonight or never, see, so don't fail.'

Well, as I said, I was barely conscious to begin with, but suddenly I came as awake as I've ever been. As he went out, he mumbled something to the turnkey about my not being quite gone yet, and he'd check again in the morning. I lay there in the dark, trying to make sense of it. Obviously, he was intending to do me a favour. Perhaps that just meant that what he'd given me would put me out of my misery more mercifully than otherwise. Yet he did say 'as you value your life,' implying that he offered some promise of saving me. That seemed preposterous, just a cruel trick, yet what did I have to lose? I could not possibly keep awake until the appointed time, but the dim light of hope stood watch over my subconscious so that when the midnight watch tolled, I was alert and counting. Four. Yes, that was it! I had not missed any. I opened the packet in my palm and without wasting a moment, licked up every bit of the vile-tasting powder. I have no idea what it was, but in a very short time, I felt myself losing consciousness again. This time, I could feel my pulse slowing dramatically along with a gradual stiffening of my limbs. I remember thinking to myself, Well, that's it, now we'll just see, or perhaps we never will see. *I don't know how much time passed, but I suppose I was examined by the prison doctor—perhaps not the cleverest in his profession—and pronounced dead. No doubt if the dose had not been quite correct, I would have been. All I know is that I gradually came to, as I was being jostled around in a stifling box. I didn't have to think too long to realize what was happening. I was in a sealed coffin, probably in the back of a mule cart, bound for somewhere. In a while, the vehicle jolted to a halt, and I heard the now-familiar coffin-builder's voice say, 'That's close enough, chum, now help me lift it* down in.' I remember feeling a thrill of horror: was I about to be buried alive? But I lay still and quiet—I don't believe I could have done otherwise. I was aware of movement: a bit of tipping and grunting and a gravelly thud on the bottom of the box. Then Newt's voice again. 'Thanks a lot. I'll take it from here.' A second voice. 'But we're supposed to stay. We got orders to help with the filling.' Even through the box, I thought I could hear a nervous edge to Newt's voice as he said, 'Bah, orders! You fellers even let someone tell you how to handle a hunk of dead meat! I'll do it myself. I get paid aplenty for these jobs. Here, you boys take a few coins and have a drink on me, won't you.' Another voice.' Heck, sure, why not? Never known the day Newt Hobbling would pay someone else to do his drinking for him!' When the chuckling had died away in the distance, I heard or rather felt a heavy thud as Newt jumped into the grave. A careful creaking as nails were pried and the lid was slowly raised. The bright light was blinding, and I blinked hard.

'Aha! So it worked. My old buddy is still with us. So how d'you feel?'

I tried to smile. I've never felt worse, and I've never felt better.'

'Well, well, we don't dare get you out of there just yet, but you can breathe some fresher air for a few minutes. I bored some air holes in the bottom of this thing, but you've probably been lying on most of them. See here, there is a water jar and some biscuits—don't worry, there ain't no pig fat in it, I made sure. Soon as you're done, we best put the lid back on, in case anyone happens along as we're waiting.'

'Waiting?'

'It'll be a few minutes. This driver made better time than I calculated. But you leave that up to ol' Newt; if you've gotten this far, the Brothers will see you the rest of the way.'

In a few minutes, a hay wagon pulled up alongside the cemetery, and the driver appeared to be checking his harness. Another man showed up as if from nowhere, and he and Newt carried me—I could not walk—to the back of the wagon where I was hidden in the loose hay. That was the last I saw of Newt Hobbling.

For the next several days, I did exactly as I was told by complete strangers. By means of a secret network of which I knew nothing, I was handed along a chain of clandestine hideouts. I never had any idea where I was as I slept in attics, caves, and false passageways. Most of the time I spent buried in the backs of farm wagons and oxcarts, lumbering through one checkpoint after another. My conductors were constantly changing, though I gathered they were all part of the "Brotherhood", as the Amanita calls itself. One day I was told that I was in Tramont, so I realized that I was being carried north. A couple weeks ago, I was finally delivered to the Coaldale River where a man waited to row me across to Lacustria. There my injuries were given emergency treatment, and I was finally sent on to Esperia. So that's my hard story.

"We heard some confused rumours about the orphanage being shut down, but we understood it had something to do with the *Dauntless* incident."

"A mere coincidence. I never heard about any of that until I arrived back here. The other facilities had their staffs deported, not massacred."

Chapter 57

As pained as I was to hear Faring's litany of horrors, I could hardly conceal my joy at finding him alive at all. His tale of survival was hardly less improbable than my own. There was no question of my leaving him to return home, at least not immediately. I accompanied him and his caregiver back to his stead. He had moved there instead of to Otterbank because his parents were both now dead, and he had other family and friends here in Longfield. His sister, the one who had disliked me so, had also moved elsewhere, and upon her brother's return, she had either forgotten or neglected to tell him about me. We spent the rest of the day together, reminiscing over the life we had shared at Cleftridge. Things had seemed so difficult in those days, but in retrospect, they seemed almost idyllic. The more time I spent with Faring, the more I realized that his health was hopelessly broken. His hair was prematurely white. Numerous broken bones had healed improperly. The soles of his feet were scorched and scarred, and his fingernails were deformed. He could only urinate with difficulty. The psychological damage was even more severe, although it did not show at once. He had a very low tolerance of bright light or loud noises. I noticed that when anyone or anything near him moved suddenly, he would cringe and throw both hands over his groin. His emotions were fragile; in the course of an ordinary conversation, he might unaccountably break into a paroxysm of sobs.

At one point in our visit, it occurred to me to ask him something.

"You said that after hearing about my banishment, you went to Dryford?"

"Yes, I spent a whole day there."

"How long was that after I left?"

"About a month, I guess. They were watching me at first."

"I'm just wondering . . . did people there think I was guilty?"

"Certainly no one that I talked to. In fact, your half sister was quite distraught, and wishing she knew some way to help you."

"She helped me plenty as it is. If it weren't for her statement at the trial, I surely would have swung. And by the way she's not my half sister."

"What do you mean?"

"Melody is my adopted sister. That's not the same . . ."

Faring was staring blankly at me; and he slapped his forehead and gasped. "I completely forgot! You don't know anything about all that."

"About what? Whatever are you talking about?"

"Look, Yaro, it's you who needs to sit down now. I have a startling story to tell you."

My joints turned to rubber as I realized that he had somehow learned some shocking information about those close to me. I found a chair and waited for him to begin.

"Dear, dear, where to start. All right now . . . after the murder, of course, there had to be a settling of the estate. No will could be found, but that became a moot point when the accounts were all settled. Yaro, the man was awash in red ink! His widow had no idea how bad things were. He must've been counting on an upturn in the cotton market because he had everything signed out. In order to satisfy creditors, the whole place was broken up and put to auction."

"That truly is shocking, but what does it have to do with my own family?"

"I'll come to that. Now Mrs. Gates was, of course, left nearly penniless, and so she and her daughter were forced to move in with Melody and her boyfriend Crag. They took in laundry to make ends meet. Meanwhile one of the pieces of furniture—an office desk, I believe—was purchased by a businessman over in Shoatmart. Soon after acquiring it, he discovered a folded paper stuck behind the drawer. Recognizing its great importance, he promptly returned it to Mrs. Gates. It was in part a will and in part a confession. In it, Jasper owned up to some romantic liaisons of his youth, one of which had borne fruit. He expressed remorse for his weakness in not divulging the fact while still alive. Obviously he expected to live much longer and disentangle himself from his financial worries because he expressly left his entire estate, not to his only daughter—which was impossible anyway—but to his biological son: Yaro Seekings."

I had begun to feel the hair rise on my neck even before these last words. Faring had well advised me to sit down.

"You mean," I mumbled through a fog, "that Jasper Gates was my birth father?"

"So it would appear."

I just sat there stunned, trying to grasp what that meant. Finally I blurted out, "Fawn . . . I almost married my sister?"

"From what I was told. Of course, whose fault was that, if no one let you know?"

"And only he knew. I wonder how he could have been so sure. I mean, I've seen my birth mother, and there's a strong resemblance, but . . . oh yes, he knew where I came from and when I was born . . . but still . . ."

"He knew more than that, Yaro. In that document—confession, will, whatever—he mentioned that when he was courting . . . seducing . . . the young Miller girl, they were walking alone on a rocky hill, and he impulsively looked around for something to make a bouquet. All he could find was some pink achillea growing among the ledges."

"Achillea . . . isn't that the same as . . . ?"

"Yes. It's another name for *yarrow*."

A flood of new-old connexions was flooding through my brain. Casual remarks Jasper had made, generous favours to me and my adopted family, and of course, his adamant opposition to my marriage to Fawn.

"But how could he not have told us?" I moaned. "Something terrible might have happened."

"I can't defend the man, Yaro. From what different people tell me about him, I piece together a rather complex character. Many admirable traits certainly, but a dark side that finally caught up with him. Although they never were able to prove the real murderer, in a sense Jasper Gates may be said to have taken his own life. Arrogance is a sword which often destroys its wielder."

"You said they never were able to prove the real murderer; does that mean they found another suspect?"

"Well, at least not . . . someone told me in confidence that one of Gates's tenants had a wayward wife, and it was rumoured that Jasper was seeing her secretly. Sometime after the murder, the tenant had gotten drunk and was overheard confiding to a friend that he had beaten his wife because of her penchant for sleeping with rich man—once with a landowner and before that with a judge. The tenant was questioned and denied ever saying it. For some reason, it was never brought to trial."

"And what about my adopted family? How were they getting along?"

"Mr. Seekings died just before I was there—not unexpectedly, I gathered. Heart failure or something. The girl seemed to have her hands full, keeping the place together, but she and her boyfriend were trying to make a go of things. As I said, Mrs. Gates and your half sister had just moved in with them. Quite a comedown for them, I'm sure, and a scandal to anyone who doubts your innocence, if there are such."

This last revelation was even more upsetting to me than the first, if only because it had consequences. The orphanage debacle and Faring's woes were horrible, but it was over with; there was nothing else to be done. However, this business about my unknown family connexions, it was fraught with implications for me. Faring's crisis was as much in the past as it could be; my own flight from Anagaia, it seemed, was not quite over yet.

Although I stayed that night with Faring's stead family, I could hardly sleep. My brain was too clouded by new uncertainties. I needed to ponder, to reconsider everything, but it was impossible to do it there. I felt too much of a need to release my emotions, away from anyone I knew, away from anyone at all. I had to get away as fast as I could. In the middle of the night, I woke Faring and tried to explain my feelings to him. He seemed to understand better than I what I was going through. Borrowing a carbide lamp to hang from my handlebars, I set out immediately and reached Ravenswing just before dawn. I didn't even go in; I met Herald heading for the springhouse and gave him the briefest explanation of what has happened. Then I headed up the Calliope Falls Road toward Candid's old cabin. Nearly breathless, I turned into the forest where hurrying seemed both impossible and unnecessary. Rays of first light were streaming over the Calendar Hills, and some of them probed down through the dense canopy. From the moment I'd left Faring, I knew where I had to go: the place where Candid had gone to ease his own pain, to grasp a new perspective when the old perspective had run aground on the ledges. At first I climbed up onto East Wisewoman Peak. It was a long hard ascent, and for a couple hours, it helped take my mind off anything else. I soon realized that it would not do to simply take my mind off. I had not come here to forget but to decide. I sat down on the summit and looked out at the glorious panorama. All the peaks: Wisewoman, Misery, Chairback, the Colliers—rose resplendent in the morning light. I could peer down into three large river basins at once: the Laughingwater, the Weasel, and the Rampant—while off to the south I could catch glimpses of the Broadlea. But this too was not what I had come for. I didn't need sweeping vistas; the soaring peaks did not speak to me. Soon I left the summit and picked my way down the north side, down through wind-stunted junipers and gnarled knee-high spruces. Down through spindly birches and mountain ash, until I came to a spring. It seeped out from cracks in the rock and gathered in a tiny moss-lined pool. When it had mustered enough strength, it formed a rivulet which tumbled down into a branch of Misery Brook. It was not only quiet here, it was still. Some bugs, too small to identify, flicked over the surface of the pool; but there was no other motion to distract. I sat down.

Start at the beginning, I told myself; don't get sidetracked. Review all of this, take it in, accept it, be methodical. I tried to, I really did, but some part of me had its own priorities. The whole orphanage thing, that one could be set aside. Not that it wouldn't give me nightmares for a long time to come—I already did have nightmares about it, ever since reading the news bulletin, only now my nightmares would have more detail. Then there was Jasper Gates, another spectre who had already darkened my dreams on occasion. So he was my father, or at least my sire or progenitor or whatever you want to call it. That was a heavy one. Frankly, I'd never before given much thought to the man who begot me. He was a mystery, never to be solved. But now I tried to imagine that dashing hard-driving landowner lying with that frumpy half-crazed woman, that fragile shell I'd found broken at the foot of the cliff. Of course, they both must have been much different twenty years earlier, before life had worked its separate moulding on them. One side of me hated Jasper; what kind of a man could have his own son right under his eyes, working for him, visiting his family, accepting his favours, yet never telling him the truth? Another side of me looked at him, not for himself, but for what might have been, if only he had stayed with Serene Miller and been my "real" father.

At that point in my contemplation, an image flashed before me, and just as quickly it was gone.

And then there was Fawn—and I thought I had mixed emotions before! There was joy now, of course, in the certainty that she believed me innocent; that was one nightmare that would never recur. But then there was the thought of her and Rose, torn from their comfortable home and thrown onto the charity of "our family"—what irony!

The subliminal image flashed again.

So we were brother and sister, eh? Half siblings anyway. Of course, she knew that too now. How did she feel about it: amused or humiliated? How did *I* feel about it?

The image again.

Well, Fawn, I still love you, even as a sister, and I hope you still love me as a brother. Jasper was right after all; it just wasn't meant to be. If he hadn't said so, I probably would've said it myself, hopefully in time to stop—

The image flashed one more time, and this time I knew I must confront it.

"Yes, I know," I acknowledged the image before me. "And then there is you."

She did not reply; an image can only speak the words you put in its mouth, and I didn't know what words to put in.

"I know this changes everything with us, but which way is it changed? How bizarre: you and she. I was her lover, and now I learn that I'm her brother. And you, I tried to be like a brother to you, but I can't lie to myself any longer. I didn't dare admit it, to myself or to you, for fear of losing you. What good would it have done? I was not free, and you were not interested. And what good will it do now? It will clear the air, I suppose. I owe you that much."

There is a feeling that I imagine a soldier might have as he marches toward a battle in which he knows he will die. He has been terrified, but now he quietly accepts his fate. The end is near, and his only care now is to finish what he must do. He is not brave, but he is bold. That is sort of what I felt like as I climbed back over the peak and down the other side. Three hours after leaving the spring, I was at Ravenswing. Everyone looked concerned as I walked into the house. They had only heard about my returning in the early hours, looking very upset, and leaving immediately for the Sacred Groves. Finding Cherish, I said to her quietly, "I must talk to you . . . alone."

There was a hint of alarm in her face, but then she assumed an unconvincing attitude of composure. As I led her gently up toward the orchard, she said simply, "I wasn't sure you'd be coming back."

I almost said, "Should I not have?" but held my piece until we reached the first row of apple trees. We sat on the new-mown hay, she leaning against a trunk.

"I don't quite know where to begin," I stammered. "You see, I've just received some unexpected news."

"Yes, yes, how wonderful," she encouraged me, though her lips were quivering. "News from Anagaia."

"Oh, you heard, then?"

"Well, Father said you met someone you used to know from back there, someone you never expected to meet again."

"Yes, that's true. Well, you see, it has changed the way I felt about some things."

"I expected so," she choked on an ill-suppressed sob. "But, Yaro," she added slowly, "we've been such dear friends, surely that needn't change?"

"Surely not, at least for my part, but I wasn't sure you would feel the same way."

"But why shouldn't I? It's just that I'll miss you so badly when you go away to be with her."

"With whom?"

"Your fiancée. Isn't that what you found out at Longfield? Aren't you going to join her?"

"That's not at all what I found out. It's a long story, but I learned that my so-called fiancée happens to be my half-sister. Even if we ever met again, nothing more could . . . but . . ."

I gave her a brief explanation of what Faring had told me.

Cherish gasped. "But I was so sure you were going to leave us. They said you were very upset. Then why did you run away to the mountains?"

"Don't you see, I had to be alone to deal with all that stuff. All this time I've been feeling like a crumb for leaving Fawn when it was never meant to be anyway. It's hard to explain why, but as I thought about it, I realized that it was good news after all."

"Good news that you have been loving the wrong person?"

"No," I said quietly. "Good news that I have been loving the right person. Cherish, I'm not sure you understand. What I'm trying to say is that I love you."

"But of course, I love you too. You're like a brother—"

"I don't want to be like a brother! I . . ." She was standing stock-still now. "I mean I love you . . . you know, in a different way, as a man loves a woman."

Suddenly she was crying, shaking with crying. I grabbed her hand hurriedly.

"There, there," I soothed. "I realize it's not mutual. You don't have to do anything about it. It's just that I can't carry it around inside any longer—"

She snapped her head up impatiently, almost angrily.

"And what about me? What have I been carrying around inside? Don't you think I love you in the same way? All this time I could never tell you because you were all tangled up in your memories and stuff! Instead, I had to always keep my distance, trying not to be pushy!"

"But . . . you already have someone, right? I mean . . . that guy Wells that comes to visit you . . . and whom you go to visit—"

"What are you talking about? I never went to visit him. I go to visit my great-aunt. He just lives in the same stead. I never encouraged him to come around; he's just persistent, like I always wanted you to be."

"But if you felt that way about me, why did you never let on?"

"For fear of chasing you away. I knew you still felt tied to an old relationship. Even if I could never really have you, I was determined to practice the charade rather than risk losing you altogether."

We clasped each other tight and gave vent to all the inner feelings we had both been holding in against our wills. I'll not embarrass the reader or myself by describing what followed. Suffice it to say that when the household of Ravenswing beheld us reentering with tear-streaked faces, they all fell into a hushed anticipation of some sad tidings. When instead we announced our plans to be married, there was a surprise gasp followed instantly by a shrieking applause and teary hugging and backslapping. Only now did I learn that there were some in the stead who were not so surprised after all: Herald in particular had long surmised how things stood but, in recognition of his daughter's dilemma, had kept up a pained silence.

Two days before Summer Solstice, the household and many guests gathered up back in the memorial garden for a traditional Steward wedding. We declared our intentions before the rest, and the Keeper of the Vision declared a blessing over us, followed by feasting and music that lasted into the night. The following day, many of us walked the fifteen miles down to Laughingwater Fair to be there in plenty of time for the Banner Day festivities. Everyone slept in tents, and when Cherish and I were quite late emerging from ours, we took a bit of teasing. However, we did come out in plenty of time to make the traditional announcement; and at the end, with Cherish's guidance, I got to join in the swirling whorls of the Sunflower Dance. It was my very first time, and somehow it seemed only natural.

THE END

Appendix

To follow the events in this story (especially diary entries), the reader may find it helpful to consult this table. The Esperian calendar is based on 13 months of 28 days each, beginning on the winter solstice. An extra day is added at the end, and a second day is added for leap years.

1/1*	Dec22	1/21	Jan11	2/13	Jan31	3/5	Feb20
1/2	Dec23	1/22	Jan12	2/14	Feb1	3/6	Feb21
1/3	Dec24	1/23	Jan13	2/15*	Feb2	3/7	Feb22
1/4	Dec25	1/24	Jan14	2/16	Feb3	3/8	Feb23
1/5	Dec26	1/25	Jan15	2/17	Feb4	3/9	Feb24
1/6	Dec27	1/26	Jan16	2/18	Feb5	3/10	Feb25
1/7	Dec28	1/27	Jan17	2/19	Feb6	3/11	Feb26
1/8	Dec29	1/28	Jan18	2/20	Feb7	3/12	Feb27
1/9	Dec30	2/1	Jan19	2/21	Feb8	3/13	Feb28
1/10	Dec31	2/2	Jan20	2/22	Feb9	3/14	Mar1
1/11	Jan1	2/3	Jan21	2/23	Feb10	3/15	Mar2
1/12	Jan2	2/4	Jan22	2/24	Feb11	3/16	Mar3
1/13	Jan3	2/5	Jan23	2/25	Feb12	3/17	Mar4
1/14	Jan4	2/6	Jan24	2/26	Feb13	3/18	Mar5
1/15	Jan5	2/7	Jan25	2/27	Feb14	3/19	Mar6
1/16	Jan6	2/8	Jan26	2/28	Feb15	3/20	Mar7
1/17	Jan7	2/9	Jan27	3/1	Feb16	3/21	Mar8
1/18	Jan8	2/10	Jan28	3/2	Feb17	3/22	Mar9
1/19	Jan9	2/11	Jan29	3/3	Feb18	3/23	Mar10
1/20	Jan10	2/12	Jan30	3/4	Feb19	3/24	Mar11

3/25	Mar12	5/10	Apr22	6/23	Jun2	8/8	Jul13
3/26	Mar13	5/11	Apr23	6/24	Jun3	8/9	Jul14
3/27	Mar14	5/12	Apr24	6/25	Jun4	8/10	Jul15
3/28	Mar15	5/13	Apr25	6/26	Jun5	8/11	Jul16
4/1	Mar16	5/14	Apr26	6/27	Jun6	8/12	Jul17
4/2	Mar17	5/15	Apr27	6/28	Jun7	8/13	Jul18
4/3	Mar18	5/16	Apr28	7/1	Jun8	8/14	Jul19
4/4	Mar19	5/17	Apr29	7/2	Jun9	8/15	Jul20
4/5	Mar20	5/18	Apr30	7/3	Jun10	8/16	Jul21
4/6	Mar21	5/19	May1	7/4	Jun11	8/17	Jul22
4/7	Mar22	5/20	May2	7/5	Jun12	8/18	Jul23
4/8	Mar23	5/21	May3	7/6	Jun13	8/19	Jul24
4/9	Mar24	5/22	May4	7/7	Jun14	8/20	Jul25
4/10	Mar25	5/23	May5	7/8	Jun15	8/21	Jul26
4/11	Mar26	5/24	May6	7/9	Jun16	8/22	Jul27
4/12	Mar27	5/25	May7	7/10	Jun17	8/23	Jul28
4/13	Mar28	5/26	May8	7/11	Jun18	8/24	Jul29
4/14	Mar29	5/27	May9	7/12	Jun19	8/25	Jul30
4/15	Mar30	5/28	May10	7/13	Jun20	8/26	Jul31
4/16	Mar31	6/1	May11	7/14	Jun21	8/27	Aug1
4/17	Apr1	6/2	May12	7/15*	Jun22	8/28	Aug2
4/18	Apr2	6/3	May13	7/16	Jun23	9/1	Aug3
4/19	Apr3	6/4	May14	7/17	Jun24	9/2	Aug4
4/20	Apr4	6/5	May15	7/18	Jun25	9/3	Aug5
4/21	Apr5	6/6	May16	7/19	Jun26	9/4	Aug6
4/22	Apr6	6/7	May17	7/20	Jun27	9/5	Aug7
4/23	Apr7	6/8	May18	7/21	Jun28	9/6	Aug8
4/24	Apr8	6/9	May19	7/22	Jun29	9/7	Aug9
4/25	Apr9	6/10	May20	7/23	Jun30	9/8	Aug10
4/26	Apr10	6/11	May21	7/24	Jul1	9/9	Aug11
4/27	Apr11	6/12	May22	7/25	Jul2	9/10	Aug12
4/28	Apr12	6/13	May23	7/26	Jul3	9/11	Aug13
5/1	Apr13	6/14	May24	7/27	Jul4	9/12	Aug14
5/2	Apr14	6/15	May25	7/28	Jul5	9/13	Aug15
5/3	Apr15	6/16	May26	8/1	Jul6	9/14	Aug16
5/4	Apr16	6/17	May27	8/2	Jul7	9/15	Aug17
5/5	Apr17	6/18	May28	8/3	Jul8	9/16	Aug18
5/6	Apr18	6/19	May29	8/4	Jul9	9/17	Aug19
5/7	Apr19	6/20	May30	8/5	Jul10	9/18	Aug20
5/8	Apr20	6/21	May31	8/6	Jul11	9/19	Aug21
5/9	Apr21	6/22	Jun1	8/7	Jul12	9/20	Aug22

9/21	Aug23	10/24	Sep23	11/26	Oct23	12/28	Nov22
9/22	Aug24	10/25	Sep24	11/27	Oct24	13/1	Nov23
9/23	Aug25	10/26	Sep25	11/28	Oct25	13/2	Nov24
9/24	Aug26	10/27	Sep26	12/1	Oct26	13/3	Nov25
9/25	Aug27	10/28	Sep27	12/2	Oct27	13/4	Nov26
9/26	Aug28	11/1	Sep28	12/3	Oct28	13/5	Nov27
9/27	Aug29	11/2	Sep29	12/4	Oct29	13/6	Nov28
9/28	Aug30	11/3	Sep30	12/5	Oct30	13/7	Nov29
10/1	Aug31	11/4	Oct1	12/6	Oct31	13/8	Nov30
10/2	Sep1	11/5	Oct2	12/7	Nov1	13/9	Dec1
10/3	Sep2	11/6	Oct3	12/8 *	Nov2	13/10	Dec2
10/4	Sep3	11/7	Oct4	12/9	Nov3	13/11	Dec3
10/5	Sep4	11/8	Oct5	12/10	Nov4	13/12	Dec4
10/6	Sep5	11/9	Oct6	12/11	Nov5	13/13	Dec5
10/7	Sep6	11/10	Oct7	12/12	Nov6	13/14	Dec6
10/8	Sep7	11/11	Oct8	12/13	Nov7	13/15	Dec7
10/9	Sep8	11/12	Oct9	12/14	Nov8	13/16	Dec8
10/10	Sep9	11/13	Oct10	12/15	Nov9	13/17	Dec9
10/11	Sep10	11/14	Oct11	12/16	Nov10	13/18	Dec10
10/12	Sep11	11/15	Oct12	12/17	Nov11	13/19	Dec11
10/13	Sep12	11/16	Oct13	12/18	Nov12	13/20	Dec12
10/14	Sep13	11/17	Oct14	12/19	Nov13	13/21	Dec13
10/15	Sep14	11/18	Oct15	12/20	Nov14	13/22	Dec14
10/16	Sep15	11/19	Oct16	12/21	Nov15	13/23	Dec15
10/17	Sep16	11/20	Oct17	12/22	Nov16	13/24	Dec16
10/18	Sep17	11/21	Oct18	12/23	Nov17	13/25	Dec17
10/19	Sep18	11/22	Oct19	12/24	Nov18	13/26	Dec18
10/20	Sep19	11/23	Oct20	12/25	Nov19	13/27	Dec19
10/21	Sep20	11/24	Oct21	12/26	Nov20	13/28	Dec20
10/22	Sep21	11/25	Oct22	12/27	Nov21	13/29	Dec21
10/23	Sep22						

*New Year's Day, Deliverance Day, Banner Day, Harvest Feast.

Printed in the USA
CPSIA information can be obtained
at www.ICGtesting.com
JSHW022108270723
45523JS00001B/14